Seventeen years of relative peace have passed in Belega while the Karthagans thrive. But this hard-won respite is drawing to an abrupt end. The Red Twins have come of age. Aiden is chosen to lead his people, as is his right as the older twin. But Ethan disagrees. Driven by jealousy, not only of Aiden's status and friendships but also of his new lover, Ethan attacks, seeking to destroy all Aiden holds dear. But Aiden's powers are growing, and at the moment, are far stronger than Ethan's. Thwarted, Ethan flees Karthag, leaving Aiden alone to care for their people.

Things aren't going any better for Natan on Sennia. Old jealousies are revived, and the Vice-King imprisons all with the ability to bend nature to their will. So far, Natan's successor, Niko, has escaped capture, but his wife has been taken, and lies dying alone in her cell. Enraged, driven mad by grief, Niko attacks the Vice-King and flees to Belega, there to lick his wounds and gather his strength to return, seeking vengeance.

The Karthagan power over nature is stirring to life once more, and Aiden finds his people besieged from all sides. Niko takes refuge on the Isle of Wind, power and death in his hands. Ethan is in Siagan, calling up the power of the lake. And another enemy emerges: the lords of Fredrik's Hall, set to learn the Karthagan secrets. Natan joins Aiden, and together with the Belegan armies, they strive to overcome the madness threatening their very lives. Aiden holds the power, but only Natan with his pure heart can heal the wounds of the earth. And then, only if he has the strength to do so.

Note: This story takes place seventeen years after Belega, book one in The Karthagans series.

THE RED TWINS

THE KARTHAGANS, BOOK TWO

DIANNE HARTSOCK

A NineStar Press Publication
www.ninestarpress.com

The Red Twins

CONTENT WARNING:

This book contains sexually explicit content, which may only be suitable for mature readers. Depictions of graphic violence and gore, torture, kidnapping, off-page rape, attempted rape, death of secondary characters, and war.

Chapter One

NATAN STOOD AT the prow of the swift schooner and leaned over the rail, excitement coursing through him, with the sea spray stinging his cheeks into glowing life, his chestnut hair streaming as a banner behind him. He wished once again Kavi was with him. Kavi would love this. The morning sun glinted on the clear water and a few tattered clouds gave depth to the blue vault overhead. Natan drew a deep breath and laughed aloud in the pure joy of life.

His pulse sped as they approached Belega's white shores after having been at sea for over a week. The anchor dragged, slowing the schooner, and men rushed to lower the sails and make ready the small boats to take the passengers to the dock. As they neared the harbor, Natan climbed onto the railing, gripping the rigging as he leaned out over the water, straining to see. His heart gave a bounding lurch when he spotted Kavi on the sand, and he leaped into the air, diving effortlessly into the deep sea.

He swam to the beach with practiced strokes. Kavi waited, flushed and smiling, as Natan climbed from the water and strode purposefully to him. Natan's wet clothing clung to his lean body, and Kavi's color deepened when he drew close, stirring Natan's blood. Even after seventeen years together, Kavi still stole his breath. Engulfing Kavi in his arms, Natan lovingly whispered his name. He found Kavi's lips and kissed him mercilessly before he pulled away with a self-conscious laugh and touched Kavi's bruised mouth. "Sorry."

"I'm not." Kavi ran his fingers through Natan's dripping hair. Natan's chest heaved, and Kavi made an appreciative sound as he pressed against him.

A polite cough separated them. The remaining passengers had been rowed ashore along with Commander Cecil, who watched them with a grin on his face. Kavi gave Cecil a friendly nod, then turned to the young man at Cecil's side and pulled him into an embrace. "I'm glad you came, Ellis. How was the voyage from Sennia?"

"Too long. It's good to be on dry land again."

"He never did gain his sea legs," Natan divulged with a teasing smile.

"Ha!" Kavi kept Ellis at his side. "I'll tell you a secret. No one enjoys the ocean like our dear Mage here."

Natan's face heated. "Probably true, Kavi."

Ellis chuckled, warming Natan's heart. Until recently, Ellis rarely smiled, never allowed anyone to touch him. Several years ago, he'd been made to watch his parents' torture and murder by the Vice-King's men for sedition. Only Natan's impassioned plea to the court had saved his young life.

Natan had once again roused the animosity of Vice-King Danul that day, but well worth it. Ellis had his mother's joyous features, his unique amber eyes standing out against his black hair and golden-brown skin, a combination of his mother's fair Belegan complexion and his father's darker Sennian heritage. Although not a tall man, he was agile and fearless and easily a match for the men he sparred with back home.

Natan glanced around expectantly. "Alek isn't meeting us?"

"He was detained and sends his apologies," Kavi told him. Natan wondered what was behind the shadow that fell over Cecil's features on hearing his lover hadn't come. As the head of the Karthagan people, Alek would be needed in the city. Especially these last few days, arranging for Aiden's ascension ceremony. The Red Twin had come of age and would assume his role as leader. It was why Kavi had been with his kin a month now. To help with preparations.

Kavi held horses ready for the short ride to the city of Karthag. It delighted Natan to see Syros waiting for them at the city gates as they approached, and he slid from his mount. He hadn't expected the Regent of Barkuit to meet them.

"My lord!" He bowed quickly, and Syros pushed the hand he held out aside to embrace him.

"How are you, Mage?"

"I'm well. How is your little boy?"

A tender smile touched Syros's lips and he answered eagerly. "Excellent. I would have brought him, but Dani's teething…" Syros flushed. "Forgive my enthusiasm, but of course I find him the most wonderful child on the planet. His mother would be proud—" Syros pressed his lips together, pain shadowing his gray eyes.

Natan touched his arm, compassion tightening his chest. Syros's wife had died giving birth to their son. "I grieve for your loss, Syros. We all miss Sharana."

The earnest young man waiting with Syros stepped forward and stretched out his hand. "Hello, Mage." He nodded his head to Cecil and Ellis.

"My lord Willum." Natan bowed to the Governor of Barkuit. At seventeen, Willum was a fit, muscular man of medium height, with the light attractive features of his mother, though there was a firmness to his lips that spoke of his strong-willed father.

He grinned at Natan now, eyeing his wet clothing, then flicked a glance at Kavi's damp tunic. "Impatient, my lord? Never mind. Will you come to the castle? The air can turn chilly on the coast." Willum's mouth quirked and Natan's smile broadened at the teasing.

"You know Ellis." Natan pulled Ellis, who had been standing behind him, to his side.

"Of course." Willum shook his hand while Syros bowed in his grave manner.

The group made their way to the courtyard, where they parted to clean up from the voyage. Natan noted the tiny smile playing on Kavi's lips and caught his heated glances as Cecil led them up a stairway and down a long hallway of the castle, talking animatedly with Ellis all the while. Cecil paused outside the door to Kavi's room and motioned them in but inexplicably remained in the doorway to belabor a point with Ellis. Natan watched them through narrowed eyes, then reached around Kavi to swing the door shut, Cecil barely managing to save his fingers as the heavy wood slammed on their grinning faces.

Once they were alone, Natan pulled Kavi close and Kavi laughed, tugging on Natan's shirt. "Out of these wet clothes, Nattie."

He helped Natan remove his sodden tunic, a hiss of anger escaping him on seeing the scars and fresh welts crisscrossing Natan's chest and back. "The Vice-King goes too far. What was it this time? You can't—"

"Hush." Natan began to undo the braid in Kavi's dark hair. He pulled Kavi into his arms as the familiar craving to have him ever closer took possession.

"The others will wonder where we are," Kavi warned with a quick breath as Natan nimbly undid the ties on Kavi's tunic, baring his torso.

"I don't care," Natan mumbled, staring at the dark nubs on Kavi's chest, beautiful against his olive skin. He leaned down to blow cool air on a nipple and watched it tighten under his gaze. His mouth watered. "I haven't seen you in a month. They can wait."

He had to take tight control of his desire, slow down before he devoured Kavi whole, to be rewarded by Kavi's gasp when he licked the sensitive point. A thrill shot through Natan. Even after all this time, his lover could still start that delicious ache inside as he anticipated Kavi's skillful touch.

Drawing the tight little nub between his teeth, Natan tugged gently, Kavi's deep moan jolting him with triumph and lust. Kavi squirmed as he licked and nibbled the tiny captive. Was he…? Natan dropped his hand and groped the front of Kavi's pants, grinning when he felt the hard length under the thin material. Setting his palm on Kavi's tight stomach, he slipped his hand inside his clothing.

Kavi's breath hitched and he moaned Natan's name. Natan momentarily lost his restraint. Kavi's skin was warm and tight as Natan licked his way downward. He tugged off Kavi's pants as he knelt and buried his face in the soft curls nestling his heavy cock. Natan's heart tripped as he breathed in the heady scent of his man: his musk and sweat.

He needed more. Turning his head, he licked along the extended vein on Kavi's hard length, took it in his mouth, and Kavi cried out when Natan lodged him in the back of his throat, swallowing convulsively. Kavi's balls were heavy in his hand and he gently rolled them. Still not enough! He needed Kavi sprawled on the bed, spread open and eager for him.

He rose to his feet and gently pushed Kavi backward onto the soft quilts of the bed behind them, the yearning to find release in his lover's body swamping him. His heart leaped at Kavi's soft laugh and Kavi splayed his legs, offering himself for Natan's pleasure. Natan widened his eyes at the erotic sight, his breath catching when Kavi lifted his hips. Moistening his lips, Natan bent and once again took Kavi's delicious cock into his mouth, allowing his fingers to stray lower.

*

SOMETIME LATER, NATAN dressed in dry clothing, still tingling from their lovemaking. Joy stirred in his heart, and he wished they could spend the afternoon in bed as he watched Kavi pull a fresh tunic over his head. They shared a smile and Kavi drew Natan against him. "Better?"

Natan's face warmed with a blush. "Yes. How could I not be?"

Kavi threaded his fingers through Natan's tangled curls, and Natan hummed with the sensual pleasure of it, letting his head fall to the side. Kavi kissed his exposed throat, trailing his lips upward to hover over Natan's mouth. "I know I don't say this often enough, Nattie, but I do love you." Kavi kissed him, tongue slipping between his lips, warm and sweet.

After a breathless moment, Natan reluctantly pushed against him.

"We'd better join the others," he said, wondering if Kavi could hear his pounding heart.

Kavi chuckled and stepped back a pace, giving Natan a slight bow. "Always doing what is right, Mage. I can't tempt you back to bed? No?" He held out his hand and Natan took it, though hot blood stung his cheeks at the desire he couldn't hide.

Alek had brought sandwiches, fruit, and wine to the courtyard for his guests, and they relaxed by the fountain in the sunshine when Natan and Kavi joined them. Cecil sat at Alek's feet leaning against his knee. Natan raised a hand when Alex began to rise. "No need to get up," he told the Karthagan lord, reaching over Cecil to shake his hand. "Thank you for having us."

Governor Willum and the Northern regent, Syros, pulled chairs close, and Natan sat at the fountain with Ellis, Kavi settling beside him. While a man on Alek's staff served them, Natan noticed Alek run a hand over the waves of Cecil's hair. Cecil raised his bright face and Alek bent to his ear. "I'm glad you're home," he said vehemently, and Cecil's eyes flashed.

"So am I." Cecil gave a roguish chuckle and touched Alek's mouth. Alek gasped and kissed him roughly, then straightened, his color high.

Natan smiled at such an intimate act from the usually reserved couple. "Is it hard for you to be gone from home so often, Cecil?" he asked gently. Cecil commanded Karthag's small fleet of ships, sailing with each in turn. They had started with two cargo ships all those years ago, added a third, and now boasted five, swift and sleek crafts built by Sennian shipwrights. Karthag prospered.

Cecil gave him a grateful look. "Yes, it is, thank you," he admitted.

"Was this last trip necessary? I didn't need an escort," Natan added, concerned by the tired lines on Cecil's face.

Cecil raised his brows in surprise. "Of course. We're honored to have the Mage with us again."

"I don't believe Natan sees it that way at all," Ellis put in with a grin. "In fact, I think he finds all this attention a trifle overwhelming."

All eyes turned to Natan where he leaned against Kavi, while Kavi ran gentle fingers through his mop of hair. He wondered if they could see his anxiety and fatigue. Probably.

Syros's eyes narrowed, and he asked abruptly, as if impatient with the niceties, "Is revolution coming to Sennia?"

Willum shot him an irritated glance, then turned to Natan, asking gravely, "If you're tired, Mage, we can speak of this later."

"I'm all right." Natan sat up and rubbed his face. He took a hard breath. "It's what I'm working to avoid, Syros."

"To any effect?"

"Syros!" Willum caught him up shortly.

"Forgive me, my lord," Syros said tightly. "But our city of Kangar is a short voyage from Sennia, mere days, and if trouble is coming, I need to know."

"In good time, Syros." The two men glared at each other, reminding Natan that Gargary's hot blood ran in his son. Gargary, a brutal leader, had been assassinated by his own people while Willum was still an infant, leaving Willum the governorship of the Northern Territory when he came of age last year. Syros had acted as his regent until then.

Syros seemed to recall Willum's temper as well, and rising, he swept the young lord a deep bow. "Forgive me."

Willum inclined his head. "Please continue, Mage, if you wish."

Natan leaned forward with clasped hands, gathering his thoughts. "I fear things are coming to a head. As you know, the Sennians are learning to control the natural world, bend it to their will, much as the Karthagans do. But there are many still without this ability, provoking jealousy and hate. The present royal family is one such. Since the previous Vice-King's murder by Danul five years ago, when Danul seized the title for himself, there has been a growing intolerance throughout Sennia for those who use their powers. Recently, people have begun to be taken and imprisoned or have simply disappeared, much as it had been when Mazzo had the old Vice-King's ear. Vice-King Jacom's daughter, Corha, was the first to die in prison, before the Vice-King himself was murdered."

Natan paused and struggled with his grief while they waited in silence. All who'd learned of the incident had been moved to pity and anger for the young woman's cruel fate. Natan cleared his throat.

"Several weeks ago, soldiers came to the school where I teach and took two of my children. I went to Vice-King Danul to petition their release. The encounter was…unpleasant."

"Papa!" Ellis jumped to his feet, a flush staining his skin, his amber eyes flashing. Natan's heart clenched. Ellis only ever called him that when he was most moved.

"They almost killed you," Ellis continued more quietly. "I remember the limp and bloodied body Kayle carried into the house. It was days before we were certain you would live."

"Perhaps."

Natan's soft reply brought an angry glitter to Syros's eyes. "Wouldn't it be better to rouse the Sennian people, remove this man Danul from power?"

Dread crept down Natan's spine. "That's sedition."

"But isn't that what you're already practicing, Mage, by teaching the children to use their abilities?"

The words stung. "Syros, I'm teaching them control. Most Sennians have the Karthagan's power as it had been before Kirstin took the madness from them. Do you wish to see that insanity loose in the world again?"

Willum put in, implacable. "Couldn't he be removed quietly?"

"We'd have to kill him and his followers." Natan covered his face with his hands. He knew Willum's own father had gained the governorship by intrigue and assassination, only to be murdered himself. Natan would find no sympathy in these hard people, though the thought of even one stolen life tore at his heart.

"What do you mean to do?"

Natan raised his head at the compassion in Cecil's voice.

"Persuade the Vice-King to change his policies. He knows the people are stirring against him. He needs to be made to see his danger. If not that, at least find a way to discredit Danul in his followers' eyes."

Natan grew discouraged by the continued silence of the Barkuit soldiers. They knew war. Natan longed for peace.

After a moment, Alek stood. "Forgive me, I have a few matters to attend to, as I'd like to leave everything in order for Aiden when he takes the reins from me tomorrow. Cecil will show you over the city, if you wish, while we wait for Governor Basal to join us. We've made many new restorations."

"Thank you." Natan climbed to his feet as well, needing the distraction. The others rose and they spent a few pleasant hours walking Karthag's cobbled streets, enjoying its gardens. The old buildings had been lovingly restored, and the new dwellings planned and constructed with care.

Governor Willum paused beside a renovated mill and ran a hand over the white rock. "Who is your mason, Cecil? This stonework is beautiful."

"That's Aiden's. About ten years ago one of the old buildings collapsed, injuring several people. Aiden petitioned for the task of restoring the old structures, and he and half a dozen of the Southern soldiers stationed at the garrison here, as well as many Karthagans, have been working on the city ever since. They've done incredible things as you can see."

"I'm tempted to steal him from you," Syros put in sincerely.

They rounded a corner in the street and watched as Aiden guided the last beam for the city's new gates into place. The wood gleamed in the sunlight, the gate so carefully balanced it could be opened or closed with a push. Natan smiled at Robin's whoop of delight and watched the young Nagal lord along with a Karthagan youth, Eon, sprint across the muddy clearing toward Aiden.

"We did it!" Robin exclaimed, then blushed brilliantly under Aiden's grin.

"That we have." Aiden held out his hand and Robin shook it vigorously. Clapping him on the back, Aiden left with Eon to help secure the ropes, but spying them, Robin trotted over.

"Mage," he bowed. His blue eyes were full of laughter, but Natan could see the earnestness of the young man hiding behind his flippant manner. The governorship of the Southern Territory would pass to him from Basal in his twentieth year, leaving only three short seasons to prepare.

A cold finger touched Natan's heart at the thought, but he shook it off. He would save that portent for its time. "When is your father due to arrive?"

Robin glanced at the sun nearing its zenith. "It could be any time now. The message we received this morning said they had waited for Lady Kirstin and Tessa to join them before leaving Nagal, but that would put them only a few short hours behind their original schedule."

"My cousins travel from Amara alone?" Kavi asked, voicing Natan's concern. It had never been completely safe for Karthagans to journey through Belega without an escort.

"No. Devon, the Amara council leader, is with them. After Kirstin lost her husband, he and Father have been doing all they can to help her."

They stood a moment in silence, Natan grieving anew for the friend that had left them last spring. Bryon had become a father to him after the death of Natan's parents when he'd been a child. Bryon's heart had unexpectedly betrayed him, stopping suddenly, shocking them all, and not even Kirstin's healing hands had been able to save him.

Presently Cecil motioned to the stairway leading to the parapet along the walls. "We can wait for them above, if you'd like."

They followed him to the comfortable benches set along the wall overlooking the soldiers' barracks and the densely wooded hills beyond. Robin and Ellis paced, speaking animatedly as they waited for their guests. Natan exchanged an amused smile with Kavi at the sight. The two young men rarely saw each other but picked up their friendship with ease.

In a relatively short time, horses appeared through the trees, and Robin leaped down the stairs before the others had reached their feet. The travelers dismounted and entered the city, the tired animals led to the stables.

Governor Basal paused to run his hands over the carved wood of the new gates. "These are incredible. Aiden's work?"

"Yes, sir." Cecil looked around. "He must have gone to help Jaden in the fields."

"Jaden's farming?"

Natan's heart warmed at the mention of his cousin. He'd always had a fondness for him.

"Yes." Cecil smiled. "The soldiers you have stationed here are extremely helpful."

"Excellent. The Barkuit soldiers in Nagal have added to our city as well," Basal assured him.

"It's good to see our treaty is working," Willum put in.

The two governors, William from the North and Basal from the South, had believed exchanging soldiers, learning each other's ways, would unite the two countries. Natan readily agreed. If they could keep the lines of communication open, they had a fair chance of maintaining the peace between them.

He bowed to the Lady Kirstin. "It's good of you to come."

"We couldn't miss Aiden's ascension ceremony."

Natan gave her a light kiss, and Kirstin smiled at him. "How have you been, Mage?"

"I'm well, though I wish to tell you in person how truly sorry I am about Bryon. His death is a loss to us all."

Kirstin nodded and embraced him again, sharing her pain. Her daughter, Tessa, a young woman of sixteen, hugged him warmly, then turned to the others. Syros and Willum greeted her, Willum bowing over Tessa's hand, making her laugh.

"Enough," Robin muttered, and they broke apart with a chuckle. Ellis elbowed him and Robin fled to Tessa's side, managing to come between her and Willum. Basal didn't comment, but his stern glance told of a future lecture for his impetuous son.

Cecil led them back to the courtyard, where Natan gratefully sank onto a bench by the fountain. He was growing tired after his long voyage. Ethan, Aiden's twin, lounged against a pillar close by as if waiting for them. Natan avoided his gaze. Whereas Aiden was open and friendly, Natan sensed a darkness around Ethan, something secretive and dangerous. He wasn't sure he was up to any games Ethan might want to play.

Kavi squeezed his hand, and not for the world would Natan admit to the pain starting in his ears. He felt Ethan's stare and reluctantly met the intent gaze of his golden eyes, shivering at the Red Twin's attention on him, sensing his animosity.

Ethan straightened when Basal and Kirstin came up to him. "My lord," Ethan bowed to Basal. "How are you, Auntie?" he continued and lightly kissed Kirstin's cheek.

Natan watched in amazement as the others spoke pleasantly with Ethan. They couldn't feel it. A cold draft swept around Ethan, and an aura of cruelty clung to him even now. Perhaps Ethan only allowed Natan to see it. Ethan slid him a look during a lull in the conversation and winked mockingly. Natan acknowledged the antipathy with a short nod.

Footsteps sounded outside the courtyard, and Commander Jaden's voice reached them, answered by an attractive laugh. The two men blithely entered the garden but stopped in dismay on seeing them. Aiden recovered first.

"Your pardon, Alek. I thought your guests would be resting after their eventful day." He gave them a courtly bow.

"Obviously," Alek chuckled. Their boots and britches were caked with mud, and though their hands were clean, their hair was matted to their foreheads with sweat.

"Well, since you're here, say hello," Alek prompted.

Jaden made a gallant bow, and Aiden inclined his head to Kirstin in apology. "My lady." He went to Natan and surprised him by taking a knee in deference. "My lord Mage."

"Aiden." Natan touched his dark head and looked kindly into his golden eyes. Aiden smiled and stood, embracing him.

"Oh, I'm sorry," Aiden apologized ruefully as he pulled away and saw the mud he'd left on Natan's tunic. Natan shrugged, unconcerned, and glanced at Ellis when his adopted son stepped to his side.

Aiden stared at him, clearly alarmed, his face paling. "Ellis?"

Ellis gave him a startled look, then grim lines settled around his lips. Aiden's eyes slid to Natan in a question, and Ellis gave an imperceptible shake of his head. Natan wondered what the exchange meant.

Aiden recovered, though his voice shook when he addressed Alek. "Please excuse me. I had a question about the irrigation, but it can wait."

"Of course." Alek let him go.

Jaden hesitated, then spoke in an aside to Basal. "I'll return once I've washed and make my report," he said softly. He approached and gave Natan a quick embrace, laughing at the mud he left on his clothing.

"Thank you," Natan said dryly, brushing at his shirt. "It's good to see you, Jaden."

Jaden winked, grinning. "It's good to see you too, cousin." He added warmly, "It's been too long. You look tired." He hugged Natan again, then turned and followed Aiden from the courtyard.

Alek rested thoughtful eyes on Ellis.

Natan studied Ellis as well, noting the pain that darkened his eyes. He wondered how Ellis knew the Red Twin, though to his knowledge Ellis had never met Aiden before that day. He ached suddenly to embrace Ellis and chase away the demons he saw in his eyes, as he'd done when Ellis first came to them. What was going on between him and Aiden?

Alek's staff entered the courtyard with a repast for the newly arrived travelers. As Natan nibbled a slice of sharp cheese, he caught Ethan's golden gaze on him again, and a cold shiver traveled through him.

"I think I'd like to rest," he confessed to Kavi, more to escape the Red Twin than needing sleep.

"Of course, Nattie."

They took their leave of the others, and Natan sought refuge from his worries in their comfortable room and Kavi's eager arms once again, having missed his husband more than he cared to admit. Kavi drew him to the bed, stripping as he went. Natan brushed Kavi's bare nipples with a thumb and Kavi's breathing hitched. He moaned Natan's name. Hearing his need, Natan's pulse leapt, racing. He lowered Kavi onto the mussed quilts.

Removing his own clothing, Natan crawled after him, pinning Kavi to the mattress. He moved against Kavi, delicious friction, pleasure bursting through him to mix with the pain tightening his chest. Ethan had rattled him. So had the talk with Syros and Willum earlier. What was he to do about the Vice-King? How could he make things right back home in Sennia?

He'd been so alone! Trapped in that dark room after Danul was through with him. He'd begun to say goodbye to this precious man in his arms. Tears burned his eyes and he clutched at Kavi's shoulders, needing him closer.

"Natan, what is it? Look at me."

Kavi's worried voice penetrated the desperate panic swirling in Natan's thoughts. He swallowed his sobs and didn't resist when Kavi cupped his chin and raised Natan's wet face.

"Darling." Kavi gently kissed him. "Tell me."

"Danul meant for me to die this time. I was locked in a dank cell for days, beaten and starving, no water. Kavi, I was so afraid! I thought I would never hold you again, tell you how much I love you—"

Kavi's mouth stopped his broken words with a savage kiss. Kavi rolled to his side, holding Natan close, cradling the back of his head. "But Kayle spoke to the Vice-King and had you freed. As the son of Sennia's former mage, Gregor, our Kayle has the people's love. Danul dare not ignore him, thank the stars. And now I have you safe in my arms. I won't let you go."

Natan sighed, relaxing against the warmth of Kavi's chest. He scrubbed at his eyes like a child, laughing slightly to relieve the intense emotions boiling through him. Kavi's warm breath tickled his ear. "Tell me what you need," Kavi urged.

"I need to be inside you," Natan confessed, heart pounding. "I'd melt into you, if I could…"

Natan turned his face away, embarrassed by the intensity of his desire, but Kavi made him meet his gaze. Fondness and lust gleamed in his dark eyes. "I want that too," he admitted, voice gruff with passion, and kissed Natan in earnest.

Chapter Two

HEARING FOOTSTEPS IN the hall, Syros looked up from the littered table in the library while Alek slipped a black book into a drawer as Ethan strolled into the room. They'd retired there while the others rested, Alek wanting to go over the shipping schedule with Syros before the coming distractions of dinner and guests and Aiden's ceremony tomorrow.

Ethan gave them a sour look, his tone patently bored when he spoke, "Are you two staying indoors the rest of the day? I've already been out riding twice, and Aiden's busy with his irrigation contraption. I was hoping you'd come to the inn for a drink, my lord Syros."

"I'm sorry, Ethan," Alek put in hastily. "I don't mean to monopolize Syros's time, but I have so few days to—"

"Never mind." Ethan put up a hand to forestall Alek's explanation. "Let me know when you're free, my lord." He gave the men a desultory wave and left by the garden door. They watched his departing back, and

Alek retrieved his book only when Ethan had passed from the garden.

"You don't trust him."

"No," Alek answered curtly. "I've managed to keep him disinterested in our trade concerns, but I fear it's only a matter of time before he interferes." He opened the ledger.

Syros spent some time every summer in Karthag, working out the trade schedule with Alek for the coming year. He studied Alek's bent head. "You know of Ethan's cruelties to Aiden, of his manipulation of your people's loyalties," he stated after a moment.

Alek flinched, raising pain-darkened eyes. "Yes, though I've only become aware of it recently. Ethan's arrogance is growing." He ran a hand through his hair, and Syros frowned at the helplessness in his expression. "Aiden has always been like my own son in my heart, and I can't help him. Ethan has the power to raze Karthag to dust, but as yet is still content to play his little games. When I take him, it will have to be quick and sure, or many more people besides Aiden will suffer." His voice broke to a whisper. "I must sacrifice Aiden a while longer."

Syros put a hand on his arm. "I'll help you find a way, Alek, you can be sure."

Alek nodded, though he wouldn't meet Syros's gaze.

The men worked quietly, going over timetables and the rate-of-exchange on cargo and, at last, closed the books and moved to the garden to clear their minds. Syros eyed the Karthagan curiously. At forty-four, Alek was in his prime, vigorous and strong, and beloved by his people.

"Alek, why are you giving up your rule to Aiden? You've built Karthag into a fair and prosperous city, the people free and independent. How can you let it go so readily?"

Alek laughed abruptly. "It's done with relief, my lord. I never wanted the rule."

"Then why did you take it?"

Alek shrugged. "I love my people. When…" He cleared the gruffness that had come into his voice. "When the horror and madness on the Isle of Wind was over, when Kirstin took our power from us, we were broken and homeless and in pain. With our leader, Gavin, dead, I was the only one they would follow. What else could I do?"

Syros looked at him gravely, then stood and bowed to the ground. He could only hope to be such a leader. Alek grumbled in embarrassment.

"Tell me, my lord," Syros asked as he resumed his seat. Alek eyed him warily and Syros chuckled. "If you could have your heart's wish, what would it be?"

Alek raised his brows at the question, and then a slow smile spread on his face. "There's a small meadow in the hills overlooking the harbor," he began. "I have often thought to build a home there such as Aiden has with a garden in the back and a wide porch in front. I could manage the exports from the dining table and spend the rest of my time watching the sea for Cecil's return."

A blush tinged his olive complexion at having revealed so much. Syros knew he didn't often speak of his fondness for the commander, but Cecil had been gone overmuch, and Alek would send him out again in a day's time.

"Can't you keep him home?" Syros began, then answered the question himself. "Ethan."

Alek shuddered. "So far, Ethan has ignored him, but if the Red Twin was to play his games with Cecil… I can't risk that. I couldn't bear it."

"Have you explained this to Cecil?"

"I daren't. Ethan would read it in his honest eyes." Alek covered his face and Syros stood abruptly.

"Let's walk before we're called to dinner. There must be a way for us to protect both Cecil and Aiden from Ethan's grasp."

*

AIDEN WATCHED IN dismay as the fields flooded yet again. What was he doing wrong? The slush gates were in place, the channel from the river clear. He rubbed his face. He was hot and dirty and tired and vaguely disappointed no one had asked him to dine at the castle. He thought of one guest in particular and laughed dryly. He wasn't a boy to be foolish over a man's eyes, no matter how intriguing.

He wiped the sweat from his forehead and went to check the gates once more, though it would be morning before he could test them again. As the afternoon turned to evening, he sent the soldiers home and began the trek up the mountain to his cabin, pausing when he heard a horse approaching. He smiled as Robin tumbled from the saddle.

"Lord Aiden." The lad bowed gracefully, a reminder to Aiden he was a governor's son. He bowed formally in return, and Robin surprised him by flushing.

"Don't do that. I'm not my father and won't be governor for many long years yet, the fates willing."

"As you wish. Did you need something?"

"Yes. Alek asks that you join us for dinner."

Aiden's heart quickened. "Very well. Thank you for carrying the message."

"At your service." Robin swung effortlessly into the saddle and trotted away, and Aiden whistled softly as he climbed the path.

He took care with his attire, and it wasn't until he stood on the porch and watched the sun set as he braided his wet hair that slow color mounted in his cheeks. What was he doing? The Sennian wouldn't even notice he was there.

Aiden hurried to the city all the same and entered the dining hall as the guests were sitting to table. It troubled him when he was seated beside Ellis, opposite the Barkuit governor, Willum. His hands fumbled as he pulled out his chair, and he flushed darkly when the attendants mocked him under their breath in front of Ellis.

The meal proved excellent and the company merry, but as the evening progressed, Ethan directed frequent barbs Aiden's way from farther up the table, and the attendants slighted him. Nothing the others would see, but Ellis was watching and caught the spilled soup and empty glass, the soiled plate that somehow never managed to be cleared.

Aiden knew his face flushed and began counting the time until he could tactfully leave. This was not how he'd wanted his second meeting with Ellis to go. He risked a glance at him, and Ellis gave him a tentative smile.

"How did your day go?" Ellis asked, clearly trying to engage him in conversation.

After a brief hesitation, Aiden found himself telling Ellis of his and Jaden's difficulty with the east field. Ellis's questions were thoughtful, his observations intelligent and useful. He laughed often and made Aiden laugh. He was enchanting.

Aiden followed the chattering group as they retired to the drawing room after dinner and stood against the wall in the shadows outside the fire's glow. He watched Ellis's radiant face. The Sennian was lovely, the fire-light a soft blush on his cinnamon-brown skin, his voice warm and musical. Aiden felt as if he'd waited his whole life to hear his laugh. He wondered if Ellis's dark hair was as soft as it looked, pictured it clinging to his fingers.

Lingering longer than he was wont, Aiden stayed until his heart ached with longing, and wistfulness dimmed his joy in the evening. At long last, he slipped from the room and stumbled out into the night. Making his way half blindly to the redwood tree in the heart of the city, he dropped on a stone bench and covered his face. His heart had been stirred by Ellis, but what did it matter? It didn't change who he was nor wipe away the horrors he'd once done.

"What more do you want of me?" he asked the night in a broken voice. How much more did he have to suffer before it was enough and he could find peace? He thought of Ellis's sweet face, amazing eyes, soft voice, and knew his pain would never end, not now. He struggled to his feet and made his way from the sleeping city, and the walk to his home in the hills had never seemed so long.

*

AIDEN HESITATED AT the entrance to the courtyard the following morning. If he didn't need Jaden's advice on the slush gates…

He glanced at his rough clothing. At least he was clean this time. He found Willum, Alek, and Syros lounging on the benches in the sun. Apparently, it had been a late night. Aiden grinned at their sleepy faces.

"Tired, gentlemen?"

"Yes." Alek opened a dark eye. "Can I help you?"

"Have you seen Jaden? I need him."

Alek sat up. "I'm sorry. I sent him with Cecil to overhaul the schooner. Governor Willum and Syros will take the ship to Kangar at first light tomorrow morning."

Willum opened an eye and closed it again while Syros struggled to sit up. "Is there something we can do?"

Aiden chuckled and pushed him back to the bench. "It's nothing that can't wait."

"Aiden!"

He trembled at the voice but clenched a hand and turned as Ellis came up to him.

"Ellis." He sketched a bow. Ellis had tied his dark hair back with a golden string that set off his amber eyes. Aiden was unaware he'd taken a step closer until he nearly touched Ellis's face with his upraised hand. His smile widened. There were flecks of gold in those incredible eyes.

"Have you come for breakfast?" Ellis asked a trifle breathlessly, and Aiden recalled himself.

"No. I ate ages ago." He waved his hand in a vague motion to show the great passage of time. Ellis moved a few steps away and took a seat on a bench while Aiden leaned against a pillar near him, fascinated by this softer side to Ellis, as if they could be…friends.

"If you're implying that I'm lazy, sir, I'll have you know that Robin and I watched the sun rise from the tower," Ellis told him with a sniff.

Aiden snorted. "I wouldn't have the courage to imply anything, sir." Sunlight touched his face, and he blinked in the bright light. Ellis's eyes narrowed, studying him, and Aiden lifted a brow, then watched in fascination as color rose in Ellis's cheeks.

Ellis shrugged. "Forgive me for staring. I couldn't decide the color of your eyes. Like gold diamonds."

"Oh." Aiden's heart pounded, though he warned himself not to be a fool. Voices approached the courtyard, and he straightened from the pillar. "I should go. I hope your day is pleasant."

"Thank you." Ellis smiled at him, and Aiden turned away with reluctance, then jumped back as he almost collided with his brother. "Good morning, Ethan."

"Aiden." Ethan gave him a cool stare, making Aiden conscious of his course appearance. "Not joining us for breakfast, I hope? If you have no respect for Alek, at least have some for his guests."

"I was just leaving." Aiden gave him a curt bow.

Ellis looked curiously at the brothers, and Aiden knew what he saw. Even though they appeared similar, there were great differences as well. Aiden was solid and muscular, his skin darkened by years in the sun, his hair lighter than Ethan's for the same reason. People called him handsome, but he lacked the beauty of Ethan's face, the grace of his slim body, and Ethan's air of control and confidence.

Ethan smiled down at Ellis. "I hope my brother hasn't been a bore," he apologized with a bow. Hot blood flooded Aiden's face as Ethan took Ellis's hand, when he would have given his life to hold it for a single moment.

He flung away from them and almost trampled the men approaching. He bit his lip, chagrined. "Good morning, Mage. Kavi."

Natan looked tired, but his grip on Aiden's shoulders was strong as he embraced him. "You left too early last night. I didn't get the chance to speak with you."

Aiden's face heated, knowing it would have been impossible for him to talk to anyone at the time. "Perhaps this afternoon?" he asked tentatively and was relieved at Natan's friendly nod. His scalp prickled suddenly, and he searched the immediate area with his eyes, shocked by the surge of power he felt in the air. A cry of pain burst from Natan, startling him, and he watched in disbelief as the Mage clutched his head and fell to the stones.

Kirstin pushed by him, and Aiden stepped back out of the way, dazed, as she and Kavi knelt at Natan's side, Kavi clearly panicked. Frantic for answers, Aiden swept his gaze from Ellis's stricken face to Ethan beside him, catching a strange glitter in his brother's eyes. Grabbing Ethan by the collar, he shoved him against the pillar.

"Let Natan go," he said hoarsely, sickened as Ethan's eyes became glazed, and a hiss of pleasure escaped his slack lips.

"Let him go!" Aiden violently shook his twin, raising his fist. Ethan blinked, then cringed back and broke his link with Natan. Aiden pushed him away and hurried to the Mage, ignoring the hate that had filled his brother's eyes.

Kirstin placed her palm on Natan's glistening forehead, then ran her fingers over his scalp. "He's bleeding inside. I think I can stop it, relieve the pressure, only…"

"What?" Aiden's heart pounded. Kavi's broken sob tore his heart. Ellis came and knelt beside Kavi, and Aiden couldn't look at him. So much pain…

"If Natan should wake up while I'm healing the wound, I'm afraid the shock could kill him."

Aiden winced at Kirstin's blunt words.

"Can't you tell him to stay asleep?" Ellis asked, sounding lost. Aiden closed his eyes.

"I haven't the gift to call spirits," Kirstin answered in distress. "Natan could, at one time." Her voice trailed off. "Aiden, you must help me."

Ice slushed through Aiden's blood, and he stared at his aunt in horror.

"You must," she said firmly and motioned to Natan's side. Aiden dropped to his knees as Kavi made room.

Panic churned inside him. "I'm afraid," he said. "I can't do this."

"I'm right here, Aiden. I'll watch over you."

Kirstin's voice was sure, but Aiden bowed his head. She couldn't save him anymore. He knew of only one man with enough strength to overcome him, should he lose control and try to seize power, and Kayle of Sennia was far away. Tears burned his eyes.

"Aiden?"

His name was the barest of whispers on the air, and he felt the light touch of Ellis's hand on his arm. He took a shuddering breath and began. Instantly, the air became charged as life's energy stirred and flowed into him. He wept… It was glorious! His blood hammered and he was filled with a joy so intense he nearly lost himself. Ellis's strong fingers pressed the tense muscles of his arm, and he drew back from the edge. Gaining control, he sent his spirit out to find the Mage…

Natan sat on an outcrop of rock overlooking the sea. He gave Aiden a curious glance as he joined him. "Why are you here?" he asked, then laughed quietly. "Never mind. You're here to take me back."

"Actually." Aiden glanced appreciatively at the scene. "I need to keep you here. This is a lovely spot."

"This is my home in Amara. My parents are buried in the next cove over, and I have a little shack in the hills behind us." They were quiet a moment. "Why do I need

to stay here?"

"Kirstin found bleeding in your head. She can stop it and relieve the pressure, but there will be pain."

"Obviously."

They fell silent and Aiden knew by Natan's quickened breath that Kirstin had begun. Natan tried to be brave, but in the end Aiden had to take the sobbing man in his arms, and at first implore, then command that he stay with him.

When it was done, he cradled the Mage like a child. He brushed the damp hair from his eyes, dull with pain, and pulled the trembling body closer. "Sleep, Natan," he urged.

"Thank you," Natan managed to say, and his eyes fluttered shut as his spirit settled into quiet rest.

*

NATAN'S FACE GREW pale, slick with sweat, and Ellis's heart constricted "Why doesn't he wake?"

"I'm not sure," Kirstin murmured. Aiden had taken Natan's hands when he'd begun, and Kirstin seemed hesitant to break the bond. The Red Twin appeared to sleep as well, though Ellis could sense the power still moving through him. Self-conscious, Ellis took his hand from his strong arm as Aiden's lids began to flutter. Golden eyes opened, bright with tears, and Aiden leaned forward and kissed Natan's forehead. As the Mage awoke, Aiden sat back with a sigh and let the energy of life flow out of him.

He turned to Ellis then, and Ellis saw the pallor of exhaustion in his face, the trickle of sweat he absently brushed away before it reached his eyes. Aiden smiled tentatively, and Ellis took a quick breath. He was so near...

"We should take him inside," Kirstin said gently, and Kavi pulled Natan into his arms as others stepped forward to help. "He'll be well. He only needs to sleep now." Kirstin assured those standing around them.

Ellis stared at Natan's pale face, then turned his gaze on Aiden, who rose to his feet at whatever he saw in Ellis's eyes. Ellis remained kneeling while Natan was carefully lifted and taken to his room.

"I am your man, Aiden," Ellis said suddenly, voice ringing in the courtyard, and prostrated himself. Aiden cried out and stepped back.

"No," he croaked.

Ellis leaped to his feet. "It's done," he said fiercely.

"You can't do this!" Aiden shouted with alarm and moved closer. "I beg you."

"Do you think I would do less?" Ellis asked, all pride and scorn.

"For him, no. He deserves our devotion." Aiden nodded to the doorway through which Natan had been taken. "But for me, you cannot." His voice turned hard. "I won't let you."

"It's done," Ellis hissed, and the two men glared in mounting anger. Aiden swore bitterly and turned on his heel to leave, and all moved aside at the anguish in his face.

"I don't understand," Willum said into the silence. Ellis sighed and rubbed a hand over his face, erasing the anger.

"Aiden saved my father's life," he began. "I'm his man, now. Where he goes, I go. He's just being…stubborn about it. Aiden risked more than his life when he went after Natan. I owe him my loyalty at the very least."

Willum looked grave. "I saw fear in his eyes."

"Perhaps," Ellis shrugged, heart burning, and would say no more about it.

Chapter Three

THE KARTHAGAN PEOPLE gathered midday at the redwood tree in the heart of the city to take Aiden as their leader and lord. As the governors of Belega, Basal and Willum waited within the low stone wall encircling the tree. Natan stood just outside the enclosure with Cecil. The commander's eyes were anxious, and Natan touched his arm. "He'll be well."

Cecil smiled faintly. "I know. I just wish it were over." He gave Natan a concerned look. "And how are you, Mage?"

"I'm doing better. Kirstin believes it was an old injury from my imprisonment and also fatigue from the voyage that caused the episode. I'm to relax and avoid stress the rest of my stay." He didn't tell Cecil he knew Ethan had attacked him. It would only worry the commander, and Natan wanted to learn the Red Twin's motive first before accusing him.

A commotion rose on the street leading from the castle, and silver bells chimed on the air as the procession approached the tree.

Tessa came first in the black and silver livery of her grandfather Kayden's house, and the people clapped and cheered for her youth and prettiness. Little bells adorned her ankles and wrists and twined in her hair, and she laughed gaily at the bright day and the happy crowd.

With smiles on their faces, Kavi and Kirstin walked arm in arm in the respective colors of their houses. Kirstin's fair hair streamed behind her and caught the sun like a maiden's, the black and silver of her dress hugging her slim form.

Natan's heart rushed at the sight of Kavi, handsome in the black and crimson of his father's house. Every inch a Karthagan lord, from his proud bearing to the slight arrogance on his face, the amused lift of his full lips, he bent to whisper something to Kirstin, who covered her mouth on a wide smile. Natan assumed he'd said something biting about the crowd, and though he shouldn't admire Kavi for it, it was this very confidence and wicked humor he found dangerously attractive. He wanted to kiss that sarcastic mouth into submission.

Silence suddenly fell. The Red Twins were there in their gleaming black and silver livery, their eyes bright golden disks in the sunlight. A ripple of apprehension passed through the people. Natan knew they had not forgotten the devastation on the Isle of Wind, and these proud lords filled all who saw them with foreboding. Ethan's head lifted in arrogance and a mocking smile twisted his lips.

Aiden strode in silence at his side, the leather showing his muscular body, his face somber and distant, his dark hair loose down his back. The Karthagan people fell grave. He appeared a warrior on his way to the battlefield.

A murmur rose as a last and lonely figure trailed the twins. Alek wore unrelieved black, his hands bound with silk at his back. A sheer scarf covered his eyes. His stride was loose and sure, his head tilted proudly as if daring them to do their worst. A shout went up at his boldness, and then cheers and affectionate cries filled the air for the well-loved man.

Alek paused, clearly startled, but Natan wasn't surprised by the crowd's reaction. The Karthagans knew who had saved them from the Isle and brought them to their present home, giving them a new beginning. Alek's bow swept the ground, and he hurried on.

Silence fell once again as Alek joined the others under the ancient tree. Aiden stood apart and stern, and Alek stopped before him and fell to his knees. He prostrated himself with his face in the dirt.

There was a frozen heartbeat as Aiden stared at the prone figure; then suddenly he raised a jeweled dagger high in his hand. Sun glittered on the sharp blade, and with a swift lunge, Aiden dropped on one knee and plunged the knife into the dirt inches from Alek's neck. Another heartbeat, then Aiden rose, and cries rang out for the new Karthagan leader.

The abrupt, on-the-edge-of-dangerous Karthagan ceremony, depicting a time when rule was passed through assassination, was over, and Natan was more than glad for it.

The circle emptied and the people dispersed, until only Cecil and Natan remained with Alek still prostrated on the ground. Cecil knelt beside him and gently undid the silk at his hands and unbound his eyes. Alek rolled to his side.

"I'm free, Cecil," he said with quiet excitement.

"Yes, you are," Cecil laughed and brushed the hair from his smiling face. "Now kiss me and go celebrate with your people."

"You don't mind?" Alek played with the wisps of light hair against

Cecil's cheek.

"No," he assured him. "You need to show yourself in the city and assure the people you hold no bitterness toward their new lord."

Natan sighed. "Aiden will need all our support."

They parted at the courtyard, Cecil heading to the schooner to see that all was ready for the morning, while Alek and Natan went inside to join Alek's guests.

*

AIDEN DID HIS duty, though every moment in the city burned his heart as the people drew away from him, and dark looks shot at him from every side. Being a few minutes older than Ethan, Aiden had been named his successor by Alek. Caught up in the moment, the people had cheered him, but no one wanted it, least of all Aiden.

At last, in misery, he wandered into the courtyard and leaned wearily against a pillar. His brief glimpses of Ellis had sent his heart pounding, and he groaned in desperation. Would Ellis ever see him as a man he could care for, or did he already despise him for his past, like the others? He closed his eyes at the desolate thought.

Approaching footsteps reached him, and he raised his head, a slow smile crossing his face when the man he'd just been thinking of entered the courtyard. His joy fled at Ellis's tense expression.

Ellis stopped before him. "We need to talk," he said by way of greeting and moved off down a side trail leading into the garden. Aiden followed and nearly trod on Ellis's heels when he stopped abruptly in a secluded spot surrounded by trees and the rose hedge.

Ellis swiveled to face him, but Aiden couldn't read his mood. Anger?

Fear? "What do you want from me?"

Ellis folded his arms on his chest. "I know it's your Ascension Day, but you have to listen to me. You've been avoiding me. Stop as of this moment. I won't deny I'm beginning to care for you, but that doesn't change the fact that what is to come is inevitable, and time's running short. We need to plan."

Aiden drew a sharp breath at his words, and Ellis's eyes flashed. "It's not today, Aiden."

Aiden sank to a nearby bench and covered his face. "Why don't you go away? I don't want you here."

Ellis laughed harshly. "You've had the same dreams, Aiden. Nothing we do will change things."

"You don't know that."

"I do."

Aiden looked up at the bleakness in Ellis's voice. Ellis's hazel eyes softened. "All Sennians have a power of some kind, Aiden, as do the Karthagans. My special gift is I have nightmares that always come true."

"Always?"

"Without fail. Once, when I was a child, I saw a man adding wood to a fire, and in my mind the fire roared up and burned him to death. I jumped to my feet and screamed at him to get away from the flames. I frightened him so badly he ran out into the storm, and lightning struck and killed him."

Aiden swore softly, pity stirring in his heart. Ellis moved impatiently, and Aiden caught his wild gaze. "You don't like me."

"I'd hoped never to set eyes on you," Ellis admitted. "My dreams of you are horrible. On the other hand, for two years I've lived with uncertainty. That's now over."

"Why don't you go far away? If we're not together… Or do you accept this fate?"

"Accept!" Ellis clenched his hands. "I'm nineteen, Aiden. I've hardly begun life." He raised a tortured face to the sunlit sky.

"Ellis!" Aiden stood quickly. "I won't let it happen."

"It has happened. Every night, over and over. I shall go mad soon."

"No!" Aiden's voice boomed, and there was an answer of thunder in the distance.

"You can't stop it."

"I can try." Aiden sprang suddenly and tackled Ellis to the grass, his arms tight around him. He pressed his fingers on Ellis's temple. "Let me in," he urged, and Ellis whimpered as he stopped his struggles and opened his mind to him.

"Show me," Aiden commanded, and the nightmare rose to life around him, all the horror and violence and madness and death. He felt Ellis sobbing against him, but he pushed him to the end until every detail had been examined at length. Aiden then gathered the black mass of it and had Ellis watch as he crushed it to ash in his hands and let it blow away on the wind.

Aiden flung away from Ellis and sat with his head pressed against his bent knees, shaking with reaction. He hadn't known it would be like that. The memory felt real as if the horrors had actually happened and to this beautiful man.

Ellis rolled into a ball, weeping. Moving with difficulty, Aiden knelt beside him and touched the tears glistening on his lovely brown skin. "Ellis," he mourned. Ellis turned his head and there was a dawning joy in his eyes. Aiden helped him to his feet.

"You took it," Ellis breathed and laughed shakily. "The horror is gone." He chewed his lips. "You realize, though, that nothing has changed. Even if I no longer have the vision, it will still come to pass."

Aiden drew himself up, the proud lord. "If it is in my power to stop it, I swear I shall, Ellis," he promised.

Ellis's whisper was a breath of fear. "We shall see."

*

THE AFTERNOON GREW warm, and Natan and Kavi sought the coolness of the garden. The faint breeze from the coast was heady with the scent of roses and Jasmine. Finding a bench in the shade, Kavi sank on the stone surface while Natan sat on the grass at his feet and leaned his head against his knee. Kavi ran his fingers through his long curls and tilted his head back to kiss him. Natan murmured with pleasure. When they drew apart, Kavi played with Natan's hair and began an intricate braid.

Sorrow touched Natan's heart. He'd known for a long time that Kavi loved him, but he'd scared his lover badly today when he fell unconscious, and Kavi took special care of him now. Natan sighed. He would never willingly put Kavi in danger but didn't know how he could help it with what was to come. Alek had called a meeting with Kavi and Kirstin in attendance. Natan's presence had been requested as well.

Kavi touched his arm. "Are you ready?"

"No, but we'd better not keep Alek waiting."

They saw Ellis talking with Aiden as they returned to the courtyard, and a ripple of apprehension passed through Natan. He wanted desperately to take his family far away, somewhere safe, though he knew soon there would be no such place.

Alek and Syros were having coffee in the courtyard when they arrived, and Natan helped himself, bringing cups to Kavi and Kirstin where they shared a bench. He sat at Kavi's feet, and they turned expectantly to Syros.

The regent cleared his throat. "Do we know where the Red Twins are?"

"Aiden is resting in the garden," Alek said, and Natan nodded agreement. "Ethan said he was going to the harbor to walk on the beach. I didn't question him further. I stopped asking him his plans long ago." His voice held the regret of an estranged and heartsore father.

"Are you ready?" Syros asked him, and there was compassion in his eyes. Alek's face turned bleak. Kirstin looked from one to the other and stood quickly.

"Alek, wait. If you set a ward, as I suspect, Ethan will know it was you."

"No one else here has the talent, cousin," Kavi reminded her. Natan looked at his own hands. He'd had the power, once, and gave it away. He feared he'd soon come to regret that choice.

"But, Alek," Kirstin tried once more. "What of Cecil? Ethan would—"

"It is done," Alek said viciously, and Natan felt a prickling of his skin and a pressure in his ears, and then it was gone. But Alek's ward was good, and Natan knew no one outside the circle could hear what was spoken or sense their thoughts. He quietly wiped the blood that trickled from his ears, confident no one had noticed.

Syros looked around the group. "Governors Willum and Basal have been purposely kept from this meeting for their own safety, in case Ethan learns of it, but I'll convey any pertinent information to them. I'd like to begin with the trouble in Sennia. Anything new, Natan?"

"Kayle was in my dreams last night," Natan answered, and Kavi put a hand on his shoulder.

Syros lowered his brows. "Are you regaining your powers, Mage?"

The party fell silent, and Natan knew the question was one Syros would never have asked except in extreme need. He climbed to his feet.

"No, my lord." He bowed low. Syros smiled ruefully and thanked him. Natan remained standing. "Kayle is afraid. He fears Niko has lost himself in his hatred for the Vice-King, and that a crisis is coming, of Niko's design. Kayle is uncertain what form it will take, but Niko has grown cruel and cold, and Kayle fears for Danul's life, as well as that of anyone who gets in his way." Natan's voice broke, and he covered his face.

"This is not your doing, Natan," Kirstin spoke up. "Niko has always been ambitious. Corha's death has turned that ambition into the need for revenge. You haven't done that to him."

Natan nodded but couldn't raise his face, not when it showed his heart so plainly.

Alek drew a breath, gathering their attention. "I've been hesitant to bring this up, what with everything going on here, but I fear Niko's attention is already turning to Belega. His thoughts have brushed against mine, seeking entrance. And yes," he answered Natan's concerned inhalation, "I will let you know the moment I can no longer keep him out."

Syros studied Alek's face. "What news of the Red Twins?"

Alek shrugged helplessly. "Ethan has grown arrogant, my lord. He's unbalanced, and if we push the wrong way, he'll slip once again into madness. And take us with him," he finished.

"How do we control him, then?"

"Only Aiden can do that, and I won't ask it of him."

Kirstin frowned. "But why not? Surely he can see the danger Ethan poses?"

Alek avoided her eyes.

Natan asked softly, "You don't trust him?"

"We trust Aiden; we just can't predict his reaction," Syros explained. "Despite everything, Ethan is still his brother and twin, and one of the few Karthagans who speak to him. There is no one outside the city walls who will, except the soldiers Aiden works closely with."

"What can we do?" Kirstin asked with pity.

"We'll set a trap for Ethan," Syros replied. "We must either catch Ethan in one of his lies in front of the people or lure him to a chamber from whence there's no escape."

"Is there such a place?" Kavi asked dubiously.

Kirstin shivered. "My father had such a room, but I don't know his secret."

"We'll need you to remember," Syros told her gently. Natan's heart filled with dismay, knowing the horrors it would rouse in her mind.

Kirstin closed her eyes. "I'll need time," she whispered.

The group quieted at her obvious distress, and Syros soon ended the discussion. Natan gave Alek a puzzled frown as they left the courtyard. "Why did you do it? You know Ethan will be relentless until he knows what you were hiding at the meeting."

"Perhaps." Alek paused at the door to the library. "What else could I do? There's so much more at stake than my own happiness."

"And Cecil's?"

Pain touched Alek's face. "Do you think he will understand and forgive me?"

Natan squeezed his arm. "He loves you, Alek. You'd have to tie him to a horse to make him leave you."

"Or send him away on a ship," Alek said bleakly and left the sunshine for the library and a desk littered with papers.

*

ALEK SLIPPED NOISELESSLY into his room that night. Cecil slept in the wide bed, and Alek knew he'd fallen asleep waiting for him. He ached to hold him, but if he lost himself in Cecil—his pulse jumped; he was sure to—then Ethan would find a way into his mind.

He groaned and strode restlessly around the room. Unable to think with Cecil so near, he went down to the drawing room and sprawled on a couch before the dying fire. Ethan must have fallen asleep because the pressure in his mind eased, but he feared to let his guard down and fought his drooping lids during the long hours of the night.

Early morning found him pacing in the garden, and he finally returned to the library to brood. Syros and the others would be there shortly to plan their next move, but he didn't know if he could bear another day with Ethan probing into his thoughts. He feared he would soon break, and the Red Twin would know all the secrets he'd buried so carefully.

There was a tapping at the garden door and Cecil hurried in, his face alight with anticipation. Alek swore softly and caught the joy dimming in Cecil's gray eyes as he turned back to the papers on his desk.

"The schedule's tight, Cecil. Once you're home from taking Willum and Syros to Kangar, I'll need to send you out again almost immediately."

"So soon?"

"We need to take some long beams from the newly cut wood to Amara and pick up a shipment of grain. You can take Kirstin and Tessa along with Governor Basal home at that time as well." He didn't dare look at Cecil and hated himself for the cruelty he did. There was silence in the room for a moment.

"Will you not miss me at all, Alek?"

He looked up quickly on hearing the broken whisper and saw the bewildered hurt in Cecil's face. With a cry, he left his chair and pulled him into a hard embrace, pressing kisses to Cecil's cheeks and eyes and lips. "Every instant," he growled against his sweet mouth. "I miss you every moment you are gone."

Steps sounded in the hall, and Alek swore again and buried his face in Cecil's hair. "There's no time." He looked into Cecil's eyes. "Will you come to me before you sail today?" he urged. Cecil nodded, and seeing Alek's panic as the door opened, slipped out the back exit.

Ethan entered the library, and they both watched the gleam of bright hair as the door to the garden closed. Alek shuddered at his slow smile.

"Good morning, cousin." Ethan perched on the edge of the desk with a leer on his handsome face.

"Sleep well?" Alek returned. Ethan's eyes narrowed to golden slits and Alek knew he had made a mistake. Ethan would only probe the harder. He let out a breath of relief as Syros came into the room with Kirstin. Kavi and Natan followed moments later.

"Well, well," Ethan drawled, swinging a foot. "Everyone's here. Oh, wait, where's that fool Jaden? Surely the Southern soldier is part of your little conspiracy?"

"We'll see him at breakfast," Alek said irritably.

"I'm sure. Well, I'll leave you to your little plots. Good luck." He reached over and patted Alek's cheek and laughed as he jerked away.

Syros broke the silence left after Ethan's departure. "What does he know?"

"Nothing, except for finding us all together on several occasions." Alek looked at Kirstin, noting the strain in his cousin's face. "How are you doing?"

"I know what Father did to seal the room at the lake under Siagan," she said quietly. "But I don't have the strength to hold the energy needed."

"Somehow we must convince Aiden to help…" Alek abruptly sat back in his chair, stifling a moan as Ethan's life force began to claw at his mind to gain access. Niko was there as well, scraping, scraping.

"We'll take him now," Kavi declared in a voice laced with pity.

"No." Alek clenched his teeth. "Not until after the ship sails."

"We shouldn't wait," Natan warned, concerned by Alek's obvious pain.

"No." Alek straightened as the pressure in his head lessened slightly. "I don't want Cecil here."

"Alek—" Natan began.

"No! Not while Ethan can reach him. I won't risk it."

"Very well." Natan eased his tense stance. "But I'll speak with Aiden as soon as Cecil is gone."

Alek nodded and sank into his chair as exhaustion swept over him. He jumped a little as a gentle hand touched his forehead.

"Get some sleep, cousin," Kirstin whispered and kissed his cheek. "We'll keep Ethan preoccupied."

"Thank you," he managed. He followed them from the library and accepted Natan's help into a chair in the garden. He was asleep as soon as he closed his eyes.

Chapter Four

AIDEN SPENT THE early morning walking in the forest, trying to bring some order to his jumble of thoughts. He knew Ellis planned to go back to Sennia with Natan in a fortnight. His heart squeezed, feeling no closer to Ellis than he had when they'd first met. Maybe he should tell Ellis how he yearned for him. He smiled grimly, fearing Ellis's ridicule. Ellis said he was beginning to care, but that could have been a thought of the moment. Aiden was still one of the Red Twins. Why would Ellis want anything to do with him?

Restless, discouraged, he returned to his cabin. It was an attractive place with a long front room containing a stone fireplace and comfortable furniture. There was a well-lit kitchen at the end and several bedrooms off a short hallway. His forceful steps brought him to the spare bedroom next to his own. Extra chairs and a few trunks were stored inside, as well as a small dresser that matched the furniture he'd made for his room.

He pulled a blanket off a piece leaning in the corner and stared at the frame of a child's bed. He touched the roses and trailing vines carved into the wood, darkened with age. For a moment he recalled the eager young man he'd been, full of plans and hopes as he built his home for the wife and child he never found.

His heart twisted in sudden pain as he trailed his fingers over the lines he'd carved with such care. This was to be his child's room. He wondered if Ellis would want a family with him, their child sleeping in the little bed while they lay nearby. He pictured Ellis's hair, a dark fan around his sweet face on the pillows. Aiden wondered if Ellis's eyes would smolder as he touched him.

A small sound of torment escaped him, and he fled the room, his rapid strides matching the hurtful pounding of his heart. Stopping on the porch, he gripped the railing until his knuckles whitened. He took several deep breaths to ease the tightness in his chest. Aching and lonely, he sent his thoughts out to Ethan, hoping the contact with his brother would comfort him as it had done so often in the past.

He rubbed his neck, admitting he hardly recognized his twin anymore in the cruel person Ethan had become. Aiden sighed to himself, thinking that soon he'd have to take him away. A madness was growing in Ethan that Aiden could no longer hold in check. He bit his lip hard, knowing he'd have to entrap Ethan on the Isle of Wind somehow. There was no other place to keep him safely.

He touched Ethan's mind with sorrow, and the violence of the encounter wrenched a cry of horror from him. He watched in shock as Ethan smashed a fist against his captive's mouth and sent him to his knees. The man's head hung loosely while blood dripped to the ground. With his hands bound at his back, he seemed unable to stand on his own. Ethan hauled the exhausted body up against him and jammed a rag between his bloody teeth, laughed as he pushed the failing man against a wall and ripped his shirt, running a hand over the lean muscles, feeling him shudder.

"No!" Aiden leaped the railing and sprinted down the trail, heedless of the danger to his limbs. He felt trapped in a nightmare; it took an eternity to reach the city and another one to cross the distance to the courtyard.

He burst into the garden, and a frantic motion with his hand brought Alek to his feet. "What is it?"

Aiden fought for breath. "It's Ethan…and Cecil."

Alek gave him a frightened look, but Aiden avoided his eyes as he led him to a door in the castle wall and down into the cellar. The damp rooms below weren't even good for storage. He opened doors and looked into dark recesses, becoming unsure as he found them empty. He flung open a final door and cried out. Up until then he'd hoped it had been a dream. Pale light from a narrow window shown on a single blanket and the battered form sprawled on it.

Alek dropped to his knees and pulled the knife from his boot to slit the tight leather binding Cecil's hands. He gently removed the bloody rag from his mouth.

"Darling," he mourned and drew Cecil into his arms. Dark bruises covered Cecil's trembling body, his face swollen from the beating. Alek brushed the light hair from his forehead and Cecil blinked and opened heavy lids. Panic filled his eyes, and he pulled away with a small cry.

Alek held him tighter. "It's me!"

"Alek?" Cecil clutched feebly at Alek's coat and pressed his face to his breast.

"Hush. I'm here." Alek stroked a bruised cheek. He raised his eyes to Aiden and fury swept his face. "Find him."

With a last desperate look at Cecil, Aiden left the cellar, ran along the echoing halls and chambers of the castle, and slammed through Ethan's door without pause. The Red Twin was at a window and turned to face him. He laughed at Aiden, then stepped back with raised hands.

Aiden balled his fists. "What did you do to him?"

"Why nothing. Well, nothing he hadn't deserved, presuming as he did to take a Karthagan for his lover. Like that dog Natan had done. These Belegans need to be taught their place." Ethan moved closer to confide. "The cur's grunts of pain when I touched him were intoxicating as well."

Blind fury hit Aiden. He grabbed his brother by the throat, pushing him against the wall. The amusement left Ethan's face, his eyes widening with surprise. Aiden tightened his hold. There was a deep rumble in the earth as Ethan tried to shake his grip. Aiden smiled unpleasantly and pressed harder.

"Don't," Ethan gasped out. "Brother?"

Aiden flinched and wept in his heart. "My brother died as a child," he stated sadly. With his free hand he touched Ethan's chest over his pounding heart. "Be still," he whispered. The earth heaved violently as Ethan struggled; then his heart slowed. "Stop," Aiden commanded, and Ethan's strong heart stumbled. There was the crash of falling stone in the city as the earthquake rumbled into the distance and Ethan's life began to slip away.

No! Aiden buried his face against Ethan's shoulder and, for an instant, longed to follow his twin into the grave. Instead, he made Ethan sleep, unable to wake until Aiden released him. He looked at the cold pale face, a death mask. Ethan would appear so to the others when they came.

A sob broke from him and he gathered Ethan in his arms and carried him to his bed. He rested his head on Ethan's chest where a heart had beaten with love for him, long ago. Now there was only hate. Aiden suddenly fell apart, couldn't stop crying. He felt he was going mad.

He drew away from his brother in sudden fear, his thoughts wild. He couldn't be losing his mind as well, could he? Aiden ran a trembling hand over his face, knowing he needed to find Alek. He made his way downstairs but hesitated as he approached the door to the courtyard. There were distressed voices and torchlight outside, and he recalled the quake that had shaken the city. What had Ethan done? Alek passed him and Adain followed as if pulled by invisible strings to the people he suddenly feared, not knowing how much more he could take.

Syros and Natan were already there, and Natan broke away and bowed to Alek, flicking Aiden a glance. "There's been an accident, my lord. One of the older houses collapsed, and a boy is missing in the rubble."

"Any other injuries?" Alek asked as they hurried through the crowded streets. The Karthagans were out examining their city, marveling at the small amount of damage the shaking earth had actually caused.

"Only minor," Natan assured him.

The collapsed stonework was near the older part of the wall. Aiden had begun repairs in the area, but because the irrigation project took longer than expected, he hadn't reached that section yet. Commander Jaden was directing the people searching the debris, and they joined the group.

Aiden had to pause often to brush at his eyes, feeling battered and dazed. Ethan had done this trying to escape Aiden's hold, without a thought to any he might injure. With his brutal assault on Cecil, Ethan had taken his final step into madness. There would have been no stopping the horrors he'd inflict on the world, if free. *But can I save him?*

He stumbled on a loose stone and fell to a knee, then cried out at the sight of little fingers protruding from the rubble of bricks. The others hurried to him and helped free the small boy. Heartbroken, Aiden lifted the crushed body and carried him to his mother, gently placing him in her arms.

He was suddenly aware of the silence of the crowd. Looking up, he met the angry glares of the people around him and knew they laid the death of the boy at Aiden's own feet. After all, who else could call an earthquake? He glanced around anxiously, but his friends had gathered with the grieving family, and he was alone. Suddenly cold, he began to tremble uncontrollably. Drawing himself up, he walked with raised chin through the crowd of hostile observers, who quickly averted their gaze, not bothering to mask their superstition and fear. None dared approach him as he strode through the city, grim, with blood on his garments.

*

AIDEN DIDN'T SLEEP and dressed with care in the black and silver of his father's house the next morning. He fumbled with a braid, then gave up and tied his long hair back with a strip of leather. They would bury Ethan that day, thinking him dead, with all the ceremony due to a Karthagan lord. He wasn't sure how much longer he could bear the emptiness in his heart.

He walked in a daze to the city, but painful emotion swept back into him as he entered the courtyard to join the others and came face-to-face with Cecil. The commander took a startled step back, then reached a hand for him as he turned wretchedly away.

"I'm sorry," Aiden managed, afraid to look at Cecil. He didn't want to see the condemnation in his gaze.

"Aiden."

Cecil touched his hand, and Aiden trembled as he glanced up. The bruises were ugly on Cecil's fair complexion, but the compassion in his gray eyes spread a warmth through Aiden's frozen heart.

"I hold no blame against you," Cecil urged.

Aiden cried out in pain. "But I knew something was wrong with Ethan. I felt his madness." He covered his face. "I meant to take him away. I swear! But I waited too long—"

"Aiden," Cecil spoke sharply, and Aiden struggled for control. Cecil pulled him into a tight embrace and murmured, with a catch in his voice, "I'm so desperately sorry it was you who had to stop him."

Aiden's heart overflowed, and his hot tears fell on Cecil's neck. Cecil spoke words of comfort and stroked his hair, much as he'd done when Aiden had been a child and gone to him when the coldness of the people had hurt and confused him.

Aiden clung to him a moment longer, then took a deep breath and stepped back, and found that the panic in his breast had eased a little.

"Thank you." He smiled tentatively. Cecil nodded and remained at his side as the company made their way through the city streets to the ancient, secluded graveyard north of the city. Alek spoke quiet words to lay the Red Twin to rest, though deep anger simmered in his voice. Aiden kept his eyes on the dark hole they'd put his brother into. He couldn't look at the others.

They expressed soft condolences to him when all was over. As the group departed, Syros put a hand on his arm, startling him. "I'm sorry for your loss, Aiden," he said, and Aiden remembered the recent loss of Syros's wife. "If I can help in any way…"

"Thank you," Aiden told him but couldn't tear his eyes off the pit in the ground. He remained behind when the others left, taking the shovel from the men who would build Ethan's carne. "I'll do this."

Ellis touched his hand. "Let me help."

Aiden shook his head. "No. This is for me to do."

Ellis pressed his hand, tears on his sweet face, then followed the others. Aiden waited until he stood alone on the silent hillside. The sun felt warm on his neck, a slight breeze ruffling his hair. Birds chirped in the nearby trees.

"Are you ready to wake, Ethan?" he asked and blinked at sudden tears.

*

AIDEN SET ASIDE the shovel, sat at the edge of Ethan's grave, and slid into the hole. It took little effort to open the wooden casket, and he stared at his brother's still face, peaceful in sleep. For an instant he wanted to close the lid, bury Ethan, finish what he'd started. But he remembered giggles and shared secrets and sweet embraces from when they were children and Ethan his only friend.

He bent and kissed the pale face so like his own. "Wake, Ethan," he said and waited while Ethan's chest rose and fell on deep breaths. Ethan's lids fluttered and opened. Golden eyes peered at him, dreamy, confused. Then they cleared. "Aiden, what—" With a cry of horror Ethan scrambled up, dislodging clods of dirt as he climbed out of the hole. Aiden followed more slowly, a wary eye on him.

Fury mottled Ethan's beautiful face. "What have you done to me, Brother?"

Aiden held his emotions in check. He mustn't let Ethan sway him. "You attacked Cecil. Nearly killed him! Alek would have murdered you. I almost did."

Ethan's face softened, and he stepped closer, touching Aiden's arm. "But you didn't. You forgave me. I have an idea," Ethan's voice pitched higher with excitement. "Let's run away together. Go someplace no one knows us. Think of the fun we could have! No one can stop us when we're together."

Aiden's heart clenched at the wild look in Ethan's eyes. He truly was mad.

"Go to my cabin, Ethan. Wait for me there. We'll discuss this further," he said, working to keep the sorrow from his voice, praying Ethan would be there when he arrived. He'd take him to the Isle of Wind where he could live out his life…

Ethan studied his face and slowly nodded. "As you wish." He looked at his fine clothing, now covered in dirt from his climb from the grave. "I need to clean up anyway."

Aiden watched him walk into the forest, then picked up the shovel to bury an empty coffin. When he'd placed the last stone, he returned to the city. The Karthagan people were silent as he passed along the streets. He knew they feared him, refusing to meet his gaze, as if his golden eyes were a curse. Hunching his shoulders, he walked on. It was no more than he deserved. He had done terrible things as a child, and though he'd tried to make it up to them, it hadn't been enough.

He passed the fountain and stopped to watch the sunlight glittering on the cascading water. Maybe it was time to give up. He'd begun to believe he'd found forgiveness with the people, that they would finally accept him, but Ethan had destroyed that, and he was too worn to start over.

He should leave, but there was no place in Belega he could go and be welcomed. He thought once more of the Isle. There would be life there again. Surely enough for him and Ethan. He sat on a bench and stared at the cracks in the flagstone, trying to gather the courage to go. After a time, he walked toward the gates. He'd almost managed to escape when he heard Ellis call his name, and he winced in fresh pain. Would it never end?

Ellis caught up with him. "I've been looking for you. I wanted to ask if you'd sit in the garden and talk to me awhile. I have several questions…" His words trailed off as the sun glinted in Aiden's eyes.

"Your eyes are so beautiful," Ellis said in wonder. "Like burnished gold."

Aiden flinched at his words and sucked in a breath. "I know my people are bitter toward me," he said softly. "They despise me and have every right to fear my golden eyes when I look at them. But I'd hoped to not have mockery from you as well." His voice broke. "I can't bear it from you," he finished on a raw whisper.

"Aiden."

Ellis touched his arm, and Aiden cried out, feeling as if Ellis had struck him. He glanced involuntarily at him but turned quickly away, hoping Ellis didn't see the hopeless love in his eyes. Hurrying from him to the gates, he started at a fast jog up the trail into the woods. Ellis shouted something after him, but he chose to ignore it.

He was out of breath by the time he reached his cabin. The rooms were as empty as he'd feared; no sign Ethan had been there. After grabbing a jug of water, he went out onto the porch and sat on the wide railing. The brisk air, fragrant with pine and the fresh tang of the sea, cooled the sweat on his forehead. He sent his thoughts out, brushing on Ethan's energy. Aware of him, Ethan suddenly slammed a wall up between them, cutting Aiden to the heart. For the first time since he and Ethan were conceived, he felt absolutely alone.

It took a moment before he became conscious of the footsteps approaching up the trail. He watched, heart pounding, as Ellis rounded the corner and marched purposefully toward him. Aiden looked away, staring into the distance while his pulse raced madly. With a breath of impatience, Ellis climbed on the rail beside him. Aiden couldn't help the slow grin that spread on his face as Ellis sat so close his thigh pressed against Aiden's. *Darling!* So brave. But what if…

"The way I see it," Ellis began brusquely. "You have two choices. One is to leave the city and be miserable and alone and empty and all kinds of horrible things. Or, you can kiss me and—"

"Ellis!" Aiden jumped from his perch and stood looking at him, breathing hard. Ellis blushed as he slid to his feet, standing close. Aiden realized Ellis still waited for his answer, and in awe, Aiden touched his hair. The silken strands curled instantly around his fingers, and he trembled, anxious. He'd been alone a long time and could easily devour Ellis.

Ellis's breathing hitched as he stepped into Aiden's arms and raised his chin. "Kiss me," he demanded, though Aiden heard the uncertainty he tried to mask. Cupping Ellis's face with both hands, Aiden's pulse rushed at how light his olive skin looked against Ellis's umber brown complexion. He suddenly pictured them in bed, Ellis's darker body twined with his paleness, and a moan escaped him before he could stop it.

Ellis's eyes flamed and he laced his fingers around Aiden's neck, pulling his head down. Their lips brushed, then Ellis pushed into him, making

Aiden aware of his hardness against his thigh. Aiden laughed in sudden joy and swept Ellis up in his arms. Ellis laughed against his neck as Aiden carried him swiftly into the cabin. He crossed the room in three long strides, then shoved a shoulder against the bedroom door. Entering, he tossed Ellis into the middle of the bed and climbed in after him.

He pinned Ellis under him with his heavier body, reveling in the contact. Looking into Ellis's glorious eyes, he read the apprehension and elation swimming in the amber depths. He meant to be gentle, but Ellis arched up against him, seizing his lips in a fierce, needy kiss, snapping Aiden's restraint. He plundered the eager mouth, nerves sparking at the twist of tongues, forgetting to take a breath as Ellis's sweet taste filled his senses.

Ellis lifted his knee, and Aiden cried out at the friction. Head swimming, he pulled back from their kiss. "You've been with men before," he panted. It wasn't a recrimination; he was just surprised.

Ellis shook his head, and Aiden watched a dark blush sweep up his skin. *Gorgeous!*

"No, but my visions didn't only hold terror, Aiden," Ellis assured him, his tone sultry, sensual, and Aiden moaned against his neck when Ellis slid fingers under his tunic, trailing them up Aiden's back as if he couldn't stop touching him. "Sometimes my visions filled my nights with passion and sweat, hardness, and sweet ecstasy." He held Aiden's gaze and moistened his lips, hunger in his eyes. "I dreamed of you."

Gods! It was too much. It took mere seconds to strip off his clothing while Ellis did the same, and then Ellis lay in his arms, silky skin sliding against his own.

"So beautiful," Aiden whispered hoarsely and licked down Ellis's neck, savoring the salty taste of his warm skin. His heart lurched at the catch in Ellis's throat when he dropped his head and nipped one of the little nubs on Ellis's chest. A thrill shot through him, knowing he'd be the first to have Ellis's love.

He jumped in surprise, a deep moan wrenched from him when Ellis reached between them and took him in hand, stroked him haltingly and then faster, making Aiden's head spin.

"Honey, slow down," he begged, wanting it to last, wanting to taste Ellis everywhere. "I want you in my mouth."

"And I want you in mine," Ellis countered. "Shall we wrestle for dominance?"

Aiden blinked, hardly believing as he glanced at Ellis's face and took in the bright, teasing smile, the joy in his eyes. His heart stumbled. He'd never had such an enthusiastic lover, enchanted that Ellis wanted to play as well as make love.

An idea came to him, though it was his turn to blush. Ellis lifted a brow as Aiden's face heated. "What are you thinking?"

"Umm… We could do it together…" His words trailed off when Ellis looked uncertain, but then comprehension dawned and a brilliant grin lifted his lips.

"We certainly could," he said, laughter in his voice. "How—"

Aiden kissed him, stopping his words, needing to gain control of his galloping heart. No one but Ethan had ever wanted to spend time with him, offer him friendship. The few lovers he'd had were swift and hot and well compensated afterwards. That this beautiful man…

Tears threatened. With a desperate knot forming in his chest, Aiden licked a long path down Ellis's toned body, making a beeline for the dark cock jutting from its tangle of curls. Shifting around so his feet touched the headboard, he rolled Ellis on his side and licked him. Ellis moaned, music to his ears.

The tentative licks on his own hard member sent joy snapping through him and his tears spilled over. How was he to give up this sweet, sensual man? Pushing away the pain, he took Ellis into his mouth. Ellis's shudder and cry of bliss undid him. He sucked and licked with purpose, adding his fingers, determined to give Ellis every ounce of pleasure he could before the man remembered who Aiden was and left him.

Chapter Five

SYROS SLOWED HIS horse to a walk through the dense trees in the Dakon Forest, giving the animal a chance to catch its breath from the long journey from Karthag. He cautiously approached the border between the Northern and Southern Territories. He'd hoped to run into Commander Tyrel before he crossed into the South. The treaty still held between the two countries, but it was better to have a Southern soldier as escort, all the same, and Tyrel had shown an interest in the task, at least according to the messenger.

The sun was lowering to evening as he dismounted and pulled the saddle from his tired roan. As he built a fire, he wondered what Willum suspected. Before Willum had left Karthag, he'd asked Syros to pay a visit to the different cities in the Southern Territory, get a feel for the people's mood. Especially at Lord Fredrik's Hall and the capital city of Nagal. Willum had then set off for the North's capital city of Barkuit on horseback, rather than wait for a ship, thereby allowing Cecil time to heal.

Syros scowled into the growing flames of his fire. Dark rumors had been coming out of Fredrik's Hall for some time now. Fredrik had never ceased his aggressions toward the Karthagan people, which had lately been increasing. There was talk of prisoners being taken and tortured. Syros had his suspicions why. Fredrik had always envied the Karthagans their fearsome abilities and was trying to gain them for himself.

That couldn't be allowed to happen. Belega had enjoyed relative peace for the past seventeen years, ever since the Karthagan, Camron, had been thwarted in his attempt to gain control of the continent. Niko had proved the more powerful that day, removing the threat. But now it seemed Fredrik was bent on Camron's same course, wanting total power and dominance.

Were the Karthagans regaining their abilities? That business with Ethan and Cecil had been ugly. And for Ethan to attack the commander with all of them there… That spoke of arrogance and madness, both products of unbridled power.

"But I never have trusted the Red Twins," he confessed to the flames and added another stick of wood. He liked Aiden well enough, admired his work in Karthag, but Ethan had been another matter, his softly spoken words dripping like poison into the calm waters of Belega.

He jabbed a stick into the fire, stirring the coals. "And what is Aiden up to? He grieved for his brother, but there was something…off, about his actions. I wonder…"

Syros ran a hand over his face and rubbed his neck, tired. Nothing was simple. He thought of his baby son born into this tumulus time and hoped he wouldn't be gone from home too long. But this was a soldier's life. He rolled a half-rotted log onto the fire, wrapped in his blanket, and wiped away a stubborn tear as the familiar ache of loss tightened his chest. It was foolish. Sharana had told him not to grieve, to find someone new with her last labored breath.

"And if I don't want to?" he challenged, staring at the cold stars, and took that pain with him into his dreams.

He awakened in the morning by something tickling his ear, and he scrambled up with an oath, batting at it before the insect crawled inside.

"Morning, Syros," Commander Tyrel chuckled, tossing a feather into the bushes.

"About time you showed up," Syros grumbled, smoothing his hair to hide his discomfiture. "I thought I'd have to catch the trees on fire to gain your attention."

"You have it now, my lord. Why are you so far from home? Lost?"

"Maybe," Syros drawled. "Care for some coffee?" He waved to the glowing embers of last night's fire. Tyrel shrugged and sat cross-legged as Syros stirred up the flames and set a pot on the stones, adding water from his flask. When the water was heated to his satisfaction, he added grounds, then turned his attention to the commander squatting across the fire and quickly summarized Willum's misgivings. He jumped at Tyrel's sudden bark of laughter.

"Forgive me, Syros. It's just that I've had the same concerns, but about your eastern city of Siagan. There have been many Northerners from that region crossing the border to Fredrik's Hall. Oh, nothing against treaty," he assured Syros at his frown. "But enough to arouse my interest. And you say Fredrik is trying to increase his influence in Belega? Maybe wrest control from the governors?"

"Willum suspects it, and I also believe his actions have to do with the

Karthagan's abilities, at least how they'd been at their peak. Fredrik has always coveted them and is making a play to acquire the power himself."

Tyrel drained his mug. "In any event, I think Fredrik's Hall is the place to start our inquiry; then we'll check on Siagan. Shall we go?"

Syros smiled slowly. Commander Tyrel would be a good man to have at his side, even if he was a Southerner. He doused the fire, packed his few possessions, then fetched his mount from the nearby meadow. They rode at a swift pace, only stopping to allow the horses time to rest and eat, and arrived at Fredrik's Hall the evening of the second day.

It surprised Syros when the soldiers stationed there ignored them as they trotted through the barracks. The wall encircling the city was unmanned as well, except for a drowsing soldier atop the stonework, and they drew to a halt in the tall grass outside the gates.

"Lieutenant!" Syros called sharply, startling the soldier, who almost fell from his perch.

"May I help you?" the young man asked after a cool survey of them from sea blue eyes. He stood on the stonework, his red hair lifting in the faint breeze.

Tyrel scowled. "I don't know you."

"Korin, sir." The soldier bowed. "Do you wish to see Lord Fredrik?"

"Yes, and could you send someone for Commander Jacksan as well?"

Korin's eyes narrowed, hiding their expression. "As you wish." He bowed again and jumped lightly to the grass, disappearing from view behind the wall. In a moment, the gates swung open. "If you'll come with me? You may leave the horses here. Someone will care for them."

They dismounted, handing the reins to a bored soldier who came from the nearby stables, then followed Korin's easy stride the short distance to the Hall. Korin led them straight through the residence to the back parlor, where he flung open the door without knocking. Lord Fredrik rose from his chair, then sank back with a scowl. The man with him dropped a hand to the knife at his belt. Korin gave a mocking bow to the heavyset men.

"My lords, Commander Tyrel with Lord Syros," he announced loudly, and Syros looked at him more closely. Did Korin know him?

"Come in, come in." Fredrik motioned impatiently.

"And sir," Korin hesitated at the door. "They'd like to speak with Commander Jacksan as well." He closed the door softly but not before Syros saw the grim expression that settled on his attractive features.

Fredrik looked them over. "What brings you here?" he asked, though he seemed strangely indifferent to their presence. "Nelson, dear cousin, you may go."

Syros glanced at Tyrel with a raised brow. The commander waited until Nelson left the room, then cleared his throat. "Where is Commander Jacksan?"

"The guards will be here shortly to take you to him," Fredrik said with an unpleasant smile. There was a commotion at the door and five soldiers entered the room. To his dismay, Syros recognized the archer, Carrow, in the rear with his short bow. Carrow was deadly accurate with both bow and sword.

"Take them below," Fredrik instructed, and Syros knew better than to challenge Carrow as he notched an arrow.

"You have us for now, Fredrik," Tyrel acknowledged coldly. "But be assured Governor Basal will hear of this."

Syros shook his head in exasperation as they trailed the soldiers from the room to the stairwell leading to the cellars. For an instant, he contemplated making a dash for the front entrance, but that wouldn't give them any answers. He followed without protest as they were led below, then shoved unceremoniously into one of the rooms. Tyrel muttered under his breath and paced, out of sorts, but Syros leaned against the wall and cursed himself for a fool, Tyrel for leading them into a trap, and Fredrik for a traitor. The soldiers had left a sputtering torch at Carrow's insistence, but it didn't quite penetrate all the corners. After a time, Syros took it out of its sconce.

"Don't let it go out," Tyrel groused. He sat on the floor and tilted his head back against the cold stones. Syros circled the empty chamber. A dark recess in the far wall caught his attention and he lifted the torch, and his harsh cry brought Tyrel instantly to his side. The commander swore savagely on spotting the crumpled form in the alcove. Syros set the torch aside and helped him lift the limp body into the room, setting him on Tyrel's hastily removed coat.

"Jacksan?" The man's head lulled when Tyrel shook him.

Syros ran his hands over the unconscious body and frowned, puzzled. He could find no injuries on him.

"Commander?" Tyrel put his mouth close to his ear. "Jack?"

A tremor passed through the soldier, and they saw him struggle to respond. His eyes fluttered open, but even that proved too much. He cried out in pain, his eyes rolling back in his head as his body began to convulse. Syros gave him room while Tyrel protected his head as well as he could as Jacksan flailed on the hard stones. The seizure stopped and Jacksan arched his back; then his body collapsed, his last breath a rattle in his throat.

Tyrel stared at him, then turned his gaze, full of horror, to Syros.

"What happened?"

Syros lifted his shoulders, helpless, as he watched the bright red blood slip from Jacksan's ears. "I saw no injuries. Maybe something wrong inside his head?" There was a scraping sound at the door, and Syros sprang up and darted across the room to plaster himself against the wall by the entrance, expecting treachery. He held his breath as the door swung inward.

"I'm not fool enough to walk in there, sirs."

"Korin?" *What trick is this?*

"Yes, sir. We have only a few moments to reach the gates before Fredrik's men swarm us. Will you come?"

Syros thought quickly as his gaze shot to Jacksan's body. Tyrel looked grim, seeming as uncertain as Syros.

"Very well," he said and stepped into the Hall. Korin waited a good ten paces away and waved them to follow. Syros and Tyrel hurried after him as he slipped along the corridor. They passed a fallen guard, his throat slit, and Syros watched Korin with speculation as they climbed the stairs.

Korin hesitated at the top, then motioning for silence, led them quickly through the entrance hall and outside. They sprinted across the open field and crouched against the stone wall.

"Your horses are just there, in the forest, if you can reach them."

Syros turned to thank him and shut his teeth on a sharp hiss. The bruising mark of a hand adorned Korin's face, and the blood on his lips was fresh.

"The guard?"

Korin shook his head and gave a sudden fierce grin that surprised Syros, under the circumstances. "Our beloved lord when I asked him why you'd been imprisoned. Fredrik doesn't like to be questioned."

Syros studied him. "How would you explain what's happening here?"

"If you're looking for answers, my lord, go to Siagan." There was a disturbance at the Hall's door. "Go!"

Syros ran into the tall grass with Tyrel on his heels. As they passed beyond the gates, he saw Korin hitch himself on the wall and lie down as if he'd been there all day. Fear stung him for the soldier's safety, but it would be folly to return.

They reached the forest and waiting horses and flung to saddle, racing into the thickening trees. Syros cursed long and low with feeling as he recalled Korin's warning about Siagan. Messages had been coming steadily from Commander Davis stationed there, but he realized it had been over a year since he'd actually seen the man. What was going on that he was missing?

*

CARROW LOWERED HIS arm. Korin would be an easy shot with the borrowed long bow. What was the fool up to? If Fredrik found out what he'd done… The swine took pleasure in torture.

He leaned the bow against the wall and dismissed the soldiers with a wave of his hand. They knew better than to question him, and he sneered after them. The soldiers who served Fredrik were cowards and bullies, and he had no use for them.

When alone, he returned to the Hall and entered the cool cellar. He stopped beside the slain guard. Neatly done. Korin had promise. He continued on to the chamber where the prisoners had been kept, and a small breath of dismay escaped him when he discovered Jacksan's body. He'd been a good commander and hadn't deserved the horrors obviously done to him.

Carrow clenched a fist, berating himself for not having moved against Fredrik before it had come to this. The slovenly lord had been meeting secretly with visitors from the North. Messages sent back and forth. Carrow should have known something was up, but he hadn't been sure what, or in which direction he must jump.

There was a storm door at the far end of the cellar. Carrow retrieved the guard's body from the Hall and bore him across the meadow to an old well that contained many such inconveniences.

Returning, he wrapped Jacksan gently in Tyrel's coat, left behind, and carried him from the Hall. Dry grass crunched under his boots as he crossed the yard with his burden. As he approached the gates, Korin sprang from the wall to open them. He fell into step behind him, neither speaking. Soldiers stared at them as they passed through the barracks to the cemetery on the hill, but Carrow chose to disregard them. Korin fetched shovels, and they began to dig a hole beneath the spreading branches of an oak. Carrow studiously ignored the small grave on the hillside behind them holding his young wife many years now. He still couldn't bear to think of her there, her vibrant, beautiful presence gone from him forever.

The Nagal soldiers began to trickle up and looked at Jacksan's body and bloodied face with shocked expressions. Fredrik came just as they were lowering the body into its grave.

"Where are the prisoners?" Fredrik demanded hotly. Disgust swept Korin's bruised face, and Carrow kept a curious eye on him as they began to cover the commander with the dark soil.

"I asked a question!"

Carrow leaned on his shovel and gazed about the cemetery with an insolent eye. "I don't see them here. We were told Jacksan had been transferred. Can you explain this?"

Fredrik stiffened at his tone, then turned his back to him. "Korin?"

"Fredrik?"

Blind rage suffused Fredrik's face, and he narrowed his eyes, clenching his large hands. He was strangely quiet, then began to shake, sweat bursting out on his skin with his concentration.

In sudden realization, Carrow cried a warning, but it was too late. Korin's slim body gave a violent jerk, and he dropped to his knees, a horrible cry bursting from him. He clutched his head, and Fredrik stepped closer, seeming to drink in the agony on his face. Fredrik trembled as he touched the dark bruises stark in Korin's ashen skin.

His pleasure in Korin's suffering sickened Carrow. "Let him go," he hissed. Fredrik ignored him, and Carrow swung his shovel, clipping the man's temple. He watched dispassionately as the large body fell to the ground. Korin swayed, dazed, as blood trickled from his nose and ears.

Carrow took a knee beside him. "Can you stand?"

At his nod, Carrow pulled Korin to his feet. He studied the silent soldiers gathered on the hillside.

"Korin." He held his gaze. He was an unusually comely man, the copper hair and fair skin standing out, but it was the strength in the sea blue eyes that had always caught Carrow's attention.

"I need your help," he said without preamble.

"My lord?"

"I need you to ride after Commander Tyrel and Lord Syros with a message. I believe I know who's been teaching Fredrik such dangerous tricks."

"And Lord Fredrik?"

"You're in charge here, Lieutenant."

Korin inclined his head. As Carrow started back for the Hall, he paused to watch Korin, who stared at the black soil of the freshly dug grave. Korin nodded sharply as if reaching a decision, and Carrow felt sure no one grudged him the deed as he slipped the knife from his belt and made it impossible for Fredrik to hurt anyone again.

*

IT TOOK SEVERAL days of travel for Syros and Tyrel to pass through the Southern Territory into the North, and another to arrive in the late afternoon at Siagan. Syros sat on an outcrop of rock overlooking the city, squinting in the bright sunlight, while Tyrel scouted the area. Nothing seemed out of place in the quiet buildings behind the tall walls.

Hearing the crunch of a boot on gravel behind him, he turned and gave Tyrel a cool look. "I've killed a man who made less noise than you," he observed.

Tyrel shrugged. "I've killed a man with a softer tongue than yours."

Syros chuckled as Tyrel crouched beside him. Tyrel waved to the plains stretching into the distance on their left. "We have company," he said, then slipped off the rock back into the woods.

Syros waited and nearly laughed aloud as a lone horseman came into view. The young soldier rode with complete indifference to his surroundings, slowly and easily, as if he felt no danger in being a Southerner in the North. Syros watched in puzzled fascination as he drew closer. Copper hair fluttered around a pale face, and when the soldier raised brilliant sea blue eyes to him, Syros let out a grunt.

Certainly, Korin was in no danger. With that graceful body and pretty face, he would be an asset to any Barkuit ruler. Think of the intrigues he could carry out! In Gargary's time, he would have instantly been made a member of the court. Syros chuckled to himself. Willum would have had to keep on his toes, then. If he'd been allowed to live. Gargary could easily have replaced him with Korin as his son, if he'd so chosen.

Korin brought his mount to a stop at the foot of the rocks and slid lightly to his feet, then swept a courtly bow. "My lord Syros, may I speak with you?"

Syros grinned viciously. *So polite!* He wondered if the lad had any fight in him.

"If you wish."

Korin effortlessly climbed the rocks to his side, and Syros nodded approval. There was some strength in the lean body after all.

Korin sat, leaned back on his palms with a contented sigh, and drew in a breath of warm, pine-scented air. "This is nice." He turned to Syros. "Fredrik is dead."

Syros raised his brows. "Indeed?" The Southerner was surprising him more by the moment.

"It happened while we were burying Commander Jacksan." There was pain in his lovely eyes, gone in the next blink. "Fredrik had done something to Jacksan's mind, built up pressure or something. You saw."

Tyrel came up and joined them, his face grim. "And Fredrik?"

Korin gave him a piercing glance. "I slit his throat."

"Good." Tyrel's tone was emphatic.

"It was a pleasure." The men shook hands in complete agreement.

Syros watched them curiously. He still didn't understand Southerners.

If they despised the fat lord, why hadn't they disposed of him long ago?

"Why are you here, Korin?" he asked abruptly.

"I have some information Carrow thinks you're missing. He's concluded that Fredrik has been learning his tricks from a certain man here in Siagan."

"Davis?"

"No, sir. A soldier named Mandel. We fear something may have happened to Council Leader Davis. And after Jacksan—" Korin broke off, pain once again in his expression.

Syros scowled darkly. Mandel was another man who should have been killed years ago. If he were governor…

"There's one more thing," Korin turned to Tyrel. "Carrow asks that you return immediately and take command of the garrison at Fredrik's Hall, now that Fredrik is gone. He's sent a runner to Governor Basal with the news of Fredrik's death as well but would prefer to have someone of authority there until Basal decides what to do."

"Very well." Tyrel rose. "Can you children take care of things here without me?"

"We can only try," Syros answered dryly and rose to shake his hand. "Thank you."

Korin lounged on the rocks with his face to the sun after Tyrel left. Syros wondered how much of his careless pose was an act.

"How do you know me?" he asked in a moment.

Korin shrugged. "Everyone in the South knows the description of the North's governor, Willum, and his excellent regent."

Syros frowned. That wasn't much of an answer, but probably all he would be given. "Shall we go?"

"Surely." The apathy fell from Korin in a breath, leaving his eyes sharp and alert. They descended to the ground, and Syros retrieved his mount from behind a large boulder. After hiding their packs, they quickly mounted and started for the gates of the city. The tall stone walls reflected the sunlight, grim and unwelcoming. Syros dropped a hand to his knife hilt, uneasy as soldiers hailed them from the gates, but luckily he was recognized at once. They were let in without question, the wide doors swinging open, though brows were raised at Korin's uniform. Not many Southerners passed that way without being expected.

"I wish to see the council leader at once," Syros informed a soldier as the hostler took their horses.

"He's at the castle, my lord."

"Korin," Syros glanced at him and scowled, impatient with him again. Korin leaned against his roan, whispering in its ear and stroking the soft mane, the picture of indolent, spoiled youth.

"When you're ready, Korin," he snapped.

Korin stretched lazily. "Yes, my lord."

He strolled into the street, and Syros had trouble controlling his features. The North had a strict law that all visitors should surrender their weapons, and here Korin passed within two feet of the guards with a long knife sheathed at his belt, and they never saw it. Probably took him for the pampered son of some nobleman. Syros coughed to hide his delighted laughter. The man certainly had him intrigued.

Korin slanted him a look. "We'll get your friend back if it's at all possible."

"What's in this for you, Korin?" Syros asked curiously. "Why are you here?"

"Commander Jacksan was a good man and a close friend. I want to find the beast responsible for his death."

Syros nodded at the hard tone.

The courtyard stood empty, and Syros flung open the doors to the castle and strode into the hallway. A fire burned in the large hearth despite the warmth outside, and several men sprawled in chairs, wine at their elbows.

"Syros," a voice drawled, and a stocky man eased to his feet and looked them over with an insolent eye.

"Mandel," Syros acknowledged. "Where's Davis?"

"Are you the governor, Syros? What business do you have here?"

Syros took a threatening step. "Where's the council leader?"

The air crackled with sudden energy, and Korin placed a restraining hand on Syros's shoulder.

Mandel laughed gleefully. "Your pretty friend has it right, Syros. I'm not the same man you sneered at years ago. As for Davis, if you want to see him, I'll gladly take you."

Syros exchanged a look with Korin, who shrugged as if it was no more than he expected. Syros controlled his anger at the familiar situation. "Very well."

The guards moved forward, and Syros spread his hands from his weapons. Korin leaned languidly against the doorpost as they searched Syros, taking several knives.

"And you?" Mandel held out his hand, and Korin gingerly drew the long knife from its sheath as if afraid it might cut him.

"Be gentle with it, lord. It was a gift from a delightful lady. Oh, I shan't tell you who," he tutted as Mandel arched a brow. Mandel chuckled and slipped the blade in his own belt. Syros caught the satisfied gleam in Korin's eyes.

"This way." Mandel gave a short bow and led them from the room. It didn't surprise either of them when he stopped before the entrance to the cellar and unbolted the heavy door.

"In you go," he said genially.

Korin grimaced into the fading light at the bottom of the long stairway. "May we have a torch?"

Syros stirred, thinking Korin had pushed his luck too far, but blinked as Mandel laughed indulgently and handed over a torch and tinderbox from a nearby sconce.

"Don't worry, dear. The monsters aren't out tonight." He touched Korin's copper hair, then motioned them in and slammed and bolted the door. Syros looked from it to Korin, baffled.

"He flatters himself." Korin shrugged and sprang down the steps.

A little light filtered through small windows along the ceiling, and Syros did a thorough search of the stone room while Korin watched him. He returned in dismay to the gaping hole in the wall at the back of the cellar opening to the tunnels beneath the city.

"Do you think your friend is in there?" Korin asked, and Syros saw the shudder that passed through him.

"I believe so, yes."

They stared at the aperture another moment.

"Well…" Korin removed the tinderbox from a pocket and crouched to light the torch. Syros doubted Mandel would find the lad so harmless if he saw the grim set to his lips or the steel deep in his blue eyes as Korin stepped through the hole.

The smell of damp, rich earth filled Syros's nostrils, almost choking him as he followed Korin in. They moved carefully down the steep incline, and Korin held the torch aloft when they reached the bottom. The flickering light showed a small space with the tunnel continuing into darkness.

Syros caught Korin's shaky breath.

"What is it?" he whispered, unnerved.

Korin's face was white. "Don't you feel it? It's death."

Syros stared at him and caught the sudden wicked gleam in his eyes while an irrepressible grin leapt on his face. Korin covered his mouth to stifle a laugh. "Sorry."

Syros cursed under his breath, wanting to strike the impudent smirk from his face.

Korin took a quick step back and raised his hands. "Forgive me, lord. Fear always makes me slightly stupid."

"No doubt," Syros growled. Then he grinned reluctantly and cuffed the lad. "Don't do it again."

They followed the low tunnel around a curve and came to a division where the main passage continued ahead, and a narrow tunnel branched to the right. A chill crept over Syros as he looked into the dark artery, recalling all the terrible stories he'd heard of the lake under Siagan. He'd hoped never to set eyes on the still, dark surface of the subterranean waters.

Korin stirred restlessly at his side, and Syros shot him a glance, but bit back his harsh words. The soldier was genuinely afraid, the hand holding the flickering torch unsteady as he peered into the darkness. Damp air wafted from the cavern below, and Korin cleared his throat. "We'd better go down there before I can't."

Syros nodded in agreement.

They walked with caution down the steep incline, stopping when the tunnel opened into a wide cavern. The surface of the lake spread out at their feet like black ice, a deep and silent death. The Karthagan spirits once trapped in the lake had fled long ago when Kavi released them, but the lingering horror of their passage still pervaded the cold air. Both men were breathing hard in the strange quiet, and Syros jumped violently at a low moan that throbbed with hopelessness and pain in the darkness. Korin sucked in a ragged breath.

"Steady, lad." Syros put a hand on his shoulder and felt the shivers that ran his body.

Korin pulled his gaze from the lake. "How they must have suffered."

"Yes." Syros was purposefully curt. "This way."

They rounded the lake to the right, coming upon an opening set in the cave's wall. The rotted wooden door of a small room had been smashed in and the splintered boards set to one side. The torch light illuminated a pit dug in the earthen floor that brought to mind a shallow grave. They found Davis hanging by his wrists on the far wall. Giving a startled cry, Korin dropped the torch and slipped a small knife from his boot, its bitter sharpness slicing the tight leather straps binding the council leader's hands. Davis pitched into his arms, and Syros helped him carry the limp man out of that terrible place.

It amazed Syros how much easier he could draw a breath by the lake. The room had been oppressive, and he'd quickly become disoriented and forgetful. Sleep and the comfort of death had begun to creep into his thoughts.

By mutual consent, they skirted the lake and bore the man into the dark tunnel leading back to the main passage. They'd left the torch by the shattered door, and its light was cut off as they rounded the curve. Davis made no further sound as they stumbled through the darkness, and Syros feared his friend had already died. As they approached the larger passage, the barest hint of light reached them from the cellar. They scrambled up the slope with their burden. Once through the wall, they laid Davis on the stone floor, and Korin pressed fingers to his neck.

"He's alive," Korin said with relief. Syros sat back on his heels while Korin ran his hands over the unconscious man and frowned, perplexed. "There's no broken bones, and see—" Korin moved aside the ragged tunic to show slightly discolored skin and mostly healed wounds. "—the bruising and sores on him were inflicted weeks ago."

Syros touched the haggard face, the eyes sunken and bruised. He carefully turned Davis's head and fresh blood trickled from his ear and slid down to join older stains on his tunic.

Korin swore viciously. "Very much like Jacksan. He needs water," he continued, and darted a glance around the cellar. His gaze traveled up the staircase and Syros watched a puzzling bleakness and resignation come over his features. Korin shook his head and laughed mockingly under his breath.

"Keep him warm," Korin stated flatly and stood, straightened his uniform, and climbed the stairs. He gave a sharp knock, which was answered almost immediately, as if the guards had been waiting for it. They exchanged low words, and the door banged closed again. Korin sat on the top step with his hands clasped between his knees, the copper hair swinging down to hide his face.

"What are you doing?"

Korin didn't reply, and in a moment the door opened, and Korin slipped out.

Time passed slowly. There wasn't much Syros could do for the injured councilman. The leather had bitten cruelly into Davis's thin wrists, and Syros ripped part of his tunic to bind the open sores. He ground his teeth in frustration that he couldn't clean them first. Davis didn't seem to have a fever… Muffled moans escaped his parched lips on occasion, but mostly he lay still and unresponsive.

The evening light faded from the high windows before the door rattled, and Korin stumbled in, only a quick grasp at the railing saving him from a hard fall down the stairs.

"Thank you, gentlemen," Korin said, and bowed with a flourish. The soldiers answered with angry mutters and left, though one remained. Korin took a basket from him, the soldier clasping Korin's hands longer than necessary. Then he disappeared, and the door slammed shut, vibrating in the silent room. Korin laughed softly and trotted down the stairway, nearly colliding with Syros waiting at the bottom, hands on hips.

"Good evening, sir." Korin made his sweeping bow and skirted around him. After dropping the basket beside Davis, he knelt and withdrew a warm blanket, then fumbled with the stopper on the water skin until Syros took it from him.

"Korin?"

"I got the ugly man very drunk and then stole his dinner." Korin stifled a giggle and his eyes danced. "It was very good wine."

He dug into the basket, and Syros grabbed his arm. "Korin, are you all right?"

Korin gave him a strange look, then drew a quiet breath. "Would it matter?"

Fury burned through Syros. "It was foolish and dangerous—" He bit off the words and scowled. "Your life is just as important as Davis's, and you're not to be so careless again." He leaned closer. "You're not to sell yourself in this manner while in my company. I won't tolerate it—from anyone. You could have put us in danger."

"Yes, sir." Korin blinked, confusion in his eyes. "It's not what you think, Syros," he offered after a moment. "The knife I carried had several fine gems on it, and I let Mandel believe I knew where others might be had. A business arrangement. He never touched me. As for the soldier…a pleasant distraction, enjoyed by us both."

"Good." Syros continued to glower as he opened the water skin, though unaccountably relieved by Korin's admission. The lad should take better care of himself. He wouldn't wish Mandel's lascivious advances on anyone. He knelt by Davis and put an arm under his head to lift it. Davis managed a few swallows of the precious water. The hard knot of worry in Syros's chest loosened on hearing the delighted giggles that escaped Korin as he drew fruit and cheeses and the last of the sweet wine from the basket. Syros ruefully shook his head. The lad certainly didn't lack courage. He patted Davis's cheek, wondering if he could wake long enough to eat a little.

Chapter Six

SYROS SAT BACK against the cellar wall the next morning watching Korin through narrowed lids, not quite sure what the soldier was plotting. They'd spent a long night in confinement, and he wondered if it wasn't already beginning to tell on the lad. Korin passed the time by dividing the remaining contents of the basket into tiny piles. He inspected the basket as well, shrugged, and set it aside.

He then searched his pockets and Syros was amazed at the things he drew forth: flint and tinder, several colored stones, bright string, and some hard candy. He had strips of thin leather, a small silver spoon that looked suspiciously similar to the ones in Fredrik's kitchen, a few loose buttons and silver pieces that Korin sorrowfully let drop onto the blanket.

Korin scratched his bright head, then grinned and began to unbutton his shirt. Catching Syros's gaze on his white skin, he batted his lashes and turned modestly away. Syros chuckled even as he wanted to smack his pretty face.

From an inside pocket, Korin withdrew a thin sheet of parchment and charcoal. He sprawled on the blanket and smoothed out one of the papers, showing a map he'd been sketching. Syros got up to look. It showed the land beyond the border, all of the Southern Territory where Syros assumed Korin had traveled so far. He added a few dashes to represent Siagan and drew frightened eyes and something that looked like the deep lake under them.

"I could hang you for a spy," Syros said pleasantly.

"You'd have to catch me."

Korin added a few mountains in the distance then sat up and tossed the charcoal into one of the piles. He looked over the small collection ruefully. "I don't suppose you have anything to contribute?"

Syros blinked. *To what end?* He ran through a mental list and took out a clean silk handkerchief from his pocket and a few copper pieces. He thought of Sharana's ring over his heart. He could easily replace the fine chain. He pulled it over his head and Korin's eyes widened in greedy delight.

Syros held the silver band in his palm and stared at it with hungry eyes, remembering the glorious day Sharana had given it to him. He brought it to his lips and kissed it fervently, then slipped it on a finger. He felt Korin's gaze and expected derision, but instead saw the first glimmers of compassion.

"Is she waiting at home for you?" Korin asked kindly, unwittingly twisting the knife in Syros's heart.

Syros ran a thumb over the ring, throat tight. "She died in the spring, giving birth to our son."

He heard Korin's sharp breath. Looking up, he met the sheen of tears in Korin's sea blue gaze. "I'm truly sorry," Korin murmured.

Syros inclined his head. He usually despised the pity shown him, but he had glimpsed the tender heart Korin hid behind the sarcasm, and somehow it didn't hurt coming from him.

Korin retrieved the basket and lined it with Syros's handkerchief, adding the firmest grapes and sharpest of the remaining cheeses, the bright stones and string, buttons and copper and half the silver, the spoon and hard candies. Syros expected the chain to be laid over the top of it all, but instead Korin had it peeking tantalizingly from beneath a tart apple. He looked critically over his handiwork.

"That should do it."

Once again Korin climbed the stairs and pounded on the door. He hid the basket behind his back when it opened. There was a quick exchange of words and a vigorous shake of the guard's head. Korin flashed the silver in his hand but pulled it out of reach. With an angry oath the guard slammed the door.

Korin rocked on his heels and hummed as he waited. In short order, the door flung open again. Korin handed over the coin, and the guard was replaced by the one Korin had dealt with the previous evening. Korin pitched his voice low and earnest, and he handed the basket to the man with a bow. The soldier was clearly startled, but a glance at the contents brought a smile to his face, and he nodded readily to whatever Korin was saying.

The door shut again, and Korin skipped down the stairs.

"Well?"

"Now we wait." Korin sat on the blanket and returned the remaining items to his pockets.

Davis sighed and stirred.

"Davis?" Syros softly called his name and felt his forehead. No fever. The man's eyelids fluttered and there was the flash of blue eyes, dark with confusion and panic.

"It's Syros," he assured his friend, and Davis's breathing eased as he stared at him. Recognition dawned, and Syros helped him to sit up. Davis rested against his shoulder, even that little effort exhausting him. Korin aided him with the water flask, then sat back on his heels and patiently peeled the remaining grapes and fed them to Davis one at a time.

The man blushed faintly. "I feel so helpless," he croaked and managed a weak smile.

Korin shrugged. "That's because you are, but we'll build up your strength." He searched the bloodshot eyes. "Any headache? Are you dizzy?"

"No. Simply tired." Davis closed his eyes. "Mandel kept me trapped down here for months. I tried to tunnel through a cave-in, but then Ethan came…" A shudder passed along his emaciated frame, and for a moment his face was gray and old. "It was…painful."

"Ethan?" Syros took him up sharply, on a surge of fear and anger. "The Karthagan? One of the Red Twins?"

"Yes. He came a few days ago, and that bastard Mandel welcomed him like a brother. Laughed when Ethan—" Davis's voice broke, though his remembered horror was obvious.

Korin turned suddenly away, and Syros saw him struggle with his expression. His hands shook, and Syros remembered Jacksan. How close had the two been?

The door rattled, and Korin leaped up with a forced smile. "Ah."

He waited at the bottom of the steps and pushed the bright hair behind his ears. The sea blue eyes gleamed in the half light. The door swung open, and the guard Korin had given the basket to stood in the doorway with a laden tray.

"Here, let me help you." Korin sprang up the steps and took the heavier items.

"Hurry," the guard urged. Syros was surprised at the voice and watched the man closely as he followed Korin down the stairs and set the tray on the blanket. He was younger than Syros had thought, no older than Korin, with a comely face.

"Thank you," Korin said earnestly, and the young man reddened at the touch on his arm. He nodded and quickly fled back up the stairs.

Korin hummed contentedly as he took stock of the miniature feast, clearly delighted when he uncovered a thick warm stew.

"This is what we need." He rubbed his hands together. "Try to eat as much as you can, sir."

Davis struggled to sit upright, and Syros had him lean back against his chest. Korin's patience was inexhaustible as he fed him. Syros's back began to ache long before Davis had his fill, and he swallowed a sigh of relief when he could lay him back down. Davis drank greedily from the water flask, then covered his eyes with an arm and drifted back to sleep.

Syros joined Korin where he plundered the remaining items on the tray, smiling as Korin handed him the last of the stew. "All this for a bit of silver and trinkets?"

Korin nodded, a smug look on his face, and whooped as he discovered a berry pie under a cloth. "This, and something more. But that's for later."

Syros had come to realize Korin loved his surprises and stifled his curiosity.

Finally replete, they leaned back against the cellar wall, and Korin yawned and licked the crumbs from his fingers.

"Are you ready?"

Korin eyed him suspiciously. "For what?"

Syros grinned. The lad could look more indolent than anyone else he'd known. His lids were drooping, and he seemed on the verge of sleep.

"To explore Davis's tunnel, of course."

"Oh, that." Korin stretched and climbed to his feet, awake and alert, once again all smiles. "Very well."

Syros chuckled to himself as he retrieved the torch the young guard had provided along with their meal.

Neither smiled as they stood in the dark entranceway to the tunnels below the city. Korin cleared his throat. "I guess daylight wouldn't make it any brighter in there."

"I shouldn't think so."

Korin lit the torch and took a tentative step forward. Syros watched his hesitant progression, then swore impatiently and took the torch from him. "Come on!"

Korin followed with a growing smirk on his face Syros ignored.

The thick air of the tunnels caught at their throats, making it difficult to breathe. They avoided the passage to the lake, the path ahead growing narrower the farther they traveled, until they invariably came to the cave-in.

"You can see where Davis was tunneling." Syros lifted the torch to show a small gap at the ceiling, enough for a man to crawl through. He cast about. "What tool did he use?"

"His hands," Korin answered, sounding strangled, and pointed to the gouge marks in the dirt and a broken nail, pale against the rich soil.

Syros looked Korin up and down and then surveyed his own stocky frame. A wicked smile touched his mouth.

"In you go, lad." He nodded to the opening.

Korin took a hasty step back. "Why me?"

"You're slimmer, and besides, beauty before age, my young Southern friend." Syros sketched a mocking bow. He set the torch in a nearby sconce and laced his fingers to boost him up. Korin's sigh was audible.

*

KORIN KNEW HE'D made a mistake the moment he squirmed into the narrow passageway. The blackness was complete. He couldn't breathe! Panic swept through him, and the only thing that kept him from scrambling back out was the thought of Syros's derision.

He laid his head on his crossed arms and worked on his breathing. This wasn't the hole in the ground his father had thrown him into when he was a boy and in the way. That one he'd had to share with whatever pitiful creature had fallen in since his last entombment. There had been a rat, once… Enough! That wasn't helping. He was a grown man and a soldier… Ha! He inched his way into the darkness.

He traveled some distance in this manner, beginning to wonder if screaming would help after all. But suddenly loose soil from another cave-in blocked the remainder of the tunnel. He almost sobbed in relief, realizing he could go back.

But the dirt was soft and easy to push aside and pack down. Korin swore long and creatively as he burrowed forward. It wasn't until his mind began to wander that he realized the air had become thin, and he was breathing too quickly. Cold sweat broke out on his body as panic once again washed through him. He dug frantically, his mind a chaos of fear and superstition.

He thought he was hallucinating when his hand touched empty space and sunlight poured through the tiny hole he'd made. He took several deep breaths of the sweet, fresh air, then started the long struggle back to Syros. He'd never been happier than when his legs swung into emptiness, and he dropped to the tunnel floor. He frowned. The torch still cast its flickering light, but Syros was gone.

Snatching up the torch, he began to trot toward the cellar, slowing when he heard voices echoing from the passage leading to the lake. At a sharp cry of pain from Syros, he strode down the tunnel and swept into the midst of the gathered men. "Am I missing the fun?" He dropped the impish grin from his face at the sight of a Karthagan standing over Syros and swallowed a sudden fear. "Who are you?"

Cold golden eyes looked him over. "There you are. Playing in the dirt, are we?"

Korin made a feeble effort at brushing the mud from his tunic and trousers, his mind racing. "All for nothing. The way is completely blocked, like I told him."

He glanced at Syros and winced. The regent was on his knees, hands bound behind his back, and an ugly bruise marked his white forehead. Korin watched blood trickle beside his furious eye. Two guards stood sullenly behind Syros, with a third coming up to Korin, the one who'd accepted the basket from him. He gave Korin a look filled with fear and yearning before dropping his gaze. A fourth stood at the Karthagan's side. Korin grimaced at the odds and wondered how to change them.

The Karthagan took the problem out of his hands by stepping closer to him. "You needn't be here. Go on to the cellar and wait for me."

"And Syros?" Korin asked carefully.

"Korin!" Syros interjected, tone frantic. "This is Ethan of Karthag. Please, just do as he says."

Korin swallowed a burst of terror. But he had to keep his wits and distract Ethan, if he wanted any chance of saving Syros. "One of the Red Twins?" he asked, derision dripping from his voice.

Syros groaned even as Ethan sucked in an angry breath. His handsome face mottled with fury and he clenched trembling hands. Korin screamed as pain burst in his head, driving him to his knees. His sight darkened as fire raced along sensitive nerves, and he fell, twitching, to the earth. Blood flowed from his nose and ears and eyes.

Ethan stood over him, watching dispassionately as consciousness began to leave him.

"Take him." Ethan motioned, and guards picked him up, their grip painful, and hauled him to the dark chamber beside the lake. Ethan followed.

*

KORIN ROUSED ONCE again during the long torment of the night, body shaking as he hung on leather straps that might have previously held Davis captive. He felt the jab of small knives under his skin. Ethan was unusually cruel, and more than once fire had poured over Korin's body. He'd watched as his skin blackened and split and fell from the bone. Of course it wasn't real, and the pain never enough to kill. Only enough to send him into blessed darkness, to be awakened and tortured again.

It was an effort to open his eyes this time. Ethan lay prostrate in the shallow grave at his feet, embracing the ground. The air thrummed with the energy he was drawing from the earth, and to Korin's horror, from him as well. He could feel his life slowly leaking into the pulsing air to be at once pulled into Ethan.

Ethan was suddenly in his mind, and he cried out in agony as the crawling fingers probed violently into his darkest dreams. He sobbed aloud as the black memories of his father were brought out and gloated over, replayed until Korin felt the allure of madness creeping at the edges of his reason.

Fire burned him once again, and he slid into darkness, floating in pain and fear, to awake shivering. The air wafting from the lake was icy, and a cold mist swirled into the room. Exhaustion and pain muddled Korin's thoughts, and he shrank back in fear from a voice reaching through the pounding in his head.

"You must leave now," the voice urged from nearby. "The night can hide you."

It surprised him to hear Syros's voice in answer. "How can I trust you? I don't even know your name."

"It's Derik, sir. Please, there's no time. Ethan means to kill him. I saw it in his eyes. He's already killed Mandel."

Korin's sight cleared, and he saw the soldier who'd befriended him earlier standing in the room with Syros. Syros looked at Korin and nodded. "Release him."

Derik didn't hesitate. He handed Syros the torch he carried and drew a knife from his belt. The cords were off Korin in an instant, and Derik caught him as he fell, a rag doll in his arms. The soldier's face was a white mask as he dealt Korin a stinging slap, rousing him further.

"We need to go," Derik said tightly, and Korin nodded, struggling to gain his feet. Syros led them from the room, skirting the lake, but Derik hesitated as he took the left-hand branch of the tunnel.

"Korin has opened the passageway," Syros told him.

Korin grew disoriented and confused as they walked, hearing Ethan's voice in his mind. Derik led him, but his thoughts wandered into dark dreams. It was a relief when they finally reached the cave-in.

"Are you up for this?" Syros asked Davis, who waited at the opening. The man was still pale and drawn, but he had gained a little strength from their care. He nodded grimly, and Syros at once boosted him to the ledge.

The movement caught Korin's eye, and he cried out in fear. "Don't make me go in there."

"It's the only way out," Syros said quietly.

"No," Korin pleaded, an anguished whisper. A black memory bubbled to the surface. "Don't put me in there again." Tears fell from his hot eyes. "I'll be good, Father. I won't *tell.*"

They stared at him in stunned silence while Korin struggled to stay in the present.

"Go on," Derik choked out. "I'll take him another way and meet you. I've staked horses just outside the gates."

"We should stay together."

"I'll bring him!"

Syros looked from him to Korin, who hung limply against his side. "You'd better," he warned and pulled himself onto the narrow ledge.

Korin followed Derik through the tunnels back to the cellar and up into the castle's many corridors. They hid in the shadows several times to avoid guardsmen, and Korin's heart raced by the time they reached a door opening onto the quiet city streets. As they approached the gates, Derik put his own cloak around him, covering Korin's bright hair. The guards merely grunted as Derik gave the password, and they were let outside the walls. Korin groped in the darkness, and Derik took his hand, guiding him to the trees where Syros restlessly paced.

Derik hesitantly touched his arm when they parted. Glancing up, Korin was startled by the soldier's quickly drawn breath. Derik cupped Korin's cheek and looked at the blood that came off on his fingertips. With a soft cry, he pulled Korin close and awkwardly kissed him, then hurried away with a stifled moan.

"Syros?" Korin asked, bewildered as he stared after the retreating figure. Used to dealing with the corruptions and dark passions of men, he had no defense against a genuine affection. His eyes prickled with tears.

"It's all right. Let's go."

"He risked his life for us, and I didn't even thank him."

"It's all right," Syros reiterated and put an arm around him as he led him toward the horses. He helped Korin into the saddle, then sprang up behind him in time to catch him as he swayed. Davis climbed onto his own mount, grabbed the reins of the spare horse, and they started off. Korin fainted with the first movements of the animal.

*

SYROS RAN THE horses and rested, then ran them again, more than anxious to reach Kangar and home. But by noon they needed to stop. The others were drooping in their saddles, and the animals were exhausted. He fumed at the delay, but there seemed little choice.

Finding a small glen with a clear stream, they stripped their mounts and let them loose to graze. The men sprawled on the soft grass in relief. Korin's mind had cleared during the ride, and he seemed almost cheerful as he rummaged through the packs Derik had provided. Plenty of food, and he whooped in delight as he discovered a packet of garments clearly meant for him.

"I think I'm in love!"

Syros gave him a wry look. "Over a bit of clothing?"

Korin jumped to his feet. "I'm for a bath." He laughed as he ran across the glen, losing his filthy garments along the way until, with a flash of white skin, he dove into the stream, cursing loudly at the cold water.

Davis chuckled and leaned back on his hands. "Have you known him long?" he asked, and Syros could tell the mercurial temperament of the Southerner left him slightly bewildered.

"No, only the last few days. Actually, he came to Siagan for you."

"What?"

Syros bent closer. "We heard rumors that Lord Fredrik was learning to use the Karthagan powers against the rest of us. And it was someone in the North instructing him. That's why Korin is here. To warn us it's Mandel who's been teaching his tricks to others. Or it was. Davis…" Davis looked up at his intense tone. "Commander Jacksan is dead by Fredrik's hands. We feared the same for you."

"Yes," Davis whispered. "I could feel my life draining away in that dark room. If you hadn't come… I've felt things weren't right in Siagan for a long time, but I didn't know what, or why. Just a vague uneasy doubt. You know I've kept my family on our land outside of Kangar for that very reason. I didn't dare bring them to Siagan. Mandel finally showed his hand and trapped me in the cellar months ago. And then the Red Twin came."

They looked up as Korin dropped beside them. He'd dressed in the new clothing, and Syros eyed him closely. He looked better, the stark fear gone from his eyes, though a sneer marred his attractive features. "Fredrik was dangerous, and the inhabitants of his Hall are corrupt. But don't worry." Korin leaned back on his hands and crossed his ankles. The cold light that entered his eyes chilled Syros. "I've already taken care of Fredrik."

Syros coughed into the silence. "We should sleep. It's still some way to Kangar."

The other two readily agreed, and they lay in the grass where they were, eschewing a guard. Syros dozed in the warm glen, dreaming of his home and child.

"Syros."

He stirred on hearing his name, blinked, and rose swiftly. "My lord." The smile left his face. "Willum?"

"When you didn't return at the arranged time we came after you. Who's this?" He nudged Korin with his boot.

"His name's Korin, from Fredrik's Hall." Syros remained cautious, eyeing the guards. "Is there a problem?"

"I found this." Willum unfolded the map Korin had been making of the Northern Territory. Syros drew a careful breath. It could mean death for the lad if Willum's suspicions weren't alleviated.

"He meant no harm, my lord."

"We shall see. Get him up."

Korin grumbled and swatted at Syros's hand but finally opened an eye, then slowly sat up before climbing to his feet, his gaze intent on the map in Willum's hand.

"Korin, this is Willum, Governor of the Northern Territory," Syros introduced them, and Willum's eyes narrowed as Korin bowed respectfully.

"Whose man are you?" Willum asked abruptly, and Syros caught the flicker of pain in Korin's face.

"I was Commander Jacksan's, my lord."

"Was?"

"The commander is dead, my lord."

Willum glanced at Syros in surprise. "What happened?"

"It was Mandel of Siagan and Lord Fredrik that were attaining the Karthagans' powers and misusing them," Syros offered. "We lost Jacksan to their experimentation, and nearly lost Davis as well. Korin helped us escape." Syros quickly outlined the past events for him. "The Red Twin, Ethan, is now in control of Siagan."

Confusion touched Willum's face, and then his lips thinned, anger glinting in his eyes. "Ethan? I thought he was dead. What treachery is this?"

"I do not know. Willum, we must move cautiously. If Aiden is involved—"

"Indeed." Willum's voice turned icy. "What is the map for, Korin?"

"It's nothing, my lord. Merely for my own use. I didn't want to lose myself returning home."

A dangerous light flickered in Willum's blue eyes. "On whose authority did you enter the North?"

Korin tensed, and Syros saw him glance quickly from man to man, weighing his options. Though he could probably outrun any of them, one of the archers would have an arrow through his back before he took two steps.

"I explained that," Syros interjected hurriedly before Korin did anything foolish. "He came because—"

Willum stopped him with a sharp motion of his hand. "Korin can answer."

Syros closed his eyes briefly in dismay. The lad would run and be killed, and he realized in that moment he'd be missed. He wished Korin was one of his soldiers so he could beat some sense into him.

"Who are you?"

Korin shrugged eloquently. "No one of importance, my lord."

"I think perhaps you should elaborate. I'd like to know why I should trust you."

Willum motioned for them to follow and sat down in the grass some distance from the still sleeping Davis. Korin hesitated and Syros nodded encouragement, willing the Southerner to comply.

"Very well." Korin sat cross-legged beside the governor, poking a stick at the dirt while Syros sat on his other side. He spoke in a rush of words as if to get it over. "My mother was a Northern woman taken in battle by a Southern soldier and forced into marriage. She took her life when I was four, and I traveled with my father from outpost to outpost until he was killed in a drunken fight a few years later at Fredrik's Hall."

Korin jabbed at the ground until the stick broke. "I was six years old and alone. A pretty child, they said, passed around the Hall like a favorite toy. That continued for several years until I came under Commander Jacksan's notice. He caught me stealing his lunch one day and took me into his home. Things got better after that."

He paused at Syros's hiss. "It wasn't what you think. He was a good man and took pity on me. He gave me a safe home and friendship and honest work when I was old enough. He…" Korin's voice broke, and he stared at his clenched hands.

"And Fredrik?" Willum queried.

Korin's eyes flashed with contempt. "That fat, stupid man? Some flattering words and I was his loyal follower and free to do as I liked." His attractive face sobered. "I like to think I was able to help a few of his miserable subjects because of it." He gave a mocking little laugh. "Perhaps not." He covered his eyes.

Willum watched him, asking Syros, "Do you believe him?"

"I trust him."

"But?" Willum had heard his hesitation.

Syros chose his words with care. "He thrived in that cesspool. I suspect deception and intrigue are an art to him, any game that will put a few silvers in his pocket. On the other hand, he would have sold himself for water and food for Davis, if necessary, and purposely angered Ethan so he would be sent to the chamber instead of me." Syros looked at Korin's bowed head, the glorious copper hair hiding his face. "I think he values life above all things, except maybe his own."

"That can be dangerous as well."

Korin shook himself and glanced up. The vulnerability showing in his beautiful face shocked Syros, and then Korin winked outrageously and sprang to his feet.

"Satisfied?" he simpered and turned on his heel and sauntered down to the river.

Syros chuckled despite the grave conversation. "That man will go far in the world, Willum. You might want to keep him at your side."

"Perhaps, if I didn't fear he'd slit my throat."

"Gain his trust, and he'll be the one to protect your precious neck."

Willum inclined his head.

Davis woke soon after, and Syros called Korin back so they could eat and be on their way. Davis expressed his anxiety to return to Kangar as soon as possible and see to his family's safety.

Willum passed him the water flask. "Of course. You may travel with us."

After a sparse meal provided by Willum's men, Korin saddled the horses. Syros frowned at a tuft of grass as he waited, reluctant to say goodbye. He feared the lad would get himself killed without a friend to watch over him.

Korin came up to him. "What is it?"

Syros shook his head and held out his hand. "If you ever find yourself at loose ends, Korin, you'd be welcomed in Kangar."

Korin looked at his hand, and a wicked grin sprang on his face. He whooped and pulled Syros into a tight embrace.

"Give your son a kiss for me," he teased as he let him go.

Syros cuffed him. "Mind your place."

Willum walked over with Davis, who was leading Syros's roan. Looking between them, Davis lifted a brow, and Syros felt heat rush to his face when Korin snickered.

"Sir?" Syros inquired of Willum as he took the reins of his mount.

"I'm sorry, Syros. I know you want to go home and see Dani. But I still need to know what is happening in the South. Find out what's going on in Nagal. I need to know if Fredrik's corruption has reached there. Can Basal still be trusted? Peace." Willum held up a hand at the anger flashing on Korin's face. "I'm only looking for information. I'm not accusing the South of anything."

Korin lowered his gaze but not before Syros saw his sudden panic. The man didn't know who to trust, and that wouldn't do. "I will go gladly, Willum, if only to prove Basal is a man of honor. I hold no doubt of it myself."

Korin gave him a grateful look and Syros nodded. "Let's go."

"One more thing," Willum added. "After I take Davis to Kangar, I'll be in the city of Karthag for a few days if you should have need of me. I want to see if Alek is aware of Ethan's return."

"My lord." Syros nodded, then climbed into the saddle and trailed Korin's mount while Davis left with Willum and his soldiers.

Chapter Seven

AIDEN THOUGHTFULLY WALKED with Alek through the trees, conscious of Ellis on Alek's far side. They were engaged in pleasant conversation, but Aiden had a hard time concentrating when all he wanted was to take Ellis to bed and continue the pleasures of the other night. If only he could be sure Ellis wanted the same. Too many people had always been about for them to speak of it.

He drew a breath of the salty air. The trail was a steeper climb than the one to his cabin. They'd have to add several switchbacks to lessen the incline to Alek's new dwelling, once it was built.

They at last reached the top of the hill, and the seascape spreading below the fir grove stole Aiden's breath. "This is wonderful, Alek. And I've noticed you have a fine view of the harbor as well," he teased and enjoyed the slow blush in Alek's cheeks. Aiden had always found his cousin's reticence about his affection for Cecil amusing. And sweet.

"Aiden tells me you start building today, Alek?" Ellis inquired with interest.

"Yes. We're setting the stakes this morning, and Aiden will take charge of clearing the plot later today." Alek didn't mask his excitement. "I haven't told Cecil yet."

"He'll love it."

"I hope so. I want to make up to him for these last few hard weeks. He's been very patient with me." Alek's voice dropped lower, the loneliness and insecurity of the long days and nights betrayed in his last words, "I miss him."

"Is Cecil on his way back?" Ellis asked kindly.

Eagerness brightened Alek's face. "He's arriving from Amara tomorrow. Despite not being completely healed, the dear, stubborn man insisted on seeing Governor Basal and Kirstin home himself."

The joy left his expression, and the deep sadness that took its place startled Aiden. "What is it?"

Alek shrugged and took a seat on an old stump. Aiden settled on a large rock nearby, smiling slightly when Ellis sat cross-legged at his feet. "Tell me."

"Because I was afraid of what Ethan might do to Cecil, I kept him away from home. But Ethan hurt him anyway. And now I fear what Niko—"

Aiden slipped off his perch to Alek's side in one smooth motion, Ellis scrambling to his feet in alarm.

"Is Niko in your head?" Aiden accused in low tones, betraying his instant anger. "You said you'd tell us if he were."

"He's pushing." Alek drew back when Aiden reached a hand. "Aiden, no. It's too dangerous. Niko could find you through me."

"I hope he does. Let me in, cousin."

Alek whimpered slightly when Aiden touched his temple and pushed inside. Aiden sympathized, remembering the crawling sensation, as if fingers traveled over one's mind. The bright light and warmth that was his cousin's memory of Cecil made him smile, but he moved on, stalking the dark shadow lurking in the corners. He'd only met with Niko a few times and suddenly realized they had been purposely kept apart.

He thrust the sting of that away. They had a right to fear him, though he'd never wanted the Mage's power; that Niko now held. He curled his lips in a sneer. Niko wasn't aware of him. It would be easy—

Niko turned on him, his dark gaze piercing through the shadows, pinning Aiden in place. His brown eyes widened with surprise, then Niko raised his proud head. "What are you doing here, child?"

"I think you know," Aiden countered. "Let my cousin go."

"If I refuse?"

Aiden smiled coldly. "Then I will make you."

Niko narrowed his eyes to glittering slits. "You can try."

Without hesitation, Aiden shoved at Niko with all his strength and cried out in sharp pain at the brief clash of wills, though he managed to drive Niko's strong presence from Alek's mind. He quickly sealed the pinprick through which Niko had entered.

Aiden withdrew, sucking in air to calm his racing heart. Pride and arrogance were in his stance, every inch the Red Twin to be feared, but he pushed down that image he'd shown to Niko. He never wanted to be that man, and he gave the others a tentative smile, taking in Ellis's wide gaze. "That's given Niko something to think about, anyway."

"Aiden," Alek remonstrated. "That was reckless. Why did you do it?"

"I hesitated with Ethan. I won't hesitate again."

Alek nodded, though his eyes were sad. Aiden sighed. He loved Alek as a father, and there were times like this when he felt he disappointed him. Sudden voices on the trail reached them, and he watched as a group of men carrying surveyor's equipment came into view.

Alek put a hand on his shoulder. "Thank you for coming to see the land. Shall I send a runner for you once the stakes are set?"

"That would be ideal. I'll probably be home for the rest of the day. I have a few small chores to finish."

"Excellent."

Ellis embraced Alek, then started down the trail with him, Aiden thrilling when Ellis twined their fingers.

"Will you come home with me?" Aiden asked and held his breath.

Ellis flashed him a grin. "Try to stop me."

It was a beautiful morning and Aiden set a leisurely pace, letting the anticipation build between them, Ellis seeming content at his side. Soon enough, they climbed the road to his home. Aiden let them into his cabin, and Ellis surprised him by continuing on to the bedroom, losing clothing along the way until he stood naked at the foot of the bed, his slim, exquisite body bared to Aiden's hungry gaze.

"Ellis," he murmured, heart full. He quickly stripped, pulse pounding under Ellis's appreciative gaze, cock thickening. Ellis's eyes darkened, and he moistened his lips, drawing a groan from Aiden. He climbed swiftly onto the bed, pulling Ellis with him.

"How can this be real?" he asked on a shaky breath, with Ellis pinned beneath him, smiling into his eyes.

"I'm not sure." Ellis slid his fingers down Aiden's chest. "Why would I possibly want to be in the bed of a strong, gorgeous, virile man…" His voice trailed off, and he captured Aiden's gasp in a kiss as his fingers grazed Aiden's cock.

They made love with joy, Aiden swallowing Ellis's panting breath as Aiden eased into him, using plenty of oil, and they moved together. Ellis's soft cry as he came with Aiden buried deep inside was ecstasy. They lay in each other's arms afterward, Ellis warm and sleepy beside him. Soon a sigh escaped Ellis, betraying his pleasure and happiness. He rose up on an elbow and played with Aiden's hair with his free hand.

"When will you marry me?" he enquired in an offhand fashion.

Aiden drew back, hardly daring to hope. "Ellis, you don't know me—" A painful tug on his hair stopped his words.

"I've dreamt of you for years, Aiden. Don't tell me I don't know you." Ellis continued forcefully, "Or do you think I would sleep with just any-one?"

"No! Of course not." Aiden swallowed sudden tears. How could this beautiful man want him? "I could speak with Natan," he offered tentatively.

"Do that." Ellis rolled to his back. A smile played on his lips, but Aiden watched a crease form between his brows, a troubled expression re-placing his joy.

"What is it, darling?" he asked, brushing wisps of hair from Ellis's wondrous eyes.

Ellis shrugged slightly. "It may be nothing, but I can't hear my brother Kayle anymore."

Aiden looked a question.

"When my nightmares first began, I didn't understand what they were. I don't think I slept for more than a few hours at a time. Anyway, Kayle touched my thoughts during a particularly scary vision, and put the tiniest bit of himself in my mind. He said that when I was afraid, to think of him, and it would be as if he were right there with me, standing guard.

"It's always worked, too, until now. I've searched for him, and he's there, but it's as if he's asleep or can't communicate. I'm worried." He laughed self-consciously. "I haven't been sleeping."

"Ellis," Aiden murmured, dismayed. "Have the nightmares gotten worse?"

"Worse? No, you took the worst one away." Ellis sighed and continued under his breath, "I wish you could take them all."

"I think you need a husband to distract you," Aiden teased, heart sore, wanting a smile but unprepared for the bleakness that dimmed Ellis's brilliant hazel eyes.

"Will you have me, Aiden? I don't sleep, or when I do, I wake up screaming, and the visions haunt me for days." His laughter was forced. "A catch for anyone if you don't mind when I go insane."

Ellis had wrapped his arms tightly around his chest and rocked slowly, fighting for control. Aiden pulled him closer, and Ellis leaned against him.

"Have you spoken to Natan about this?" Aiden wiped the tears from Ellis's face with gentle fingers, not knowing what to do.

"He has enough to worry about. I'm all right. I've simply panicked a little, not having Kayle's help. And I would like to sleep."

"Go ahead, Ellis. I'll keep watch." Aiden leaned closer to whisper in his ear, "I'll watch over you the rest of my life if you'll have me."

Ellis sighed and settled comfortably against his shoulder, the tension slowly leaving his slim body. When his breathing settled into sleep, Aiden sat against the headboard with his hand in Ellis's dark hair. He dozed a little during the long afternoon, but mostly he listened to the low moans, sharp cries, and desperate breathing of his lover's nightmares. He would soothe Ellis's brow and murmur encouragement, and Ellis would calm and sleep, then dream again.

A runner came with news that the stakes had been set for Alek's home, but Aiden sent him away. His thoughts became grim as the slow hours passed, and a coldness settled in him as Ellis's broken sobs dripped into his heart. It wasn't to be borne. He clenched his hands in growing resolve. As the evening light entered the room, Ellis seemed to calm, and Aiden kissed his white face and left him to seek out Natan.

His thoughts churned as he strode into the city; he didn't see the people he passed. Natan sat with Alek and Governor Willum in the garden, Kavi at his feet, and they rose as he approached. Aiden went directly to Willum and bowed. "I didn't know you had returned, lord."

"I've only now arrived. What is wrong?" He motioned Aiden to a chair while the others resumed their seats.

Aiden sat and clasped his hands between his knees, deciding to be blunt. "Ellis's nightmares have worsened, and he says he's lost contact with Kayle." He wiped his face with a trembling hand and turned to Natan. "I fear for his mind, Mage."

Natan looked troubled. "My dreams have also grown strange. I believe Niko is making his move and is somehow blocking Kayle from contacting us. We will need to act soon."

"The plan has not been agreed upon by all," Alek said sharply. "I still have questions."

Willum cleared his throat. "Do you have something you'd like to add, Alek?"

Aiden frowned at the sudden tension between them. "What plan is this, lord?"

The men shared a look, then Kavi cleared his throat. "He needs to be told, sooner rather than later."

Willum sat forward, and Aiden widened his eyes in growing shock as the Barkuit governor outlined his strategy for dealing with Niko. But he also spoke of Ethan, who had taken up residence in Siagan, the bigger threat to the peace on Belega. Willum avoided Aiden's gaze as he talked of his brother, and Aiden's heart filled with misery and fear, though they didn't seem to hold him to blame. He had hoped Ethan would find a quiet place to live out his life. Instead, the worst had happened. And now their beloved mage, along with others, would pay the price for his mistake.

As Willum continued with his plans, his words became more desperate, and his voice suddenly broke. "Forgive me, Mage," he said roughly, "Every ounce of my being is against this, but I need to use all my resources now to stop the unfolding events."

"Willum, I'm yours. Just tell me what to do," Natan assured him.

"Alek?" Willum prompted.

Alek ran a hand through his hair, his agitation evident. "How has it come to this? Natan, you can't—"

Natan lifted a hand, stopping his impassioned words. "Peace, Alek. Willum, please go on."

Thunder rumbled in the distance while Willum added the final touches to the daring, dangerous strategy. Aiden sent an anxious glance at the sky as the wind picked up. Would every hope he had end in despair?

Natan gave him a kind look. "You have something more to share with us, about Ellis?"

"We're to marry," he answered softly, self-consciously.

Kavi snorted. "So Ellis has told us, repeatedly. I take it he has informed you as well?"

Aiden's face heated, but he pushed on. "Yes. And though I know it's short notice, we wish it to be soon."

"Tomorrow would be best," Alek put in unexpectedly and tapped a finger against his lips. "Events are moving swiftly. If you are to marry, do so at once, before we are swept into Niko's machinations, Ethan's madness, and Willum's perilous counterstrike."

Thunder crashed again, closer. Aiden wondered if it was an omen.

Natan's gaze gentled. "Alek can still marry you and Ellis in a storm, Aiden." He leaned closer. "Tomorrow will come. You'll see. You deserve to be happy."

Aiden frowned, thinking of the sacrifice they were asking of Natan. "And what of you, Mage? If Willum's plan is brought to fruition—"

Natan opened his arms, stopping his words. "How could I not be content, Aiden? This is what I am meant to do. I think Gregor had foreseen this from the beginning, when he first gave me his powers."

"My lord." Aiden rose and made his deep bow, his braid sweeping the floor at Natan's feet. They spoke a while longer, Aiden's heart growing heavier with each word spoken, and he stayed late in the garden when the others had left, searching his mind for alternatives.

Tomorrow he'd marry Ellis. Aiden's heart flooded with joy and pain. Ellis would be in his home, bringing laughter and love to the quiet rooms. He hoped Ellis wouldn't be lonely. Aiden hadn't many friends. He laughed, disconcerted. Ellis drew people to him with his kind smile and gentleness.

He'd already made many friends amongst the soldiers and the people in the city. His heart eased a little. Maybe Ellis could be happy with him, after all.

He rose and made his way home as the first raindrops struck his face. He lingered on the porch to watch the storm travel down the valley and, finally, sought his bed and Ellis's sleeping, warm presence as the moon set deep in the night.

*

ELLIS WAS MISSING from his bed in the morning, and Aiden dressed, then went into the city to pace the castle gardens with anxious steps. He didn't understand why Alek had insisted he breakfast with them. His cousin should have known his nerves would be in tatters.

He turned a corner in the path and almost collided with Kavi and Ellis coming toward him. He drew a quick breath at the sight of his husband-to-be, drank him in, his beauty bewitching him over again. "Good morning." He bowed, and his discomfort deepened when Kavi gave a soft laugh.

Then Kavi linked their arms. "Are you coming to breakfast?"

"Darling?" Aiden held out his free arm to Ellis, and Ellis's color heightened, stealing Aiden's heart once more.

"We'll be right there," Aiden murmured distractedly to Kavi, releasing him, and Kavi's merry laughter followed them as Aiden pulled Ellis behind a screen of climbing vines.

"Ellis!" he whispered as he held him loosely. He watched, enchanted, as Ellis's eyes slowly darkened with passion under his gaze. He pressed their foreheads together with a soft groan.

"This is torture, love," he murmured, his lips brushing Ellis's. "Can't we run away?"

"If you wish." Ellis smirked, and his eyes danced as Aiden gave a shout.

"Dearest," he chided and kissed Ellis's tempting mouth. He followed Ellis to the courtyard to join the others, and ate an informal meal, not tasting a thing. And then it was time. They were to be married in the rose garden with the heady scent of blooms filling the air. Sunlight shown on the happy faces watching them, but Aiden saw only his young lover as Ellis took his hands and they stood before Alek.

"Darling," Aiden murmured with awe. Tears filled his eyes and dropped on Ellis's fingers as he brought them to his lips. Ellis ran a hand over Aiden's bowed head and smiled when he raised his face.

Alek cleared his throat to gather their attention and begin the ceremony, when the unmistakable clatter of hooves on the cobblestone street outside the garden gave him pause. Concern touched his face.

Aiden turned to the pathway. It sounded as if the riders had their mounts at a dead run, and he wondered with trepidation what news came so swiftly.

The horses drew to a halt and two men burst into the garden.

"I hope we're not too late?" Robin inquired and gave the assemblage a dazzling smile.

Cecil brushed by him and strode directly to Aiden and embraced him, and then Ellis in turn. "Forgive us for being late. We pushed the ship, though we struck a head-wind last night."

"You sailed in the storm?" Alek asked in surprise and censure.

"Of course. I sensed you wanted me here. Then the men at the harbor told us of the wedding." Cecil grinned at Ellis's bright face before turning to wink outrageously at Alek, who drew a startled breath. Lithe and tanned, Cecil was glorious, his gray eyes bright crystals filled with mischief. Alek flushed slightly and collected himself.

The ceremony was eloquent and beautiful with Alek's happiness spilling out in his words. His glance strayed to Cecil as he spoke of love and the need to cherish and protect each other, and Cecil smiled at him, his heart showing in his eyes.

At Alek's last words, Aiden took Ellis in his arms, yet couldn't speak. He looked into his husband's hazel eyes—his husband!—and touched his face, then suddenly laughed and gathered Ellis close, kissing him repeatedly while his heart sang. The company cheered and clapped, then wandered into the courtyard for brunch.

*

IT WAS LATE afternoon before Aiden and Ellis were able to slip away and the last of the guests departed from the garden. Cecil settled more comfortably on the bench, his head on Alek's thigh. He opened his eyes a slit when Willum spoke.

"That was beautiful, Alek." Willum leaned back in his chair and put his feet up on a nearby bench.

"Thank you. I've never seen Aiden so happy."

"Nor Ellis." Willum smiled. "I—" A slight snore interrupted him. Robin lay sprawled on a bench fast asleep in the sun. He looked younger than ever with his sandy hair tumbled over his face and a tiny smile playing on his lips. Alek glanced at Cecil, who gave him a drowsy smile, and Alek and Willum exchanged an indulgent look.

"Come on, my boy." Willum shook Robin's shoulder. Robin grunted and covered his eyes, and Willum chuckled rougishly as he pinched his nose.

Robin snorted and sat up. "What?"

"This way." Willum pulled on his arm. "Your bed is much more comfortable."

"Hmm…" Robin rubbed his eyes. "Oh, very well."

Willum caught him as he staggered to his feet, and they were both laughing as Robin stumbled up the path, leaning heavily on his arm.

Alek ran a hand through Cecil's hair and bent to his ear. "Come inside."

Cecil mumbled sleepily as Alek took his hand, not even sure what he was trying to say. Their room was cool and shadowed when they reached it, and Alek undressed Cecil and pushed him gently on the bed. As he fell, Cecil pulled Alek down with him, and Alek laughed softly even as he pressed kisses to Cecil's warm neck. "Don't you need to sleep?"

"Later," Cecil assured him and raised Alek's face for a kiss. They made love, slowly, leisurely, then frantically, Alek holding him close, kissing his tears away as Cecil slowly returned from ecstasy. Afterward, the afternoon slipped by as Alek dozed, and Cecil pounded the pillows, unable to get comfortable. A strange anxiety plagued him, waking him time and again. He wondered what it meant and would have asked, but Alek woke with a soft smile and eager arms, and he forgot.

He slept a little after Alek left the bed, but his dreams grew uneasy and sent him from the covers when next he woke. He dressed, and his uneasiness grew with each step he took in the quiet hallway, so he was almost running by the time he reached the stairs. Robin stood on the top step, tense, his hair rumpled from his bed. He followed on Cecil's heels without a word when Cecil motioned for silence and descended the empty stairway.

The rooms below appeared deserted, their footsteps a hollow echo.

"Hello?" Cecil called as he eased open the kitchen doors. An attendant glanced up from the counter, startled. "Everyone's at the harbor, my lord. A message arrived."

"Thank you." He and Robin exchanged a worried glance and rushed to the stables, the empty streets adding to their trepidation. Without bothering to saddle the horses, they swung up on the sleek animals and raced the short distance to the harbor, where they found Alek and Willum in grave discussion on the beach.

Leaving his mount with Robin, Cecil hurried to Alek's side. His lover didn't say a word to him, only laced their fingers.

Willum nodded to Cecil and continued, "I don't know how long we'll be gone. I'm leaving Commander Jaden here with the Southern garrison to supplement our own soldiers, but perhaps you could send word through your bond with Cecil if you need me."

Alek drew a sharp breath as if to protest when Captain Daran strode up to them. "We'll be ready to sail, Commander, when you say."

Cecil didn't try to hide his bewilderment.

"Kayle has called to the Mage," Willum said quietly.

"Do we know how bad it is?"

Willum rubbed his face, his concern evident. "Natan was quite specific. Niko's ambition has led him to kill the Vice-King in a play for power, but the people are against him, and he's subsequently been forced to flee Sennia. Apparently, he's sailing to the Isle of Wind. Kayle promises to arrive here in three days, and we'll go after Niko then."

Cecil sent an appraising glance over the ship. "How many are going? Daran, are there enough provisions?" He took a step but Alek's grip on his hand tightened.

"You're not going."

Cecil stopped in surprise at the fear in his voice. "Alek?"

"You're not to go," Alek said stubbornly.

Cecil's heart lurched. "What is it?"

Alek looked at the ground. "I've had terrible dreams. It's perilous for you to go. I want you safe."

Cecil put a hand on his shoulder. "I won't go, then."

He looked at Willum, who shrugged. "I won't make it a command, Cecil. It's your decision."

"No." Daran stood his ground when they stared at him. "The crew won't sail without the commander."

"They'd refuse to take the Mage?" Willum asked in disbelief.

"They'd sail the Mage around the world, if he asked," Daran replied. "It's the other one they fear."

Cecil followed his gaze to where Aiden stood alone on the beach and watched the sea. Ellis joined him and slid an arm around his waist, but no one else drew near or had a word for him. Daran scowled. "We need the commander to balance the scales."

Cecil began to protest but shut his mouth with a hard click of teeth. He knew better than most the dark superstitions that ran rampant in a crew who risked their lives on the changeable sea.

"Will you give me a moment?" he asked with his eyes on Alek's averted face. Willum bowed and moved off with Daran. Robin followed them with a troubled expression, letting the horses free for the time being.

"You know I have to go," Cecil began when he and Alek were alone.

"No! I know no such thing. You need to stay with me."

"But what of…"

"Leave, then." Alek flung off Cecil's hand.

"Alek! Will you walk away in anger?"

"Does it matter?"

The cold tone struck Cecil, and with an oath, Alek grabbed his shirt and gave him one hard kiss. Cecil tasted blood as a sharp tooth cut his lip but didn't care as Alek strode up the beach away from him. After a moment, he joined the others on the ship and went over the preparations for the coming voyage with the captain.

Heart sore, he stayed on the ship that night when Alek didn't send for him. Fetching a blanket, he lay on the deck with his head on a coil of rope. He knew very well Alek was afraid for his safety. Cecil would give him time to come to terms with his decision to go, though it hurt to be separated from him yet again. He sighed and let the sea lull him to sleep as he watched the stars wheel overhead.

*

NIKO EASED THE small craft into a cove just out of sight of Karthag's harbor. He was still six days from the Isle, but he needed fresh supplies. The moon and stars shone brightly as he slipped onto the beach and headed for the pier. He would surely find what he needed there. As he approached the harbor, he curled his lips in a sly smile at the lovely ship in dock.

Approaching cautiously, he discovered the gangplank conveniently down. A few sailors lay about the deck sleeping, and he crept quietly into the galley and filled a sack with all the delectables he could find.

When finished, he strolled in the moonlight, in no hurry to leave the ship, and almost tripped over the man sleeping on the aft deck. He stared at him a moment, puzzled, and then an unpleasant smile slid on his face. He knew that light hair and fair skin. Apparently Alek wasn't taking very good care of his pet. Shocking. Anyone could walk off with him. Niko cocked his head. Would Alek even notice if Cecil was gone? It would be interesting to find out. But what…ah. He hefted an oar in his hands.

*

WILLUM SAT IN the garden with the morning sun on his face and a heavy heart. He'd heard horrible things about the Isle of Wind and had no wish to follow Niko there. But as the governor of the Northern Territory, it was his duty… He glanced up as Natan and Alek joined him. Alek took a seat beside him, but his grim features did nothing to assuage Willum's fears.

"Good morning." Natan took the bench opposite. He glanced around. "Where's Cecil? Didn't he come in last night?"

Alek sighed. "He wouldn't presume."

Natan gave him a confused look, but before Alek could elaborate, they heard quick steps on the path.

"There you are!" Robin fought to catch his breath. "Something's happened on the ship. Daran's requested that Alek and the commander come immediately."

Alek stared at him, clearly baffled. "Cecil stayed with the ship last night."

Robin paled. "Cecil's not on the ship, my lords." He spoke carefully, "Food is missing from the galley, and we searched the ship. There is blood smeared on the aft deck."

Alek parted his lips in a soundless cry and hurried from the garden, catching up Robin's horse. Willum and the others followed as quickly as they could be mounted, Willum's heart threatening to pound out of his chest. Reaching the harbor, he slid from the saddle and strode across the sand toward the ship with Natan at his side and Robin on their heels. The silence on the deck as he climbed the gangplank unnerved him. He made his way to the stern, and the sailors watched with grim faces as he approached Alek, already speaking with the captain. He noted Aiden and Ellis at the rail close by. They were all there, it seemed.

"Daran?"

"My lord." Daran bowed to him. "We've searched the ship and harbor. We can't be certain who was here."

"It was Niko."

Willum frowned at Alek. "How can you know?"

"Because Cecil is far away and in pain—" Alek broke off and stared at the sea. "We need to go after him. Daran, pull the anchor. We leave immediately."

"No." Willum made his tone adamant, though he knew the danger of rousing Alek's anger. "We wait for Kayle. We won't sail without him."

Alek's eyes glittered. "They're my ships."

"We can't take Niko without Kayle's help. No one here is strong enough, alone," Willum insisted, hating that he had to take this stand against his friend.

Natan stepped between the two men. "Alek, we'll get Cecil back, but Willum's right. We must have Kayle or our carefully laid plans will fail. We can't risk losing Aiden over this. We need him for…later."

"But Mage," Alek dropped his gaze. "He's frightened, and… I can't bear it." He covered his face with shaky hands.

Aiden's soft voice startled them as he came up. "Go after him, Alek.

Go by land," he directed, and Willum shivered at the glitter in his golden eyes. Alek came to life, and without a word sprinted for the horses. He stumbled and brushed at his eyes before mounting.

"He mustn't go alone!" Robin cried, his voice catching on a note of pity.

Willum gave him a piercing look. "Go."

Robin bowed and raced after the retreating man.

The silence seemed to deepen on the ship after they'd gone. The captain's daughter, Riana, joined them with an accusing look at Willum. Willum took a deep breath and directed his questions to Daran, "What is it? What do the sailors want of me?"

"That coward has our beloved commander. We want him back—at any cost."

"We'll leave as soon as Kayle arrives."

"And can we find Cecil? You'll help us do that?" Riana spoke bitterly, her eyes on the dark smudges staining the deck.

Willum shook his head, out of his depth. "I can't promise that."

"Then who'll take us? Who can find Niko for us?" Daran voiced the sailors' fear. The Isle was a terrible place to them, full of horror and strangeness.

"I can find him," Aiden said, looking over the sea.

Daran shivered but pressed his lips together in a grim line. "I will follow the Red Twin," he said for all to hear and dropped to a knee. A murmur of assent ran the ship, and one by one the crew followed his lead. A cold finger touched Willum's heart.

Natan glanced at him. "Watch."

Willum's gaze swept the kneeling men and back to Aiden and realized the Red Twin didn't see them. He bent his gaze on some distant point on the ocean. Ellis touched his hand, and Aiden blinked and seemed to come back to himself. His eyes lost their piercing light as they fell on his husband.

"Come home," Ellis said. Daran and the crew rose, but still Aiden paid them no mind. Willum scrutinized the couple as they made their way across the deck with laced fingers, and he almost laughed in nervous relief. He'd thought for a second that Aiden…

He jumped when Natan placed a hand on his shoulder. "You'll have to learn to trust him, Willum. He's not his brother."

"I know. I'm trying."

Natan walked away, but Willum stopped him. "You're not to blame here, Mage."

"No one's to blame but that monster," Daran stated, and Willum had never seen such fury in his eyes before.

"We'll bring Cecil home, if it's at all in our power to do so," Natan assured the listening men.

"We'll bring him home," Daran vowed, his hands clenched.

Willum bowed, then he and Natan joined up with the others at the horses. Ellis mounted, and Aiden stood at his stirrup speaking softly. Willum caught Aiden's eye and walked over to him. "I'd like to ask why you sent Alek across the country. He won't arrive at the Isle of Wind any sooner than we."

Aiden answered in his grave manner. "I'm not sure, my lord. There was a vision in my eyes of a man needed. Alek will find him on the way to the Southern harbor outside of Amara."

"Do you know this man?"

"No, my lord. His features were indistinct to me, as if seen from a great distance, but his hair was a flame in the sun."

Willum swore with frustration. "Nothing's simple anymore."

Aiden's harsh laughter startled him. "It's never been simple, my lord," he replied. Willum glanced at Natan, who spoke quietly with Ellis, and nodded. It would be a difficult two days of waiting for Kayle's arrival, and a hard ride for Alek to reach Amara and then the sea and the Isle of Wind in a timely manner. The peaceful days in Belega seemed about to be shattered.

Chapter Eight

KORIN LAY ACROSS the top of the wall in the hot afternoon sun, dozing after a restless night. His dreams had been terrible, of war and death, playing in his mind again the minute he closed his eyes. He'd arrived yesterday at Fredrik's Hall while Syros continued on to Nagal. They'd reached the conclusion he'd do better to spy out the situation in the Hall and report his findings to Syros on Syros's return.

He was supposed to have presented himself to Commander Tyrel that morning for his duty assignment but overslept, and then the warm stones had tempted him. He'd just about made up his mind to take a horse and ride away, see where he ended up in the world. Anywhere would be better than the Hall with its dark memories and loneliness. Nagal was nice this time of year. And Syros was there with his piercing eyes and taut body and stern tone Korin wanted directed his way.

"Hello?"

Korin ignored the voice. He wasn't a messenger. But there had been a tiredness in the youthful tones. He swore softly and rolled to his side. "Can I help you?"

Blue eyes blinked up at him. "We've been traveling for more than a day and wondered if perhaps there was a room we could use for the night?" The young soldier chewed his bottom lip. "We haven't much to pay…"

Korin frowned, noting the absence of packs on the animals. The soldier's companion raised his face at that moment and Korin drew a hard breath and darted a look around. The Karthagan's life was in danger every moment in the open.

"You mustn't stay here," he said urgently. The young soldier slumped in exhaustion but nodded as if he'd feared that all along.

"Could we have some water, then?" the Karthagan asked softly, his striking face pale, driven. "We have a long way still to go."

Korin stole another glance toward the Hall, heart thumping. Heaving a sigh, he dropped lightly to his feet. "Come with me." He led them to his cottage near the soldiers' barracks, careful to stake the horses in the small yard in the back, where there was some grass for them. He was fairly certain Fredrik's men hadn't spotted them or there would have been an outcry, and Commander Tyrel's soldiers would never talk.

"Leave them," he said as the young man began to rub one of the roans down with his coat sleeve. "I'll take care of them in a moment." He took them through the back door of the cottage to the kitchen and bade them sit at the table.

"I'm sorry I haven't anything more," he chatted as he set fruit, wine, and a pitcher of water down. "I only arrived home yesterday. I'll run over to the Hall in a while and see what I can find for dinner." Korin hesitated, wanting to ask who they were, but there was a quiet dignity about the Karthagan that kept him silent.

"Forgive me," the young soldier rose to his feet and bowed. "I'm Robin of Nagal, and my companion is Lord Alek of Karthag."

"My lord." Korin felt a sudden urge to drop to a knee. Instead, he made his most eloquent bow and blushed to the roots of his copper hair at the gleam of humor in the Karthagan's dark eyes.

Alek motioned to a chair opposite. "Sit a moment, please. We haven't learned your name, and I'm curious why a soldier at Fredrik's Hall would welcome us into his home. Isn't it dangerous for you?"

Korin shrugged. "You've nothing to fear from the soldiers, my lord, though it would be deadly for you at the Hall. They have no liking for your people." He held out his hand. "I'm Korin."

Robin looked at him with interest as they shook hands. Korin stared at him with equal curiosity.

"You're Governor Basal's son, aren't you?"

"Yes, sir." Robin nodded.

"I've seen you around Nagal. Well, my young lord, there's fresh towels in the cupboard if you and Lord Alek care to wash. I'll see to the horses and find us some dinner."

His tone had been faintly mocking, and Robin's candid eyes narrowed, but he merely inclined his head. "Thank you."

Korin scowled as he went outside. There'd been no need to be rude. Must be more anxious about their presence than he realized. Grabbing some old cloth, he then methodically rubbed down the animals and made sure there was water in the trough. No one was in the kitchen when he returned, and he went through to the great room.

He couldn't quite stifle his laughter. Robin had rubbed his damp hair into a tangle on his head, and a few freckles stood out on his freshly scrubbed face. "You look about ten," he told the flustered soldier. "Do you need a comb?"

"I have one in my pack at home," Alek volunteered dryly. He was braiding his dark hair that fell in strands of silk over his shoulders.

Robin shook his head. "The Mage advised me to always keep a bag close at hand, in case I had to leave somewhere in a hurry. I never learn."

"The Mage?"

Korin knew their eyes were on him as ice flushed through his body, but he couldn't see them as the dreams from the previous night sprang to life in his mind. He whimpered and sank to his knees as the images overwhelmed him.

"Korin?" There was a kind voice in his ear and warm hands touched his face. "Let me in."

He cried out as the fingers seemed to push into his mind and the vision played once more…

The clouds tore open and great drops of rain fell on the men scrambling over the white sand, their screams terrible as the downpour burned flesh to the bone. The earth heaved and spouts of molten rock spewed into the sky and raced across the terrain, devouring men and animals alike.

A pale man sat alone on a cliff's edge where the earth dropped suddenly to the sea. Wind whipped the pale tangle of hair from his face; his crystal gray eyes were wide with despair. The blue-tinged lips opened in a soundless cry and the man's gaze pierced Korin's heart. "Find the Mage."

The anguished words reverberated in Korin's head, in his soul. The rain reached the man and his beautiful pale face dissolved before Korin's horrified sight…

Korin was suddenly released from the dream, still weeping as the pale man lost his life. He slipped to the floor and struggled to retrieve his scattered thoughts.

"Are you well?" Robin helped him into a nearby chair. "It's always strange when they do that," he offered, rubbing Korin's back. "It's lucky I don't have any dark secrets to hide."

"Does it happen often?"

"Occasionally, though I'm afraid they're usually disappointed by what they discover in my head."

Korin chuckled at the dry tone and felt better. He glanced around. "Where's Alek?"

They found him in the yard sitting with his back to a tree, tears on his face. Robin sat respectfully beside him.

"Do you know the pale man, my lord?" Korin asked gently.

"His name is Cecil," Alek said, grief in his tone. "Niko has him."

Korin shuddered. He'd heard the Sennian spoken of in horrifying terms. "Can we get him back?"

Alek clenched his hands. "We will."

"And the Mage?"

"He's in Karthag."

Korin started to his feet. "I must go to him."

"He'll have sailed by the time you reach the city." Alek nodded as if a question had been answered. "I think you're meant to come with me."

Korin felt as if a trap were closing around him. "Where?"

"To the Isle of Wind. You're why my heart led me here instead of straight to Amara."

"I only had a dream," Korin protested, and ran a hand through his hair in agitation. "It didn't tell me to go anywhere."

"You dreamed of the Mage. I wouldn't shrug that off lightly."

Alek's answer frightened him, sounding like prophesy, and the pity in Robin's eyes did nothing to help.

"I'll think about it," he said grudgingly. Robin rubbed surreptitiously at his eyes, exhaustion gaining the upper hand, and Korin's anger dropped from him as he realized the lad had forsaken everything to help Alek. Was he expected to do the same for the Mage? That was absurd. He motioned to the house, abruptly changing the subject. "Come inside and rest. I'll see if I can find us some dinner."

"Thank you," Alek said, not pursuing the matter, to Korin's relief. His guests rose and followed him into the cottage, where Robin helped him set up an extra cot in the spare bedroom. After seeing them comfortable, Korin made his way across the field to the Hall's large doors. It didn't help his mood when the guards let him through with sly looks, knowing what lay in store for the errant soldier. Korin paused and blew them a kiss before he slipped around a corner with a grin for their outraged expressions.

He stopped in his tracks as he bumped into someone in the hallway on his way to Fredrik's den.

"Korin." The man's voice was a soft caress and Korin's stomach knotted.

"My lord Ashel." He bowed and made to pass. A touch on his arm froze him, a conditioning left from childhood.

Ashel stepped closer and Korin shuddered at the brush of his warm breath on his cheek. "We've missed you in the Hall, pet. I've missed you."

Korin jerked his arm away, and Ashel's mocking laughter chased him as he stumbled down the corridor. He reached the den and fought the latch; then the handle gave way and he staggered inside, only to swallow convulsively as Commander Tyrel swiveled to him. He caught the angry glitter in Carrow's light eyes as well and shivered. He hadn't known the archer would be there.

"Forgive me, sirs." He bowed and almost missed the startled exchange between the men.

"What is it?" Carrow stepped closer, studying his face.

Korin cleared his throat. "Lord Alek of Karthag and Governor Basal's son are in my cottage. Terrible things are happening, and they need to speak to you straight away."

"What things?" Tyrel asked.

"Don't ask me! I'll only muddle it." Korin anxiously rubbed his face.

He flinched when Carrow took his arm. "Have you eaten today?"

"What?" His voice slurred. He felt overwhelmed and suddenly panicked. They were asking too much of him! He'd seen what the terrible powers of the earth had done to Jacksan and Davis. He'd felt it stealing the life from his own body at the lake. They couldn't expect him to travel willingly to that horrifying Isle…

Commander Tyrel's voice came from far away. "What's wrong with him?"

"I'm not sure. Best you keep an eye on things here. I'll return shortly with some answers. And please have some food sent over."

Carrow had sounded worried, confusing Korin further.

"Come with me," Carrow said in his ear, and Korin knew he'd disappointed the archer. He was a coward and a failure, and no one would be proud of him, not anymore. He was fiercely glad Syros wasn't there to see his shame. Tears slipped unheeded down his cheeks as Carrow led him home.

Robin met them at the door and helped Korin to the table. Food was soon pressed on him, and suddenly Alek stood beside him and put a hand on his shoulder, his touch on Korin's mind bringing unexpected peace.

Carrow took the chair opposite. "What happened?"

Alek shook his head with regret. "Niko was able to reach into Korin's mind through my earlier contact with his dreams. I'm sorry, Korin. Truly. I hadn't realized the Sennian had grown so powerful and cruel." He stared at the floor as he described Cecil's capture to the archer in clipped tones.

"And where does Korin come in?" Carrow asked into the quiet that followed. Korin choked on the bite of stew he'd just taken and gratefully took the cup of wine Robin put in his hand.

"I don't know, but every instinct I possess tells me the lad must come with me. There can be no mistake."

"Your instincts are always right?"

Alek gave Carrow a haughty look and ignored the question. He leaned over Korin's shoulder. "You should sleep. It will be an early morning for us."

Carrow narrowed his eyes. "I think I'll come with you as well."

Alek inclined his head, then glanced at Robin. "Will you return to Nagal with us?"

Robin surprised them. "I don't think so, my lord. Even I, with no abilities at all, can sense the wrongness here. I should remain until my father can reach the bottom of it."

Carrow bowed to him. "As you wish, lord," he said and chuckled when Robin blushed. "But keep out of the way. The lords of the Hall can be dangerous; Fredrik's cousin, Nelson, the worst of the lot."

Korin pushed his plate away, feeling tired and confused, his thoughts skittering in every direction as sleep crept relentlessly over him. He thought he was a child again when gentle hands helped him from the table to his room and waiting bed, and blankets were tucked under his chin. He sighed and rolled over.

"Goodnight, Father," he murmured into the pillow.

There was a pause, and then "Goodnight" came a husky reply, sounding strangely like Carrow, and Korin smiled as a hand ruffled his hair. He slept.

*

THE TWO DAYS ride to Nagal passed uneventfully, and Carrow watched Korin closely as they entered the city. The brash soldier had been growing increasingly quiet as they neared the capital. Carrow touched his arm as they dismounted at the stables and ordered, "Keep out of trouble."

Korin widened his eyes in surprise, and even Alek chuckled at the relief showing on his face. "You won't make me go to the court?"

"Fool."

Korin dodged his jab and Carrow shook his head as he went whistling down the street. What was to become of the lad? There was courage and intelligence there, but also a recklessness of spirit that could very well get him killed.

"Hello!" Governor Basal strode toward them and made a bow, which included them both. "Alek, I couldn't believe the guard when he said it was you. What could possibly have brought you out of Karthag? Alek?"

"I'm sorry." Alek brushed a hand across his face. "The news gets harder with each telling."

Basal's smile disappeared altogether. "Come to the courtyard."

Basal led them into the walled garden and drew Alek to a bench by the fountain, while Carrow leaned against a nearby tree. Emile, Nagal's council leader, joined them almost at once. Alek leaned his head back and closed his eyes.

"What is it, Carrow?" Basal queried when the Karthagan remained silent, his face a pale mask.

"Niko has stolen a ship and is making for the Isle of Wind," Carrow answered, a soldier's gruff, succinct reply. "He apparently stopped at Karthag's harbor for supplies and has taken Commander Cecil."

"To what purpose?" Basal began, then drew a sharp breath.

Emile swore darkly, running a hand through his red hair. "Is Niko with you now, Alek?"

"No," Alek roused. "He can't breach my thoughts, though he tries every moment. I believe he means to use Cecil as a link to me."

"Will it work?" Emile pressed.

"I will not allow it."

Carrow shivered at his cold, adamant tone.

"How can we help you?" Basal prompted with concern. Carrow knew his keen mind would already be at work, searching for solutions.

Alek looked startled, then rose and bowed to them. "Thank you, my friends," he said from the heart. "But I believe there is a danger growing on Belega that needs your attention just as urgently."

"You mean with the Red Twin, Ethan," Basal acknowledged. "Syros has spoken of him. A strange turn of events, to be sure."

"Yes, but there's a darkness in Fredrik's Hall as well, a malady in the air," Alek pressed. "Tension that speaks of the powers of the earth being misused."

"Pardon me," Carrow interjected and turned to Basal. "Commander Tyrel requests that you return to the Hall in all haste, sir. Robin remained in the city as your representative, and though the lords of the Hall seem content for the moment, Tyrel urges you to hurry."

"You left Robin in that foul place?"

Basal's eyes glittered dangerously, and Carrow pushed upright from the tree, hands open. "Robin was determined, and I agreed with him."

Basal clearly struggled with his temper, his mouth set in a grim line. "Of course, Carrow. My apologies." He scowled at the dirt, then raised piercing eyes to Alek. "Forgive me," he said tightly. "I had planned to go with you to the Isle, but now I must leave immediately for Fredrik's Hall. I'm torn in two."

Alek shook his head. "No, Basal. You must go. There's a strangeness in the Hall and, I fear, peril."

"Emile, will you please show Alek to a room?" Basal bowed and hurried inside. Carrow reluctantly followed him with a last glance at Alek. His first duty was to the governor, but Alek's plight tugged at his heart.

*

KORIN PAUSED IN the archway of the great hall. He refused to admit even to himself he'd spent the day roaming the city in hopes of running into Syros. He was being a fool to fall for the Northern lord. But his concern he'd leave in the morning without even a glimpse of Syros brought him to the castle now.

"Korin!" A friendly voice rose over the myriad conversations and his gaze searched the crowded room. Commander Jaden's daughter, Nikki, waved from a chattering group of young women, and he smiled at the lovely picture they made.

"My lady." He bowed over her delicate hands as she came up to him, and she laughed as he gazed soulfully into her eyes.

She blushed as he continued to hold her fingers and pushed him away. "Stop teasing."

Korin rested his head on her shoulder. She'd been kind to him the few times he'd come to Nagal, and he found her delightful. "I wish you'd let me sketch you," he drawled. She clucked her tongue at his brashness, but he loved the flush of rose in her umber brown complexion.

"What are you two conspiring at?"

Korin drew a startled breath and struggled frantically for composure as he straightened.

"None of your business, sir," he said, admiring Syros's strong, trim figure in his dark uniform. He tried to slow his racing heart. "How have you been keeping yourself while here?"

Syros looked confused and shook his head. "What are you talking about? Do you have anything to report?"

Korin pulled himself together. "The Hall is in chaos, as we thought, the lords vying for supremacy. But Commander Tyrel has things under control for the present."

Silence stretched between them, and Korin rocked on his heels, searching frantically for something to say. He groaned inwardly.

"Will you be returning home soon?" he asked politely, the last question he wanted an answer to. If Syros returned to Siagan, he might never see him again.

"I'm undecided; waiting on Governor Basal's advice."

"And what have you discovered?" Korin asked in an aside.

He stared as Syros thoughtfully chewed his lower lip and had to turn his eyes away as his blood rushed.

"I find him an honorable man, untouched by the madness infecting Siagan and Fredrik's Hall."

"To your liking?" Korin couldn't help but tease. He was staring at his boots when he asked the question and barely caught Syros's swift movement in time to dodge his hand. He backed away, laughing. "You're always trying to strike me!"

"And you're always trying to anger me."

Korin stepped right up to Syros and looked into his gray eyes. "Can we not be friends?"

The eyes softened. "Perhaps."

He was so close! Syros's breath stirred his hair, and Korin ached to pull him into his arms. *Fool!* A bell rang to announce dinner and Syros retreated. "Shall we?" he said, and held out an arm to Nikki, hovering nearby, who readily agreed.

Korin watched them walk away from him without even a backward glance, and he was a boy again in a deserted hallway. The light and warmth and laughter were behind the closed doors, and he was alone with no one to give him a thought.

He flung off the mood, poured a glass of wine from a sideboard, and joined the soldiers at the hearth for a good gossip. There was no telling what juicy divulgence he could wheedle out of a man, given enough drink and conversation. But he was often lured from a quietly uttered confidence by Syros's voice, and twice he caught his eyes on him. The third time he blushed to the roots of his copper hair. What did it mean? Was Syros drawn to him, even a little? Should he go to him?

He took a few hesitant steps in his direction and was jolted as a heavy hand landed on his shoulder. "If it isn't Fredrik's little pet."

"Carrow!" Korin embraced the archer in exaggerated delight and laughed at his annoyance in the display. "I was afraid you'd leave with Governor Basal without saying goodbye."

"Basal won't be ready to leave for a few hours yet. And you?"

"Alek wishes to depart at dawn."

"You'll take care?"

A wicked smile sprang on Korin's face, but he closed his teeth on a flippant reply as dismay darkened Carrow's light eyes.

"I will," he promised gravely. "And you also."

They found a table and called for wine. Korin searched the room with his eyes for Syros but couldn't spy his trim form anywhere. He sighed and dug into the food placed before them. The Hall grew merry as the evening progressed and the wine flowed, but he found he hadn't the heart for it. When he'd eaten, he bid Carrow goodnight and made his way to the barracks to find an empty bed and what sleep he could get.

Morning came too soon and Korin grumbled as he dressed, his eyes slanting to the soldiers on their separate cots. They all seemed wrapped in slumber, and piqued, he helped himself to the few trinkets left carelessly on a bed stand. He stuffed someone's extra clothing into his pack as well, and scurried from the quarters as a snore from a corner rattled the silence. The streets were empty except for a few early risers, and Korin hurried when he spotted Alek already riding toward the gates in the distance.

His heart gave a delightful little skip as he neared the stables and discovered Syros holding the bridle of his roan. He flung the saddlebags over the bay and turned to him with a tiny grin, braving to touch his dark hair. He'd never been in love before, and it made him slightly giddy.

"Alek saw me in the courtyard and asked me to help with the horses," Syros began.

"Have you come to kiss me goodbye?" Korin asked, all eagerness and smiles. Syros took a shocked step back, and Korin dropped his hand heavily to his side. For an instant he felt stricken and bewildered, a child hurt once too often. He blinked, and leaped on the roan with a desperate laugh and rode quickly away, not looking back.

When he drew his mount alongside Alek, the man swallowed his greeting on seeing his face. Korin didn't know what his expression betrayed, but the small kindness helped ease the hurt in his chest. Especially since Alek's lover was in dark peril, and he had no reason to spare Korin any consideration. Korin shrugged into his coat. There was no one in the world to spare a thought for him. It took a long while to push off his melancholy.

Chapter Nine

CECIL ROUSED WITH effort. Niko had been brutal with the bindings, and the leather at his wrists bit into his skin. The noose on his neck tightened with every shift of his body as the boat rocked beneath him. He lay on his side on the oaken floor and followed the strip of leather with his gaze from his neck to a hook high on the wall. Effective. His tired glance wandered the room and fastened on a bowl set several paces from him on the polished floor, clear liquid lapping at the brim with the movement of the ship. He gave a slightly hysterical laugh as he measured the distance.

He began to squirm toward the container as thirst drove him, but the leather at his neck tightened until he could scarcely draw breath. He hesitated, though he was so close to the bowl it filled all his sight. In desperation he gave a final lunge. Blood roared in his ears, and he fought unconsciousness, then tried to move back but the leather wouldn't loosen at his neck.

Cecil panted against the floorboards, becoming aware of the pool of water against his cheek, smelling of wet wood and life. He must have over-turned the bowl on his last effort. Pressing his mouth to the floor, he lapped up as much of the liquid as he could before it dripped between the cracks.

His head pounded with his heartbeats, and he closed his eyes as black spots swam in his vision. The short breaths he managed didn't fill his lungs, and though the water had briefly revived him, he grew cold and numb and slipped into the blackness behind his lids.

He woke slowly, hearing whispered words in his ear, and shrank back, Niko's face too close to his own.

"Careful," Niko cautioned and rose to his feet. "Don't want to strangle yourself."

Niko held the end of the leather strap around Cecil's neck and tugged gently, forcing Cecil to stand, then laughed unpleasantly and led him on deck as he would an animal. Cecil winced in the bright sunlight. Niko tied him to the railing at the prow of the ship, and Cecil raised his face to the spray of the sea, wishing for one full breath of the tangy air as it stung his skin.

He wanted to go home, yearned with all his heart to see Alek again. He feared he would die on the ship. A small, wounded cry escaped him at the thought, and he sank to his knees, head bowed. The panic could be one of Niko's tricks, but he was too far gone with exhaustion and pain to care. It was frightening either way.

Niko slipped with ease into his mind and found the old phantoms in Cecil's nightmares where Cecil had hidden them, then drew them out. The dead rose from the lake under Siagan, rotten with age, crowding Cecil's sight. *They weren't real!* Niko laughed cruelly at his desperate sobs as Cecil fought his terror of them.

At long last, Niko bent to his ear. "Sleep," he commanded and withdrew the terrible images, leaving Cecil shivering on the deck, desperate for his friends to hurry—surely Kayle had reached Karthag by now?—and for Alex to come and find him.

*

KAYLE WISHED AGAIN he was back home in Sennia as he pulled the string from his hair and let the stiff breeze sweep the heavy strands from his forehead. As the sea spray cooled his hot skin, he glanced across the sleek ship to the horizon, his restless gaze catching Belega's approaching shoreline. For a panicked moment he wondered if he'd ever see his country or darling wife again. Last night he'd watched Jena in the moonlight while she slept, and a terrible longing came over him to take her somewhere beautiful, to build their home and have children with her. He'd wanted to stay in their bed, pull her into his arms, and hold her forever…

He drew a quick breath when he heard the step he'd been waiting for. Light from the new moon shown on the path, and his pulses rioted as he watched Jena approach him. He couldn't speak as he pulled her into his eager arms and buried his face in the waves of her hair. She gave him a shy kiss, and he trembled as he led her into the concealing darkness under the trees where he'd set a blanket. He picked her up in his arms and lay with her gently cradled against him.

"Don't cry, darling," he said brokenly as he felt her shake in his arms. His heart twisted. "I think I've done a terrible thing in marrying you, when I have no place to keep you safe."

"I'm not crying," she said. "I just miss you when we're not together."

"Darling," he murmured against her soft throat. "Can you be patient a little

longer? If Niko…"

"Hush." She put her fingers against his lips. They both knew the cruel weapon she'd be in his hands if Niko discovered their attachment.

"I can wait forever," she promised, and he kissed her eyes and cheeks and sweet mouth. He pulled her closer against him and for a time there was only the two of them in all the world.

"Dearest?" he called to her in the morning and touched her lips with his. She murmured sleepily and snuggled against him. He almost wept. "I have to go, my dearest."

"I know." Her voice had been a bare wisp of sound. Her lids fluttered but the effort to wake seemed beyond her. He had kept her up late, sharing their love, talking until the wee hours. "Kiss me goodbye."

His tears fell as he kissed her gently, passionately, and held her to his heart until he had no choice but to go…

The ship floated into Karthag's harbor, and a shudder ran over Kayle when he spotted Natan waiting on the sand. *Now it begins.* He scrambled over the rail before the gangplank lowered fully, jumped to the dock, and then rushed to him. The strain of the past weeks caught up, and he went straight into Natan's close embrace.

"Papa," he choked out, and sobbed brokenly against the comforting shoulder. He'd watched Niko, dear to him as any brother, fall into madness. And now he had to hunt him. It was too much!

Natan asked no questions, simply held him, stroking his hair. In time he said Kayle's name, easing the crush on his heart.

"I'm sorry, Papa," he murmured, feeling he was again the orphaned child Natan had taken into his home.

Natan wiped his own tears and smiled. "I'm not, dearest boy. This is a terrible time. We both needed this connection. It's good to see you. I've missed you. We've missed you."

Kayle looked around eagerly. "Is Kavi here?" he asked, wanting to see him, Kavi being as much a father to him as Natan.

"He's in town with Ellis."

"Is it true Ellis is married?" Kayle asked and laughed at Natan's rueful nod. "I can't believe it, after all the young men he declined at home."

"Aiden is exceptional."

"He must be."

Natan chewed a lip. "Who's in control, Kayle, now that the Vice-King is dead?"

"The council is holding things together as best they can, but…"

"Niko wants you on the throne."

"Just because my father had once been Mage doesn't signify I would make a good Vice-King," Kayle pointed out.

"And in any event, the council won't give up their authority easily." Natan stared thoughtfully at the sea, then roused. "Well, we must deal with Niko first and foremost."

They mounted the waiting horses, and Natan explained as they rode toward the city how Captain Daran's ship stood ready to leave for the Isle.

"You're to rest during the afternoon, and we'll start at twilight. I'm to go with you," Natan said firmly as if Kayle might have objected. "As will Aiden and Ellis. Willum will stay here, along with Kavi, though he's furious. But for us to take him back to the Isle of Wind…"

"Understood," Kayle said, hearing the strain in Natan's voice. A grin leaped on his face when they approached Karthag, and he saw his family waiting to greet him at the city gates. They hurried forward as he dismounted, though Ellis was the first to reach him.

"Kayle!" Ellis flung his arms around him.

"Are you well?" Kayle searched his open face. Ellis appeared pale and tired, and there was a strain in his eyes. But his spirit seemed good. He reached past Ellis and gripped Willum's hand. He felt someone's gaze and found the golden eyes of the Red Twin on him and shivered, sensing immense power kept carefully controlled, guarded.

"Kayle, this is my lord Aiden of Karthag and Ellis's husband," Natan introduced them. "Aiden, my son Kayle of Sennia."

"My lord." Aiden bowed, and his long braid brushed the ground at Kayle's feet. They studied each other until Kavi impatiently pushed between them, reaching for him.

"Kayle," Kavi said warmly as he took his hands, his gaze piercing. "Are you well?"

"Well enough." Kayle frowned. "Though I could wish this done and all of us home and safe."

"As do I," Kavi agreed and clasped him tightly in his arms.

Kayle returned his embrace. "We'll end it this time, Kavi, one way or another."

He felt Kavi tremble slightly at his words, and then Kavi stepped back, brushing at his eyes. Willum, watching them, motioned toward the castle. "We have set out a light repast. Shall we go?"

The afternoon was pleasant, the sun warm, breeze soft, and they decided to eat in the garden, reclining in the grass or on the benches. They talked of trivial matters, reluctant to disrupt the joy at being reunited. At last Kayle stirred. "Where's Alek? I thought he'd be the first to greet me after Papa and Kavi."

Willum sat forward, his face grave. "Niko stopped here two nights ago. Alek is certain beyond doubt he took Cecil, who'd fallen asleep on the deck after readying the ship we're to take. He sensed Cecil's fear and pain." Kayle felt a coldness seep into his heart as Willum continued, "Alek rode to the coast outside of Amara at Aiden's suggestion, from where he'll take a small craft to the Isle of Wind, while we'll travel from the harbor here."

Aiden's head had jerked up at the mention of his name. "I felt it was necessary. I saw a man in my mind's eye, someone key to our success, whom Alek needs to find before he goes to the Isle."

Kayle nodded, knowing the value of premonition, then sighed, suddenly weary to his bones. He grieved at the loss of Niko, who'd been such an intricate, joyous part of his younger years, whose mind had grown unsound through grief and helpless rage. The thought of Cecil in his hands chilled him.

Natan rose to his feet. "We'll get Cecil back, Kayle, but for now you need to rest. Come with me."

Kayle obediently stood, and Natan took him to a cool room in the castle with a soft bed and the forgetfulness of sleep.

*

GOVERNOR BASAL SHIVERED, ice touching his heart as they crested a hill and Fredrik's Hall came into view. What was happening to Robin in that hateful place? Carrow swung from his saddle as they reached the gates, pushed them open, and they urged the tired horses inside the walls. They rode straight to the Hall, leaving the animals to graze on the overgrown grass as Basal shoved apart the massive doors. Two guards jumped to attention on seeing them.

He glowered at them. "Take me to Commander Tyrel. Now."

The soldiers dropped a hand to their swords but took a step back as Carrow drew the short bow from his shoulder and notched an arrow. Basal's knife gleamed in the sunlight spilling through the open doorway as well, and the guards fled. Basal and Carrow advanced several paces before a lisping voice halted them, and Basal spied a stout, rather short man leaning against the wall. "Welcome, my lord Governor."

"Nelson." The archer drew the bow back full length.

Lord Fredrik's cousin squeaked. "Governor Basal, tell him to wait!"

Out of patience, Basal strode up to him and pressed the blade of his knife to his throat. "Where's my son?"

Blood dripped from the dagger's edge onto his white tunic, and Nelson's breath caught on a sob. "Please, my lord! I don't know. There are many ambitions in the Hall. Governor! I can take you to Commander Tyrel."

"Please do." Basal shoved the insipid lord down the hallway, cringing as the man halted twice to try to kiss his hand. "Go."

Basal's fear formed a hard knot in his chest as they followed the man down a flight of stairs to the cellar rooms. Where was Robin? The thought of his incorrigible son in the hands of the Hall's corrupt lords made him ill.

Carrow swore under his breath as they entered a bleak chamber and spotted Tyrel against the far wall. "This is where Commander Jacksan was held."

Basal shuddered even as he hurried to Tyrel's side where he sat propped with his back against the stones. He called Tyrel's name, but it wasn't until he raised the commander's chin from his chest that Tyrel's gray eyes focused. "Governor?"

"Yes," Basal confirmed in a tight voice and slit the leather binding his hands. Carrow helped the commander to stand. Nelson had deserted them, so seizing the chance, they made their way up the stairs to Fredrik's den with Carrow's arm around Tyrel's waist for support. Tyrel sank into a chair and touched the purple contusion on his forehead, wincing in pain.

"Are you well?" Basal asked.

"Well enough." Tyrel slid to his knees before Basal. "I'm sorry, my lord. We were at dinner last evening when two men burst into the room." His handsome face flushed, shamed. "I never made it from the chair before they were on us."

"Who?"

"A lord named Ashel and one of his lackeys. They didn't hurt him," Tyrel rushed to assure Basal. "They threw a sack over Robin's head, and the knife at his back convinced him to go quietly."

"At least he had that much sense."

"Don't underestimate him, lord," Carrow put in softly. "Robin's a shrewd man under his foolishness. He'll keep his skin intact."

"They've left the castle," Tyrel continued. "I know that much. But to where, I couldn't learn."

Basal took a deep breath. "Carrow, call your men. I want them in the fields within the hour. Find Robin, if you have to search every inch of Belega, the South and North."

"Yes, my lord."

"Tyrel, I want you at the border again. Question the guards on both sides to see if anyone's crossed over in the last few days. Send a message to Governor Willum, as well, informing him of what's happened here."

"As you wish." Tyrel bowed.

"I'll question the remaining lords of the Hall myself," Basal said grimly, tightening his fist.

*

ROBIN STRETCHED HIS bound legs in front of him and leaned against the boulder, resting his tied hands on his lap. So far, his captors had been pleasant enough, not paying him much attention. He hoped that continued. He'd met most of the men at the Hall, but these two must have kept out of the way. He had no idea what to expect from them. They'd been camping in a copse of trees a few leagues from the Hall, though for how much longer, he couldn't guess. Hearing their raised voices, he set his features to one of boredom and sleepiness as the two men entered the small clearing.

"So, the little puppy is awake," the tall man observed, the one Robin hated, and squatted in front of him. "How's our boy tonight?"

"Leave him alone," the handsome one growled.

Robin shuddered as the man in front of him traced his cheek with a finger. "Why? Aren't you going to share?"

"Leave him, Corhen," the other said, disgusted.

The tall man shrugged and moved away. "Why so fussy, Ashel?"

"Because, as the boy is, the governor will scatter his men to find him, giving us the time we need to set our plans into motion. Damage him at all, and Basal will spend his life to see us dead."

"You're afraid of him?"

A knife appeared in Ashel's hand, and Corhen stepped back with a white face. "Know your enemy, Corhen," Ashel advised softly. "If you don't fear the Governor, then you're more of a fool than I believed. If we hurt his precious boy, we may as well slit our own throats." Ashel flicked Robin a glance. "That doesn't mean I won't kill you if I deem it necessary."

Robin nodded. Ashel studied his face a moment, and Robin drew a breath of relief when he scowled and turned away. He found it hard to play at being harmless when he felt like roaring at the praise to his father.

Corhen grumbled as he brought wood into the clearing and started a small fire. "How long do we have to do this?"

Robin choked back a laugh. Obviously, the man had never left the comforts of the Hall before. His laughter died at the look on Ashel's face. He knelt beside Corhen and the man never sensed his danger. At Ashel's silence, Corhen tilted his head back to see his face, and his scream choked off as Ashel slid the edge of the thin knife neatly across his throat.

Ashel watched dispassionately as the hot blood poured over his hands. He lifted the man in his arms and crossed the clearing to dump him into a small hollow between two trees. He was whistling as he returned to the fire.

Robin turned his horrified gaze away with effort. He'd never witnessed murder being done, or seen a life counted so cheaply. He couldn't control the trembling that ran through his suddenly weak body, and he shrank back with a cry as Ashel appeared over him.

"Quiet," Ashel said amiably as he crouched at Robin's feet. He looked at Robin with a strange light in his eyes, blinked, and the madness seemed gone. He smiled crookedly.

"I'm trusting you," Ashel said as he sliced through the leather at Robin's feet and hands. "I want you to make us dinner and do the various chores around camp that Corhen used to do. If you behave yourself, I won't kill you. Try to run, and…well, I'm very good at throwing knives as well."

He stood and held out a slim hand. Robin stared at it a moment, then climbed unaided to his feet and stomped some life back into numb limbs. Ashel shrugged and took parchment and quill from his pack and made various notations, ignoring him. Robin watched him a moment, then sighed and searched the packs for food.

They sat in the gathering darkness and drank hot tea, and Ashel spoke to him in a companionable way and told a few stories. Robin listened intently, never having felt more terrified in his life.

Chapter Ten

NIKO STOOD AT the tiller and guided the small craft onto the white sands of the Isle. *At last!* His heart rushed with an excitement he couldn't contain. He'd waited a lifetime to step foot on the beach where the Karthagans had lost their powers. He never should have listened to the Mage; Natan was weak with his talk of peace and unity. Those with power should control. The others were nothing.

He jumped from the deck and ran a line to a nearby tree. Glancing back at the ship, he grimaced with distaste at the sight of the crumpled figure bound to the mast. Why had he even brought the thing with him? In the end, he hadn't proven much fun. He'd withdrawn into himself only a few days into the voyage, as if he couldn't be hurt any deeper. Niko had tried! But to no avail. The man simply endured with empty eyes. If he didn't have one final use for him…

He left the man in the sun and took a leisurely walk in the cool under the trees. It would be another day before the others caught up to him. Time enough to set the stage.

*

NATAN STOOD AT the prow of the schooner as they dipped through a wave and laughed with irrepressible joy as the spray washed over him. He couldn't help it. His heart was lifted by the sun and the sea, the white sails against the evening sky, the sting of salt water against his face.

He wondered if Niko ever felt such simple pleasure anymore. He remembered the first time Niko had sent his spirit out to sail on the wind. The awe and rapture in his expression! Natan had known that feeling once upon a time. Did Niko find joy in his gifts now?

He missed his old friend. Perhaps if he had done more to save Corha… Useless regret. The Vice-King hadn't listened to his pleas, and there wasn't much he could do for her from the cell they'd thrown him into.

He gazed over the endless blue water and wished Kavi were with him. No. He wanted the world sound and whole, and he and Kavi on their way home to Sennia.

He stayed on deck to ride a few more waves, heart rushing, then made his way below and tapped on Aiden's door. Aiden had kept to his room for most of the voyage at the captain's request, but Natan knew it was time they spoke together.

"Come in, Mage," Aiden called softly, and Natan saw him struggle to smile as he entered. He sat at the head of the bed with his knees drawn up tight against his chest, his head back against the oak wall. The golden eyes were dark smudged and full of shadows.

Natan noticed the untouched tray on the bedstand. "You're not eating?" he asked in concern

"No. I'm afraid it would choke me."

Natan settled at the foot of the bed and searched Aiden's gaunt face. "Is Niko with you?"

"No, Mage. He surrounds the ship with terror, but so far I've kept him at bay. He's very powerful."

His tired voice held a note of warning. Natan sighed as tremors passed through the strong body opposite him. They sat quietly and he hoped his presence was some comfort to the suffering man.

"Was Niko ever on the Isle, Mage?" Aiden asked some while later.

"No. He's been to Belega once before, but never to the Isle of Wind."

Aiden nodded to himself. "Then it's my cousin Camron's memories he's sending me. The ones he received in their last moments together, before Niko killed him."

"Aiden!"

"It's difficult, Mage."

"What do you see, my boy?"

"I'm on the Isle." His voice sounded like a lost child's, without hope. "Ethan is with me. The hill burns. Father burns. But it's as if someone's watching these events, reveling in our madness."

"No, that can't be," Natan protested, distressed by the implication. Had Camron watched and done nothing?

"It's only the truth, Mage." Aiden pressed his eyes to his knees and wept soundlessly.

Natan's heart broke. This was his fault. He'd made the grave error of passing Gregor's powers on to Niko, and now this good man was suffering. Ellis lived with nightmares. Kayle was far from home…

He ached to set things right, but feared he wouldn't prove strong enough in the end. He despaired. Willum had chosen the wrong man for his plans. A bleak moment passed, then Natan took a breath and gathered his courage to go on. He touched Aiden's arm and drew the molten eyes to him.

"Try to rest, if at all possible," he said kindly. "Aiden, you're not alone."

"Yes, Mage," Aiden said on a sigh.

Natan left him and joined Ellis on the deck as the sun sank below the horizon. They talked of home and fishing with Mika, and picnics on the beach with Tillie and her lover, Kam. Neither mentioned the morning to come.

Ellis fought to stay awake, but at last his young body betrayed him, and he blinked heavy lids. "I'm afraid to sleep, Papa, without Kayle's help or Aiden's arms around me," he confessed as he sat on the deck and rested his head against Natan's shoulder.

Natan's throat grew tight. "I know. But both men need to prepare for tomorrow's encounter with Niko. I'm here, though, and we're safe, and there's so many who love you."

"I love you too." The tired voice faded into sleep. Natan gathered Ellis in his arms and brushed the dark hair from his son's face. He hoped his touch would bring peace. Ellis's cry of fear came all too soon, betraying his nightmares as he moaned and wept. Natan spoke quietly in his ear, rubbing his back and arms. He touched his face. Ellis would quiet, sleep, then wake again to sob against him.

To Natan the night became unbearable, yet he dreaded the coming day, when the nightmares in Ellis's dreams would come true.

Deep in the night, Ellis slept, and Natan rose and stretched sore muscles. He heard a faint noise from the galley, and soon the captain's daughter Riana joined him, bearing mugs of fragrant tea. They settled by Ellis and Natan gratefully sipped the hot brew.

"Go in and sleep, Mage, if you wish. I'll stay with Ellis," Riana offered hesitantly. They looked a long moment at each other, and Natan squeezed her capable hand.

"Thank you, my dear."

Ellis stirred and muttered dark words, and Riana sat nearer and placed his head in her lap. She crooned over him and stroked his hair, and her soft voice seemed to penetrate his dreams. A faint smile touched his strained features, and as Natan left them, he saw Riana bend down and place a gentle kiss on his forehead. She watched the agony on his face a moment and kissed his pale lips as well. Natan sighed for the heartache in the world and went inside.

*

The ocean boiled. Creatures churned to the surface and burst apart, spewing blood into the water. The sky darkened, smelling foul. Birds dropped, dead, onto the deck of the ship and joined the carnage in the sea...

Aiden blinked hot eyes and the vision left him. The Isle sat peaceful in a crystal ocean. The afternoon sun kissed his face.

"Did you see, Mage?" he asked and heard the strain in his voice. It couldn't be helped. He was rushing toward his fate at a perilous speed and couldn't turn aside, or what good would he have done in the world? He would see it through, even if it meant...

No, he wouldn't think of losing Ellis, with his skin heating to Aiden's touch and his glorious eyes warm with love. A groan burst from him, and he covered his face. He would be brave, though it was hard without his twin to lean on.

"We're with you, Aiden."

The Mage's voice remained steady, firm, and Aiden clung to its echo in the chaos of his mind. He calmed. "Thank you, Natan," he murmured.

"How can I help you?"

"I'm almost blind now, Mage," he answered. "Stay with me! I can only see the visions Niko sends. Talk to me. Your voice anchors me."

The Isle burned. People fell screaming in pain on the melting sand…

Tears fell from Aiden's scorched eyes. He hadn't the strength to keep the nightmares away any longer and despaired of the insanity to follow.

"Stop the ship, Mage. I can't… I don't know what's real. We should take the small boat from here. Kayle, Ellis, you and me. No others."

"Yes, my lord."

Aiden felt on the point of collapse. If he could just get them to shore, he could let go. Someone took his arm and guided him to the dory. Aiden could barely sit still as they rowed over the swells fouled with rot and disease and filth. A child's face peered from the depths, Ethan's young features begging for his hand to lift him up.

"Father!" he cried out and didn't know if he called to Natan beside him or the one burning once again in his mind. Arms went around him—Ellis—and he leaned into their comfort, straining to hear the quiet words that brought peace. He blinked his eyes open, searched Ellis's beloved face and found strength in the love and resolve in his amber gaze.

Taking a breath for courage, he scanned the white sands of the Isle drawing closer, the green pines towering against a blue sky. "It's not right. Even after eighteen years, the Isle couldn't have recovered like this with trees a century old. Niko is stronger here. We can't trust our senses."

"Trust each other," Kayle said grimly and leaned on his oar a moment to gather their attention. "Niko will use us one against the other if a chance opens. Keep this moment in your hearts. We're united by love and a common purpose. Don't believe otherwise."

Aiden let out a frightened breath. "They're coming! Be ready." He covered his head with his arms as nightmares crashed over the prow. The others screamed as horror took over their minds.

Aiden stood with sudden resolve.

"This isn't real!" he cried as the world erupted around him with fire and storm and the anguished screams of his dying friends.

Natan groped for his hand and called over the howling wind. "Stop this! It'll kill them." He gestured to the others, who crouched in the bottom of the boat with bowed heads, overwhelmed and unable to throw off the visions that could bring madness.

"I don't know—" Aiden sucked in a harsh breath and set his lips. Raising his face to the burning sky, he flung out his arms. "Enough!"

His voice boomed across the sea and shattered Niko's control on their minds. They'd been adrift during the moments of terror, and a sudden wave caught them. Ellis scrambled for a paddle, and he and Kayle rowed with determination. The next wave cast them up on the hot sands of the Isle, and Natan scrambled over the side to haul the dory out of the tide.

Aiden swooned, spent, hardly aware when Kayle lifted him from the boat and carried him under the trees. His thoughts slipped from them and traveled the corridors in his mind, bright and airy. It was almost a pleasure to walk the quiet pathways, though he felt Ellis following him. That could be dangerous. If Ellis sprang the trap… But then he smiled a little. He'd take Ellis home…

The cabin of stone and pine logs rested peacefully on the mountainside, and Aiden sighed in contentment as he breathed in the pine-scented air and watched Ellis's sweet lips part in wonder as Ellis took the chair beside him. He licked his own in anticipation. He lived for this time with Ellis. But then his brow wrinkled. Kavi spoke to him from far away, from Karthag, urging him to wake; then he spied Natan approaching them across the wide porch. Aiden gave him one fierce glance, then buried his face against Ellis's shoulder. Couldn't he have this one moment?

"You can't have him back yet," Ellis said forcefully to Natan, and Aiden trembled, heart exalting at his sharp defense. "He needs a quiet moment if we don't want to lose him."

"If Niko comes…"

"Aiden will be there soon. Give me a moment with my husband, please." Ellis ran his hands through Aiden's hair, calming his thumping heart. Natan's footsteps retreated, then Ellis nudged Aiden's face up, and kissed him…

Aiden came back to himself to find Ellis curled against him, sleeping, and Natan sitting close by.

"I'm sorrier than I can say that you must be here. It breaks my heart," Natan told him, grief in his voice.

"Will I go mad, Mage?" he asked, helplessness washing through him. Ellis stirred and pressed a gentle kiss against his neck.

"You mustn't give up," Natan urged. "Find the one special thing in your life and cling to it. Niko can't win through that."

"I've found him," Aiden practically growled, close to tears, holding Ellis close. "But if I lose him—"

"Aiden!" Natan's urgent voice dragged him from the black pit opening before him. "You see what he does? Niko pulls out our darkest fears to use against us."

Ellis made a soothing sound, sat up, and held Aiden's gaze. "I'm not going anywhere, Aiden. Remember, I've known Niko my entire life. There's nothing he can do to take me from your side."

"We will all protect you, to the depth of our abilities," Natan promised.

Aiden suddenly remembered. "Kavi sent you a message, Mage," he said and laughed outright as Natan flushed.

"Mage," he continued gently. "Kavi was with us for the briefest moment in my mind and said to take care of yourself and to guard his heart, which you carry with you."

Natan wrapped his arms around his knees and buried his telltale face. Kayle joined them and Aiden gratefully took one of the packets of fruit and nuts he handed around.

They ate quietly, lost in their own thoughts, until Kayle reluctantly stood. "I know it's early," he began, "but I think we should sleep while we can. Ellis, I would like you to keep the first watch. I'll take the second, and Aiden the remaining. We need to be rested to face Niko."

"What of me?" Natan had been blinking his eyes, trying to stay awake, and appeared bewildered as Aiden exchanged a fond smile with the others.

Ellis held out his hand. "Come with me."

Aiden watched him lead Natan under the pines. Natan tried to protest, but Ellis merely shook his head at his slurred words and pushed him gently onto blankets Kayle had laid out for him.

"Go to sleep, Papa," Ellis commanded and fondly kissed the tip of his nose. He returned and sat beside Aiden, pulling Aiden down to rest his head in his lap.

"Sleep," Ellis commanded, and Aiden smiled even as exhaustion claimed him.

*

KAVI ROUSED FROM his vision of Aiden on the Isle, his chest once again tight with fear. It took him a moment to recall he was in Karthag, left behind, while Natan and the others walked into danger.

"I'm afraid they won't come back," he confessed brokenly to the semi-dark room. Aiden's desperateness and suffering wrung his heart. And he hadn't been able to speak with Natan directly, damn it all. Kavi wanted to be in his arms, Natan's beloved voice in his ear, his sweet moans driving away the world as they made love. His laughter. Kavi ached for him, longed for his safe return. "How can I wait?"

He kicked off the light blankets, unable to resume his rest. He hadn't been sleeping, but this attempt at a nap after dinner only served to make him irritable, his contact with Aiden compounding his fears. Willum's great plan might be unfolding as he desired, but Kavi would no longer be left out. He wasn't powerless. He understood why a Karthagan couldn't return to the Isle of Wind—Aiden and Alek the desperate exceptions—but if he didn't do something to help, he'd surely go mad anyway.

It took some time, but he finally tracked down Governor Willum at the city gates. He and Commander Jaden were in deep discussion and looked up, their worry plain to see as Kavi approached.

Kavi smiled tightly. "Aiden has reached the Isle of Wind."

Willum motioned to the causeway above the gates. Kavi ran fingers over the handrail as they climbed the steps, then touched the back of the nearest bench as he took a seat, appreciating Aiden's intricate vines and roses chiseled with care into the granite. He didn't know the Red Twin well, but if he brought harm to Natan, Kavi would make sure he paid dearly.

Willum sat against the low wall facing him while Jaden remained standing, his eyes on the gateway below, both almost lost in shadow as the sun sank behind them.

Willum sighed into the silence. "I'm not sure what is to come. The future is dark." He took a deep breath. "I'm leaving for Kangar on the Northern coast in the morning, and then on to Barkuit and ultimately the border. A crisis is coming, and I need to know where our people stand. Jaden, please move the Karthagan soldiers at the garrison into the city in the morning to fortify the walls and gates. Then take your own men back to Nagal. No Karthagan is to leave the city after that. I fear… I believe it's no longer safe for them in Belega. The hatred from the Karthagan Wars is reawakening."

"Why do you say that?" Kavi asked, dismayed. As if Niko's betrayal wasn't bad enough. Now they weren't safe in their own homes. How would they protect themselves if the Belegan armies turned against them?

Willum ran a hand through his hair, clearly agitated. "One of the Karthagan soldiers I use as scouts returned from the Southern border today, tied to his horse. He'd been questioned and beaten without any explanation as to why. No one has bothered my scouts before. He was carrying the news that Robin of Nagal has been taken hostage at Fredrik's Hall, and both armies are on edge. And it was soldiers from the Southern Territory who'd questioned him. What if it had been Northern soldiers from Barkuit who no longer trusted him?"

"He wouldn't have come back at all," Jaden supplied.

"They would have killed him, fearing he may be a spy carrying misinformation." For an instant Willum looked uncertain, then shook his head. "Jaden, you need to remove your company of soldiers. If war comes, you wouldn't be safe here."

At his words, Kavi hung his head as the walls of his world began to crumble around him. Without their powers, how could the Karthagan people defend themselves? Alek and Aiden had asked him to look after the city while they were gone, and the burden seemed unbearably heavy. He didn't know what to do.

"Natan, I need you here," he murmured, missing his friend and lover as never before and not sure of ever seeing him again. He wasn't sure of anything anymore.

Chapter Eleven

ALEK WARILY EYED the white sands of the Isle of Wind as it drew nearer. He and Korin had ridden their horses hard from Nagal to the coast, borrowed a skiff, and left immediately for the Isle. The beach seemed like a pleasant dream on the horizon, the sky blue, the tree line green. He thought he heard a waterfall in the distance. Niko had grown strong indeed to create this fantasy.

"Ready?" he asked Korin.

The soldier nodded, and they slipped the boat into a wave and rowed frantically for the shore, the water sweeping them onto the beach. They hauled the vessel above the tide line, there was no sign of another boat. The others must have landed elsewhere. Alek strode into the forest.

"Wait!" Korin had to trot to keep up. Alek ignored him. He moved with cold purpose through the pines, a fierce promise of violence in his heart to any hindrance.

They walked half the day without pause, climbing higher into the hills, until Korin stumbled in his exhaustion and dropped hard on his knees. Alek sent him a look of fury.

Korin climbed unsteadily to his feet, gulping air. "I'm sorry, lord. I'm ready."

Alek blinked, dizzy and sick and driven. What had the lad said? The red haze in his mind lifted, and he knew with alarm Niko had controlled him. In his single-minded purpose to find Cecil, it must have been easy. If Korin hadn't stopped him…

In dismay, he took in the translucency of Korin's fair skin, the tremble in a slim body worn by two days at sea and a forced march without rest or water.

"I'm sorry, Korin." He helped him to a low rock, where Korin dropped wearily, the bright hair swinging down to hide his troubled eyes. Alek brushed it aside and raised Korin's face. "Stay here," he said. "Make us a camp. I'll find Cecil and bring him back."

"Aren't you tired, my lord?"

"Do you think I could rest? I'm on fire, Korin! I feel he is near, and if I hesitate, he dies. Niko's final trick on me. If only…"

The air crackled to life, and Korin sat up as his copper hair stood on end. Energy flowed into the space around them, and Alek spread his arms wide. In a moment, a soft neigh sounded on the edge of the clearing and two horses trotted up, skittish and wild from years of freedom. Alek used soft words and caresses to steady them. He swung smoothly onto one of their shaggy backs and urged him to a trot, Korin forgotten in his urgency.

He found Cecil where he feared he would be. As Alek slid off his mount, he glanced over the precipice to the sea far below and shuddered at the violent memories that struck him. He'd been there when his uncle had lifted up his hands and sent half the Isle crashing to the bottom of the ocean. Hundreds of Karthagans had been lost that day.

He shook off the images, all his attention centering on the man whose feet dangled over the edge of the stone outcrop.

"Cecil?" he called softly, not wanting to startle him. Cecil seemed not to hear him and appeared unaware of his danger. Alek carefully climbed up on the rock.

"Cecil?"

Cecil's continued silence unnerved him, and he couldn't risk another moment so near the chasm. He flung his arms around Cecil's slight body and dragged him backward. They fell heavily off the stone to the ground and Alek rolled to his knees. Cecil had landed on his side with his back to him. Alek winced as he drew his knife to cut the leather straps on Cecil's bloody wrists. The tight cord had sliced into his flesh, and the wounds were festering. Freed, Cecil's arms fell limply, and the blue-tipped fingers twitched with returning circulation.

Alek pulled him into his arms, and Cecil's head rolled loosely against Alek's shoulder. With horror and disbelief, he saw the cord that bit into Cecil's throat, causing the tinge of blue to his cheeks and lips. Alek brushed at the tears in his eyes and tried to be careful on the tight leather, but finally just sliced through it, nicking Cecil's neck in the process.

Cecil hesitantly drew his first lungful of air, and then he was gulping it in as if he'd been drowning. His hard sobs broke Alek's heart.

"I'm here, darling. You're safe now."

Alek gently rocked him and stroked his hair. Cecil grew calmer, yet

Alek became aware of the violent tremors that repeatedly shook him. He studied the strained face so close to his own, and a sudden fear came to him.

"Open your eyes," he requested quietly and was filled with dismay at the tiny whimper in Cecil's throat. "Please, dear," he urged. Cecil turned his face away.

"Open them now," he commanded, and Cecil's body jerked in his arms. Cecil faced him and the bruised lids flew open. Alek cried out in pain on seeing the nightmares that walked in the gray depths. He put a hand on Cecil's temple and pushed into his mind, and the phantoms ran from the fury of his coming. Alek stalked them relentlessly, crushing them one by one to dust with his bare hands. The remainder fled down the dark corridors of Cecil's tortured mind as Alek strode grimly after them. There was no place to hide.

When he'd disposed of the last horror, Alek returned to himself to find Cecil sleeping in exhaustion. He rose to his feet, holding Cecil easily in his arms; grieved at how gaunt he'd become. Well, he'd would have the pleasure of nurturing him back to health. As he rode slowly toward camp, he rejoiced in the feel of Cecil against him, knowing he was alive and safe. If he stole a few kisses on the way, there was no one to begrudge him.

Korin rose from the fire as they entered the small clearing and took Cecil from Alek's reluctant arms. Alek sprang from the horse's back and spoke kind words in his ear, then sent him to his companion, nibbling grass on the edge of the glen. Korin laid Cecil on the bed he'd made of blankets over a thick layer of pine needles near the fire, and Alek knelt beside him. They looked at Cecil, hesitant to disturb him. His skin was a pale fine porcelain, the fair hair strands of white silk. Alek feared Cecil would shatter at a rough touch.

He placed his hands on Cecil's glistening forehead and felt the warmth of fever. "Could you heat water, Korin?"

"I have some ready for coffee. If I add cold water, it should be right."

"Thank you."

Alek gently removed the filthy garments from Cecil and tenderly washed him. Between their two packs, he and Korin managed a clean set of clothing, dressed Cecil, and wrapped him in the blankets. Cecil opened his dull eyes and blinked vaguely at Korin. His gaze shifted to Alek, and a wondrous smile spread on his tired face. He dutifully drank the water Alek pressed on him, sighed, and settled back into sleep.

*

KORIN CAUTIOUSLY MADE his way to a camp the next morning Alek assured him was half a league to the south. He smelled pine and a hint of wood smoke on the cool air, then spotted a man standing by a fire, mug in hand. His mouth watered at the aroma of coffee, and he watched enviously as the stranger took a sip of the steaming brew.

Preoccupied, he almost stumbled into a tent pitched at the edge of the clearing and took a hasty step back as a curly head thrust from its depths, then smiled into the hazel eyes alight with interest that looked up at him. He sketched a bow. "Yes, I'm real," he said in reply to the man's hesitant expression. "I've come to the Isle with Alek."

The man scrambled from the tent. "Cecil?"

Korin nodded. "We found him. Alek sent me to pass the news on to Natan, Kayle, or Aiden. Which are you?"

The man returned his contagious smile. "I'm Natan. Kayle and Ellis have gone to scout out the caves. I believe Aiden is by the fire. You are?"

"I'm Korin of Fredrik's Hall…" He closed his mouth with a snap of teeth, regretting the admission at a flicker in Natan's eyes.

"Is Commander Tyrel well?"

"Yes, my lord."

"We heard news of Commander Jacksan's murder. I'm deeply sorry for your loss. Jacksan was a good man and a good friend."

Korin cleared a tight throat. "Thank you."

The attractive stranger stomped into his boots. "Will you come to the fire?"

"At once," he said, remembering the coffee. He kept close to Natan's side as they approached the Karthagan tending the flames, intimidated by the intense scrutiny of the golden eyes watching them.

"Who have you found, Mage?" the man asked.

Korin stopped in his tracks, turning to Natan beside him.

"You're the Mage?" he whispered hoarsely, and fell to his knees, eyes on the ground. "I'm sorry. I didn't know. I wouldn't have been—"

"Korin," Natan protested, urging him to rise. "It's an old title, and I'm certainly no one to kneel to. Now, how have you heard of me?"

Korin had trouble meeting his eyes. "I dreamed of Cecil on the cliffs with the world melting around him." He shuddered violently. "When I awoke, I had an overwhelming compulsion to find you. I don't know why."

Natan slipped an arm across his shoulders, the gesture strangely comforting. "Never mind, lad. We'll find out together. Aiden, is breakfast ready?"

Korin ate his portion of fish and nuts in silence, awed by the man opposite. Alek had been the first Karthagan he'd met, and Korin found him intimidating at times. This man devastated him with his anguished golden eyes and proud, cold face, his dark hair a loose braid at his back. Tremors ran through his strong body.

Aiden must have felt his gaze and raised eyes where nightmares walked in the molten depths. A faint cry escaped Aiden, and he began to rise. "Forgive me. I didn't mean to disturb your meal…"

Korin stretched out a tentative hand. "Please, stay. You're not disturbing me. How can I help you?"

Aiden covered his eyes. "It's too late for that. I only need it to end."

Stricken, Korin looked pleadingly at Natan. "Why must he suffer?"

"He keeps the madness from us all. No one else can." Natan's voice dropped, pain touching his face. "We wouldn't have the strength."

Horses approached and they rose to their feet as two men entered the camp. Korin watched curiously as the men dismounted. The taller, dark-skinned man was definitely a Sennian, the other an attractive youth with lighter Sennian features and clear amber eyes.

"Ellis," Natan murmured and pulled the young man into a close embrace. He surprised Korin by doing the same to the older man, then he motioned to Korin, the smile lingering on his lips. "Korin, I'd like you to meet my sons, Ellis and Kayle of Sennia."

"My lords." Korin bowed, then grinned as the youth shouted.

"You heard him, Papa. You'll need to start treating me with more respect."

"Ignore him," Kayle advised as he shook Korin's hand. "He's still very young."

Korin's admiration for the men grew with each passing moment. There was a terrible strain in their eyes, as if they were pushed to the limit, and yet they could laugh. Their friendship was unmistakable, and a sudden thought came to him that caught his breath.

"This is your family, isn't it, Mage? Everyone you hold dear?"

"Yes," Natan said softly. "Kavi remains in the city of Karthag, but these men are the sons of my heart."

"Does Niko hate you so much?"

Natan bowed his head as he accepted the burden.

Kayle sternly took him up, "No, Papa, you're not to blame yourself."

"It was I who gave Niko his powers. I who let his wife die."

"That's not true," Ellis protested vehemently. "You did all you could to save her. The Vice-King almost killed you for it!"

"He wanted me to stop teaching the children. He wanted me to leave Sennia. I could have done that for her."

"No, Papa. That would have broken your heart," Ellis challenged.

"Perhaps it would have been better so," Natan whispered, in pain.

"And the Vice-King would have killed her to spite Niko all the same," Kayle countered, taking up the argument.

They jumped at Aiden's voice. "Quiet. Niko is here." He stood, a dark sentinel with molten eyes on the forest. He glanced at Natan and his gaze softened. His smile was almost shy. "This is not your doing, Natan. Be at peace. The lust for power would have consumed Niko whatever had happened." He turned back to the forest. "Be ready."

"Oh, yes, Mage. Be ready," a voice mocked, and Korin took a step back as the Sennian walked from under the trees and stood before them, hands on slim hips. To Korin, it was as if a mask fell over the features of his friends, cold and distant, giving nothing away.

"It's nice to see you again, Natan. And the boys are here." Niko's gaze dismissed them. "But where is our friend Alek? Did he really leave Cecil to his fate? Well, no matter."

His glance fell on Korin. "Wait. Aren't you Alek's companion?" He stepped closer and Korin felt frozen in place. "Has Cecil been replaced so soon? Who are you?"

"Korin."

He felt strangely drowsy. It seemed right to answer the man's questions, and he waited anxiously for his next words. Swift irritation seized him at Natan's laughter.

"You've always been good at attacking children, Niko."

Korin felt bereft as Niko's attention pulled from him, and then he covered his face in confusion and shame. He had no defense against the man.

"Who should I attack, then? The Red Twin?" He looked Aiden up and down. Aiden returned his gaze, but they could all see the tremble in his hands, the glisten of sweat on his lips.

"He's close to madness, Mage. Shall I push him over the edge?" Niko met Aiden's golden eyes with contempt, and Korin could have screamed from the sharp tension suddenly in the air. And then it seemed Niko became trapped, unable to look away. His face grew pallid, and a cruel smile touched Aiden's lips as Niko cried out in pain and clutched his head. The earth trembled and groaned under their feet.

"Let him go, Aiden." Natan said firmly. "It's not yet time. We're not ready to contain the power…" Neither man took any notice of him, and a rumble was heard as rocks fell in the distance. Natan grabbed Aiden's arm, and the burnished eyes turned on him. Natan's body jerked, and pain whitened his lips, but his hold tightened. "Let him go, my boy."

Niko stumbled back, freed, and he fled in fury into the trees. Aiden's eyes remained on the Mage, and Korin watched along with the others in a tableau of shock, as a crimson drop of blood appeared at Natan's nose. His mouth opened in wordless agony. Aiden blinked in bemusement. He touched the suffering face and cried out as if burned as blood from Natan's ears dripped onto his fingers.

"Mage!"

Aiden's strangled plea released them, and Kayle leaped and caught Natan as he swayed and fell to his knees.

"I'm sorry. I didn't mean…" Aiden clutched his head. He sank to the ground and hid his face in his hands, his shoulders shaking.

"Aiden." Ellis knelt beside him. Aiden scrambled back and Ellis flung his arms around him, whispering urgent words in his ear. Korin could swear he was holding the world together for him.

He heard Natan's gasp as his breath returned.

"Papa?" Kayle murmured, clearly worried as he wiped the blood from his face with a spare cloth from a pocket.

"I'll be all right. Help me up."

"You shouldn't…" Kayle pressed his lips together as Natan sat cross-legged by Aiden and took his hands.

"Look at me, please." Natan brushed the strands of dark hair from Aiden's eyes with shaky fingers. "Remember in the garden, with Willum? We knew even then it would come to this. You need to be strong, now."

"But, Mage, I'd rather die than hurt you."

Natan wiped Aiden's tears with a gentle thumb. "You don't have that option, Aiden. We need you with us. We need you to be strong, just a little longer. Kayle says Niko has taken refuge in the caves. We will seize him today and end this."

Natan glanced up and Korin thrilled at the flash in the depths of his eyes as he looked at them one by one. "We end this, one way or another. Korin, will you ask Alek to join us?"

"I'll go with him," Ellis offered when Korin agreed, and Korin gave him a grateful look.

*

KORIN GREW RESTIVE as he and Ellis made their way to Alek's camp. He felt useless and unwanted and wondered if he shouldn't just take the boat and go home.

Ellis bumped his shoulder. "What's wrong?"

Korin shrugged as tears pricked his eyes.

Ellis studied the conflicting emotions crossing Korin's face. "You understand, Korin, that you mustn't trust your perception of things, here on the Isle? Doubt your senses. Make sure that what you see and feel is real."

"I shouldn't be here! I can't defend myself. Niko can get in my head and control me any time he wishes." His voice broke. "What if I hurt someone?"

"You won't. We won't let him do that to you." Ellis's tone was sharp and bitter, pulling Korin from himself.

"Tell me," Korin urged.

Ellis's voice shook. "Niko threatens my husband. I will stop him if it's in my power." He glanced around when they reached the camp. "Alek?"

"He's in the trees over there. I'll wake him."

He went to the blanketed figures, but hesitated as he stood over them. Alek slept with Cecil wrapped protectively in his arms, and he hated to disturb them. He knew it was Niko getting in his head again, but he'd never felt his loneliness more keenly as he did then.

He clenched his hands. So be it, but if he didn't get off the Isle soon, he'd surely step off the same cliff Alek had told him about, the one Cecil had been in danger of slipping over.

Cecil stirred and blinked up at him. "Are we needed?"

"Yes, my lord. Natan calls us," Korin stammered, then fled as Alek growled and gathered Cecil closer, and Cecil hid his blush against his shoulder.

*

NATAN STOOD AT the cave's mouth in a cold sweat as the day progressed to this deadly moment. Aiden sat a small distance away with his eyes on some inner darkness. Aiden wouldn't be going in with them. He was to stand guard to keep Niko from escaping, Natan too afraid of what the Karthagan might do in the close quarters of the cave.

Ellis stood with Aiden. His face had paled, his stricken gaze darting to Aiden when Kayle asked him to keep watch at the cave's entrance as well. Then he'd bowed deeply as if accepting some long-foreseen fate. Perhaps one of his nightmares coming true.

Natan almost faltered. He couldn't sacrifice Ellis! Not his beautiful son, his joy. He dropped his gaze as tears stung his eyes. He felt Kayle's hand on his arm and wanted to throw it off, take his family and flee, leaving the world to its fate. How could they ask this of him?

"Are you ready, Papa?"

"Yes," he murmured and wiped his eyes and followed Kayle into the dark. Korin walked behind them as planned with Alek and Cecil making for the far entrance of the caves to keep Niko from fleeing that way.

He heard Korin's shuddery breath and glanced back. "Stay with me. I won't let him hurt you."

"Why am I here?"

The bleakness in his voice halted Natan, and he went to him and put a hand on his shoulder. "You brought Alek to us safely and helped rescue Cecil. And now you support us with your courage and good heart, giving us the courage to go forward. I, for one, am grateful you are here, a person outside this drama that's been unfolding for years. You help me see clearly. But don't be reckless. Niko is extremely dangerous, and I should like to have you for a friend when this is all over."

A strange pain crossed Korin's expression, and Natan feared he expected death in the caves. He wouldn't let that happen.

"Hush," Kayle warned. "He's near."

Niko's laugh rang eerily in the close cave.

"Do you see him?" Natan asked, scanning the darkness, senses heightened.

"Not yet."

Natan blinked as a tiny flame appeared in the air beside him, and his gaze was drawn from the fire dancing in Kayle's open palm up to his eyes.

"The first lesson you taught us as children," Kayle murmured gently and moved closer to kiss Natan's brow. He knew how painful it was for Natan to see him using the powers of nature, when Natan could no longer do even that simple trick with fire.

"How touching," Niko drawled and stepped into the circle of light.

"Hello." Natan searched the glittering eyes for any sign of his old friend but feared he'd died with his beloved wife.

"Mage." Niko bowed mockingly. "What brings you to my little Isle?"

"You've brought us here with your cruel games. I should like to know why."

"In time, my friend." He looked them over. "Where's Alek? I expected him to be with you. Korin?"

Korin jumped at the harsh tone, and he spoke, the words seeming torn from him, "He's at the far entrance with Cecil."

"Is he?" Niko stepped closer to him. "Does that make you sad?" He touched the copper hair gleaming in the flickering light. "Does that leave an emptiness inside, dear? An ache in your heart that grows unbearable?"

Korin parted his lips on a breath of pain, and Natan took a step toward them, his temper flaring, but Kayle gripped his arm. "Wait."

Kayle then clenched a hand and energy crackled in the air. Niko leaped back, startled.

"Hello?" Niko's voice rang in the cave, and his eyes darted frantically into the shadows. Kayle's lips moved and Natan could hear a well-remembered voice in his head, Corha, soft words of love and comfort for Niko, standing tense with wild, desperate eyes.

"Darling?" Niko's soft plea whispered in the complete silence as tears streamed down his anguished face.

"I'm here," Corha's voice came from behind him. As he swiveled toward the sound, Kayle dived for him, and they both crashed to the floor. Niko escaped his grip with a violent wrench, fury and hatred distorting his features as they regained their footing, and Kayle kindled light once more.

The earth heaved, evidence of Niko's fury as he sprinted for the entrance. Natan made a desperate lunge for him, but the stone floor cracked, throwing them off-balance. Natan fell, jarring his knees on a sudden upthrust of rock. He cut his hands on shards of stone as he scrambled from the widening pit behind him.

Staggering upright, he saw Kayle trapped on the far side of the fissure, cut off from the entrance. Korin lurched to his feet several steps from Natan and shouted something Natan couldn't hear over the crash and grind of stone. He felt a breath of movement and dodged as a rock struck the side of his head. The motion saved his eyes, but he was smashed to the earth by its weight, and the blinding pain nearly sent him into darkness.

Hanging onto consciousness, Natan blinked at the tingle in his hands and legs, licked his lips and tasted blood. The crimson streak on the rock near his head brought his thoughts into focus, and a terrifying image came to him. Ellis!

He clambered toward the cave's mouth, crawling and stumbling, ignoring his injuries. Sprawling from the opening, he pushed to his knees only to watch helplessly as Korin raced after Niko, and Ellis sprang across the clearing to intercept him. Niko lifted his hands, and Natan cried out in horror as Ellis fell as if made of straw. Niko raised his hands to strike again, and Natan pushed to his feet, then froze. Korin had reached Niko, knocking him off-balance even as Aiden stepped between Niko and Ellis.

Aiden's body flinched as the energy struck him, though Korin had disrupted most of the deadly flow. Then the Red Twin smiled, and Niko cried out as the pulse of energy turned on itself. Niko staggered up, and as Aiden approached, he fled into the trees. On his face were the tears of an inconsolable grief that tore Natan's heart to shreds.

Aiden walked a few paces into the forest and watched his flight while Natan staggered to Ellis's prostrate form. Korin joined him, taking Ellis's hands while Natan knelt and pressed fingers to his neck, searching desperately for a pulse. When Aiden returned, Natan shot him a pleading glance. "Can you help him?"

The Red Twin sat cross-legged beside them, seeming emotionless, and touched Ellis's face with its streaks of blood from nose and ears. He bowed his head for a moment, then looked at Natan.

"He'll be well. What of you?"

Natan held still as Aiden felt along the swelling on his right temple down to his chin. "The bones are intact," Aiden said abruptly, then rose to his feet, his eyes going to the cave's mouth.

Natan made sure Ellis lay comfortably against Korin, all the while mourning Aiden's seeming lack of emotion. What damage had Niko done to him? He feared what else might be taken from Aiden as he followed him to the entrance. The flame that ignited in Aiden's hand lit the cave sufficiently to show Kayle waiting on the far side of the wide fissure.

Aiden studied the crack. "Brace yourself," he cautioned as he knelt on the stone. He placed his hands palms down on the rock, and the earth gave a violent lurch that caused Natan to stumble. The gap closed enough for Kayle to leap over.

"Ellis needs you," Aiden murmured as Kayle joined them, and Natan frowned, realizing that Aiden seemed hardly aware of them.

Kayle touched his arm. "Where are you, Aiden?"

Aiden lowered his head, his strength ebbing.

Kayle pressed. "What's happened to you?"

"I had to save Ellis."

In sudden fright, Natan sought Aiden's eyes, and he blinked sleepily. "I drew Niko's energy to myself. He's quite powerful. Korin deflected the worst of it, saving my life, but still…"

He placed Natan's hand over his faltering heart, and Natan cried out as Aiden slid unconscious to the floor.

Chapter Twelve

CECIL CAUGHT HIMSELF nodding sleepily on his horse's back and knuckled his eyes. After Alek had heard Kayle's urgent warning in his mind of Niko's escape, he had become desperate to rejoin the others. But exhaustion chased Cecil, and his hands loosened in the horse's mane. He wasn't sure he had the strength to continue. But Alek rode grim-faced beside him and Cecil set his lips. He wound his hands tighter in the coarse hair, hardly aware when Alek urged his mount faster.

After a time the horse stumbled, and Cecil jerked awake with a cry as he slipped from the wild stallion, landing hard, the ground jarring his bones, and he winced at a bitten tongue.

"Can I help you up?"

He scrambled to his feet at the unexpected voice, ignoring the aches in his body, and put his back to a tree, the mocking laughter that followed a sharp blade scraping along his nerves.

"Surely you're not afraid of me?" Niko stepped closer and touched Cecil's mouth. "I really didn't mean for the horse to throw you," he apologized, his eyes on Cecil's blood, staining his fingertips.

Cecil felt frozen in place, ashamed of the fear that held him, his terror leaping to Alek as he heard his mount returning. A knife appeared in Niko's hand, and he pressed it against Cecil's throat, and Cecil swore under his breath, angry with himself, as the color drained from Alek's face at the sight of them.

"Close enough," Niko said softly.

Alek dismounted and held up his empty hands. "What do you want of me?"

"Only a horse, my friend. I guess the question is, what do you want in return?"

"I should like Cecil back, please."

"What, this pale man?" Cecil remained still as Niko looked him over. "Don't you care for the vibrant boy you had in your camp yesterday?"

"I care for every person on the Isle."

"Would you die for this one?"

"If necessary."

"Is that so?" Niko's smile was unpleasant. "I wonder how long it would take for you to die without him."

Niko made no move, but a current of energy struck Cecil, leaving him dazed. Rough hands gripped his tunic and hauled him toward the horses. He saw Alek's face and knew death was very close to them. Planting his feet, he threw all his weight to the ground, breaking Niko's hold. Niko ran for the equine, and with a shout, Alek raced after him.

"No!" Cecil scrambled to throw himself in Alek's path. He snagged

Alek's foot and they went down in a tangle of limbs. Niko's laughter floated back to them as he swung onto a stallion and kicked to a gallop. Alek swore savagely as he struggled to break Cecil's hold, and his boot caught Cecil in the head. Pain exploded through Cecil, but he reached desperately and managed to tangle his hands in Alek's shirt, pulling him back down.

Cecil flung his arms around Alek's slim waist and held tight. Alek's heart thundered wildly under Cecil's ear, and he concentrated on that as Alek kneed him cruelly in the stomach. Again, and Cecil gagged on the bile that rose in his throat. But he daren't let go, Alek seeming lost to a blind fury Niko roused in him. A fist smashed against Cecil's ear and blackness swam in his eyes.

"Alek! Stay with me," he begged as his hold loosened, his limbs growing weak. He knew without a doubt that Niko would kill Alek should he follow. "Please, stay."

Alek heaved under him and threw him off, and his footsteps hastened away. In a brief moment, Cecil heard the clop of hooves fade into the distance. Dirt filled his mouth, and he pushed up on his elbows and spat. *Alex, why did you go?* When the spots lessened in his eyes, he climbed to his feet, wrapping his arms against the agony in his middle. It was growing dark and he looked in despair at the tracks disappearing into the trees. Sweat and tears stung his eyes, and he wiped them with his sleeve, then started doggedly to follow.

Darkness descended, and at last pain and exhaustion forced Cecil to stop. He found a hollow spot under a tree and lay down to sleep, worn with suffering and grief.

Sometime in the night he lifted his head and coughed roughly, wiping his mouth with the back of his hand. He huddled into himself on the cold earth. Had he heard… But no, he was alone, and his body hurt, and Alek was far away. He coughed again, drew his knees up to his chest against the sharp pain, and fell at once back into exhausted sleep.

His dreams were strange, and a fit of coughing woke him in the early morning. Cecil lay a moment and watched the flames of a small fire in bemusement. Another cough shook him, and he winced at the raw soreness in his throat, then sat up gingerly, his abdomen bruised and tender to the touch. It was some time before his muddled thoughts finally cleared, and he saw Alek sprawled on the ground beside him. He'd come back! Cecil caught his breath, undone with relief. He'd been so afraid. Alek's face was gray, his eyelids bruised with exhaustion.

Someone cleared their throat, and he flicked a glance across the fire, fumbling for the knife at his belt. An unusually attractive man sat opposite, his copper hair framing a pinched face.

"Korin," he murmured with surprise.

"I thought you two would never wake. Not that I blame you…"

Cecil blinked and turned to Alek, who still slept curled toward him. He reddened at Korin's chuckle.

"Alek," Cecil called softly.

Alek stirred and murmured something as he woke. He looked at Cecil, and suddenly his expression grew disconsolate. "I'm so sorry, Cecil! I never would have— Niko confused me—"

Cecil grabbed his arm, stopping the flow of words. "We're not alone," he warned.

Alek's lips thinned, then he turned, rising up on an elbow. "Hello, Korin. What are you doing here?"

"Kayle sent me. You didn't arrive when expected, and he grew concerned."

"We encountered Niko," Alek told him grimly.

Korin rose and scanned the area with a piercing gaze. "Are you well?"

"Well enough, but I'm furious with myself. I allowed him into my head. We couldn't hold him."

Cecil climbed to his feet and surreptitiously pressed a hand against the sore muscles of his abdomen. He stifled another rumbling cough and became aware of their eyes on him. "What?"

"You're bleeding," Korin commented with a sidelong glance at Alek, who murmured a wretched oath. Cecil touched his face and grimaced at the dull pain of an abrasion.

"I fell off my stallion," he said, aware from the pain there was probably visible bruising around his eye running up beneath his hair toward his ear. Korin gave him a close look but didn't comment.

"Shall we go?" Korin asked instead and confused Cecil by the quiet care he took of him on the journey back to the others: helping him mount the horse he'd share with Alek, passing the water flask to him first.

*

HIS HEAD BOWED, Natan sat on the sand beside Ellis, who'd awakened for a short time and spoken to him, but now lay unconscious once again. Nothing had gone right. They'd almost lost Aiden, his heart struggling to beat strongly again. It had been too close. First, Kayle had had trouble finding Aiden's fierce spirit as it flew on the wind. Then it had only been Natan's quiet reminders in his ear that Ellis feared for him, that had brought the Red Twin back.

The group had returned to their boat waiting on the beach, the injured men needing to be half carried. Kayle remained with Aiden in the tent now, hand on his breast as he slept, keeping his heart beating. After seeing the tired, discouraged faces of the company, Natan acknowledged it was time to retreat. They'd rescued Cecil from Niko as they'd set out to do. As soon as they were able, they needed to leave Niko for Kayle and Aiden to deal with, men with the necessary power to do so, much as Natan hated to abandon them. But he had to keep the others safe.

Ellis cried out in his sleep, and Natan clenched his hands. He ached to pull Ellis into his arms and comfort him, but Ellis no longer knew him. Niko's thrust of energy had been hard enough to steal his memory and leave him bewildered and frightened of them.

Natan stirred up the fire and then, discouraged, stood and crossed to the tent where Aiden lay. Kayle sat quietly beside him with his light touch over Aiden's heart, their spirits in the far world where Natan could no longer go. He didn't want to disturb them. Kayle was doing his best to heal Aiden's wounds. The warm afternoon was fading into evening and Natan left the area of the tent and walked under the trees, at last finding a comfortable rock on which to sit and still keep an eye on camp.

Lonely, he wondered what Kavi was doing. He pressed a hand to his chest. Kavi said he carried his heart, but at that moment he seemed so far away. Natan's tears fell unheeded, and for an instant he gave in to the despair lingering on the edge of his thoughts.

But then Ellis stirred and sat up by the fire, making his heart leap. *He's awakened!* Natan jumped from the rock, dashing the tears from his eyes in preparation of joining him, and didn't hear the horses until they were upon him. Natan looked up to find Korin studying him from horseback. Alek and Cecil shared a separate mount, with Cecil asleep on the stallion's neck.

A dark scowl swept Korin's face. "We need to get off this Isle, Mage."

"Yes, we do." Life stirred in him again at Korin's emphatic tone, and he smiled faintly.

They went over to the fire and Natan took Cecil in his arms as Alek handed him down from his mount, then laid him by the fire near Ellis. "Niko's doing?" he asked, indicating the dark bruises on Cecil's fair skin.

Alek shook his head, his eyes full of sorrow. "It was I. We need to leave here, Mage. Niko has us at one another's throats. I no longer trust my own thoughts."

"Let me speak to Kayle, and we'll go as soon as possible."

Korin muttered under his breath, his concerned gaze on Ellis, who ignored them and stared moodily at the fire, his hair tangled with sweat. "What's wrong with him?"

"Niko's attack hit him hard and seems to have stolen his memory," Natan explained. "At least for the present."

Ellis glanced at Korin as he stepped up. "You mean you've forgotten me, darling?" Korin cried out, arms spread, and Ellis surged to his feet in utter confusion. Korin clapped a hand over his mouth on a fit of giggles. Natan cuffed him smartly.

"I'm sorry!" Korin held up his hands. "I couldn't help it."

Ellis gave him a hard look, but the mischief dancing in Korin's eyes would be irresistible to anyone, and a slow grin took over Ellis's face. "We must have been friends."

"It's my honor," Korin said with a short bow.

"We should have a meal before we sail," Alek advised, opening his pack.

They ate on their feet, then gathered their few belongings. While the others made their way to the skiff, Natan returned to Aiden's tent. He sat beside Kayle and put a hand on his arm, drawing Kayle's attention. Kayle blinked, and Natan could see his consciousness returning. "Papa?"

"Hello. Are you well?"

"We are. Aiden's heart has strengthened, so he should be waking soon."

Natan studied the lines of suffering in Aiden's face. "You know we're leaving?"

"Yes, Mage. It's for the best."

"Shall I stay, Kayle? It worries me to leave you and Aiden here alone."

"Papa." Kayle embraced him. "You need to go. Niko would only use you to hurt us."

Natan returned his embrace. "Take very good care of each other."

As he touched Aiden's face in farewell, the golden eyes opened, and the Red Twin sat up with his help. "Hello, Father."

"My son," Natan hugged him. "I feared we'd lost you."

"Not yet," Aiden said and struggled to rise. Kayle helped him to his feet.

They went with Natan to the beach to say goodbye to the others. Kayle put an arm across Natan's shoulders as they walked to the boat. It was a solemn farewell.

"My dory is landed farther down the coast, for you and Aiden," Alek told Kayle as they parted.

"Thank you." Kayle rubbed his tired face.

Aiden stood a little apart with Ellis, holding his hands loosely, their foreheads touching as if searching each other's eyes.

"You don't remember me," Aiden said on a note of sadness.

Ellis shook his head. "I do not, though…" A soft blush stained his cheeks, his smile tentative as he took in Aiden head to toe. "I don't see how it is possible to forget you."

Elation flashed over Aiden's face, and he kissed Ellis's fingertips. Ellis joined the others, joy and worry vying in his expression as he climbed into the boat beside Natan. Kayle and Aiden pushed them into the waves while Korin and Alek used the oars. Cecil held the tiller. Once past the breakers, Ellis helped Natan set the sails.

Ellis stood at Natan's side and watched until the beach was a smudge in the distance. The two solitary figures lifted their arms in farewell, then sprinted up the coast like deer and were soon lost in the shadows. Natan worried for them, then sighed, took a seat, and turned his attention to Belega and whatever troubles waited for their return.

*

ROBIN SAT AT Ashel's feet and listened intently as he described some incident at Fredrik's Hall. Ashel had been in a good humor all morning but seemed to recall himself when Robin laughed at one point in his narrative.

Ashel gave him an unfriendly look. "Don't you have work?" he snarled, rising to his feet. Before Robin could move, he drove a fist into his upturned face, knocking him to the dirt. Robin picked himself up, gathered wood from the nearby pile, and returned to the fire, keeping his face averted to hide the anger in his blue eyes.

He'd almost had the information! Ashel rambled in his dementia, on the brink of revealing his plans. Robin knew that Ashel had stolen him to obtain his father's attention. The man was ambitious, wanting Fredrik's Hall for himself. But there was more to it. Ashel had experimented with the energies of the earth, sometimes with Lord Fredrik, more often alone. But to what purpose Robin had yet to discover.

He'd begun to fear that the man, in his instability, would begin to practice on him, something he strongly desired to avoid.

Dusk settled in and Robin built up the fire. He saw the bit of stew Ashel had left in the pot, and with a sidelong glance at him, ate it in quick bites. In the few days of Ashel's company, he'd learned to eat when he could and drink whenever possible.

He rose and stretched a body sore with bruises and hunger and lack of sleep, and took a few steps into the forest for more wood. The nights proved cold. Movement caught his eye, and he blinked stupidly as Carrow appeared several paces away, then grinned suddenly. He should have known.

The archer came silently to his side. "Are you well, Robin?"

"I'm all right. You shouldn't be here, you know," he said but couldn't hide his delight. It was horrible being with the madman.

"Come away with me."

Robin was sorely tempted. "I can't," he said before he gave in. "Ashel has a terrible stratagem in mind. I feel it, but he hasn't revealed it yet. If I can stay a little longer—"

"He may kill you."

Robin winced at his abruptness, and Carrow put a finger under his chin, raising Robin's face, bruised and bloody. "I may kill him first," he murmured, his voice icy.

"Thank you, sir." Robin bowed, moved by his concern. "I should like a few more days. After that, if you still care to rescue me…"

Carrow chuckled. "I see Governor Basal in you. It'll be as you say, for the moment. But see that he doesn't strike you again, or I'll surely put an arrow through his heart."

Even as Robin's eyes widened in surprise, Carrow slipped back into the shadows and disappeared. Robin thoughtfully gathered wood. Carrow had disturbed him. The archer's loyalty to his governor clearly extended to his son. Robin had never thought of the people before. They had always been his father's concern. Shame flushed through him. He'd spent the summer playing soldier when he should have been learning how to govern their diverse territory.

Ashel sat at the fire when he returned, and he quietly laid the wood down and added a few sticks to the flames. Ashel looked up, his blue eyes clear for the moment.

"Come sit by me," he invited, and Robin swallowed nervously, unsure, as he settled beside the lord on the log they had rolled up to the fire. Ashel gripped his chin and turned his face to the fading light.

"You shouldn't anger me," he chided, then swung a fist, the blow smashing against Robin's chin, knocking him to the ground. Ashel rose, towering over him. "On your feet."

Robin pushed his aching body to stand, feeling sick as Ashel hissed with impatience. Ashel's next blow landed beside his ear and pain exploded through Robin, driving him to his knees. He would have stayed there, but Ashel gripped his collar and hauled him up.

"What more do I have to do?"

Ashel's mumbled words bewildered him. "I don't understand—"

A jarring slap silenced him. His head rang and Robin realized with dismay that his one chance to fight back had come and gone as blackness began to swim behind his eyes. Ashel's knife slid into his vision, and he braced for the inevitable.

"Hold."

Ashel drew a satisfied breath, and Robin parted his lips to warn Carrow. A sharp jab to his stomach stole his air and he doubled over in agony.

"Move away from him, Ashel."

"I don't believe I will," Ashel drawled. He jerked Robin's head back by his hair and Robin felt the cold blade settle at his throat. "Did you truly believe I was unaware of you out there, Carrow?" Ashel continued with a lazy drawl. "Your reputation is well known in the Hall."

"I'm honored," Carrow said dryly.

Robin straightened painful limbs. As his sight cleared, he saw the archer on the edge of their camp, his bow stretched in his hands, the arrow's tip glittering in the fading sunlight. Ashel's grip on Robin's hair tightened and he winced as the knife pricked his skin.

"Put the bow down, Carrow."

"I can kill you where you stand, Ashel, make no mistake."

"One slip and the boy dies. Do you really wish to chance it? No, or you would have shot me already." Ashel was suddenly impatient. "Come now, Carrow, I'm not the man you want anyway. Can we not talk?"

"Speak."

"Surely we can be comfortable." Ashel gestured to the cheery fire and the coffee bubbling over. He tugged gently, and Robin stumbled with him to the log. They sat close and Robin felt the knife press against his side.

Carrow studied them with narrowed eyes. Giving a slight shrug, he leaned the bow against a tree and sat on a rock across from them. "Well?"

Ashel laughed softly. "Serve the coffee, Robin," he said, giving him a shove off the log. Robin landed hard on his knees and swallowed a cry. He held still, fighting nausea, and spat blood and bile from his mouth. By the time he could see again, Carrow had already poured the dark brew. Robin sat with his back against the log, holding his stomach. It was a moment before he could understand what was being discussed.

"Tell me again why I shouldn't kill you?" Carrow asked conversationally.

Ashel chuckled and leaned to run a hand through Robin's hair, damp with sweat. Robin barely suppressed a shudder, not wanting to antagonize him further.

"I would hate for something bad to happen to little Robin. Or to his dear father," Ashel answered in an offhand manner.

He had Carrow's full attention. "Please explain."

"What about Father?" Robin had forgotten himself, and Ashel's boot caught him in the ribs. Carrow sprang to his feet with an oath, and Robin struggled to his knees, wiping desperately at the tears blurring his sight. "Carrow!" he cried out and clutched the archer's cloak as he skirted the fire.

Carrow had his long knife pressed on Ashel's chest, and he looked at Robin in disbelief.

"What of Father?" Robin begged. He groveled at Ashel's feet. Father mustn't die. Not for him, a son who was surely a disappointment. He pressed his face to Ashel's knee. "Please."

Carrow drew back with a dark scowl as Ashel bent to Robin's ear. "I'll tell you, but you must sit quietly now. No words."

His voice was a gentle rebuff, and Robin nodded and sat back against the log, dizzy. He forgot the aches in his body as his fear grew.

"It was kind of you to leave Robin with us," Ashel began whimsically.

"Everything just fell into place after that. With Fredrik out of the way…" He inclined his head, and Carrow's face whitened with anger. "Well, I have you and Robin here with me, while the governor is with my close friend and cohort at the Hall. And believe me," Ashel sat forward, his voice ice. "He's not as tolerant as I. If I'm harmed in any way, Nelson will slay Basal out of hand."

Robin let out a whimper, and Ashel patted his bruising cheek. "Don't worry, dear. I doubt Nelson has killed him yet."

Robin clutched that hope to his heart as Ashel continued his dreadful conversation with the archer.

*

BASAL SCRATCHED HIS week's growth of beard. He knew he needed to pull himself together, clean up and get some sleep, but he would do neither. The last of the scouts had come in that morning with still no sign of Robin. Carrow was his last hope, and though he had faith in the archer, the waiting was killing him.

He strode from the den. He needed to be outside, moving. Maybe he'd take a horse, and…

He nearly knocked into Nelson in the hallway.

"Pardon, my lord."

Basal nodded and would have passed the stout man, but Nelson touched his arm. Basal eyed him with distaste, repulsed as always by the dissipation in the man's sallow features. A strange expression crossed the lord's face, and he seemed to struggle with some inner battle. A hard glitter came into his pale blue eyes. "May I speak with you a moment, Governor?"

Basal was instantly on his guard. What game was this? The man had stopped trying to curry favor and been infuriatingly insolent up to that point.

"Of course." He followed Nelson to his rooms.

A quick step at his side as he entered Nelson's private den was the only warning he had, but he managed to get his knife into someone before he was overwhelmed by several others. Rough hands held him as he struggled, while another man bound his arms tightly behind his back.

Nelson's short dagger flashed near his eyes. "Very foolish, my lord Governor."

Nelson nodded to the men holding him, and Basal was hauled across the room and forced into a chair. His quick glance around revealed others in the room with Nelson, his many cousins, the lords of the Hall.

Nelson toed the man bleeding on the floor. "Remove him," he said as if he were speaking of refuse. Basal's knife had sliced wickedly across the man's abdomen and upward to lodge under a rib. He breathed his last as two of his cousins struggled through the doorway with him. Basal shuddered. They seemed to have no care for each other. He was less than nothing to Nelson.

"What now, my lord?" he asked quietly.

"Haven't you guessed?" Nelson mocked. "Why would we have taken Robin, do you think?" He laughed at the flash of fury Basal couldn't control. "Don't worry. Ashel won't hurt him. No, I take that back. Ashel wouldn't kill him, but he has his little vices, and Robin is sweet—"

Basal flung out of the chair with a roar, and Nelson stepped back, knife at the ready, halting him.

"Very good," Nelson said coldly, though rage blazed in his faded eyes. "Ashel will kill him, if I'm harmed. Now, sit down."

Basal resumed his seat and stared at a knot in the pine flooring, fighting for control. He would need a cool head to get Robin back safely. If they harmed him… He wouldn't think of that. Listen to the cur.

"What do you want?" he bit out.

"Only what I deserve, my lord. I want to be the new ruler of Fredrik's Hall. I want the soldiers removed from the barracks and from the area. I want to be in charge of the Hall with no interference from you or any future governor. I want this done immediately."

"And what does your kin make of this?"

"They'll have no choice with you to back me."

"I'll do nothing until Robin is returned."

"Of course." Nelson stepped forward and backhanded him, cutting his lip. "Don't push me, Governor. I may just kill Robin out of spite."

Basal felt sick. "You know the consequences of that."

"They may be worth it." Nelson leaned closer. "Behave," he lisped in Basal's ear, and Basal wanted to put his hands around his throat even as Nelson set him free.

The afternoon stretched endlessly, and Basal shoved his dinner away untouched. He spent the long hours of the evening pacing before the gates. Finally, he climbed on the wall and strained his gaze into the distance.

At long last he was rewarded when two horsemen came into view. He eagerly scanned the men, then an angry shout broke from him as he spotted a slim figure stumbling behind one of the animals by a rope binding his wrists. Heart burning, he leaped to the ground and ran to them.

The riders halted as he approached, and Carrow and Ashel slid from their saddles. Carrow instantly raised his hands, signaling his powerlessness in the situation, though fury smoldered in his eyes. Ashel held up a hand to stop Basal, but Basal simply brushed past him and dropped to his knees, gathering Robin's drooping body in his arms.

"I'm here, Son," he murmured in an excess of relief.

"Father?" Robin blinked at him, and Basal saw the slight glaze in his blue eyes. A hard knot of anger settled in his chest. Robin's face was bruised and swollen, and he favored his side as he slumped against him.

Basal raised a face of stone, his emotions masked. "Kill him."

Carrow nodded and pulled the bow from his shoulder.

"No!" Ashel backed away. A sharp hail from the gates gave Carrow pause, and Basal turned in swift anger. Several archers stood poised on the wall, arrows trained on them.

Ashel smirked. "Put the bow down, Carrow," he admonished. "As I've warned you, Nelson won't hesitate to kill us all, if he feels threatened."

Rage blinded Basal, but then he nodded, and Carrow slung the bow on his shoulder. He twirled the arrow in his fingers though. Basal removed the rope from Robin's wrists, but Ashel walked at Robin's side with his hand on the butt of his knife. After a few stumbling steps, Basal's patience snapped, and he swept Robin up in his arms. Ashel closed his mouth on his words at the murderous look Basal threw him. Nelson greeted them at the gates and led them inside to Fredrik's den, which proved quiet. Basal lowered Robin into a chair and knelt by his side while Carrow stood at his back.

"Be still, Son," he murmured as Robin stirred and tried to speak.

"What a touching scene," Ashel sneered. He moved closer to them. "You mightn't be so affectionate, Basal, if you'd witnessed him on his knees to me earlier."

Robin's head jerked up, but he looked at Ashel with cool eyes. Basal saw the tinge of red in his bruised cheeks when Ashel gave a low laugh.

"He's right, my lord," Carrow spoke softly. "Robin had prostrated himself to the man, on your behalf. I could only hope my own son would have acted in such a manner."

There was silence in the room, and Robin's broken lips parted on a small gasp. They were all aware Carrow's young wife had died giving birth to his infant son, who'd followed her to the grave a few moments after.

"Enough," Nelson swore in disgust. "Ashel, take the boy downstairs."

Basal rose and stood between them. "Strike him again and you will surely die."

"Yes, yes." Nelson said impatiently. "Ashel, lock him in and return promptly. Carrow, assist him. And keep in mind—cause any trouble whatsoever, and I'll have no trouble killing the lot of you."

While Carrow supported Robin and followed Ashel from the room, Basal took Robin's vacated chair and coldly studied Nelson.

Anger mottled Nelson's face but then he laughed. "You shan't goad me into a foolish act, Basal. Your son is returned to you, and as soon as the Hall is mine, you'll be free to go."

"And I have your word?" Basal said dryly, and Nelson's eyes narrowed.

"Indeed." Nelson slurred the word into an obscenity. "Now, you're to return to your pretty soldiers and tell them they are recalled to Nagal."

"It will take weeks to disband them."

"You have days," Nelson said with finality. He fussed with some papers on his desk, darting glances at the door as the silence stretched between them.

"Where's that fool?" he muttered at last. "Excuse me," he snapped and stormed from the room. Basal watched him go, realizing there was no love lost between him and Ashel. Restless, he paced the room while he waited and frowned as the moments lengthened and still no one came.

At a prickling along his scalp, he swiveled to find Ashel standing in the doorway. He knew that feeling. The man had tried to probe his thoughts.

Ashel smiled lazily at Basal's scowl and made a small bow. "Shall I take you to the boy?"

"If you would," Basal said carefully.

"Say please."

"Please." Basal gave him a bland look.

Ashel chuckled in delight. "Robin is more like you than I thought. I love a man without pride. So easy to direct."

Basal sketched a bow. "May I see my son?"

"Oh, most definitely."

Basal didn't like the gleam in his eye. They went to the cellar, and Ashel led him to the same room that Tyrel had been held in, that Commander Jacksan had died in. Basal almost shouted his relief when the door opened, and he saw Robin sitting on the edge of a cot.

"Where's Carrow?" he asked in instant suspicion when he didn't spy the archer in the room.

Ashel waved a languid hand. "I sent him to the stables. It amuses me to think of the proud man raking out the stalls."

"Father!" Robin rose to his feet as they entered, and Basal went to him and held him tight.

"Are you well?" His eyes searched Robin head to foot.

At an unpleasant laugh behind them, they turned to Ashel.

"Oh, please continue," Ashel jeered. "This is quite touching."

Basal put his back to him and Robin hissed urgently while his father stood between them, "He's the one to fear!" Basal widened his eyes in question and Robin nodded and stepped back to sit on the bed. Basal shivered when he found Ashel at his side.

"Mustn't have secrets," Ashel chided softly. They heard a commotion in the hall and Ashel rubbed his hands in glee. Basal shuddered at the strange low laugh in his throat.

"Now we can play," he told them in a sly whisper and hurried across the room, slipping against the wall, hidden as the door flung open.

Nelson swept into the room, face mottled with temper. "What's going on? Where's Ashel? I can't find the man anywhere." Nelson's eyes darted to Basal. "How did you get down here? Ashel warned me you'd try something like this."

Ashel stepped swiftly from behind the door, flinging an arm around Nelson's neck. He jerked the man's head back, and his knife blade left a neat red line across his exposed throat. Ashel put his cheek against Nelson's and listened to the gurgles and sputters from his bloody lips as if it were music. He slid with Nelson's convulsing body to the floor and laid him down, watching the eyes glaze over with death.

"Goodbye, cousin," he murmured in the deaf ears. He stood, all his attention suddenly on them. "Go upstairs, Basal," he said curtly as he stared at Robin. Basal took a step between them, and Ashel laughed. "I won't hurt little Robin," he promised, and then his tone turned to ice. "Unless you make me. Go upstairs."

"Please go, Father," Robin whispered urgently. Basal swore and brushed by Ashel in fury and desperation, the man's mocking laughter ringing in his ears as he climbed the stairs to the rooms above.

Chapter Thirteen

NATAN JUMPED FROM the skiff and helped Korin drag the boat onto the beach outside of Amara, very close to the spot where Kavi had first stepped onto Belega's shores years before. The others disembarked, and Alek carried Cecil's limp body to the trees and laid him on the blanket Ellis placed out of the midmorning sun. Korin dampened a cloth and hurried to them. Alek thanked him, clearly distraught, and wiped the sweat from Cecil's waxen face. Cecil burned with fever and muttered in delirium, having fallen ill during the voyage, and Alek winced at every deep cough that shook his frame.

Hearing hoofbeats on the forest trail, Natan loosened his knife, then let out a relieved breath as Devon burst from the trees leading a small group of horses. Worry etched the Amara council leader's lean face as he drew to a stop beside them.

"You have to go at once. Thankfully, Lady Kirstin sensed your coming and sent me, but it will be only a matter of time before the soldiers get wind of your arrival."

The anxiety in his voice and the fearful way he scanned the enclosing forest drove them all to their feet. Without a word, Korin and Ellis ran to the boat for their few provisions. Cecil muffled a groan when Alek lifted him, and Devon eyed him with concern. "Can he be moved? Then hurry," he urged at Alek's nod. "The world has gone mad."

After mounting the animals he'd brought them, the company raced into the woods. Natan crouched in the saddle, hardly aware of Korin's arms around him. He knew the paths as well as Devon and took the lead, while the council leader protected their backs. It became a frenzied rush, the animals stumbling with exhaustion before they reached the Lake of Glass.

Sunlight filtered through the trees and turned the lake to gold. Natan slipped from his saddle and stood a moment in awe. He hadn't been there in many years. Alek brushed by him with Cecil and entered the water. He sat with Cecil's head resting on his thigh and cupped the clear liquid, bathing Cecil's forehead and pale hair.

Natan sat cross-legged in the sand and put his hand on Alek's shoulder. "We're with you," he murmured. They remained that way for several moments, and then Alek sighed. "The lake has helped remove his fever, but there's a sickness in his chest. We should get him to the fire and keep him warm."

Korin and Devon made camp while Alek wrapped Cecil in a blanket and settled with him by the fire Ellis built up. It was quiet at the lake, and Natan drew a steadying breath as one by one the exhausted company rolled in their blankets to snatch a few hours of much needed rest before traveling farther.

It seemed a matter of moments, but it had become late afternoon before Natan woke in terror and scrambled to his feet. The air vibrated with a tension that was unbearable. *It is happening.* He frantically searched the camp with his gaze. Alek lay nearby with Cecil in his arms, though both were rousing. Ellis and Devon were some distance away, speaking urgently. Where was Korin?

He spotted him at the water's edge, and something in his stance sent Natan hurrying to his side. "Korin?"

Korin looked at him with such hopelessness in his eyes Natan's heart twisted. "Korin! Niko is here in our minds," he said. "This is Niko's doing."

Korin drew a shaky breath. "Yes, Mage. What should I do?" He threw out his hands in a helpless gesture, and Natan knew he was beyond rational thought.

"Come with me." Natan took his hand and led him to the fire as if he were a small child. "Sit here, Korin. You're safe here."

Korin nodded and watched the dying flames, then shut his eyes as if closing out the flowing currents of energy pulling reality apart.

Natan studied the sky and sent his thoughts out to his boys on the Isle. He wanted to fly to them. The air stretched taut, and a sudden low boom echoed across the sky. Natan wept at the release of pressure. Alek and Cecil climbed to their feet while the others hurried over. Natan stretched his hands to the horizon. "Can no one help them?"

Alek sent his gaze to the southwest, but in a moment shook his head in despair. "It's as if the Isle is encased in glass. No one can reach them."

*

AIDEN LEANED AGAINST a tree to catch his breath. He knew the dark shadows under the overhanging limbs hid him from Niko's view, but a nervous chill seized him anyway, and he pushed off the trunk. The sky split with a deafening crash and lightning burst the tree end to end. The shock knocked him to the ground, dazed. Hands reached under his arms and pulled him up, and he scrambled to his feet and ran with Kayle. They flung themselves into a ditch and crouched in the scrub brush.

"That was too close, Aiden. You're not concentrating."

"I'm sorry, Kayle. It's hard…"

"I'm here." Kayle's hand gripped his. "Use my strength. You must win."

Aiden groaned and covered his face, trembling head to foot. Kayle's arms went around him, and the energies of life began to flow into him from Kayle.

"Enough!" He pushed Kayle away and glared into his dark eyes. *Was he killing himself slowly?* "You must keep some for yourself."

Kayle glanced away. "It's not important. You must be strong."

"I don't think Jena would agree, dear brother."

Aiden touched the bowed head and Kayle looked up with a flash in his eyes. "You're right. I let Niko in again. I need to concentrate as well."

"He'd have you give up your life; then I'd be alone."

They started at a sudden roar in the distance, riding the wind.

"Climb!" Aiden yelled. The sound grew closer, bringing heat and the crackle of flame. Fire swept the gully as they slipped over the far ledge. Aiden rose to his feet, all emotion cold. He searched the opposite bank with his gaze and spotted a darkness through the smoke, a shadow, a man…

He smiled, and the earth screamed as it tore open. Steam burst into the air, molten rock, and Aiden lost sight of the shadow in a spew of lava. His pleasure was fierce, then gone. He could sense Niko in his mind, laughing, mocking.

"We have to go!" Kayle pulled on his arm, wrenching his mind from chaos. As they dodged into the forest Aiden's thoughts slipped into the past. He ran with Ethan, and his heart sang. Power flowed in his young body, in Ethan's, and all fled from the light in their eyes. They ran, singing, and tumbled into a wash overrun with fern, laughing as it tickled their faces.

Aiden raised his head. "Father's calling, Ethan. Let's hurry home."

Silence answered and he turned curiously to his brother.

"Father's dead, Aiden. Don't you remember the pleasure we had watching him burn? Oh!" Ethan struggled to his knees, his boyish face alight with smiles. "Remember when we made Natan think he was on fire? He made the funniest squeals!"

"Ethan! Father's calling. Time to go in."

"Father's dead."

Aiden turned on him angrily, and cried out as Ethan's face contorted, grew older...

"You've killed me!" Ethan gasped from his bed. "Why have you killed me, dearest one?"

Aiden felt his brother's heart slow, stop. He sank to his knees, covering his eyes in grief.

"Aiden," a voice whispered close to his ear. Strong arms held him, strangely tender.

"I killed them, Kayle," Aiden mourned. "Everyone I love." His heart ached. He was so lonely. He wept.

"Close your mind, Aiden. Don't think. Don't let Niko win." Kayle stroked his hair, soothed the dark memories until they slipped out of reach. Aiden took a shuddering breath. He felt so tired.

"Sleep now, my friend." Kayle's voice was a gentle murmur, irresistible. "Niko is far away. I'll keep you safe."

Aiden's thoughts wandered out and brushed against Niko's, then tip-toed away. The man had found a shallow cave somewhere in which to sleep, a good league away. He wondered if they were secure enough for him to fall asleep as well. He had never been more tired.

He felt Kayle's push into his mind and slipped into dreams without a struggle.

It seemed only moments before Aiden roused, though, adrenaline keeping him from rest. Kayle slept, but tossed restlessly beside him, and Aiden put a hand on his shoulder...

"Is it really you?" Jena asked in wonder, and Kayle felt her fingers as she touched his face. He couldn't speak through the tears in his throat, and then she was in his aching arms and her sweet lips were on his. He didn't know how he was there; he didn't care. She was warm and unbearably alive, and he wanted to stay with her forever. He drew his head back, just a little.

"I can't stay," he groaned against her mouth.

"He needs you," she acknowledged even as her arms tightened. She pulled his head down for another glorious kiss.

"I don't want to leave," he begged and didn't know whose permission he was asking...

"Quiet," Aiden warned as Kayle jerked awake. They could plainly hear the footsteps on the ledge above them. The steps paused, and a trickle of rocks slid down the embankment. Aiden held his breath until they moved on; then he gave Kayle a little smile. "I was afraid you'd cry out when you woke."

"I shouldn't have slept. I apologize."

Aiden gave him a sly look. "I sent you home. You seemed to need it."

"Aiden!" Kayle sobered at the revelation. "Have you been home?"

"No." He turned his face in shame. "I wouldn't come back."

"That's not true—"

Aiden's abrupt laugh stopped him. "I may have more ability with life's energies, Kayle, but you're the better man." He picked up a few pebbles and stared at them. "I would have sunk the Isle long ago to destroy Niko." He closed his fist and the rocks crushed to dust. His thoughts turned bleak, and he shook himself when Kayle made no reply.

"We should go," he said, and they crept in the direction Niko had taken. Aiden's heart filled with dread as they slipped over the silent ground.

They chased the shadow man for hours while the forest burned around them. Mires of quicksand lay behind them. Boiling pits of tar vomited from the earth, and jagged crevasses opened at their feet, some of their own atrocities against the earth in their struggle to stop Niko.

At last, Aiden leaned heavily against a rough boulder to keep from falling. They'd found Niko at the cliff's edge, and for a brief instant the sky had splintered and deafened him. His mind still reeled from the attack. Did Niko mean to destroy the earth rather than give in? Niko stood at the brink of the abyss, a shadow against the ocean and brilliant sky; an enigma, not a real man at all.

"Are you ready, brother?" Kayle's steady voice brought him from the lure of mad dreams.

"No," Aiden laughed tensely. "I'm not strong enough."

Kayle turned to him with glittering eyes, yet there was a fondness in his smile. "You're one of the Red Twins, Aiden. If not you, then no one."

Aiden gathered his tattered courage. He wished Ethan were holding his hands. A thrill shot through him at the memory of their power together. Power surged to life once more in him, and he raised his proud head. Kayle gave a yell and stepped from cover.

"It's done, Niko!" he shouted as if a promise had been kept. Niko's cry of triumph roared on the wind and slammed into him. Kayle laughed in release even as he fell to his knees, and the energy of his life began to bleed from him.

In that moment of distraction, Aiden stepped forth. Niko turned all his strength against him, but it was too late. Aiden simply drank it in along with the energy Kayle seeped into the world. He opened his arms and called Niko's name, and Niko walked unresistingly to him. Bewilderment creased his ebony face. "I don't understand."

"I've always been the stronger," Aiden chided. "Gregor of Sennia felt mine and Ethan's power all those years ago. Knew there was something…dangerous on the Isle of Wind. Sensed me." He leaned closer to whisper. "I'm afraid you never stood a chance."

He took Niko's face in his hands and focused, until Niko's eyes filled all of his sight, and there was nothing left in all the world. Niko's gasp was a whimper of pain yet somehow a strange joy as Aiden drained the energy of life from him. Aiden made sure all fear and uncertainty and loneliness slipped from Niko with his last breath, and he died in peace.

Aiden lifted the shell of the man and walked to the edge of the Isle.

He kissed the dead eyes for the life that had once dwelt within, and let the body fall from his arms to the sea far below.

He turned back to what remained of the Isle of Wind, and his eyes fell on the slumped form of a man close by. He went to him and rolled him onto his back on the springy moss, sitting cross-legged beside him to brush the hair from his handsome face.

Aiden searched his thoughts, realizing he should know this man, but couldn't recall him. He was too tired to remember. He placed a hand on the cooling forehead, and another over the faintly beating heart, and spent the last of his strength in returning life to him. The man stirred and Aiden helped him to sit up, wondering at the intense stare from his brown eyes.

"Aiden?" the man whispered, breaking loose a flood of memories in Aiden's mind.

"Kayle? How do you feel?" he asked kindly.

Kayle leaned against the tall pine behind him and rubbed his face, wiping impatiently at the tears that would come. "My powers are gone, Aiden." He shrugged helplessly. "I knew you would have to take them, but I'm so empty…"

"Peace." Aiden's throat tightened with pity. He reached a hand. "Come. Alek will send a ship for us."

Kayle blinked several times as if considering, then permitted Aiden to help him to his feet. They made their torturous way to the beach and found an old log in the sand to rest their backs against. Having no strength to make the journey themselves, they waited patiently for the ship to come, letting the sun bake the weariness and sorrow from their battered bodies and troubled minds.

*

NATAN LET OUT a shuddering breath. Then another. He met Alek's gaze, seeing his own awe reflected in his face.

"Is it done?" he asked, doubting the relief flooding through him.

Alek cautiously nodded. "Aiden is exhausted, confused, as is Kayle. I don't sense Niko at all. It must be over. I'll have Kavi send a ship for them immediately."

Natan turned his face away as fierce jealousy and pain unexpectedly scorched him. He ached suddenly to speak to his lover as Alek could. To reach the men on the Isle of Wind and check on them personally.

"Father!"

Natan's heart jumped as Ellis raced to him, and he caught his son in a close embrace as Ellis's arms went around him. "I thought I'd lost you," he managed to choke out.

"I felt lost. I couldn't remember anyone. But Aiden somehow reached me, made me whole again."

They separated, and seeing his tears, Ellis gently chided him, wiping Natan's cheeks with a thumb. "You can't cry now."

"Hey, that looks fun. May I?" Korin teased as he walked up, lifting a hand. Natan raised his chin, and Korin blushed to the roots of his red hair. "Devon says we should move on, Mage," he said hurriedly.

The Amara council leader joined them. "We have to get you safely to Nagal. The South is rising against the Karthagan people. The North as well, most likely."

Ellis looked from him to Natan. "But Niko was a Sennian."

"It doesn't matter," Devon urged. "Most won't distinguish between the two. I can tell you that few soldiers from either territory trust the Karthagans nor the Sennian people, except maybe those who live with them daily. They find their abilities too frightening. And after the intensity of power we just felt from the Isle… I'm sorry, but we'd better get Alek hidden somewhere quickly."

A stubborn line settled on Alek's lips. "I won't go with you to Nagal. I'm taking Cecil home to Karthag and preparing for Aiden's return."

Natan shook his head. "But the road is perilous."

"No matter."

"You need protection," Natan pressed. "I'm going to Nagal to speak with Governor Basal, see where things stand in the world. Come with me."

"Excuse me, Mage," Devon said. "I could take them to Karthag by way of the coast. There are very few people who dwell along that route, and they know me. Perhaps my presence will be enough."

Natan frowned. "Are you willing to risk it? They may turn against you."

"It's a far less dangerous path than your own," Devon reminded him gently.

Natan chewed his lips. "Very well, though I'm afraid for you." He looked thoughtfully at Ellis. "Will you go with them?" He took Ellis's hands, stopping the protest forming on his lips. "Aiden will need you when he returns. And Kavi will need to see that you are well. He needs to know that I am. I sense… Something is wrong. I wish I had my powers!" The words broke from him against his will. "Kavi comes to me in my dreams, and I can't understand what he says. He's in great distress, and I can't… Please, go to him in my stead." His voice dropped to a broken plea, "Keep him safe for me."

Ellis put an arm across his shoulders, hugging him to his side. "Of course, Papa."

Korin stepped up and met Ellis's anxious gaze. "I'll keep the Mage out of trouble," he promised gravely. Ellis nodded.

Natan took a steadying breath. "Alek, will you wake Cecil, please?"

"At once, Mage." Alek bowed and moved to Cecil's side as the others retrieved the horses. Kneeling, Alek murmured in Cecil's ear, "Wake up."

Cecil stirred and opened his eyes. "Alek," he said hoarsely.

"Can you stand?"

Cecil nodded and Alek helped him to his feet. "Niko has stirred up the old animosity against the Karthagans. We need to go home at once."

They took a few hesitant steps, then Cecil stumbled, and concern touched his face. "Shouldn't you go without me? I can follow…"

"No!" Alek lowered his voice at Cecil's startled face. "I left you once. I won't do that again."

"That was Niko's doing, and this is your life at stake."

Natan cleared his throat, needing to interrupt. "It's your life as well, Cecil. I'm afraid you're linked with the Karthagans in everyone's mind."

"Rightfully so," Alek muttered, urging him to their mount. He swung up into the saddle and held out a hand. Cecil looked uncertainly at him.

Korin moved to his side. "Let me help you, my lord," he said and laced his fingers.

Cecil settled behind Alek and touched Korin's shoulder when he would have turned away. "I need to thank you for taking care of Alek on the Isle of Wind for me. He must have been desperate and would have been reckless."

"It was my pleasure, my lord," he answered with his incorrigible grin.

Alek leaned from the saddle and gripped Natan's hand. "Goodbye, dear friend. Take very good care of yourself."

"And you, Alek. Please give Kavi my love."

Devon mounted his horse and the group parted, Natan swinging into his own saddle with a heavy heart.

Korin mounted behind him and they traveled slowly, sparing the roan as they climbed the winding forest path toward Nagal. At one point they had to leave the trail to avoid a party of soldiers from Amara. Natan soothed the animal as they hid in the trees, conscious of Korin's curious eyes on him.

"Do you have the Karthagan's powers, Mage?" Korin asked as they resumed their journey.

Natan flinched, though he should have expected the question. "No, though I could desperately use them now."

"I wouldn't wish them on anyone," Korin countered. "They seem to bring nothing but trouble."

They fell silent with their own thoughts as they rode and didn't stop until long after dark, when they built a fire and ate a meager dinner. Afterwards, Korin disconsolately poked the fire. Natan worried about him, wondering what part he still had to play. There was courage in the boy, and selfishness…

Korin glanced up and Natan laughed self-consciously. "I'm curious about you. Anyone special in your life?"

"No. Well, no one who returns the sentiment," Korin answered, jabbing at the coals.

Natan studied the beautiful face across from him. "I have trouble believing you," he teased.

Korin shrugged and looked uncomfortable. "I suppose I've had…admirers," he admitted. "But no one who's loved me."

"Maybe you've never given them a chance."

Korin looked troubled.

"We've all grown fond of you," Natan told him. "And I could easily count you as a son, if only for the care you took of the others when I couldn't."

"But you love everyone," Korin scoffed.

Hot blood flooded Natan's face, and he drew back, stung, then stared into the fire. He hadn't meant to presume on Korin's friendship. He was lonely and frightened and needed… He closed his eyes tightly. He needed to hold Kavi in his arms and feared he never would again. He needed someone to tell him all would be well when it was over, after he'd…

"Mage!" Korin said, distressed. "I didn't mean it like that." He cleared a husky throat. "It's in me to make a joke when I'm most moved. I'm sorry."

Natan laughed at himself. "And I'm a fool. If I weren't so caught up in my own troubles, I would have remembered that. Friends?" He held out his hand, and Korin clasped it in relief.

*

THEY TROTTED THROUGH the lush fields of Nagal late the next morning and drew to a halt outside the opened gates of the city. There seemed to be an unusual amount of activity, and Korin sent him a questioning look. Natan lifted a shoulder.

"Let's go in, lad," he murmured and leaped off the horse. "Stay close to me if you wish."

Korin flashed him a dazzling smile, and Natan blinked; then his face heated. "Behave yourself," he warned with a small laugh. Looking closer, he saw Korin's features brighten with mischief. "Korin!"

Korin looked surprised. "Mage, don't worry about me. I have some friends here."

Natan was dubious. "I'll be in the castle should you need me."

Korin stared at his outstretched hand, then stepped back and gave him a low, eloquent bow. "I am your servant, Mage. Send for me when you will."

Natan watched as he swung down the crowded street and wondered what drove Korin so relentlessly, as if there was an underlying desperation. He led the roan to the stables, then continued on foot to the castle.

"Natan!"

He looked around to find Commander Jaden trotting down the cobbled street toward him, arms outstretched. Natan grinned widely as they embraced. He'd always had a fondness for his brash cousin.

"But what brings you to Nagal?" Natan asked. "Is there trouble in Karthag?"

"There's trouble everywhere. Willum has sent every Southerner from his lands."

Natan sighed, discouraged, and Jaden quickly took his arm. "Never mind that now. It's good to see you, cousin. Come with me." Jaden pulled him into the courtyard.

Mirah, Jaden's wife, rose from a bench and kissed Natan's cheek, urging him to sit. "Will you have something cool to drink?"

"Thank you." He stretched out his legs with a contented sigh and closed his eyes. Shutting off his mind, he enjoyed the soft touch of a rose-scented breeze on his face. Birdsong reached him, the hum of small insects, and he took a moment to simply be. In time, he drew a lungful of fresh air and opened his eyes and smiled, slightly embarrassed. Jaden and Mirah had moved a few steps away and were talking quietly. Noticing his attention, they took the bench opposite him.

"How can we help you, Mage?" Jaden asked, earnest and troubled, probably by the stress Natan couldn't mask.

He shrugged helplessly. "I don't know! I thought I'd be with Aiden until the end, but things turned out otherwise. I'm unsure of my next step."

"Where is Aiden now?"

"He and Kayle are still on the Isle of Wind, awaiting a boat from Karthag. Alek assures me that Niko is no longer a threat…" Natan stopped and swallowed painfully. It was the first time he'd had to say it aloud.

"Oh, Natan, I'm so sorry." Mirah touched his arm. "I know he was a friend."

He nodded, drawing a steadying breath to continue. "I'm assuming once Aiden reaches Karthag, he'll leave immediately for Siagan and deal with Ethan."

"Then you'll be going?"

"Perhaps." He rubbed his face. "I'm too weary to decide today. And who knows—" Natan smiled painfully. "—maybe I'll be inspired by my dreams." He leaned toward them. "It's hard without my abilities. I feel so very inadequate."

Jaden said fondly, "You've always felt that way, Natan. We have faith in you. Trust in that."

Natan felt crushed under the weight of that belief. He was only a man! What if he did the wrong thing? What if he did the right thing for everyone else, but Kavi no longer… The thought was hard to bear, and he thrust it to the back of him mind, changing the subject. "Nagal seems very busy. What's happened?"

"We received word from Basal a few days ago. Nelson demands the lordship of Fredrik's Hall and the disbandment of the Nagal outpost there. They've taken Robin as hostage to ensure his cooperation. Basal's unsure of Nelson's next move but wants Nagal prepared for any contingency."

"As well he might."

They jumped as the door to the castle banged open.

"Mage! Forgive me. They didn't tell me you'd arrived. Will you come in for some lunch?" Emile took Natan's hands, kissed his cheeks, and pulled him toward the doorway.

"Are you well?" Natan asked the Nagal council leader as they entered the castle, his heart lightened by the exuberant greeting.

"Yes, thank you." Emile ran a hand through his flame of hair. "Shocking about little Robin, isn't it? But never mind that—" He hurried on. "—Tell me about yourself. Everything's all right?"

"Yes." Natan laughed a little as Emile rushed him into the kitchen as if he were a young lad in need of nourishment. He sank gratefully into the cushioned chair Emile offered and begged the council leader to sit and tell him all the gossip. Emile eagerly pulled up a chair as Jaden and Mirah sat opposite. Anxiety had etched lines into Emile's attractive face, but for the moment he seemed genuinely happy, and Natan would do his best to let them have this moment of peace. They could all use it.

Chapter Fourteen

KORIN SAT ON the edge of the fountain and counted the newly won silver in his pocket. He'd bluffed his way into the game, and though he'd lost a little gold ring on one toss, it hadn't been his to start with, and silver was much easier to spend anyway.

He glanced up when someone called his name. "Korin, what are you doing here? This is an unexpected pleasure."

"My lady Nikki!" Korin rose to his feet with a smile for Commander Jaden's daughter as she came up to him. Then his heart skipped at the sight of her companion. "Hello." He bowed to them.

"Have you abandoned your friends already?" Syros asked coolly.

The contempt in his voice tore Korin's heart. Where was this coming from? "Perhaps," he managed and cleared his throat. "Why are you still in the South? Isn't it dangerous for you here?"

"It may be, but I will stay until this issue with Robin is resolved."

Korin couldn't stop himself from looking at him, so damned handsome in his uniform. Syros frowned, his lips parting as if he were going to speak. Then he blinked and his eyes grew cold as they rested on him.

"Syros," Korin said in dismay. "Can we not at least be friends?"

"I'm sorry, Korin, but I can't give my friendship to a man I have no respect for."

Korin felt numb and put his trembling hands in his pockets as he walked away from them. He wondered, with distraction, why his heart thumped so painfully. It didn't matter. Nothing ever mattered.

He walked aimlessly along the streets, his wandering feet leading him into the castle. He climbed the long stairs to the tower and sat on the parapet, kicking his heels against the aged stone. The sun was going down in the far distance and little lights flickered in the houses below his feet. He giggled a little as he held the wine flask he'd appropriated from the kitchen on his way through to his lips. He never realized before how empty and alone a man could feel in the vast space of the world. But the wine was sweet and cool and brought the return of blessed numbness.

"Will you come down?"

He froze at the voice, the one he longed to hear, but now it only filled him with a blinding anger. He stared fixedly at the lowering sun.

"Korin?" There was a worried note in the voice. Must be the wine.

"I'll not apologize for who I am!" The words burst out of him in a harsh whisper, and he trembled with emotion. Why was Syros tormenting him? He'd not endure it! He slid to his feet, but his traitorous body wouldn't walk away. He stood with averted face, his heart pounding in his ears.

"I'm sorry, Korin. When I heard you called Lord Fredrik's 'pet' last time you were here, and after the way you behaved in Siagan..." Korin flinched as Syros's words cut into him but held his breath as Syros continued, "I thought it was true. I thought you were Fredrik's lover. And…it hurt. I hadn't expected that. Nor had I expected the biting jealousy."

Syros made a frustrated sound. "I know I should have talked to you personally, but…" He paused, then finished with a small catch in his voice that sent Korin's pulse hammering. "The Mage waylaid me after you left us earlier, demanded to know the reason behind my foul mood, then made me see the truth. In fact, he gave me a whole lecture on trust and couldn't praise you enough. Won't you look at me?"

Korin raised his eyes, a gasp escaping him when Syros cupped his hot cheek and ran a finger over his lips. His was the first gentle touch Korin had ever received. It overwhelmed him, and he couldn't help himself. Tears filled his eyes.

Syros studied his face, then unexpectedly kissed him, softly, searching. Could this be happening?

"I'm not your wife," he blurted out, his uncertainty strangling him.

Syros gave a half laugh, his smile tender and sad. "I know you're not. And Sharana will always hold a place in my heart. But she was so full of life, so loving, she would be angry if I denied my feelings for you. In fact," his heated gaze swept Korin head to toe. "I think she would approve of my choice. Come with me."

Syros took his hand, and Korin followed in a daze as he led him inside, down dark hallways to his room in the castle. Once there, Syros lit the candles and drew Korin into the warm glow of the fire crackling on the hearth.

A smile lifted the corner of Syros's mouth, and he ran his fingers through Korin's hair. Korin trembled at the touch, moistened his lips as

Syros raised a few tresses, holding them so the firelight flashed in the red strands.

"You're so beautiful," Syros murmured, and Korin's heart jumped, then thumped madly. It wasn't the words themselves. He'd been called beautiful the whole of his life, from the men who'd taken him as a child to his many trysts as an adult. But it was the way Syros said it, with awe and delight, as if Korin was a gift.

Korin raised his own hand, then hesitated. What did Syros expect here? He was a proud man, the regent to a fierce people. Did he want Korin to be submissive? Take what he gave without—

Syros shook him slightly, breaking the poisonous spiral of thoughts and placed Korin's hand against his cheek, his skin warmed by the fire.

"Touch me all you want, Korin. We're equals, here. In fact," he stepped closer, his body heat scorching Korin, his gray eyes flashing. "I insist."

The unwelcomed insecurity holding Korin frozen shattered at Syros's words, and a delighted grin leaped on his face. "Oh, I intend to, my lord," he promised and dropped a hand to cup Syros while licking a slow path up his neck, across his jaw, loving the hitch in Syros's breathing, the salty tang of his skin under his tongue. He knew many ways to please a man, and he'd use all his gifts to—

"Stop that."

Korin paused, momentarily bewildered, especially when Syros gripped his shoulders and pushed him back against the nearest wall. Firelight flickered on Syros's face, the gray eyes flashing with desire and temper. Syros shook him again, then bent to kiss him, not the rough kiss he expected, but something tender, deliciously sweet. *Oh gods.* Syros kissed him like he dreamed a lover would, as if he cared. Korin didn't know what to make of it, and a whimper rose in his throat.

Syros ran a soothing hand over his hair, making Korin shiver, and his gaze warmed. "Don't be troubled, sweetheart. I want you here with me, right now: not thinking of past lovers; not distracted by what we'll do an hour from now or tomorrow morning. This single moment, right here, with only the two of us in your mind."

Korin couldn't speak but nodded. With a quick movement, he pulled Syros's shirt loose from his pants, lifting it over his head. He allowed himself the pleasure of running a slow gaze down Syros's toned, muscular chest, over the rippled muscles of his abdomen. Old scars and several new ones stood out on his taut skin, a soldier's body, with a scattering of light curls disappearing into the hem of his pants, making Korin's mouth water.

"Your turn," Syros demanded, though his voice was a trifle unsteady, his gaze piercing; controlled passion. Korin laughed suddenly and ran fingers through his hair, shaking out his worry. He'd undressed hundreds of times for men, sometimes quickly, other times with deliberate slowness, teasing, drawing that sweet moan of impatience from them.

But somehow it was different this time, with Syros. He felt unaccountably shy. Not to show Syros his body. He knew he was an attractive man. His cock more than adequate. But Syros's gaze devoured him. What if he saw more than Korin's bare skin? Saw all the way through to the twisted blackness inside him—the corruption of a boy passed between bedrooms by the men of Fredrik's Hall like a favorite toy? Would Syros be disgusted...

Syros swept an arm around Korin's waist and yanked him against his hard body. His hands splayed on Syros's chest, Syros's heart pounding under his fingertips.

"You're thinking again. Guess I'll have to make you stop," Syros murmured against his lips, then turned suddenly, swirling Korin around. The bed struck the back of his knees, and Syros shoved him onto the thick blankets.

"In the center of the bed, undressed. Now."

Korin stared at Syros standing over him, hands on hips, then scrambled back, stripping clothes on the way. Men commanded him all the time, usually with a slap or kick. But not like this, not with that passion and promise on their face that Syros wore as he removed his own clothing and crawled on the bed toward him.

Heart racing, Korin licked his lips and moaned aloud when Syros nudged between his legs.

"You are not to think of anything but what we do right now," Syros warned him.

"Yes, sir," Korin answered glibly, though his pulse rushed madly. Syros's laugh was a low growl, heavy with lust. Korin clenched the blankets, wondering…and lost the ability to think when Syros kissed his inner thigh. Tears stung his eyes. Did Syros mean to make love to him? He didn't deserve…

Syros licked his skin, igniting a flame of pleasure inside, then drove him mad by licking and kissing him everywhere, teasing his nipples with teeth and tongue, saving his cock till Korin squirmed with need. The flick of a tongue over the head of his cock made him cry out, then moan when he was swallowed down, Syros's throat tight and hot around him. He drowned in soft sheets and heated skin and hard cocks after that, both of them slick with sweat. They writhed together, Korin taking what Syros gave and giving back with joy until they were satiated and fell into exhausted sleep.

*

KORIN DIDN'T WAKE until morning, then stretched his sleek body, paused, and quickly turned to Syros, who leaned on an elbow watching him. "You're still here."

"You seem surprised." Syros leaned close to whisper in his ear, "But I know you've had many lovers. You can't tell me you've never woken with someone in your bed before."

Korin shrugged away a prick of pain. "No one's ever stayed until morning." He ran a finger down Syros's molded chest, feeling helplessly vulnerable, then laughed and rolled Syros under him.

"I'm glad you stayed," he confessed. Syros studied his face, then kissed the tears from his eyes.

"I'm being an utter fool," Syros confessed. "But there's something about you, Korin. You get under my skin, and that rarely happens." He played with a strand of Korin's vibrant hair and laughed slightly. "You make me happy."

Korin kissed his mouth, terrified he'd confess his love and hear Syros's reply. They were dressing when someone pounded on the door.

"Go away," he called pleasantly.

"Open the door, Korin, or I'll knock it down."

"If that is your wish, Jaden, you brute." Korin grinned at Syros, inviting him to share his mirth.

"You'd better open it," Syros warned, though the corner of his mouth twitched with a smile.

Korin crossed the room and flung open the door, and was taken aback by the commander's glowering expression. "What is it?"

"You're needed." Jaden looked over Korin's shoulder, caught Syros's eye, and swore under his breath. "Please come with me, both of you. Ashel has returned to Fredrik's Hall with Robin."

Korin choked back an oath, moving to a window to stare unseeing at the day, ice seeping into his veins. Jaden cleared his throat. "I'm afraid things will become…unpleasant."

"To say the least," Korin said quietly.

"We'd better see what they want," Syros said in a clipped tone, once again regent, as far from Korin as the moon. "I don't know what it's like for a Southern soldier, but in the North we go when we're called or take the beatings."

That brought a laugh from Korin. "It's much the same for us. Unless," he flashed a glance at Jaden, "I can get someone to take the beatings for me."

He sobered, thinking of what might be required of him. "Let's go."

Jaden looked glum as he led them from the room to the council chambers.

*

NATAN WATCHED KORIN as he entered the room, and his heart filled with sadness. It was a terrible thing they would ask the young soldier to do. Out of all the sacrifices made, his would be the cruelest.

Korin sat opposite him and laced his fingers on the table. "Mage?"

Natan reached impulsively for his hands, then drew back and cleared his throat. "You know why we've sent for you?"

"Ashel has our Robin."

"It's been confirmed," Jaden said, taking the chair next to Natan while Syros claimed the seat beside Korin. Emile sat to the left with Sadie, captain of the battalions stationed outside Nagal's walls. She'd been in animated conversation with Emile, and now watched Korin with an anxious expression. Natan saw Korin's eyes narrow. It must seem as if they were arrayed against him.

Jaden leaned forward, elbows on the table, "We had a messenger from Fredrik's Hall last night with a note smuggled out from Robin. Ashel has Robin at the Hall. He's murdered Nelson and has claimed the lordship for himself." He drew a troubled breath, darting a glance at Korin. "Robin asserts that Ashel has a secret agenda neither Nelson nor Lord Fredrik knew anything about. Robin tried but couldn't get the information out of him."

Korin sat back in his chair and looked at them each in turn. Natan struggled to return his gaze when his accusing eyes reached him.

"You want me to find out what Ashel is hiding; is that it?"

"Yes," Natan replied and despised himself for having to involve him. If he could go in his stead… But since Robin had failed, there was no one else besides Korin who Ashel might let down his guard with and betray his secret.

The room was silent. The morning sun shone brightly through the high windows, yet Natan felt cold.

"I don't want to go, Mage."

He winced at the soft plea. "I don't want you to go, Korin." His voice cracked, and he swallowed a hard lump. "I want to go home. I want life to be simple and good. To spend my days and nights with Kavi. But the corruption would find us wherever we hid." He studied the troubled eyes across the table from him and stood abruptly. "Will you walk with me?"

Anger flashed across Syros's face. Natan held up his empty hands. "I only wish to speak with him. I shan't try to manipulate him."

"Very well," Korin said curtly.

"With your permission?" Natan bowed to Emile, who nodded with reservation. With Basal absent, as council leader, Emile would have the final say. Natan didn't envy him. He led Korin to the garden and found a bench for them to sit on in the sun to chase the chill from his bones, then waited.

"Do you know what it means for me if I return to the Hall? To him?" Korin said at last.

Natan covered his face. *Why is this the only way?*

Korin's voice dropped to an anguished whisper. "What if Syros hates me afterward? It would kill me to lose his regard."

Natan gave a small, wounded cry. He spoke gravely then, outlining the plan Willum had set in motion what seemed an age ago.

Korin listened in surprise and obvious fear, and when Natan finished, he looked at him in awe. "You would do this, Mage?"

"Yes," Natan answered simply.

"But why? You may lose everything you love."

"It needs to be done."

"It may kill you."

"Perhaps. I don't believe so." He flashed Korin a grim smile. "I'm stronger than I appear."

Korin studied his face, and Natan sat passively. He wouldn't urge him to make the same choice that was tearing his own heart to shreds.

"I'm not brave."

Natan shouted, startling him. "Do you believe I am? I'm terrified, Korin, every moment. I'm terrified of being wrong. I'm frightened for the lives I endanger by simply being with them. I'm afraid of failing or succeeding. I'm being eaten alive with doubt!" He made a great effort to calm his racing heart. "I still must go."

"How does Ashel fit in?"

"I'm not sure, but I fear Aiden will walk blindly into a trap of Ashel's design. All his focus will be on Ethan in Siagan now. He may not be aware of the danger Ashel poses. I must protect him. Our only hope is in Aiden's success."

"And yours."

Natan laughed softly. "There are many who could take my place."

Korin's gaze seemed to pierce his heart. "I very much doubt that, Mage," he murmured and rose to his feet. "When do we leave?"

Chapter Fifteen

ALEK LET OUT a relieved breath as they approached the gates of Karthag. Following the coast had been a long, dangerous journey. Many times, they'd been forced to hide in thickets or a copse of trees from searchers. The last time, they'd been able to outrun their pursuers only through Devon's knowledge of the terrain.

It had been easier once they'd crossed into the North. Alek sent Devon home then, though the man had protested hotly. But it would have been certain suicide for the Amara council leader to remain with them, with the unrest in both territories. He had bidden Devon, though, to urge Lady Kirstin to join them in Karthag immediately. Without a doubt, they would need her medical skills. And the Karthagan people should be together.

Alek shifted Cecil in his arms, and Cecil blinked sleepily, coming awake as a soldier hailed them from the walls. It was Eon, a young man who'd been accidentally injured while working on the gates with Aiden. Eon was a good man and worked hard despite his crippled fingers. Ellis stood in the stirrups and waved his hat. "Hello!"

"Welcome home," Eon called down and motioned for the gates to be opened.

They rode into the city and Ellis leaped from the saddle into Kavi's waiting arms.

"Don't cry," he begged his adopted father and laughed a little as he wiped at his own tears.

Kavi searched his face. "Are you well?"

"Yes." Ellis leaned close. "Natan sends his love."

Kavi drew a sharp breath, betraying his longing, though a tender smile touched his lips. "Come, I think you could all use a good rest."

He took Ellis's arm, and they followed Alek as he walked his horse at a quick pace to the castle, anxious to put Cecil to bed. Upon reaching the courtyard gate, he slipped from the saddle and helped Cecil down. Cecil stumbled slightly, and Alek felt the fever in his skin as he steadied him. "Go with Ellis. I'll be up after I've spoken with Kavi."

Cecil looked stubborn, then inclined his head. "As you wish," he murmured, with a flash in his gray eyes as Ellis slipped an arm around his waist.

A slow grin spread on Alek's face at his tone, relieved Cecil was recovering his spirits. A soldier led his mount away, and he turned to Kavi. "Shall we go into the garden?"

They took seats by the fountain, and Alek wasted no time in asking, "Where's Willum? He must know of our return. I have much to tell him."

Kavi shifted on the bench. "He's gathering information on the unrest in Belega to assess our danger. It seems the whole country is up in arms, distrust on both sides. He's recalled our troops, pulled every Karthagan inside the walls, and sealed off the city."

Alek scowled. "I'd better go find him."

"No, sir. The city has been sealed. No one's to leave, by Willum's direct order."

Alek looked at him, pushing down his anger. "Very well. Am I allowed to know the situation inside the walls?"

Kavi stiffened at his tone, his face showing the stress of the past weeks.

Alek put a hand on his arm. "Forgive me. This has been an unsettling time for us all. How are things in the city, and how may I help?"

Kavi rubbed the lines from his forehead and motioned to Eon at attention in the garden doorway. Eon came up and bowed. "The army's been installed in the lower section of the city, near the southern wall. They've almost finished repairs on the buildings damaged in the earthquake. We have provisions enough for two months, though we'll be left with nothing for the winter. We may have to send men out to fish in the coming week."

"Is the peril so grave, then?" Alek asked, his concern mounting.

"I believe so," Kavi answered. "The people of both the North and South have grown suspicious and wrathful. It wouldn't take much to have them turn their attention to us."

They heard voices, and Alek rose to his feet as Ellis joined them with a parting word to the soldiers escorting him.

"Cecil's fine," Ellis assured them as he pulled up a chair. "He has a slight infection in his lungs that the doctor feels is healing. He needs quiet and rest now to recover fully."

Alek sat in thoughtful silence a moment, then stirred at Kavi's troubled question, "How is Natan, and why isn't he with you now?"

Alek frowned, grown irritated with worry. "You know the answer, Kavi. Willum's plan is not yet complete. Ethan is still free, and until he's stopped, there can be no peace for any of us."

"But why does it have to be Natan? He has no power…" Kavi stopped in dismay. "Is it because he once had Gregor's gifts?"

"Partly, but more than that, there is no other with a truer heart. He can't be tempted by any allure of power."

Kavi looked stricken. "I'm frightened for him."

"So am I. For all of us."

Alek sighed internally, then outlined what had transpired on the Isle of Wind and of the hostility of the Belegan people toward them as they traveled. Dusk came, and attendants brought food to the courtyard. Alek lit a fire in the stone pit, and Cecil surprised them by coming to the garden soon afterward.

Alek gave him a keen look. "You should be in bed."

"I couldn't sleep."

His expression was defiant and desire flashed unexpectedly through Alek. He was strongly attracted by Cecil's returning independence and was finding him hard to resist. But he must never let passion control his actions, especially with what was coming. If so, he would never leave Cecil's side, though he must go. He turned his shoulder as Kavi gave up his place to Cecil and leaned toward Ellis. "Do we know when Aiden will arrive?"

Joy mingled with sorrow touched Ellis's face. "He's on his way. Maybe two or three days if Daran doesn't encounter a storm."

"How did he seem?"

Ellis's eyes darkened. "I don't know. His thoughts were confused, emotions tangled in the past and future. He is driven, Alek." Ellis pressed his unsteady lips together. "I fear for him."

Alek searched his face, strong and determined, his eyes alight with fire, and nodded in relief. Ellis would stand by Aiden, whatever would come, and be his anchor.

They spoke a while longer, until Ellis declared he was tired and left to make his way to his and Aiden's home on the hillside, and Alek and Kavi were left alone with Cecil nodding sleepily on the bench. Alek had studiously ignored him and now slid to the edge of the bench with an exasperated breath. Cecil stretched out with a faint sigh, resting his head on Alek's thigh. Alek played with his light hair as he stared moodily into the fire. Cecil wasn't making it easy for him.

"Did you tell him you were leaving?" Kavi asked after a moment.

"No, but he knows." Alek traced the lines of sadness in Cecil's unguarded face, an ache growing in his heart.

"So you mean to shut him out?"

"No!"

Cecil jumped and struggled to sit up, dazed with sleep.

"Hush. All's well. Go back to sleep," Alek assured him. His heart twisted at the extreme anxiety in Cecil's face, but his soft words calmed him, and he lay back down, though it took a while for his quick breathing to slow. Cecil slept, but his body continued to shake as if chilled.

"Let me find a blanket," Kavi said kindly. Alek sat in silence and raised a miserable face when he returned.

"You don't have to go," Kavi urged. "I know you wish me to stay with Ellis and help him govern in your absence, and I will do that as long as I am able, but you should remain in my stead. You and Cecil have given enough."

Alek laughed abruptly, in bitterness. "When Aiden calls us to war, not a single Karthagan will oppose him. I go to keep our people from rushing headlong into death."

"Willum is lord—" Kavi tried to say but broke off at his wry expression.

"Willum may be the governor of this territory, Cousin, but Aiden is the Red Twin. We'll go when he calls and leave when he sends us away."

Kavi nodded in acceptance.

Alek sat in the garden long after Kavi had gone inside and gently stroked Cecil's hair as the fire burned to embers. He regretted turning his anger at himself on Cecil, but the frustration and fear were becoming more than he could bear. He could almost wish Cecil would lose his temper, scream, and revile him. Perhaps his guilt in leaving would be assuaged, if only a little.

Cecil stirred and coughed but didn't wake. The tightness in Alek's chest eased and he smiled. Their battles had always been from misunderstandings and unintentional thoughtlessness on both their parts. Cecil would stand by him in this as in everything else.

He listened to Cecil's even breathing and bent to kiss the slightly parted lips. "Shall we go up to bed?"

"Hmmm…" Cecil rolled to a more comfortable position.

"Come on," Alek chuckled and lifted him bodily. He grieved anew at how light Cecil had become, mere bones. His skin was the finest porcelain in the starlight. Alek cradled him, this man who was his life, and took him to their room.

He wept into his pillow, as Cecil slept beside him, for the hurt he would soon cause him, though he loved him. Fingers touched his face in the darkness, and Cecil whispered his name and pulled him into his arms, and he could at last sleep with Cecil's heartbeat under his ear.

*

A MESSAGE HAD been secreted in for Carrow the previous day, so he waited outside the gates of Fredrik's Hall at the specified time for the travelers to arrive, hoping to get Korin hidden before Ashel became aware of him. As the horsemen approached in the evening gloom, he glanced back at the Hall and took a moment to string the short bow he carried. He examined the arrows and promised himself that a shaft would find Ashel soon.

He shifted his weight as Natan drew near, the mage incongruously humming to himself. Natan looked vaguely at Carrow in the fading light, then blinked him into focus, blushing slightly as he reined his mount to a stop. "Sorry. I didn't see you. I was thinking of home and…Kavi."

Anger flashed through Carrow. "Aren't you the least bit concerned with what's transpiring here?"

Natan jumped at his tone, amazed. "Me?" He laughed harshly, temper flashing in his hazel eyes. "What would you have me do? Lie prostrate on the ground, crushed by the fear that all my choices are wrong? That Ashel will prevail here, and Ethan win in the end because of my ineptness?"

Carrow lifted a hand. "Mage! I'm a fool," he said in defense, with a glance at the riders a short distance behind them. "But it shreds my heart to know…" His voice trailed off in a frustrated sigh.

The anger fell from Natan's expression, replaced by a soft compassion as he slid off the horse to his feet. "I know you are concerned for

Korin, as am I." He tilted his head. "And you're remembering the passing of your dear Lyra."

"We had less than a year together when I wanted forever," Carrow admitted, the words wrung from him against his will. He couldn't believe how much it still hurt to think of his wife and the infant son he'd lost—the son Korin had become in his heart. "I should hate to lose Korin as well, annoying as he is sometimes."

"We all have our parts to play," Natan reminded him. "But I swear I'll end Korin's portion as quickly as I may."

Carrow nodded and took Natan's outstretched hand to seal the promise. Korin and Syros caught up to them, and Carrow led them to the gates. Natan stopped them before entering, his expression thoughtful. "Korin, please take Syros to your cottage for the night. No visitors and talk to no one on the way. I should like to keep you a secret for as long as possible."

"But Mage, shouldn't I…"

Natan hushed him with a kind smile. "Go on, Korin. Tomorrow will come soon enough."

"Thank you," Korin said on a breath of relief. With a questioning glance at Syros, he headed toward the barracks. Syros nudged his horse after him while Carrow and Natan passed through the gates. After leaving their mounts at the stable, they entered the Hall, where a sullen attendant led them to the study.

After an interminable wait, Carrow stirred and glanced at Natan. "Shall I go find someone?" he asked and examined the tip of an arrow. Natan smiled grimly, seeming ready to let him. Quick steps sounded in the hall, and they rose to their feet as Basal strode into the room, his face white with fury.

Relief swept Basal's features at the sight of them. "Forgive me, Mage. I've only now been informed of your arrival."

"Basal." Natan held out his hand and then embraced him instead. "How is Robin?"

Basal clung to him a little tighter than usual. "They won't let me see him."

"Are we to speak with Ashel tonight?" Carrow put in quickly.

Basal swore. "He's put us off until the morning, a few hours after sunrise." He ran a hand over his face and dark hair. "I'm sorry. I haven't seen Robin for days, and I'm driven to desperation."

"We'll get him back," Natan said with assurance.

Basal gave him a sharp look. "What do you have planned?"

Natan set his lips. "We'll meet with Ashel and let events unfold as they may."

Anger flashed over Basal's face, quickly controlled. "As you will," he growled, and Natan closed his eyes as if in pain.

Seeing the breach growing between the two friends, Carrow took Natan's arm. "Let me show you to a room, Mage," he said kindly. Natan nodded, tired, and Carrow guided him to the room he'd had prepared near Basal's.

"I'll have food brought. Do you need anything else?" he asked as he left Natan at the door.

A helpless look crossed Natan's face, then he glanced aside, hiding his expression. "No, Carrow. We'll meet in the morning," he said and closed the door before Carrow could form a reply.

Carrow stood in the hallway a moment, then shook his head and fled the smothering atmosphere of Fredrik's Hall. Once outside, he took a deep breath of the cooling air, rubbing absently at the ache starting in his temple. He'd felt the tension between Natan and Basal and suspected another's influence. If Ashel could manipulate Basal, or worse, the Mage, then they were all in trouble. He made his way to the soldiers' barracks and his own familiar cot, where he tossed for most of the night.

*

SYROS STOMPED INTO his boots, studiously ignoring the crumpled bedsheets as morning light spilled into the room. He hadn't meant to sleep with Korin again. Fredrik's Hall was a treacherous place and they needed to keep alert, their senses sharp. But Korin had nipped at him all evening, wound up and nervous, until Syros had told him to put his sarcastic tongue to good use.

By the gods, Korin was dangerous. Bewitchingly beautiful with that fiery hair, dancing eyes, and full mouth made for wickedness. Syros could no longer resist the allure of that slim body, unexpectedly strong and limber, and that bright, quick mind behind it all. Warmth spread into his cheeks. Korin was rapidly stealing his heart, and he had no plans to stop him, whatever the outcome with his quicksilver lover.

He jumped at a sudden pounding on the door, his heart turning to lead as he opened it and found the archer, Carrow, on the steps. "Is it time?"

"Indeed." Carrow wore a scowl as he brushed past him, then stopped just over the threshold. Korin entered the room with his shirt untucked, vigorously rubbing a towel over his still damp hair. He had the look of a man happy with himself and life.

The soft smile on his face squeezed Syros's heart. He swore viciously and wanted to strike someone, hating the feeling of helplessness washing through him.

"Are you ready?" Carrow bit out.

Korin flinched as if he'd been struck through the body by one of the archer's arrows, then he laughed bitterly. "No! But you know me. I'll be late to my own funeral." He dropped into a chair and pulled on his boots. Syros watched him, lips pressed together, and slowly clenched his hands into fists, wanting to protect him and knowing he couldn't.

Korin gave him an odd look as he rose to his feet, and Syros flushed, caught staring. Unexpectedly, Korin crossed to him, lifted Syros's hand to his own cheek, holding his gaze, then kissed his palm. He touched Syros's hair, then made a strangled sound and fled out the open door.

They had to hurry to catch up, and then Syros fretted as Korin assumed a casual pace. Korin began to sing under his breath, his face raised to the sun. He stopped and stretched his lean body, grinning broadly at Syros, whose heart thumped painfully.

Carrow looked puzzled. "What are you doing?"

Korin laughed. "I plan on getting gloriously drunk, and if I remember my dear Ashel, he'll have a decanter with him, and I can start straight away."

"I don't understand…"

Korin whirled on him, his eyes wild. "I have nothing more to lose, Carrow, not one single damn thing." He glanced at Syros and bit back an oath and resumed his stroll, even skipping a few times.

Syros grew frightened for him in that state of mind. Korin slowed even further as they reached the wall and trailed his fingers over the stones, humming under his breath as they walked toward the gates. Syros didn't think he'd ever forget the scent of the tall, dried grass heated by the sun, and Korin's desperation.

"Should you keep him waiting?" Carrow finally asked, his anxiety breaking through his calm mask.

Korin winked. "I know how to manage Ashel."

They asked him no more questions as they approached the Hall and the open doorway.

Korin stopped on the threshold and covered his face. "I don't want to go in."

"Don't!" Syros interjected. "Come with me. We'll make our way north. Take a ship to Sennia, if we must."

"But where after, Syros? The Mage says the darkness would find us even there."

"Perhaps, but we would have time together, before…"

Korin dropped his hands to his sides, and for a brief instant his love kindled his face. "But I want forever, Syros," he said simply and strode into Fredrik's Hall.

Carrow shook his head, and they followed him inside. Korin hesitated only a moment outside the closed doors of the study where they were to meet with Ashel and the others, ignoring the stares of the few servants. Taking a sudden breath, he flung open the doors, entered, and made a sweeping bow.

"I'm sorry I'm late." His eyes flitted across the startled faces of those inside and landed on Ashel. He looked the man over indolently, dismissed him, then went to a window and leaned on the sill, seeming to pay them no more mind.

Syros swallowed a painful laugh. If nothing else, Korin knew how to command attention. Ashel tried to pick up the threads of a conversation, but his gaze kept sliding to Korin. The sun through the windowpanes turned his hair to flame, and the sea blue eyes were startling in his ivory face, uniquely beautiful. Carrow moved to his side and leaned against the wall, a quiet reminder to Ashel the lad wasn't without friends. Syros could have screamed at the unfolding scene, his nerves pulled taut. He should have whisked Korin away during the night, Ashel and the others be damned.

Basal cleared his throat, obviously bewildered by their presence, but determined to regain Ashel's interest. "The army is disbanded. When may I have my son?"

Ashel turned to him in distraction. "What?"

"We had an agreement," Basal growled. Natan put a hand on his arm, and he settled back in his chair.

"Ashel," Natan took up. "The soldiers have left, as both Nelson and you demanded. The remaining lords back you, and the governor will declare the Hall a sovereign region. What more could you desire?" His eyes flicked to Korin. Syros caught his glance and saw the shame and self-loathing he hid from Ashel.

Ashel followed his gaze, and the hunger on his face brought Basal to his feet. "Let Robin go, as per our agreement."

"Oh, little Robin can leave anytime," Ashel purred, "if Korin will come to me of his own accord."

Silence fell on the room. Korin clenched his hands and kept his eyes on the window.

"I won't trade one man's life for another!" Basal shouted, outraged.

Ashel mocked him. "Not even for your own son?"

"Especially not for him. Robin would understand and agree."

"What do you say, Korin?" Ashel prompted as if Basal hadn't spoken.

"Will you submit?" His voice turned to ice. "Or shall I take Robin instead?"

Korin's face turned deathly white. He looked directly at Syros, anguished, and in that instant Syros could have killed for him.

"Korin?" Ashel was impatient.

Korin threw back his head, haughty and beautiful, and glanced at him with overbright eyes. "Very well, dear, but you may come to regret it."

Ashel drew a quick breath at the challenge. "Oh, you jewel," he murmured with a widening smile and took a step toward him. "Take your brat and go," he said to Basal and waved a hand in vague dismissal, all his attention on Korin. Korin glanced around, and when Ashel reached him, he slipped away to the sideboard to pour a glass of red wine. Ashel's indulgent laugh chilled Syros as he followed the others from the room, and a knot of fury formed in his chest.

*

SYROS'S ANGER BUILT as they strode silently through the hall, Natan dodging into an archway to the cellar steps. But at the bottom, before Syros could say anything, Basal grabbed Natan's arm, halting him. "What do you mean by this? You know the cruelty of the man."

Natan's face was white. "Yes I do. Don't you think it shreds my heart to leave that beautiful child up there while we walk away?" He struggled for control, then unexpectedly flung away from them and strode to the far end of the hallway. He leaned his forehead on the cold stones, breathing hard. Giving a harsh cry, he struck the rocks several times with his closed fist, drawing blood.

Syros took a pitying step toward him, but Basal gripped his arm. "Let him be a moment. I shouldn't have pushed but tell me what this is about.

It's not like the Mage to use a man this way."

Carrow answered when Syros could only shrug helplessly. "Let's get Robin away from here. Once outside the walls, we can talk without fear of being overheard."

"I won't go without Korin. He's a Southern soldier and I won't leave him in this nightmare place," Basal countered grimly.

"You must!" Carrow lowered his voice, "My lord Governor, won't you trust the Mage in this?"

Basal let out a frustrated breath. "I don't know what's right. Help me with my son, and perhaps I can think straight again."

Syros hesitated, torn at leaving the Mage, but followed the others to a room close by. Oddly, they found the door unlocked and hurriedly pushed it open. Robin sat cross-legged on a cot, his head lulled forward as if with sleep.

Basal touched his slack face in fear. "Robin?"

"Poisoned," Syros stated bitterly when he saw the glazed eyes. Basal's patience snapped. He grabbed up his son and carried him from the room, not looking back.

They returned to the hallway, and Basal mounted the stairs with his burden, Carrow trailing, while Syros turned to Natan and cleared his throat. Natan climbed to his feet and joined him, his face working. "With all my heart I want to take Korin from Ashel's hands," he said with anguish.

"I know that, Mage," Syros told him. "But come away from here. We will speak outside, as Carrow suggested."

Syros took his arm, and they followed the others upstairs and out the Hall's front doors, Syros's heart burning at abandoning Korin, even for a moment. They approached the barracks, and Basal entered Korin's house, striding through to the couch, where he sat with Robin's head resting on his shoulder. Robin drowsed and Syros felt fever when he touched his damp forehead. "Poison can be tricky. Is he well?"

Basal set his lips in an angry line. "It appears Ashel gave him just enough to keep him complacent. I fear all we can do is let it work its way through his body."

"I'm sorry, Basal," Natan offered and flinched at his harsh laugh.

"Then maybe you can tell me what's going on?"

Sorrow touched Natan's face. "Korin will stay with Ashel for a time."

"And this is by your design?" Basal countered.

Natan nodded and rubbed his forehead. "Let me gather my wits," he pleaded, going to the window where he stared at the clear sky.

"Natan, have you regained your powers?" Basal pressed, his tone cold.

Natan looked at him. "No, sir. At times Kavi comes to me in my dreams. He sends me impressions—"

"So, exchanging Korin for Robin was done on your own council, against my wishes? Without another's input?" Basal snapped.

"Yes, sir."

Basal's eyes flashed. "Leave, Natan. Gather your things and leave us. You are no longer welcome in the Southern Territory."

Natan stared at him in the silence that followed his words, then bowed to the floor. Carrow glanced at Syros, and they followed Natan as he strode from the house to the side yard, where he dropped onto a bench.

"I stand by you, Mage," Carrow stated. "The governor is under a tremendous strain and doesn't know what he's saying. Distance is your best option at present, and I will accompany you."

"You won't be allowed to cross the border," Natan reminded him in a tired voice, rubbing a hand over his face.

"We shall see."

Natan let out his breath. "I have no authority over you, and you'll do as you please, anyway. But I would welcome your bow at my side." He reached a hesitant hand to Syros. "I have no right—"

"Ask, Mage," Syros said. The situation was quickly growing intolerable.

"Will you make sure Robin is taken to Nagal? Don't let Basal dissuade you. We don't know all that Ashel may have done to the lad, and he needs to be home. And…watch over Korin for me." His voice broke, face crumpling into lines of pain.

"Of course, my lord," Syros promised. His gaze went to the Hall as apprehension tightened his chest.

Natan touched his arm. "It will be well, Syros. Be strong for him."

Syros nodded, and Natan sighed and stared at the dirt at his feet.

Carrow watched him a moment. "Shall I saddle the horses, lord?"

Natan was still bewildered. "Why are you helping me when your duty is here?"

"Because you are right, Natan. I know Ashel. He's always been ambitious, and from the instant the energies of the world were stirred, a madness has grown in him, a lust for power even surpassing Fredrik's. If anyone can reach him now, dig out his secret, it will be Korin. And you may be assured it will be something terrible. You had no other choice."

Natan looked at Fredrik's Hall in the distance. "Thank you for that. I hope with all my heart that your faith isn't ill placed."

"It's not, Mage." Carrow bowed and went for their mounts.

Syros studied Natan's lowered head. This would never do.

"Hard decisions have to be made in times of war," he began and went on when Natan's head shot up, his pretty hazel eyes startled. "Have no doubt, we are at war here, and you are needed. The rest of us are tangled in politics and…emotion." He cleared his throat. "We need your clear thinking. As much as it hurts to have Korin here, it was the right decision."

Natan acknowledged that with a quick nod. "I would ask one more thing of you." He looked at the grim stones of the Hall. "Keep an eye on Basal. He won't comprehend the depth of Ashel's lust for power, wishing to see the good in everyone."

"You don't think he'll return to Nagal with Robin?"

"No. I love him for it, but he would never abandon one of his men if he thought there was a chance to save Korin. Whatever the danger to himself."

Syros scowled, frustrated. He needed action, not this waiting. But…

"As you wish, Mage." He gave Natan a curt bow. "These are dark times. May the gods bring us through safely."

"As you say." Natan rose to his feet as Carrow approached with the horses.

Syros watched them ride away, then turned his gaze once again on the Hall, troubled, and was on time to see Basal enter its bleak walls. What was Ashel doing to Korin at that moment? Had the vibrant, darling man managed to avoid Ashel's attention? Pain and fierce jealousy bit at him, but he pushed it down. Korin was doing what was necessary, the brave fool, whatever Syros's personal feelings. Heart sore, he found a spot in the shade beneath a gnarled tree and watched the city walls.

Agonizingly slow hours passed into late afternoon. *Enough.* He climbed to his feet, checked on Robin—still sleeping, though the drug seemed to be wearing off, his color better—and then approached the silent stonework of Fredrik's Hall. Where were the guards? He climbed the wide steps, surprised to find the door unmanned and unlocked. His steps slowed further as he walked through the hall. He hoped for a peek of Korin. Was he kept hidden? His heart ached that he might be imprisoned in some dark room. He paused at the archway to the garden, and the glimpse of lush foliage and brilliant colors was more than he could resist. He wandered the paths in the sunshine and came upon Korin in a far corner.

Jealousy stung Syros once again. He was no prisoner! He was free to walk in this beautiful garden. And when Syros thought of the handsome man inside…

"So, this is where you've hidden yourself," he said icily and watched in cold satisfaction as Korin scrambled to his feet, face averted, and swayed as if wanting to flee.

"Go on. Go back inside. There's no one here to keep you," he sneered, blood pounding in his ears. Korin made no reply and pain drove Syros's next words. "Are you enjoying yourself with him, Korin?"

"Syros."

His name was a whisper of hurt from an anguished heart. Anger blazed through Syros that Korin could still move him, and he pulled roughly on his shoulder. "At least look at me."

A sharp moan escaped Korin, and he hugged his arm and gave Syros an involuntary glance. He turned desperately but not before Syros saw the cruel bruises on his face, struck many times, the dark print of fingers on his pale neck.

"Korin!" he cried, and all his anger swept away in a rush of concern.

"What's happened to you?"

"Ashel plays rough. He always has."

Korin added the last words in a tone of despair, and Syros flared to life. "He'll pay for this."

"Syros, no." Korin took up Syros's hands in extreme distress. "You mustn't go to him. He'll kill you. I can't bear this!" The words seemed torn from him, and he dropped to the bench and covered his face. Syros sat at his side and whispered words of comfort. He couldn't tell if Korin heard, but he stroked his hair and kissed the tortured cheek, tasting his tears. Korin quieted, but turned away as Syros kissed his lips. He bowed his head in shame.

"Korin."

Korin wouldn't look at him, and Syros gently cupped his face, tilted his chin up, and gazed in sorrow at eyes that had recently been so brilliant and now were dull with the hurt and loneliness of a child lost long ago. He kissed them softly, each in turn.

"Come with me, now," he urged, pulling Korin up as he stood. Doubt swept Korin's face, longing. He bit hard on his cut lips and drew blood.

"I can't," he groaned, and his expression pleaded for understanding. "Robin was right. Ashel has a terrible secret. He laughs in madness and nearly tells me… Something about the Red Twins… Can you be patient a little longer?"

"But he'll hurt you again." Syros felt torn. He wanted to force Korin to leave with him and yet thrilled at his bravery. He put his hands on Korin's face and brushed their lips together, and though Korin drew back, Syros deepened the kiss until Korin was breathing hard and his eyes flashed. An unaccustomed insecurity prompted Syros to say, "Think of me when next

Ashel has his mouth on yours."

A painful flush rose in Korin's face. "Syros," he chided and pressed his hot face into Syros's shoulder. "It's only been you for a long time."

Syros nuzzled against his ear. "I love you," he whispered. "Take good care. I *will* free you. Have no doubt."

Korin kissed Syros's hands and drew a hard breath. "Goodbye," he said, dropping his gaze to the ground and walking with slow feet back inside. Syros's heart swelled with pain and pride; then he made his way back out of the Hall without encountering anyone else.

Chapter Sixteen

ETHAN STOOD ON the shore of the cold lake under Siagan and breathed deeply of the damp air. Life stirred in him, and he felt its energy in the air and water and in the chamber across the way. He ran his tongue over dry lips, a strange excitement stirring in him as he crossed the cavern.

He paused in the broken doorway of Aunt Kirstin's old cell, flickering with candlelight, and his heart thundered. Energy pulsed in the room, and he looked hungrily at the man shackled to the wall.

"Good morning," he offered as he went up to him. He ran fingers over the suffering face, raising the man's chin to look into the sunken eyes. "Are you awake?"

The man's lids remained closed, and when Ethan withdrew his hand, the head lulled forward, the dark hair falling in lank strands to cover his face.

"Answer me!"

His captive's body jerked as energy burst in the room. He made no sound, but the dull eyes opened to slits filled with despair.

"Ah, I thought there was still some life in you." Ethan placed a hand on the faintly beating heart. Giving a satisfied nod, he left the man and slipped into the shallow pit dug into the ground in the center of the room. Energy thrummed beneath his prostrate body, hummed in the air around him, and began to seep from the tortured man, dripping into him.

It was a long while before he climbed to his feet again, with the power flowing through him stronger than ever before. He felt as if there was nothing he couldn't do…even be merciful. He approached the man drooping on the wall, the iron clasps digging cruelly into his wrists. He touched the metal, and it crumbled to dust. The body dropped like a stone. Ethan sat in the dirt and brushed the thin hair from his captive's stark face. As he pushed fingers to the hot skin of his neck, the faint pulse of life faltered under his fingertips.

"Be alive," he whispered, and let life's energy trickle back into the man, just enough to sustain him for another day, another session. The bruised lids fluttered open and the feverish eyes stared unseeing at the candlelight.

"Would you like water?" Ethan asked kindly and lifted the weak head to his knee, then let the soldier drink from his flask. The man's whimper of relief was music.

"Sleep now," he murmured gently. "Tomorrow, we'll share your precious life again."

Ethan left him unchained. There was nowhere for the man to go. He made his way through the long tunnels and outside to the fountain in the courtyard. Smiling at the brilliant sky, he let his spirit drift out—magnificent power! He'd never felt more alive. He reluctantly came back to his body, not wanting to reveal himself, not yet. There were others out there stronger than he. But they would come to him soon enough, and when their energy merged with his own…

His daydream grew wild and strange, and he became lost in visions of power and control and pleasure, with only death and despair and blood for his enemies.

*

SYROS HUNG LOW on his roan's neck as he raced through the night, determined not to lose Ashel in the Dakon Forest. *Bloody hell.* After leaving Korin in the garden, he'd gone back to the nearly empty barracks and a desultory meal at Korin's house. Robin woke and joined him, managing to eat a little, and they made plans with the remaining Nagal soldiers to escort Robin home in the morning.

It was by the merest chance Syros had glanced out the window and spotted horses being taken to a side door at the Hall, the barest luck he'd caught Ashel and Korin stealing away into the night. He'd quickly followed, though with an anxious thought to Basal still inside the Hall. But afraid he'd lose Ashel's trail if he hesitated, he pressed on.

After an interminable time, he spotted where Ashel had veered off the main road, taking a little used path into the Dakon Forest to avoid the watchers at the border. Syros followed and fumed when he ran into Commander Tyrel on patrol. He dropped a hand to the long knife at his belt, unsure of his welcome, but instead of challenging him, Tyrel listened to his curt explanation and joined him in the chase.

Faint light shone in the eastern sky before Tyrel pulled his mount to a quick stop, and in his sleepiness Syros nearly collided with him. He straightened in the saddle and looked carefully at the silent forest, every sense prickling. Catching the scent of wood smoke, he tracked Tyrel's intent gaze eastward to the flicker of a campfire.

"Someone's been careless," Tyrel muttered and slipped from his roan, tossing the reins over a branch. Syros followed suit, and they crept through the scrub brush, halting in a thick patch to peer at a meager campfire. Syros swore under his breath. Korin sat in the dirt and stared at the flames. Exhaustion lined his white, bruised face, and the once wonderful hair hung in limp strands on his neck. His dull eyes darted to the sleeping form nearby, and he tossed a handful of pine needles into the fire. They sparked briefly, quickly burning.

Korin waited a moment, then threw on another bundle, and a nervous chill shook him. Syros realized with a flash of compassion Korin tried desperately to gain some passerby's attention—anyone's. He tossed a last handful, and Ashel stirred and muttered at the crackle. Fear swept Korin's features, and he slipped back under the blankets, covering his head, feigning sleep. Ashel rolled, finding Korin still beside him, then drifted back into his dreams, the hand clutching the gleaming knife relaxing on his breast.

"Damn you," Syros hissed, chest tight with a chaos of emotion, fury and fear uppermost. Ashel could count the days he had left to live on one hand.

"Commander," he said in a low voice, keeping his gaze on Korin. "I'm going to try to free him. Will you go on to Siagan and set up a camp overlooking the city? That is, unless you need to return to the border."

Tyrel snorted. "Just try to keep me out of this. Ashel and Ethan have a lot to answer for."

Syros nodded. "Excellent." They shook hands and parted.

*

A SOFT KISS on his neck woke Korin, and he held himself still, finding that if he stayed complacent, he could sometimes avoid the worst of Ashel's cruelties, though the last few days had been a long, continuous nightmare.

"It's time to wake up, darling," Ashel murmured in his ear. After a kiss on his lips, Ashel left the blankets and stirred up the fire. Korin lay weak with relief, then quickly rose. He swayed an instant, dizzy, and sought with his fingers the leather cord tight on his neck. He didn't dare loosen it and wearily began to fold the blankets and gather their few belongings.

Ashel stopped him with a touch on his arm as he reached for a pot to fill with water for coffee. Korin carefully met his critical eyes. Ashel lifted a strand of Korin's dirty hair in distaste. "Wash while you're at the creek. You're not taking care of yourself as you should."

"Yes, my lord."

Ashel growled and pulled Korin roughly against him, pressing bruising kisses on his mouth. "You're still beautiful," Ashel assured him.

"Thank you." Korin kissed his palm, because Ashel liked it, then shuffled to the nearby stream. He stared at the glittering water where the morning sun touched it and thought if he could only take one full breath of air, he'd feel better. He stripped out of his filthy clothes, wincing as fresh scabs were torn open, and washed them first.

The water flowed only a few hand spans deep at the bend, and he lowered himself in and stretched his length on the pebbly bed. The water was ice on his warm skin, and in an instant he was shivering. Korin scrubbed his hair with sand and rinsed it, then used the sand carefully on the open sores. Unable to reach his back, he rubbed it on the river rock beneath him.

At last, he dragged himself from the water and put on the wet clothing. He was pulling viciously at the leather strap on his neck to stretch it when he heard a step and turned in panic. His heart lurched and a trembling smile sprang on his lips. "Syros!"

"Korin, you're coming with me, now."

Syros's harshness confused him. Were they no longer friends? Feeling suddenly lost, he turned his eyes away as the scalding tears gathered.

"Korin." Syros's tone gentled. "I only want to free you from that madman."

"No. You mustn't try. He can get into my mind and see you. But listen," he stepped closer to Syros, darting a gaze around the glen. "I found out his secret. Ashel knows how to take Ethan's powers for himself the moment Lord Aiden attempts to seize them." He nodded vigorously at Syros's surprise. "He knows Willum's plans. There's little we can hide from him, but the great lords don't know how powerful he is. Tell them. Tell the Mage."

"Come with me, my dear. You can let them know yourself."

"No! Ashel mustn't find out I told. He'd change his arrangements." Korin took a step back and blinked at a sudden frightening, wonderful thought. He smiled as a strange peace settled over him.

"Korin?"

He laughed a little at the suspicion in Syros's voice, though his heart was breaking. He wished they'd had more time…

"I need to go back. Take care, Syros. You've always been kind, even when I didn't deserve it."

"What do you mean to do?"

"Nothing." He shrugged. "But if Ashel succeeds in killing me, it won't matter so much now."

He turned with a little wave, meaning to be free one way or another that day. Syros grabbed his arm, and he froze, waiting for the painful twist. He laughed shakily when it didn't come. Of course Syros wouldn't hurt him. He might even love him a tiny bit. "Let me go, Syros."

"Not until I have your promise."

"Which one?" He tried to appear indifferent but his heart thumped.

"You're to stay alive, Korin."

"I won't stay with him!" The leather tightened on his throat with his exertion and his head swam. They glared at each other.

"What of us?"

White agony poured through Korin, and he hated Syros at that moment. He spoke in a low hiss, "I can't think you'll want me after you know the things Ashel has done with me. Better he should kill me."

Syros stepped closer and clutched Korin's damp shirt. "Never say that! Never think it. You stay alive, Korin. I don't care at what cost."

"Why?"

Korin flinched as Syros touched his face, his fingers sliding to the cord binding his neck. Anger flashed over his face, quickly stifled.

"Because I love you, my dear, but you know that." Syros pressed a tender kiss on his mouth, which nearly broke his heart.

"Your lips are blue. Go back to the fire. And, Korin, trust that a better time is coming. Believe in the Mage. He'll save us. And if not," Syros added as an afterthought, "I will kill Ashel myself to free you."

Korin looked in the steel gray eyes and saw the compassion and tenderness hidden in their depths.

"Very well," he murmured hoarsely. He took a step toward the camp, and despair swept him. How was he to go back when he yearned with all his heart for Syros's arms? He drew as full a breath as he could, stood straight, and went to Ashel.

The fire was wonderfully hot, and he ignored Ashel's dark stare as he held his hands out to the flames. Unaware of the depth of Ashel's anger, he was unprepared when Ashel's fist slammed against his ear and sent him to the dirt. He instantly prostrated himself. Ashel's boot caught him in the ribs, but he bit his tongue rather than cry out.

Ashel gripped his hair and jerked him roughly to his knees, a dangerous light flickering in his dark eyes. "Were you trying to escape, my dear?"

"I was washing!"

Ashel continued to stare at him and a knot gathered in Korin's stomach. "I think you need to be punished."

"I was doing as you asked…" Korin clenched his teeth. Pleading would do no good. The tingle started in his feet this time, growing painfully hot, and suddenly flames burst to life on his skin and raced up his legs, engulfing him. He opened his mouth to scream his agony, but the leather at his neck caught his breath and he was drowning. His head roared, blinding him with pain.

As he slipped into wonderful darkness, he felt a sharp prick on his neck. Air rushed into his lungs, and he wept as he gulped in deep breaths. The fire was gone from his mind, and he sank back on his heels, wrapping his arms around a body that shook with violent tremors.

Ashel knelt beside him, raised his chin, and made a soft sound of pity as he smoothed back Korin's damp hair.

"You shouldn't anger me," he chided gently. His touch stung on

Korin's neck where the knife had cut his skin, and Korin saw a gleam enter Ashel's dark blue eyes as he stared at the crimson smear on his fingers. He shuddered as Ashel bent and kissed the spot on his neck.

"Don't," he begged as the burning mouth trailed up his neck and across his lips.

"I shall," Ashel promised. Korin whimpered as Ashel's thoughts slipped silkily into his mind and stirred confusion and powerlessness and a strange yearning, and the hands that could bring such pain brought exquisite pleasure, entangling Korin in the passions of the moment.

After Ashel finished with him, he made Korin wash in the creek again and allowed him to stand by the fire to dry his clothes while Ashel sat on a nearby rock and drank his tea. It passed noon before they broke camp. Korin dowsed the fire and turned to find Ashel at his side running a strip of cord through his fingers. He dropped to his knees without a word. Ashel patted his head as he fixed a noose around his neck and pulled it tight.

"It's to keep you docile, my sweet," Ashel explained as he wiped Korin's tears with a thumb. "Can't have you running off."

For an instant Korin thought his chest would burst, but then he adjusted to the short, rapid breathing the noose allowed. He staggered to his feet, flung the pack over a shoulder, and went to the horses staked nearby. He climbed onto his mount with some difficulty, then followed Ashel's horse through the trees as best he could.

It was twilight before Siagan's walls came into view. Ashel stopped on a small rise overlooking the city and dismounted. Korin eased down off his horse onto a rock close by and hung his head, dizzy and sick. He rubbed his eyes.

Ashel gripped his chin and Korin tried to focus on his angry face.

Why was he mad? He would like some water. The dark spots that had gathered in his eyes all day began to dance, and Korin watched them curiously. He felt the sting of Ashel's hand on his face, but Ashel was a gray blob against the darkness, and Korin almost laughed as he lost his balance and toppled sideways.

He murmured sleepily when Ashel drew his head onto his lap.

"There, there," Ashel crooned and brushed a few strands of hair from Korin's face. Korin blinked, drowsy and confused, and heard Ashel's quickly drawn breath. Ashel bent to his ear. "You captivate me, Korin. I wish things could always be as they are now, peaceful, with the man I love in my arms. But there's a churning blackness within me that's never far away. You rouse it with a single derisive glance or foolish act. Be careful! I could kill you in a rage, and then life would hold nothing for me."

He slipped the sharp little knife from his boot and carefully cut the cord biting into Korin's soft neck, admitting it may have been too snug that time. Korin drew a painful breath, and then sobs broke from him. He turned his face against Ashel's side, and Ashel stroked his hair.

"I won't put it on you again, darling," Ashel promised in a choked voice.

Korin relaxed slowly. He groped and found Ashel's hand and brought the palm to his lips. "May I have water?" he asked in a tiny whisper.

Ashel smiled indulgently. "Sit up, love," he said, and helped him sit cross-legged beside him. Korin took a swallow from the water flask, and then he drank greedily. Ashel laughed as he pulled it away. "Easy, darling! You can have some more in a moment."

Ashel stared thoughtfully at the city below. "Will you stay here while I see how my dear friend Ethan is doing?"

Korin gave a careful nod.

"Promise me."

"I promise," he muttered. Ashel touched his face, and Korin flinched, expecting pain. "I promise, Ashel," he said urgently, and Ashel nodded, satisfied.

Ashel rose and studied the city again. "I'll soon have Ethan's powers, and then you'll come to me willingly," he said. He spent several moments describing the ways he'd spoil Korin in the future, when they were together forever.

There was the flicker of movement at Siagan's gates, and Ashel narrowed his eyes, then turned and snatched up his pack.

"Wait here," he ordered brusquely and walked into the trees. Korin waited for his return, the knot in his chest tightening. Fear kept him immobile until exhaustion finally won out, and he huddled on the ground and fell asleep.

A loud crack of thunder roused him from his stupor sometime later, and he rolled onto his back, blinking at the rising moon through high clouds. Throwing off his languor, he took an anxious look around, then struggled to his feet, disgusted by his own timidity. Ashel wouldn't have everything his way. He'd promised Ashel he wouldn't leave, and he wouldn't. He was just going for a walk.

The rocky landscape appeared beautiful in the moonlight as he wandered, but he hated it. It only stirred longings for a man with piercing gray eyes and tender hands. He groaned aloud.

"Korin?"

He jumped at the voice, darting a glance this way and that. He was on an outcrop of rock; hard to distinguish shapes from shadows. A tall form detached from the darkness, and Korin held his ground with great effort, then lost his breath. Syros walked up to him, his intelligent eyes studying him, cautious. But then Syros's gaze softened, and he tugged Korin into his arms. Korin resisted out of habit, then sank his head onto Syros's shoulder.

Syros pressed a kiss to the top of his head and held him until he stopped shaking.

"I was coming for you, despite Ashel," Syros murmured fiercely. "How did you get away? Never mind that now," he added hastily. "Come to the fire."

He took Korin's hand, and Korin's heart sped as Syros led him no small distance to a clearing between tall boulders. A sparse fire burned at its center, and Korin dropped down gratefully beside it, holding out his hands to the warmth and light.

Syros crouched opposite, then handed across a water flask. Korin nearly broke down but gathered his remaining strength and sipped at the water though he wanted to swallow it all in one gulp. Syros studied him and swore under his breath. Korin watched with interest as he dug in a nearby pack and drew out a packet of dried fruit, handing it to him. Korin fumbled with the wrapping in his eagerness, and Syros came across and knelt beside him.

"Let me," Syros offered, voice gruff, and took the packet from him, deftly untying the string and handing him the open paper.

Korin stared at the bright fruit, tears blurring his sight. Gods, he was exhausted, and hunger gnawed his gut. Syros made an impatient movement and picked up a small cherry, bringing it to Korin's lips, which parted with his surprise. He bit down and moaned as the sweet taste burst on his tongue.

Syros sucked in a breath. "How did you escape, Korin?" he asked gently.

Korin shrugged. "Ashel went to spy on Ethan, so I walked away." He took up another cherry. "He'll kill me for it."

"You're not going back to him," Syros warned, a growl in his voice, matching the rumble of thunder from the passing storm.

"Doesn't matter. He'll find me eventually and kill me with a look."

Syros frowned, lines of worry forming between his brows. "I'll not allow it."

Korin nodded, having faint hope anyone could save him if Ashel decided he should die. And kill Syros for harboring him. The fire crackled and he leaned against Syros, finding a comfortable position as his lover continued to feed him. He needed to find a safe place to hide close by, one Ashel couldn't reach and would keep Syros from harm. Unbidden, the walls of Siagan came to mind. Ashel would never look for him there—he'd be too busy with Ethan—and it would give him the opportunity to do reconnaissance for Syros. He must be anxious to know what's going on behind those tall ramparts.

He sat up, drawing Syros's attention before he changed his mind. "I've thought of a place I would be out of Ashel's reach. Dangerous as death, yet…"

"Tell me," Syros said, and Korin nearly laughed at the suspicion in his tone. Syros knew him too well.

"I'll go to Ethan. Listen!" he interrupted Syros's instant objection. His heart thumped as he outlined his plan, meeting all Syros's heated arguments with cool reasoning. "I'll be perfectly safe. Ethan has no cause to do me harm. And you can't deny my logic. We need someone on the inside."

"You've given too much!" Syros scrubbed a hand over his face, then wrapped Korin in his arms, his tears a surprise against Korin's neck.

"And the Mage plans to give everything he has and is. This is small in comparison. Yes, I wish I was far from here, but we have few options, none of them safe. If there was another way… I don't see it." Korin ran out of words, exhaustion and near despair laying a heavy blanket over his abused body. He squirmed, stretching his legs out.

Syros pulled him back against his chest, and Korin heard the hitch in his voice when he spoke. "I hate everything about this. I say we run away and let the great powers fight it out." He sighed. "But I see you're committed to this battle, so I'll stay and fight with you. Yes, having someone inside Siagan would be a tremendous help. Sleep, love. I'll watch over you," Syros promised, murmuring words of love and pride in Korin's ear until sleep finally came for him.

Chapter Seventeen

WILLUM STOOD ON the wall of Barkuit in his black uniform of soft leather and linen and looked over the beautiful city, the bright buildings, and attractive roads. Syros had begun the restorations as regent, and Willum continued them as governor. His people lined the streets to see them off, the soldiers moving in ranks, silver and black uniforms gleaming in the sunlight, thousands strong. Pride stirred in him. They were the most formidable army on the continent, and if he'd had time to mobilize all of the North, they'd be unstoppable.

The Barkuit people spied him and a cheer rose on the air. Willum bowed as his name was taken up until it rang in the sky. Then he slipped from the wall, going to the courtyard below. His heart rushed as he swung into the saddle of his waiting horse and led the Barkuit soldiers onto the plains, and to war. It had been coming for some time, a restlessness in the blood, the Barkuit people growing uneasy and distrustful as rumors spread from Siagan.

They went at an easy pace, their first camp a half-day's trek south, where supplies and gear had been stored. Everything must be in order for their forced march to Siagan. They would approach the city from the north-west and engage them. Willum frowned. He'd prefer to take the city peace-fully, but he held little hope for that. It was difficult to take war to his own people, whom he'd sworn to protect and guide. He shook his head. Ethan pushed too hard, a foreigner, and some of Willum's people followed him. It was time to push back.

Once out of sight of the city, he jumped from the saddle, preferring to walk with the men rather than act the privileged lord. Evening found them at the camp set up by Captain Gael, and the men smiled in apprecia-tion for the waiting tents and a cooked meal. Willum searched out the cap-tain of his personal guard and newly appointed military advisor and found him over a fire stirring something that smelled wonderful.

"Gael!"

A grin touched the captain's attractive face as he rose, and they gripped hands tightly. Next to Syros, Gael was the one man Willum trusted—blunt and honest, without ambition for the moment beyond his present rank. More than that, Willum enjoyed his dry humor and easy com-radeship. He found they had much in common, not least of all a profound love for their country and its people.

"Why didn't you ride?" Gael inquired when Willum let out a hiss as he removed his boots, footsore.

"Ride while the others walked their horses? May as well thrust a knife into my own back," he joked, though they both knew it was close to the truth. The Barkuit soldiers were a tough lot, despising weakness. Gael reached for a bowl and handed Willum stew and some biscuits he'd hoarded.

After eating, Willum walked through the camp as darkness settled, the soldiers turning to their blankets in preparation for an early morning. He stopped outside the glow of the campfires and stared across the plains. Stars illuminated the sky, and the half-moon touched the horizon on his left. The silhouette of rocks that held Gregor of Sennia's grave, who'd been the Mage before Natan, beckoned him.

It was quiet in the small glen, and he sat with his back to a large boulder, his legs outstretched toward the carne. He hadn't known the Mage, but even so, the knot in his chest at the coming battle eased. He settled more comfortably, hunching into his cloak, and breathed deeply of the cool air. In less than a heartbeat, he closed his eyes and slept in peace.

*

SYROS SAT ON the rocks overlooking Siagan and surveyed the sleeping city as the sun rose. The air was crisp, scented with pine and faint woodsmoke; bright, unlike his tumultuous thoughts. He remembered when Davis had first taken control of Siagan's council. In a few short years he'd transformed the city from squalor to a place to be proud of. The streets and walls repaired; the buildings gleamed and gardens bloomed.

He swore softly, shouldering the blame for what was happening now. He should have paid more attention. But he'd settled comfortably into Kangar and a delightful life with Sharana and ignored any unwelcomed news coming from Siagan. Then he let an unseasoned boy become governor, taking command of the North.

Syros rubbed his face, knowing that wasn't true. Willum was more than capable of governing. Together they'd shaped the Northern Territory into something prosperous and growing. Mandel, and then Ethan, had been clever and deceitful and taken them all by surprise.

Tyrel crouched on the rocks beside him and handed him a mug. Syros gratefully sipped the coffee. "Is Korin ready?"

"Yes." Tyrel frowned. "Are you sure this is a wise move? If things go wrong…"

Syros was brusque. He'd sent men into danger before. He never liked it. And the fact it was his lover this time… That should make no difference, so he pushed the fear from his heart. "We need a man inside and Ethan won't be able to resist Korin. A pretty addition to his army of sycophants."

"Didn't you say Korin was in his hands once before?"

"Yes, and I believe he'll hesitate to kill him, curious to find out how he'd escaped, wonder how he could use him. Korin will be able to slip under his guard and get the information we need."

"And if he's caught?"

"Then we go in and bring him out."

Tyrel looked skeptical and Syros wanted to hurt him. Korin would walk a knife's edge of danger in Siagan. Tyrel didn't need to tell him that. But the world was in peril and risks had to be taken, damn their eyes. And he hadn't been able to dissuade Korin…

Korin appeared below their perch and Syros scrambled down the rock face, dropping beside him. His heart smote him. Korin stole his breath, morning sunlight turning his hair a glorious flame, but his sea blue eyes were uncharacteristically somber.

"Do you still want to do this?"

Korin nodded once. "I'll send a message when I can."

Syros gently touched Korin's neck near the angry rope burn, and his resolve faltered. He leaned to Korin's ear. "Come away with me, right now. We can be at my home in Kangar by nightfall and catch a ship anywhere we wish."

Korin's breathing hitched, but he shook his head. "Let me do this, Syros. I'm not a brave or strong soldier, able to fight off armies with my valiant sword." He ignored Syros's snort. "But I can wheedle my way into most men's good graces. I can at least do this. I will learn Ethan's secrets."

Syros growled in his throat. "That means little to me at the moment. I would see Belega sunk to the bottom of the ocean if it meant you were safe."

Astonishment and a sudden deep longing flickered on Korin's sweet face, then a brilliant, false smile lifted his full lips. "Why Syros, one would think you cared." He moved quickly and gave Syros a hard kiss, which Syros returned in kind. Then Korin jerked away and headed toward Siagan, waving over his shoulder.

"Take care," Syros whispered and climbed the rock again to watch him enter the city.

*

KORIN STOOD BEFORE the gates of Siagan and wondered what the hell he was doing there. He'd left Fredrik's Hall and a life he knew and found himself swept up in politics he didn't understand. He felt small and overwhelmed and wondered if there was a bigger fool than he in all the world. Then he remembered Syros's concern, and the cherished memory served to conquer fear and uncertainty.

He pounded on the heavy planks of the gate, and it swung open to admit him. The guards watched him closely, so Korin knew his approach had been reported to Ethan, and his entrance cautiously permitted.

They led him through the awakening streets of the city into the castle. A fire burned on the hearth in the great hall, doing little to dispel the cold, where they told him to wait. He stared at the flames and took a breath, gathering his courage as footsteps echoed in the adjoining room.

Ethan surprised him. He'd become gaunt since they'd last met, his golden eyes feverish, piercing. They surveyed each other in silence, and then Ethan inclined his head.

"Korin, well met," he murmured in a raspy voice that slithered down Korin's back. "Welcome once again to Siagan. Will you join me in the court-yard? It's far more pleasant than this cold hall."

"Thank you, lord." Korin swept a low bow. He'd need to endear him-self to the Red Twin quickly.

Ethan gave an enigmatic smile, putting a hand on his shoulder. His speculative eyes never left Korin as he led him through the kitchen to the sprawling garden in the back. He waved Korin to a bench in the shade of a tall oak, and an attendant handed Korin a cool glass of wine, then disap-peared on soundless feet.

Ethan sat uncomfortably close. "You made your escape, Korin. I'm curious to know how. But more importantly, what brings you back to my city?" He absently touched Korin's hair, shining in the sunlight, and tugged gently.

Korin studied the condensation on the wine glass. "I felt a great stir-ring of power in Siagan. It drew me here, almost irresistibly."

Ethan watched his face. "To take it?"

Korin snorted. "As if I could. But I am inclined to study its usage.

Lord Fredrik taught me sparingly, begrudging his powers. I'd like to learn from you." He slanted Ethan a heated glance, then demurely lowered his gaze. "You frightened me last time, but I believe I can be of service to you. If you'll have me."

"Perhaps. But let us speak of your escape…"

Korin's mind raced. "Mandel wanted me. I didn't want him. One of his soldiers aided my escape before we learned of the lord's death." *Not far from the truth.*

"And the soldier who helped you? After Mandel's demise?"

"I slit his throat and ran far from here."

"Wonderful! Such a resourceful man. Perhaps you can be of use to me after all." Ethan jumped up and restlessly paced a cobbled pathway and back, head bent in thought, then resumed his seat beside Korin. "I'll visit the lake tonight. Would you care to come?" he asked, sounding like an eager child.

"If you wish," Korin said, though a shudder passed through him as he remembered a dark room and his imprisonment. Ethan's unbalanced state was apparent, but there was something more, a dark unknown lurking in his glittering eyes that unnerved Korin.

Ethan chatted amiably as if they were longtime friends and offered to give him a tour of the city in the afternoon.

"I have some business to attend to at present," Ethan apologized as he reluctantly rose to his feet. "Feel free to explore the garden and dwellings, but I'll ask you not to leave the castle unescorted."

"As you will."

Ethan gave him a shrewd glance. Korin met his gaze, breath held, and felt he had passed some test when Ethan smiled, lifting a hand as he left him in the fragrant yard.

After he'd gone, Korin drank his wine. He had little doubt Ethan mistrusted him, let him live for his own purpose, whatever that might be. After a time, he rose to his feet and explored the winding pathways through tangled, flowering growth, finding that the garden opened into an apple orchard at the back. A high wall enclosed the area. Hearing water, he searched until he found a tiny stream meandering through the trees for irrigation. He stopped to watch the sunlight playing on its rippling surface. What did Ethan have planned for the future? Nothing good, he could be sure.

Movement caught Korin's eye and he spotted a young man a short distance downstream from him. He stifled a surprised cry. The figure waded into the stream, then lowered himself into the icy water, fully clothed, rubbing sand over his tattered uniform with hands that shook. He washed and rinsed his hair the same way, then pulled himself to the bank and sprawled in the sun.

Korin moved closer and saw that the soldier's cheeks were sunken, great hollows surrounded his eyes. His clothing hung loose and ragged on a skeletal frame. Korin must have made a sound because the man opened turbulent brown eyes and scrambled to his feet, panting with the exertion.

"Forgive me, lord." He bowed with painful effort. "I didn't mean… I didn't expect…" He gave up and looked away.

Korin studied him, drawing a quick breath when he recognized the soldier who'd helped him escape Siagan the first time. He put his hand out. "Derik, are you ill?" He touched Derik's arm in concern and felt the death in him. He drew back with an involuntary cry, and a sob broke from the soldier.

Derik hid his face in his hands, seeming shamed. "I'm sorry. I didn't mean for anyone to see me." His tone was proud and he bowed again, then hurried away on legs scarcely able to support him.

Korin ached to follow, but the stark fear in Derik's eyes held him in place. How had this come to be? Had Ethan found out Derik was the one who'd helped him escape and tortured him for it? No, Ethan would have called out Korin's lie earlier, when he said he'd killed the soldier who'd aided him. Ethan must be misusing Derik for some hidden purpose. He clenched his hands, determined to help the suffering soldier if he did nothing else on this strange mission.

A long afternoon passed, broken by Ethan's cursory tour of the city, as promised. Korin could see decay besetting the once beautiful streets. Sullen eyes watched them from darkened doorways. Vigilant, Korin searched for any glimpse of Ashel, but the man remained hidden, and Ethan gave no indication he'd seen the trespasser. Korin wasn't surprised. Ashel had always been sly.

They ate a simple meal, but Korin could hardly swallow as the tension grew in his chest. When finished, Ethan took him through the kitchen to the cellar doorway. It surprised him that the heavy door was unlatched.

"Who would dare enter?" Ethan queried, and then excitement seemed to seize him. Korin hid his aversion as a strange gleam slipped through Ethan's golden eyes. They descended the stairs to the empty cellar, and Ethan motioned him to the gaping hole widened in the far wall. Lifting his hand, a light too bright to gaze on filled the tunnel.

"This way." Ethan strode like a king down the steep incline. A shiver of dread ran through Korin as he followed. He remembered the knife Syros had given him, hidden in his boot. Would he need to use it soon?

The air felt cool in the passages below the city, and he grew chilled as he followed Ethan along a narrow artery that branched to the left of the main tunnel. He knew the lake waited below. The power of the earth thrummed in his body in mounting waves. Yet deep beneath that energy he sensed an intense sadness and despair. He watched the Red Twin ahead of him with horror. What had he done down there beneath the ground?

They stood at the lake's edge. Ethan raised his hand and the light shimmered across the water like starlight. Korin fell on his knees in awe and placed his hands on water that bit coldly into his palms. Without any magic of his own, he still felt a wound in the earth, not allowed to heal, kept open by the man at his side. He swooned, and it took all his effort to pull himself from the dark brink. Such power was never meant to be held by any man.

Korin staggered to his feet, slowly coming back to himself. He looked at Ethan, and the lust exposed on his slack features made him ill. The golden eyes were unfocused, and Korin backed away from him in fear.

But the lake appeared a glimmering opal, bewitching him. Korin walked in bemusement along its narrow shore, almost missing the dark shadow in the wall he'd looked for. He gazed through the broken doorway and knew it was Lady Kirstin's prison. His heart hurt for her, for himself. Her loneliness must have been complete, waiting the long years for Bryon to release her. His own short time there had been horror beyond thought.

Drawn irresistibly, Korin stepped inside, and his broken cry shattered the silence. Derik slept on the damp earth, arms wrapped around his shivering body. In the flickering light from the lake, his expression was that of a small child, lost and afraid. Why was he in that terrible place? Korin glanced back at the man at the lake, and anger rose up in him that nearly smothered his good sense.

The soft cry of pain from the sleeping soldier saved him. He'd almost given in to the lure of the immense energy waiting to be called to life, to strike out at Ethan with it. He had to leave that cave, now, or be as lost as Ethan. He gave Derik an anguished glance, but he couldn't stay, even for him. He fled the chamber, but Ethan called to him and he had to go to his side.

"Beautiful, isn't it?" Ethan murmured and slipped an arm around Korin's waist as they faced the water, but Korin's tears blurred its shimmering surface. Small and alone, he longed for Syros to come, hold him, and keep him safe.

*

KORIN SAT ON a bench in the garden the next morning and let the sun warm his face. Ethan and he had spent the long hours of the night at the lake, and he rejoiced to be outside. Ethan had spoken of the day he'd first visited the lake, learned to draw the energies of the world into himself and send it out again. He'd spoken of the people he'd manipulated, the men he'd destroyed. Korin had little doubt he himself would be used like Derik soon enough.

Once during the night, low sobs, quickly stifled, had escaped from the dark cell in the cavern. The lonely sound had broken Korin's heart.

He heard the click of the garden gate and peered through half-closed eyes, blinking against the brightness. He quickly sat up, gripping the sweet bread he'd brought from the kitchen. Derik crept down the path toward the water. His quick gaze darted around the garden, but he failed to see Korin, screened by a rosebush. His steps were cautious, his face pinched with extreme anxiety. He stopped at the water's edge, and a smile of delight touched his cracked lips, perhaps at the sunlight glittering on the clear surface.

Korin looked away as Derik stepped out of his clothes and entered the stream. He washed as before and pulled his dusty uniform into the water and cleaned that as well. When satisfied, he climbed onto the bank and dressed in the damp clothing. He sprawled in the sunshine on the grass, worn by that little effort, his expression one of content as his eyes fluttered closed.

After a moment Korin approached him—and swallowed a shout. For a brief heartbeat he feared he gazed at a corpse. Derik had grown worse during the night, body emaciated, the hands touching the soft grass, bony claws. His skull was plain to see under the tight skin. Derik whimpered, perhaps sensing his presence, and the dark eyes flew open. He scrambled to sit up with a breath of dismay.

"Don't be frightened," Korin said gently and knelt beside him, smiling with reassurance and friendship. Derik leaned back on his hands, panting hard, and slowly the fear left his eyes.

Compassion overwhelmed Korin. Derik appeared starved to death. "Will you eat with me?" He didn't know what else to say and held up the sweet bread.

Derik gave him a strange, fey look. "I don't eat…anymore," he said with slight hysteria.

"But you'll die."

"I have died! Over and over." Derik moaned into his hands. "He won't let me go."

"Derik." Korin touched his knee in pity, and Derik rose with a wail of despair and fled back to the castle, his broken sobs ringing in Korin's ears long after he'd gone.

Korin spent the morning in the garden, then reluctantly joined Ethan in the dining hall for a meal at noon. The Red Twin sat alone, and Korin took his own chair with dismay, realizing it would be only the two of them once again. He found Ethan's company unsettling at best.

Servants brought in dishes. Korin took a bite of the savory broth, then suddenly had trouble swallowing as Ethan's glittering eyes met his.

"Can I help you, my lord?" he croaked and cleared his throat.

"I think it's time." Ethan nodded and rocked in his chair. "Yes, I believe I can trust you. You're my friend, are you not?"

"Of course." Korin watched him closely. Madness had the upper hand that day.

"Come with me." Ethan abruptly left his chair and swept from the room. Korin dropped his spoon and hurried after him. He caught up to Ethan at the front entrance and followed him into the street. Ethan seemed unusually animated and muttered incessantly to himself.

It took some time to reach the eastern wall of the city, and Ethan giggled as they climbed the steps to the balustrade. Korin's blood turned to ice as he looked over the wall. Hundreds of Barkuit soldiers were encamped in the fields beyond the city.

"We're almost ready," Ethan assured him. "When the great lords come to Siagan, we'll be able to greet them properly."

"Why?" The question leaped from Korin's mouth without thought, his voice choked.

"We're the stronger. Surely the strongest should rule?"

A passing soldier raised his head at that moment, filling Korin with dread. Hate and power-lust suffused the pale face, violence promised in the blazing eyes. A hard shudder swept Korin as the man prostrated before Ethan. Clearly, the soldier would follow the mad lord to death itself if asked.

They left the wall and Korin excused himself. Sick with worry, he walked along the crumbling streets with blind eyes. At last, he sat by a choked fountain and covered his face. He didn't want to be there! He suffered a moment of loneliness and doubt and only slowly became aware of a voice calling softly to him. He raised his head. "Hello?"

He spied Derik crouching in the straggling flowers. Derik glanced keenly around and approached him, skittish and unsure. "What is wrong, my lord?"

Korin's heart ached for him. "Will you sit with me?"

Derik flushed as he sat cross-legged on the paving stones. Korin noted that he kept his face averted.

"You needn't turn away," he said softly, once again moved to pity. The tiny smile that touched Derik's skeletal, mottled face, broke his heart.

"You're very kind, but I have seen my reflection," Derik's voice caught. "I was handsome once. You might remember. Let me serve you, lord," he pleaded, and Korin realized he was begging to be treated as a man again, to have some purpose other than a crazed lord's whim.

Korin shook his head in dismay. "You can't aid me. I'm sorry. I need to get a message outside the walls. No one can help with that."

A sly smile slid across Derik's face. "I can."

Korin went still. "How, my friend?"

Derik shrugged his thin shoulders under the tattered uniform. "I can go where I will. Ethan calls me and I go to him, however far I am." His voice dropped, lost. "He compels me, and I cannot resist, wherever I may be."

"I'll be in your debt," Korin said gravely.

Derik raised startled eyes. "No, my lord. There'll be no talk of debt between us. I'll go because you've been kind when all others turn their eyes from me." He wrinkled his brow. "I'll go when I'll be missed the least, to be sure."

"Why don't you leave for good?" Korin urged.

Derik shrugged again. "I'm too much Ethan's creature. Only he can release me…to death."

Derik wept silently and Korin had no words to comfort him. Death might find them all, unless the men of power, Natan and Aiden and Alek, found a way to save them.

Chapter Eighteen

CECIL WOKE AND glared at the morning light on the ceiling. This was the day Alek would leave the city. He dressed and had to sit a moment to rest, pressing fingers to his chest where it hurt when he coughed.

After stopping in the kitchen for some sweet bread and coffee, he wandered into the garden and found Alek alone by the fountain. "Will I disturb you?"

Alek gave him a smile "No. I've been waiting for you."

Cecil sat on the stone bench and offered a slice of the flaky bread. "Where is everyone?"

"We're done, for our part. Now we wait for Aiden's guidance." He held out a hand. "Come, walk with me."

They strolled through the waiting city, and Cecil refrained from speaking, not wanting to break their tenuous connection. When they reached the western gate, Alek had it opened and Cecil followed him without question. They made their way to the harbor, in no great hurry, and Alek laced their fingers as they stepped onto the beach.

They walked a while on the warm sand, then found a place in the shade to rest. Alek sat and pulled Cecil into his arms and touched his hair. A shadow crossed his face and he gave a shaky laugh. "You seem so fragile!" Cecil's skin was translucent in the morning light, and he knew his eyes were smudged with bruises.

Cecil leaned into him and twined his hands through the dark hair surrounding Alek's face. "I won't break," he promised against Alek's mouth, and his blood raced when Alek kissed him in the old way. He coughed abruptly, breaking them apart, and he swore as Alek's heart slowed under his ear.

Alek admonished him, forcing his chin up so their eyes met. "Kavi said it will take time for you to heal. You'll regain your strength soon enough."

"I'm fine," he grumbled, but Alek's hold tightened as he coughed again. Alek murmured soft words and settled him comfortably in his arms, stroking his fair hair.

"Kirstin is on her way to us," Alek murmured against his hair. "She will know what to do."

"Of course."

Cecil grew drowsy as the day warmed, sleeping intermittently as the morning crossed into afternoon.

Alek woke him suddenly from a dream. "It's here."

Cecil peered through the trees, and though he usually loved the sight of a sleek ship and trim sail, he loathed this one. "It will be another hour before they reach us."

"I have to get to the harbor. The Red Twin calls us." Alek pushed him away and climbed to his feet. "Hurry."

Alek quickly outpaced him, and it surprised Cecil to see the crowd at the harbor when he approached. It appeared that every Karthagan had come to meet the ship and hear Aiden's words. There was a strange quietness about the waiting people, their handsome faces grave. Alek had confided to him how no one but Aiden had fully recovered their abilities, yet many had recently felt the stirring of energy in their blood. They would use it if bidden, though it broke their hearts. Many had perished on the Isle of Wind when the Karthagan people had used their powers, one against the other. At that time the Red Twins, even as children, had nearly destroyed the world in their lust for more.

"We fear it will come to that again," Alek had confessed with deep sadness.

Cecil now scanned the crowd and spied Kavi on the dock with Alek, proud lords awaiting their commander. Ellis stood a little apart from the others on the sand and seemed utterly alone.

"Ellis?"

Ellis glanced at him as he walked up, his amber eyes glowing. "Cecil." He tilted his head, and his dark hair danced on his shoulder. "You look tired today."

"I am, a little."

Ellis's attention swiveled back to the ship. The anchor dropped and soon the vessel was close enough for them to make out the sailors on the decking and the man who stood inflexible as granite at the prow. A cry went up at the sight of the Red Twin, the crowd's anticipation a prickle on Cecil's skin.

"Will you stay with me?" Ellis asked, trembling head to toe. Cecil knew it was a hard moment for him and took his hand, standing close beside him. The schooner touched the dock, and Aiden leaped over the side. The crowd parted silently for him as he passed through it. He went straight to Ellis and buried his face in his hair with a broken sob, crushing his slim body to him as Ellis clung to his arms.

Aiden smiled as he pulled away and caressed Ellis's face. He spared a glance at Cecil and embraced him as well. "How are you feeling? I'm sorry we couldn't stop Niko before he—"

Cecil interrupted him, chiding the man as he had the child, "You are not responsible for everything."

Aiden blinked in surprise, then gratefully inclined his head. He slipped an arm across Cecil's shoulders and steered him toward the city, clasping Ellis's hand as they walked. "Are the supplies and horses ready? Did you leave enough for the winter?"

"Aiden!" Cecil protested with a smile and waved a hand at the people around them. "I think they're expecting you to say something."

Only then did Aiden seem to take in the silent crowd, and a nervous chill shook him. He gave Ellis a pleading look, and Ellis nodded encouragement. "Kavi told me he was drawn here by an irresistible urge, as were the others. As if you were calling to them."

Aiden pressed Ellis's hand to his cheek and lips. "I'm frightened, darling. I don't recall…"

Ellis held him close. "It doesn't matter. We're here now, my heart. What do you need us to do?"

Aiden drew a hard breath. "Be brave," he urged and stepped away from Ellis to walk through the crowd. They gave way before him as if he carried a plague, closing behind him again as he stopped before Alek and Kavi. They bowed to him as one. Alek spoke, "How shall we serve you, lord?"

Aiden looked over the people and a cold smile touched his lips. "We are almost one hundred strong. My father, Kayden, had come close to conquering Gavin's clan with half as many. And Ethan and I—" He covered his eyes.

"There is a madness coming out of the North," he continued softly, and yet his voice resonated in the air and in Cecil's ears. "The old energies of the earth have been stirred to life in the black lake beneath Siagan. I can feel it as a sickness in my body. Soon it will spread to all, and the insanity that nearly destroyed our fathers will possess us. We'll go as one heart and mind to Siagan and stop this thing, once and for all. We will leave tonight."

He uncovered his eyes, and their molten gold shown in the sunlight. None could resist his words, and Cecil sucked in a breath as the Karthagans took a knee to him. Aiden never saw them. His gaze found Ellis, watching with pride and compassion, and went to him, lifting his hands to his lips.

Cecil gazed after them as they walked toward the city, his heart moved. Then he joined the others on the dock as Kayle climbed from the schooner and approached Kavi and Alek. "My lord." He bowed to Alek. His smile faltered. "Kavi?"

Kavi rubbed his eyes as if stirring from a dream. "Kayle?" He searched his face. "You look tired."

"I am." Kayle gazed to the northeast, toward Sennia, and a wonderful smile brightened his features. "But it's over for me. Whatever powers I had are gone. I'm going home to help repair the damage Niko has wrought. And see my wife."

Alek looked troubled but gave him a warm embrace. "It's good to have you back safely. We owe you our lives."

"No, my lord. It is all due to Aiden. He carries the burden for us."

Kavi took his arm, seeming to struggle for normalcy. "Shall we go home and have a meal before we pack the horses? You could probably use something hot and filling."

"That would be perfect."

Cecil stayed behind, forlorn in that unguarded moment as he leaned on the railing and stared at the glittering sea. So caught up the Red Twin's grave, dramatic return, Alek had passed within steps of Cecil without so much as a nod in his direction, preoccupied with unfolding events. Cecil worried for him.

He straightened, his keen eyes on the schooner as seamen came out of the hold and began to take in the remaining sail and start the chores of a ship in dock. He climbed on board and made his way to the tall man at the bulwark shouting orders. "Daran."

The captain glanced impatiently at him, sweat on his dark skin, then a smile lit his face, and he pulled Cecil into a rough hug. "Commander! It's good to see you free from that monster." His expression fell. "Forgive me. I know Niko had once been a friend."

"Yes." Cecil paused, cautious of the sailors near them. "I need to speak with you."

Daran frowned at his tone and noticed the attention of the men at hand. "At once. We can talk in my cabin," he offered and escorted Cecil below deck.

*

CECIL HURRIED FROM the docks. He hadn't meant to stay with Captain Daran for so long. The sunlight was going and Alek would be leaving soon. Upon reaching the city, he raced through the empty streets until his throat and chest burned. He didn't care. He reached the gates and fell against the framework, fighting for breath. The last of the horsemen were a dark smudge under the trees in the distance, and he thought his heart would burst with the disappointment of not saying goodbye.

"Alek," he grieved and didn't know how he would bear the separation now. Quick steps drew close, and he was pulled roughly into someone's arms. Fierce, bruising kisses were pressed on his lips and neck.

"I thought you'd gone," he choked out, his hands tangled in Alek's hair.

"Not without this," Alek growled and claimed his mouth again. Cecil held him tightly, returning his ardor, not wanting to let go. Would he ever hold him again?

"Take great care," he murmured finally and stepped back. They looked at each other a long moment, then Alek ran and leaped to his horse and raced after the torches disappearing into the forest.

Cecil watched until the last of the lights disappeared into the trees, then climbed the steps to the city's wall. Kavi was there, looking sullen, but Alek wouldn't have permitted him to travel to Siagan without Natan's approval. He trusted Natan's guidance in all things to bring them safely through the coming trial. Ellis was also there with the remaining Karthagans, the young and elderly and the ones whose health wouldn't permit the journey. Captain Daran's daughter, Riana, moved from Ellis's side and put an arm around him. Kayle pressed his shoulder in sympathy. Then his friends gathered close and fussed over him until he was laughing and blushing at their foolishness. He caught Ellis's eyes and shared a look of deep understanding, each knowing the other's grief and fear.

The sudden sound of hoofbeats on the trail approaching the city caught their attention. A barely discernable rider appeared out of the gloom of the forest. Cecil moved to the edge of the parapet, joined by the others.

"Kirstin!" he called down on recognizing the rider. Kirstin waved and Kavi descended the steps to meet her at the gates.

"Why has she come alone? That was reckless." Ellis frowned as Kavi ushered her into the city.

"She's always kept her own counsel," Kayle observed softly. "And she can protect herself. Have no doubt of that."

Cecil added, "Alek sent for her. He'd hoped she would be here to greet Aiden and ride with them to Siagan. Her healing powers will be needed." He watched Kavi and Kirstin speak with the soldier Eon, then walk with him along the wide street. "They are headed for the Redwood. Shall we join them?"

Cecil hastened his steps as they approached the tree and trotted to the woman standing beneath its wide branches before taking a knee. "My lady Kirstin."

Kirstin smiled as she pulled him to his feet. "You seem exhausted. Are you well?"

"Well enough." He motioned to the benches. "Please, sit and tell us your news."

She glanced at the assembled party. "I had hoped to be here sooner. I have a message for Aiden but it seems I am too late."

"Didn't you pass them on the trail?" Kavi asked, his tone neutral though his eyes sparked.

Kirstin bit her lip. "They'd already reached the plains when I saw them, and my horse is too fatigued to chase after. I came with all haste, but not quick enough, it appears."

"What was the message?" Cecil asked to forestall Kavi's disapproval.

Kirstin wrung her hands as she answered, her gaze taking them in one by one. "It comes from Fredrik's Hall. Lord Nelson has been killed by his cousin Ashel. Apparently, Ashel has powers even beyond Fredrik's. He's ambitious and cruel, and the Mage fears he will go after Ethan, and Aiden will be caught between the two of them. But that's not all."

She ran a trembling hand over her face. "There's something else Aiden may not know. My father, Rodrik, was a powerful, ambitious man, as was his brother, Karl. They tore our people apart. But my father had an advantage that Karl didn't. We had Siagan's lake."

Cecil's skin prickled at her words.

"That is where the madness began. Father stirred the energies of the earth." Kirstin covered her eyes in evident horror. "But he did more. He took a man, his best friend, and made him a prisoner in the dark chamber where he later imprisoned me. He took the man's life in small increments to increase his own potency, but also made him a shield between himself and any attackers. The very wrongness of it corrupted the energy flowing from the lake."

She dropped her hands to her lap and a bleakness touched her expression. "If Ethan has done this same thing, then Aiden can't hurt him. Whatever he does will be pushed onto this shadow of a man. Aiden will have to kill the Shade to get to Ethan.

"And one more thing," Kirstin added into the silence that followed her words. "Kavi, you released the spirits from the lake long ago, but it is still foul. Any man who remains near it for long will be driven mad by its corruption. There's no escape. Such men will fight unto death to protect Ethan, help him keep its twisted power. I had hoped it wouldn't come to this, not again. You can't know the horrors I've witnessed."

Kavi sat and put an arm around her while the company looked at each other in shock. Cecil cleared his throat. "Aiden must be warned of his danger."

"Kirstin and I will do that," Kavi said. "Natan is walking blind as well, and that I will not allow."

Seeing his mutinous expression, Cecil reluctantly agreed, knowing it would be futile to argue with the Karthagan in that mood. He explained, "Captain Daran and I have spoken of the safest way to reach Siagan if need arose. We'll take Daran's ship to Kangar and travel from there overland to Siagan, leaving Kayle to then take the ship from Kangar to Sennia and see his people safe."

A frown creased Ellis's brow. "What of me?"

Cecil answered carefully, "Karthag will be in your charge while we're gone—"

"I'll not be left behind." Ellis set his lips in a stubborn line.

Kavi cleared his throat. "And if you are captured by either Ashel or Ethan, what then? You would put us all in danger. You know as well as I that Aiden would lose control. Then all would be lost."

Temper flashed in Ellis's eyes, but he gave a curt nod of acquiescence.

"I'll have Eon stand at your side," Cecil continued. "Some of the elder Karthagans may still see you as an outsider, and Eon's presence will be helpful."

"I am your servant," Eon said with a bow. Ellis looked frightened, then inclined his head. "As you wish. I will remain here." He didn't add "for now," but Cecil heard it clearly in his tone of voice.

Cecil gave his arm an encouraging squeeze. "I'll return as soon as I am able."

They remained a while longer under the redwood, finalizing their plans.

"How is Tessa?" Cecil asked Kirstin, while Kavi and Ellis spoke quietly together.

"She is well. Frightened for me. Devon will escort her to Nagal, where she should be safe until this is over."

"You didn't want her here?"

Kirstin gave him a close look. "No place is safe, Cecil. But she has friends there who will see her through."

"I am pleased to hear that." Cecil ran a hand over his face. "We should prepare for the morrow then get some sleep," he said, feeling tired and ill.

"I agree," Kavi said abruptly, overhearing him, and sent them to their various tasks. Cecil walked with Kirstin to the castle, then continued on to his and Alek's room with a heavy heart.

Chapter Nineteen

DEVON DREW HIS horse to a walk in relief as he and Tessa approached the city of Nagal after several days of hard riding. The few people they'd met on the road from Amara had eyed Tessa with suspicion and dislike, and he was eager to be among friends. In his relief, the unusual quiet of the city hardly registered.

He realized his mistake in letting down his guard when they found the gates of the city blocked by several grim men, daggers drawn.

"Why have you brought that Karthagan here?"

A coldness settled in Devon's heart as he stepped in front of Tessa. She put a hand on his shoulder.

"I'm sorry, my lady," he said in regret for his blindness.

"I think I asked a question," the man snarled while the others circled them. Devon drew his knife, as did Tessa. The men laughed unpleasantly and advanced, but there was a rattle of chains and the gates flung open.

"Hold!"

All froze at Commander Jaden's roar and soldiers poured from the castle. Devon sagged with relief on seeing them, when the first soldier who'd spoken to them made a sudden lunge for him. His dagger sliced across Devon's abdomen, and Devon lost his breath in waves of pain as he sank to the ground. He struggled to rise, but a haze filled his eyes, and he slid into unconsciousness even as his attacker fell with several arrows in his body.

*

ROBIN PACED THE hall, at last sitting outside the room they'd taken Devon to, and then leaned his head back against the wall. Newly recovered from the poison Ashel had fed him, he found he tired easily.

"Robin?"

He started awake, dismayed. "I hadn't meant to sleep."

Tessa helped him to stand.

"How is he?"

"Devon's wound was thankfully shallow. He should recover with time and care." Tessa stumbled unexpectedly as they took a step down the hall.

"My lady." Robin offered his arm, and Tessa gratefully leaned on him. Robin's gaze slid again and again to Tessa's brown curls resting on his shoulder. His heart stirred strangely, and he felt heat mount in his face. He held Tessa's hand longer than necessary when he bid her goodnight at the door. "What has happened? I've never seen you so tired and worn."

"We've saved Devon," she answered sleepily. "Though he'd lost too much blood. It took all my energy until it was spent…"

"What do you mean?"

Sadness crossed her face and she let out a worn breath. "We nearly lost him. I had to draw on all my strength. It will be a while before it returns. It feels strange…"

Robin stepped back as doubt touched his heart. "You're tired, my lady. Good night," he said quietly and made a formal bow.

He wearily sought his own bed, where nightmares chased through his dreams until dawn. He'd called a meeting for the morning and, after a hasty breakfast, climbed the stairs to the council chamber. He paused a moment in the doorway to enjoy the sunlight flooding in from the high windows. There was a fire on the hearth to drive off the morning chill as well, and he smiled gratefully to Emile as he entered the room.

Jaden joined them, followed almost immediately by Tessa. Robin went across the room to greet her, then bowed to the others.

"A poor substitute for my father, I'm well aware," he said softly. "Tessa, will you please join us? There's much to discuss."

"Of course," she replied and hastily took the chair he indicated at the long table. She looked at Robin as Emile placed a cup of tea at her hand. "Why am I here?"

Jaden answered from across the table. "Devon woke for a time this morning and requested that you represent Amara in his place, if you will, until his strength returns."

"And we should like your tidings, lady," Robin put in as he sat at the head of the table and put his chin on his hand. "Have you heard anything from Lady Kirstin? Has Governor Willum or Lord Aiden made a move?"

"Lord Aiden is taking the Karthagans to Siagan. He feels it is his duty to put an end to Ethan's cruelties. What Willum's plans are, Mother doesn't know. It would be hard for him to make war on his own people. He will, though, if he feels it necessary."

They sat in silence, pondering her words.

"Jaden, in these circumstances, wouldn't it be prudent to send men to reinforce the border?"

"Your father wanted us to protect Nagal at all cost—"

"I know my father's words," Robin interrupted sharply. "I'm asking you, as an experienced commander of the Southern army, would it not be wise to send men to strengthen the governor's position at Fredrik's Hall, and to guard the border in the chance that the Siagan army flees south?"

Jaden stared at him for a long moment, then he rose and bowed. "Yes, my lord. Our position is weak, made more so by the proximity of the Karthagans. If Aiden should lose control…"

"Those are my thoughts as well."

"Your pardon, my lord," Emile hesitated and Robin turned to him. "Do you distrust the governor and his orders?"

Jaden flushed red. "Some do," he growled.

Robin pressed his lips together. "You weren't there, Jaden. Ashel is insane, and his madness spreads throughout the Hall as a noxious air, affecting everyone. I was with him only a few days and felt its influence. My father has been there many days."

He rose to his feet, his face grim. "I won't say I distrust my father, but his judgment may become confused the longer he stays there."

"I concur," Tessa told him firmly. "When I touched on my mother's thoughts last night, I felt a madness in her and in the very air around her. I believe the closer one is in proximity to Ashel, or to Ethan in Siagan, or Aiden…anyone holding onto power, the more muddled their thoughts will become. I fear none can escape it."

"What will you have me do, my lord?" Jaden asked, and they knew he had just shifted his allegiance from Basal to his son.

Robin took a breath, settling the responsibly on his inexperienced shoulders. "How many men are in Nagal, Commander?"

"There is one garrison in the city, lord, and three to the east."

"Excellent." Robin's ready smile touched his face. "More than I had hoped. Let's keep the one in the city, place one with my father at the Hall, and the other two on the border." He cleared his throat. "Jaden, will you go to my father in my stead? I wouldn't be welcomed."

"I will see him safe. You have my oath." Jaden went to him, and they gripped hands. Jaden cuffed him gently, a fond, forced grin on his lips. "But who'll keep you in line while I'm gone?"

"There's plenty here to remind me of my place," Robin answered with a sly glance to Tessa. He cleared his throat. "Commander, please advise Captain Sadie of our plans. I should like you to leave as soon as possible."

"At once, my lord," Jaden bowed and left the room with Emile at his heels.

Robin accompanied Tessa to the patio where they found Devon in the sun.

"Hello," Tessa announced their arrival. Devon shifted in the chair, and Tessa helped him sit up.

"How are you today?" Robin asked politely as he shook the man's hand.

"Very fit, considering."

Devon leaned back as Tessa touched his forehead and searched his eyes. "No pain?"

"Not to speak of."

Robin was attentive to his guests, though he soon rose and took his leave of them, ashamed he'd counted the many times Tessa had touched Devon's hand or arm. It was the last straw when she placed a blanket around his shoulders against the breeze.

He made his way to the gates and viewed the ranks of horsemen he was sending to war, giving Jaden a moment to say his farewells to his wife and daughter. Robin was miserable, full of doubts, anxious. Who was he to send these men and women to battle, many to death? He rubbed his face and hair and jumped when Jaden clapped his shoulder.

Jaden gave him a keen look. "This is the right thing to do, Robin. Have no doubts."

"I'm afraid. It's nearly impossible for me to let you go, knowing the danger I'm sending you into. How can I ever be governor when I'm so weak?"

"You're compassionate, Robin, and yet you send the soldiers into conflict when necessary and stay behind to protect the city when I know your heart burns to go with us." Jaden smiled at his blush. "You'll make an excellent governor."

Jaden gave a whoop and sprang to saddle and, with a last wave to Mirah and Nikki, kicked his mount to a gallop. A roar went up from the ranks as Captain Sadie fell in beside him, and the horsemen sang as they followed their commander. Robin's heart raced with pride and fear, and he prayed they'd be safe.

He walked thoughtfully through the city, wondering how to raise the morale of the people left behind. Though he was greeted warmly on all sides, he saw the uncertainty in their eyes, an anxiousness for the future. How could he ease their minds? He'd speak with Emile about it.

Robin chewed a thumbnail. He'd had a word with Devon. The council leader was quickly recovering his strength and eager to return to Amara. Robin had to admit he'd be glad to see him go. He flushed with sudden shame, happy that Tessa couldn't read his unworthy thoughts.

Lost in contemplation, he entered the courtyard and walked in the garden. Rounding a corner on a path, he stopped, smiling in delight. Tessa lay on the grass under a tree singing softly, and Robin had never heard anything more beautiful, but he worried about her. There were shadows in her brown eyes that hadn't been there before.

Heart thumping as he approached her, he wondered if she would walk with him. "Hello." He smiled down at her, and she dimpled and sat up, patting the ground beside her. Robin settled cross-legged and plucked at the grass.

She laughed and took his hand. "What is it?"

He played with her fingers. "Will you walk with me?"

She began to nod, then shook her curls. "Oh, I can't. I'm meeting with Devon straight away and don't have the time."

Robin swore under his breath, heart burning.

"What is it, Robin?"

"I don't know." He laughed abruptly. "I guess I always thought… I'd dreamed…" He took a sharp breath and continued passionately, flinging out his arms. "I'm only seventeen, Tessa! I won't even have a home to offer you for another three years—"

He shut his mouth at the tiny smile creeping on her face and flushed darkly. He stood and lifted his head, all pain and hurt pride, and made an eloquent bow. "I've been a fool. Forgive me. Devon's a good man, and I'm sure he can give you all your heart's desire." His voice broke on the last word, and he turned from her in misery.

"Robin! Dear…"

He stood still, his heart squeezing painfully. She rose and put a hand on his arm, drawing his eyes. "We're friends, and that's all he wants of me."

"And you, Tessa?"

"Oh, I wouldn't dream of leaving Mother for at least three years. Time enough for you—"

"Tessa!" Robin took her hands. He couldn't speak and kissed her fingertips. He stole a glance at her face. "You're laughing at me."

"Well, dear, you were rather dramatic."

"I was afraid." He pulled her slowly into his arms and gave her the tiniest kiss. They grinned at each other.

"That was nice." Tessa blushed. "I suppose you've had lots of practice."

Robin snorted. "Why would I kiss anyone but you? I've been waiting."

They held hands and walked awhile, then found a shady spot to sit and plan a delightful future, Devon forgotten. Tessa even gave him a few more sweet kisses before they went inside.

*

JADEN HALTED THE men in view of Fredrik's Hall. A more desolate and abandoned place he'd never seen. The main gates hung open with not a soul to be seen within its walls. The silence was eerie.

He turned to Sadie. The captain had her keen eyes on the walls, and the short bow she favored rested in her hands. Her fine dark hair fell in a long braid down her back, out of the way. Her calm, confident manner reassured him.

"Please take the men to the barracks, Captain."

She raised a brow. "Shouldn't I come with you?"

"No. If it's a trap…" He grinned crookedly. "You can rescue me."

"Very well, Commander." She gave a short, reluctant bow, and Jaden admired her control as she motioned to the men around them.

He carefully approached the Hall. The entrance doors pushed open at a touch, and he walked through the silent corridors in growing dread. A strong odor wafted from the stairwell to the cellar, and he wrinkled his nose. Then horror came over him. He knew that acrid tang. He'd smelled it on many a battlefield.

Heart pounding, Jaden leaped down the stairs, the lingering smoke choking his throat even as it led him to the room that had held so many captives in the past. Fire had burned through the door and he glanced in. Though he'd been prepared for the sight, it still sickened him and filled him with pity.

Charred bodies huddled in the middle of the stone floor with a few others in the corners, as if they had tried in vain to escape the flames that had engulfed the chamber. By the blackness of the stones, oil had been poured on the floor and lit. He took a breath and stepped into the nightmare.

He determined the lords of the Hall had been present, going by bits of clothing and jewelry he uncovered, along with their various lovers and servants. One body near the door puzzled him, separate from the others. He crouched and searched the form carefully. A terrible cry of recognition escaped him.

"No, no, no," he murmured in disbelief and grief washed over him.

It couldn't be true. Why would he have been included in this horror?

He roused with effort and climbed to his feet, grim with sorrow and a smoldering rage. Quick steps approached and he met Sadie's gaze through the charred wood of the door. Distress flashed over the captain's face, controlled.

Her brown eyes narrowed. "You'd been gone overlong. What has happened?"

Jaden motioned to the man at his feet and found he couldn't speak. Sadie stepped through the doorway and crouched on her heels to study the body.

"It's Governor Basal," she said in a tight voice. Hot anger swept Jaden at her indifference, but then she lifted a face white to the lips. She rose and took a steadying breath, and Jaden knew she would save her grief for a more private moment. "Let's take him upstairs."

Filled with sorrow, Jaden removed his coat, gently wrapped it around Basal, and carried him to a bedroom on the upper level. When he could speak without his voice breaking, he and Sadie went to the barracks and broke the news to the waiting soldiers. Silence fell as they each dealt with their shock and anger. It was some time before Jaden could convince them not to take up arms and go after those responsible.

"We need to adhere to Robin's plans. He is governor now," he said and choked on the words.

Jaden called Sadie to him as evening settled in. They sat on the porch of the cabin he was using and watched the stars come out in a darkening sky. A breeze rustled dry leaves in the cemetery behind the dwelling.

"I'll take Basal home to Nagal in the morning." A spasm of pain squeezed Jaden's heart. "Robin was telling me how he feared he'd never be ready for the governorship. I guess we'll learn the truth of it now." He covered his eyes a moment. "I'll leave you to take the soldiers to the border and reinforce Tyrel's men. Don't go into the Northern Territory. I suspect Ethan's tricks."

"What of the Hall, Commander?" Sadie furrowed her brow. "Shouldn't we leave a few men—"

"We'll burn the Hall in the morning, Captain. To the ground."

Sadie sent him a startled look, but kept her opinion to herself, correctly reading his expression. He wouldn't discuss this.

Jaden wandered in the cemetery later that terrible night. The moon was young but cast enough light for him to read the headstones. He found Commander Jacksan's grave at the top of the hill and paused a moment, but restlessness soon sent him on.

He walked into the grove of oaks and was startled to find Sadie there. She was standing by a grave set a little apart from the others. Soft moss had been encouraged to grow over the mound, and a wild rose of delicate pink blooms twined about the simple headstone.

"My Darling Wife and Son," he read, and his breath strangled him.

"Carrow must have loved her very much," Sadie observed softly. Jaden gave her a keen look, but her face was calm and thoughtful, giving nothing away.

"Get some rest, Captain," he said kindly and sighed, then wound his way back to the cabin and his own bed for what sleep he could find.

Morning came swiftly, and Jaden sat his horse at the gates while a few of his men laid torch to Fredrik's Hall. Flames appeared as the roof caught, and the ancient timbers crackled and sent waves of heat washing over him and the waiting soldiers. He stayed until the structure was aflame, then turned to the captain beside him. He motioned, and Sadie saluted smartly and started the companies north.

A small group of soldiers remained with Jaden. They tied a litter to several of the horses for Basal's remains and began their slow trek to Nagal with hearts as heavy as their burden. Jaden dreaded their journey's completion.

After a long and sorrowful march, Jaden drew rein at Nagal's gates and jumped from the saddle. Several soldiers did likewise and they took up the litter, dropping tears as they carried their governor home.

The gates swung open to a large assemblage of people with frightened and curious faces, but Jaden saw only the boy, still and proud, who held himself erect in preparation for the blow. They stopped before him, and Jaden never forgot that moment of utter quiet, and the terror in Robin's eyes.

"My lord Governor." Jaden took a knee to Robin and bowed his head. A cry of surprise and grief raced through the crowd, and the people wept openly.

Robin didn't move, his eyes fastened on the still form in its soft wrappings. He drew the knife from his belt and stepped closer. Jaden made a violent motion to stop him and then rocked back on his heels. Robin ran the blade of the knife through the cords binding the cloth together, and carefully folded it away from the charred face of his father. He looked a long moment, then tenderly covered Basal once more and gathered his father in his arms, holding him to his heart. Not a sound escaped him.

Jaden dispersed the crowd, and they left quietly, in respect for their grieving governor, many touching his shoulder as they passed with a murmured word of sympathy. Robin held his father until he and Jaden stood alone with the pallbearers. Robin dismissed the closest soldier and took up the pole himself, carrying his father inside the city with dry, piercing eyes.

*

ROBIN WOKE IN the morning with sunlight on his face and threw an arm over his eyes. This would be a black day. He groaned and sank into the blankets, wishing now he had brought Tessa to his room last night. He desperately needed her love at that moment when grief was an unbearable weight on his heart.

There was a tap on the door, and Tessa's sweet face appeared around the edge. He stretched out aching arms, and she ran to him, and he folded her to him and let her soft words wash over and through him, lending him comfort.

She raised his face and kissed his wet eyes. "It's time, darling," she murmured, her voice trembling.

He knew she was trying to be brave for his sake, and his heart swelled. "Will you marry me soon, Tessa? I need you so desperately."

"Of course. As soon as you wish."

Her prompt answer won a smile from him. She helped him dress in somber black and brushed down his unruly hair. He nearly broke when she placed the Governor's cloak around his shoulders, the proud falcon embroidered on brilliant blue, but she held his hands tightly and nodded encouragement.

He drew a hard breath. "Will you walk with me?"

She hesitated, and he imperiously held out his arm. Startled, her lips parted. Pretty color blossomed in her cheeks as she touched his forearm. He kissed her fingertips, and they left the room together.

The walk through the city became a nightmare to Robin. The sun shone warmly, but his face chilled as he led the funeral procession. Tessa's touch on his arm kept him sane as all eyes watched him, looking for signs of grief or weakness. But it was the speculative eyes that tore his heart, as if he could somehow be glad for his father's death. A hiss of pain escaped his clenched teeth, but he found new strength as Tessa's arm went around him.

The graveyard stood quiet as the day sped toward noon, the air warm, scented with dry grass and freshly turned earth. The Nagal people remained in the city and watched from the walls. Only Basal's family and close friends gathered at his headstone. Emile spoke a few words of farewell and peace, and they lowered Robin's father into the ground. The soldiers stepped back from the grave, and Robin realized they were waiting for him. He moved to the open plot and lifted a handful of rich soil.

"Goodbye, Father," he whispered and let the dirt fall with a dull thump as it struck the wooden coffin. He couldn't bear to stay and moved off to walk among the nearby stones as grieving soldiers lifted their shovels.

Tessa's warm hand slipped into his. "Are you ready to go back?"

He brushed the soft curls from her face. "I'm going to stay awhile," he said and wiped her tears with a gentle thumb. He touched her lips with his own unsteady ones.

After a time, they returned to the newly raised cairn and watched Emile place the last stone. The council leader turned and embraced Robin, then fell apart in his arms. Robin hugged him tightly. "We'll make it," he urged, and Emile stood back and pushed the tumbled red hair from his face, nodding curtly.

Jaden gripped his arm on the other side and gave him a close look, his own dark eyes full of pain. "The people are behind you, sir, and my sword is yours."

Robin sighed, then drew a fortifying breath, running a trembling hand over his face. "The world has gone mad. Jaden, please take a few soldiers and join the others at the border. I fear terrible things are awakening, and Sadie will need your help."

"As you wish, Governor."

A tremor passed through Robin at that. "Father!" The word tore from his lips and rang in the air with all the anguish of his young heart. An answering cry came from the walls, and Basal's name was taken up and shouted until it was a roar on the wind.

Robin stepped into a clearing and lifted his face to the city. Silence fell. He opened his arms wide to embrace them, then made the low bow he'd seen Aiden perform, his light hair sweeping the ground. There was a gasp and muffled cry, and then a cheer raced the walls as Robin took command of Nagal and moved into the hearts of its people.

He sat quietly by his father's grave when the others had gone, holding tightly to Tessa's hand.

"I'm not ready, Father," he confessed and played absently with a few pebbles. "You tried to warn me, but I thought I'd have years yet to learn to be a man."

In time he stood and drew Tessa to her feet. "We'd better go in." He saw the uncertainty in her eyes and pulled her into his arms.

"I'll take care of you, Tessa," he promised brokenly. "I've always loved you."

She couldn't seem to speak past her tears, but her sweet kiss swept away all his doubts.

Chapter Twenty

NATAN SCRAMBLED DOWN the embankment behind Carrow and threw himself under the scrub brush, fighting for breath. It was a moment before he could lift his head, in time to catch the wicked delight in Carrow's glinting eyes. He climbed painfully to his feet and methodically brushed the dirt from his clothes until he was able to control his anger.

"Was all this even necessary?" he asked and motioned up the hill. They'd crossed the border into the North that morning, slipping through the trees and up and down gullies until he was bruised and sore.

Carrow neglected to hide his grin. "Perhaps not, but we're heading into trouble, and I wanted to see if you were up to it or if you would need to be pampered."

Natan looked at him coolly. "And?"

Carrow struggled with his laughter, and Natan wanted to pummel him.

"You'll do, sir," he finally admitted and started up the next slope with suppressed chuckles. Natan stomped after him, disgusted with himself for feeling flattered by the archer.

They left the Dakon forest and carefully made their way across the Northern plains. As they traveled, Natan's respect for his companion grew. Carrow, whose keen ears and vigilance often saved them, at one time spotted a Northern patrol Natan would have blindly stumbled into. They rested and ate a scratch meal at noon.

Natan eyed Carrow where he lay on his back, staring at the few white clouds in the blue sky. There was a recklessness to the man, a careless disregard for his life that worried Natan.

"What are your plans, Carrow, when this is over?"

The archer continued to gaze at the sky. "That depends on how things work out," he answered dryly.

Natan reddened and pulled his pack closer and began to replace the few items he'd removed for lunch, angry with himself again. When would he learn not everyone invited his confidence? He glanced up involuntarily as he felt the archer's eyes on him.

Carrow sat up and dusted off his tunic. "If things go well, I intend to return to Fredrik's Hall and try to set things right for whoever the new lord may be."

"Is that where your heart is?"

"It's where Lyra and my child are."

They fell silent and Natan noted the signs of loneliness around Carrow's blue eyes.

"Do you ever think to remarry…" He paused and smiled ruefully. "You can tell me to mind my own business."

Carrow gave him a keen look. "If you lost Kavi, would you replace him?"

Natan's blood chilled as Carrow struck at the worst of his fears. He shook his head helplessly. "I can't even think of it."

"Forgive me, Mage. I shouldn't have spoken those words." Carrow bowed from where he was sitting. He continued in a moment. "I've thought of it lately. Not that I love Lyra any less, but I should like a family—" He broke off and stirred, restless. "We should go."

It was dusk when they approached Siagan. Carrow moved with extreme caution and Natan followed his movements exactly, neither of them wanting to be taken prisoner by the madman behind the walls. They stopped abruptly by an outcrop of rock, and Natan chuckled even as Carrow notched an arrow.

"I hear you, Syros," Natan said softly. He'd traveled too often with the man to mistake that footstep, stealthy as it managed to be.

"Put your hands where I can see them, both of you," Syros demanded, his tone cold, and Natan raised his hands in surprise. Carrow followed suit as if he'd expected it. Syros came out in the open and looked closely into the archer's eyes. Carrow quirked a brow, and Syros nodded after a moment as if satisfied. He stared long at Natan.

Dismay filled Natan's heart. Had he lost Syros's trust as well? His task seemed unbearably heavy of a sudden, and he blinked at the tears that stung his eyes.

Syros's aloofness melted into a fond smile. "Forgive me, Mage." He bowed low. "I had to be sure you weren't one of Ethan's creatures. They seem unable to hide their madness."

"Of course," Natan said quietly.

Syros put an arm across his shoulders. "Come to the fire, Mage. You're tired. Rest and eat something. We can speak afterward."

Carrow put his arm around Natan as well, and Natan was laughing at their foolishness as they entered the small clearing between the rocks where a fire crackled. He was glad to sink down off his feet. In a moment Commander Tyrel brought him a stew made of potatoes and some kind of small game. Natan didn't bother to ask what they had managed to catch. The food was hot and savory and filled an empty stomach.

When finished, they sat around the fire, a mug of coffee in hand, and Syros caught them up on what had transpired.

"You said Korin volunteered for this?" Natan scrubbed a hand over his face. Hadn't the lad been put through enough?

"He did," Syros confirmed, a harsh note in his voice. "We needed a way to infiltrate Siagan, find out what Ethan is plotting. Also, Korin needed a refuge, somewhere out of Ashel's reach. Siagan seemed our only recourse. And Korin claimed he would have no trouble learning the Red Twin's secrets. You know how he is… Mage, I wouldn't have let him go if I could think of any other way. But I couldn't. Believe me, I wanted to. But as Korin himself has said, there's no place on earth he'd be safe from what is to come."

For a moment Syros's guard was down, and Natan could see his worry and uncertainty and a hint of the anguish he buried in his drawn-out explanation. But then Syros drew a breath and sat up, once again the soldier and Regent, his cool mask settling into place. "If he is not back within a day, I will go after him," he vowed.

Natan nodded, having no words to ease Syros's pain and guilt. He carried enough of it himself.

"Korin is an intelligent, capable man, Syros. He'll come out of this with his skin intact," Carrow assured him.

"He'd better," Syros muttered, and stared into the fire.

They grew quiet, and in time Natan rolled in a blanket, closed his eyes, and let sleep finally take him for a few moments of peace.

*

NATAN STIRRED UP the fire in the morning and set water on to boil, wanting his tea, and stifled a yawn as he searched his bag for the packet of dried herbs. Startled by a hiss, he glanced up to where Syros kept watch on the city from the rocks above camp. Syros motioned, and Natan understood that he was to be the bait for whomever approached. He resumed poking at the fire, surreptitiously loosening the knife at his belt.

He scrambled to his feet in utter surprise as a man silently appeared on the far side of the fire, a nightmare, the bones of his skeleton pressing on tight skin. The tormented eyes were living coals in a stark, mottled face.

The creature flung out his arms in a gesture of despair. "Please, don't be afraid!" He covered his face with hands that were twisted claws.

Natan caught a blur of movement. "Syros!"

Too late. The man crumpled under Syros's weight like broken straw. Syros instantly scrambled up with an oath, stepping back as if burned.

"Peace," Natan murmured as he dropped beside the prostrate form. He ran gentle hands over the emaciated body and grieved at its thinness. Nothing appeared broken, but as he laid the man out carefully, a musky odor rose from him, not unpleasant, just strange. Faint breath escaped the soldier's blackened lips, and his eyes fluttered as he fought for conscious- ness. Transparent lids flew open and terror filled the dark eyes.

"Rest easy," Natan soothed while Syros crouched beside them. Natan brushed the thin, graying hair from the feverish brow and ached as he wiped the man's tears as well. Righteous anger swept through him suddenly, and he did something he'd kept hidden from the others. He took the man's face in his hands and stared deep into the black eyes. The soldier cried out and struggled feebly, but Natan pushed and entered the suffering mind.

It was his turn to cry out in horror. The soldier's torture—Derik's torture, by Ethan—was reveled clearly to his disbelieving eyes: the slow ebbing of life in extreme pain and fear, the touch of death, and the stirring to terrible life again. A story sprang from his memory of men like this one, a myth from the Karthagan wars, men whose lives were drained for another's potency until they were mere husks and slowly perished. Apparently, the tale of the Karthagan Shades wasn't a fabrication after all.

He probed further into the fainting consciousness and growled in satisfaction. "I see you."

He heard Derik's urgent plea. "No…please."

"It will be well," he soothed and slipped with care toward the dark essence of Ethan in the farthest corner of the soldier's mind.

"He'll know!" Derik wailed.

"He won't," Natan promised. He willed it, and the connection between Derik and Ethan snapped. He touched the tendril, numbing it, applying thoughts of submission and obedience, so that whenever Ethan reached for Derik, he would be fooled. This didn't sever the terrible bond between them, where Derik would suffer any harm aimed at Ethan, but it would bring Derik a modicum of peace.

Natan longed to stay with Derik. He felt the touch of death in him, his fear. He wanted to save him but knew the time for that had passed. It was too late even for Kirstin's aid. He retreated, and Derik rolled away from him and curled into a ball, weeping hard tears.

"Derik?" Natan feared the sudden release would prove too much for the weakened man. He stroked the brittle hair, and Derik calmed under his touch.

"Thank you," Derik whispered, seeming unmanned by the unexpected kindness.

Natan put an arm around his thin shoulders and helped him to sit up. Syros had busied himself at the fire and now handed Natan a mug of sweet tea, which he offered to Derik.

Derik turned away in distress. "I don't drink anymore."

Tears prickled Natan's eyes. "I'm truly sorry, Derik. Is there no way I can aid you?"

"You have." Derik reached for Natan's hand and then made a hurt sound and hid his own gnarled claws behind his back with a murmured apology. "I have a message for you!" he cried in quick delight as if he'd just recalled his errand.

"You do?" Natan asked gently, though his heart quickened.

Syros made a sound and Derik startled and bowed as best he could. "I didn't recognize you, Regent."

"Never mind, Derik. Please tell us what you know," Syros bid him.

Derik spoke haltingly of his brief encounters with Korin and the few things he knew of Ethan's army hidden on the far side of Siagan. His words were disjointed, often rambling, and it soon became apparent it was a struggle for him to concentrate. At one point he raised his eyes in apology for his wandering thoughts and caught the impatience in Syros's face.

"Forgive me!" he cried out and bowed to the ground, biting hard on his palm to cover a deeper pain. Natan exchanged a look of pity with Syros; then Syros set his lips.

"Derik," he said, his voice crisp, and years of service brought Derik's head up. Syros stood, and the man climbed painfully to his feet. Natan rose as well.

"You are a Barkuit soldier," Syros reminded him. "And no matter what Ethan has done to you, or will do, he can't change that. He can't take it from you. Be proud, sir. It is a position of honor."

Derik's eyes widened, and he straightened his weak limbs, raising his head a little higher. "Thank you, my lord." He bowed though the effort left him panting.

"It's my privilege," Syros said in all seriousness and held out his hand. Derik gaped and looked at his own crooked fingers, the skin tight on the bones. Syros waited patiently and clasped his hand with care when Derik hesitantly extended it.

Derik watched, bewildered, as Syros resumed his seat at the fire. Natan gave in to a sudden impulse and embraced him. Derik tried to draw away, then pushed his face against Natan's shoulder and sobbed quietly. Natan smoothed his hair and whispered soft words until the dying man grew calm.

"Will you tell us Korin's message?" Natan gently reminded.

Bewilderment crossed Derik's face. "Didn't I? Forgive me. He says Ethan's army is larger than you realize. Berserkers, he called them, fallen into madness, willing to die at Ethan's word."

Natan shared a startled grimace with Syros, then turned back to Derik. "Will you stay with us?"

Derik shook his head. "I can't, my lord. Ethan will want me soon.

He'll come for me."

They looked at each other a long moment; then Natan bowed low. "It's been my honor to meet you."

Derik drew a hard breath and gave one longing look at the clear sky and the beautiful world stretching in all directions. A shudder passed through him, then he turned to struggle his way back to Siagan's gates. Natan's heart ached, then burned for every labored step he took.

*

KORIN SAT AGAINST the damp wall of the cave and hugged his knees, chilled and afraid. Derik had returned to the city, but Korin hadn't had a chance to speak with him. He ached to hear how his friends faired. Had Syros asked about him? He watched Ethan kneel at the lake and stir the dark water with his fingertips, making a sound of pleasure. The Red Twin rose and silently left the cavern lit by a solitary torch in the wall. Soldiers filed in, eight or ten. They removed their clothing, men and women alike, and bathed in the icy water.

Others took their place. Time passed and Korin grew drowsy and confused in the flickering light as he listened to the soft splash of bodies stirring the immense powers of the lake. At one point, he thought he glimpsed Ashel peering from a dark recess far along the left hand wall of the cavern. But the form was gone in the next blink of his eyes, and he couldn't be certain of anything so close to the lake.

The day dragged on into an endless evening, and at one point he jerked awake. The torch was sputtering, and he found himself alone. He wondered what had woken him. Low sobs of a soul in utter loneliness and despair echoed faintly through the cavern. He struggled up, fetched the torch, and went to the small, terrible cell.

At first he didn't understand what the faltering light was showing him, and then he cried out in distress. Derik hung by his bleeding wrists from iron shackles in the ceiling, his legs grown too weak to hold him upright any longer. His sunken chest was bare, and blood glistened on the protruding ribs from the small lashings of a whip, as if Ethan wasn't content to steal his life's energy but had to see his lifeblood as well.

"Derik," Korin murmured, grieving, and raised the bruised and ravaged face. Dark eyes opened, glazed with pain, then closed in exhaustion. A single tear slipped down his pallid skin.

It broke him. Korin had felt the power of the lake pulsing through his veins all day. He summoned the energy and thrilled as the power filled him. He slammed a fist against the wall, and the shackles fell to dust. Catching Derik in his arms, light as a child, he strode from the room. Heart burning, he swept through the hallways of the castle, and all he encountered fled from the fury on his face. Where Ethan was, he neither knew nor cared. The streets were empty, and it took a mere thought for the gates to swing open and let him escape into the night.

Korin marched without awareness through the dark, and it was only the soft call of his name that gave him pause. He peered in the faint light from the rising moon and saw a pale face watching him from the darkness.

"Mage," he breathed, and the fierce clutch on his heart eased. The red haze in his mind thinned and dissipated. He caught his breath on a sob.

Natan reached his arms for Derik. "Shall I take him?"

"No, Mage." Korin smiled with tenderness at the unconscious man against his breast. "He's not heavy."

"Come to the fire," Natan said, touching his arm. Korin followed, unable to sort the chaos of emotions and images in his bewildered head.

He welcomed the fire. As he lay Derik on the blanket someone provided, he realized he was shivering and sat near the crackling warmth. A mug of hot tea was pressed into his hands. He raised his eyes to thank the giver and smiled in delight. "Syros."

"Hello." Syros touched his face, then cleared his throat and bent to Derik's prone body. Korin stared into the flames, sipped his sweet tea, and slowly came back to himself. He slanted a look at Natan at his side.

Natan smiled and reached to cup his face, and Korin parted his lips in a slight gasp as the Mage's thoughts slipped into his head. But the contact brought an end to the roar and rush of power and terrible visions churning behind his eyes.

Natan leaned close. "Peace," he whispered in his ear, and Korin felt released from some dark prison.

Syros looked at him from where he was tending Derik. "Are you well?"

"He's well," Natan answered for him. "There were seeds of madness in him. The power of the lake must press on the place of dreams in the mind, until reality and fantasy become mixed. I was able to release the energy back to the earth." He smiled at Korin. "You need to rest now."

"In a moment." Korin rose to his knees beside Syros and looked at the shell of a man on the blanket. His heart grieved as he removed the filthy clothing from Derik's skeletal body. As he dipped a cloth into the comfortably hot water Syros provided, he felt as if he were washing a corpse. Korin hated the thought and thrust it from his mind. He helped Natan put salve on the countless sores Ethan had left to fester on Derik's thin skin. Natan rummaged in his pack and dressed Derik in his spare clothing.

Syros cleared a rough throat. "Can you do anything for him, Mage?"

Natan shook his head. "He should have died long ago." His expression grew cold. "Ethan has no right to do this. I will stop him if it takes my life."

Syros stifled an oath. "It won't come to that, Natan. We won't let it."

They watched Derik sleep a moment, then Syros sat at the fire, pulling Korin into his arms to rest against his chest, while Natan moved a few paces off and rolled in a blanket to sleep, his back to them.

"Tell me true," Syros asked, lips pressed to Korin's cheek. "How are you faring?"

"I'm well… No, that's false. I'm scared. Terrified of Ethan. I've seen his army, Syros. Soldiers who will walk into death for him. How can we stand against that?"

Syros's arms tightened, and Korin settled into his warmth, tired and worn and unsure. He didn't think Syros would answer until he let out a shaky breath. "We can't defeat them. Not on our own. But we must trust in Willum and Aiden. And the Mage," Syros added in a gruff tone. "Natan surprised me just now."

"He's regained his powers," Korin whispered in awe, staring hard at Natan's shoulder turned toward them.

"Looks like it, though I wish he would have told us sooner."

"Maybe he didn't want to acknowledge it, even to himself," Korin defended. "Maybe it's his proximity to the lake." He would never forget how kind Natan had been to him on the Isle of Wind and afterwards.

"Perhaps." Syros gave a sudden sigh, nuzzling Korin's neck. "Let's not speak of it further. These men of power are best left to their own counsel. Korin, I'm truly sorry to have put you in harm's way again. I never should have allowed—"

Korin's sharp hiss stopped Syros's words, and he shifted in Syros's arms until he faced him. "Syros, darling, I love you, but do you honestly believe anyone can force me to do anything I don't want to? I chose to go of my own free will. That's the end of it."

Syros stared at him, firelight flickering over his handsome face; then he bent his head and pressed a kiss on Korin's lips, hard and hungry. He thrust his tongue deep when Korin murmured approval. They kissed long, desperate for connection, Korin clutching at Syros's shoulders until Syros broke off with a muffled groan.

"By the gods, Korin," he gasped, "I want to take you to my home, undress you slowly, and spend days with you in my bed."

Korin pressed his teeth against Syros's shoulder to stifle his moan of need and desire, his body coming alive as Syros's hands traveled down his chest, along his thighs. He would give anything to make love right then, escape the nightmare life had become, if only for one glorious moment.

"I want that too," he confessed brokenly. Syros put a strong arm across his shoulders, imprisoning him.

"I don't think—" he began, but Syros licked his neck, stealing his breath; then Korin collapsed into his arms with a strangled cry as Syros's hand slipped inside his clothing and stroked his skin.

"Come with me," Syros demanded after a moment, grabbing Korin's hand and a blanket. Korin went with him willingly outside the fire's glow to the mossy ground between tall boulders. They would have this stolen moment, whatever was to come.

Chapter Twenty-One

AIDEN LED HIS people across the border into the Northern Territory from Karthag's outlands late in the night without a glance for the patrols on either side, and they in turn kept their gaze averted from his golden eyes. His power was a cloak around him, and to a lesser degree, around every Karthagan. None dared stand against them. Afternoon found the party approaching Siagan's walls and Aiden motioned for a halt.

He surveyed the almost one hundred men and women who'd been strong enough to follow him. They cared for the horses first and then their own needs as they made camp. Most had fought on the Isle of Wind when he had been a child, though there were many young faces in the group as well—those who'd refused to stay behind. Aiden counted carefully. The houses seemed equally divided in the black and silver of his father's house, or the black and crimson leather of Gavin's.

He glanced at Alek at his side. His cousin had donned the unrelieved black of his station as disposed Karthagan leader. His hair was a long braid on his back, his proud face cold and distant. Their eyes met, and Aiden's fears lessened as Alek smiled slightly. Alek was his mentor and friend and almost father, despite their opposing families. Alek would stand with him and see that his house did likewise.

They moved a little away from the settling camp and sat on a ledge of granite overlooking the city. Alek's gaze swept toward Siagan, and he hissed. Aiden followed his keen glance, tensing as he spotted someone approaching.

"Mage," he breathed in relief and rose as the solitary figure scrambled up the rocky slope toward them. Natan didn't stop until Aiden found himself caught in his tight embrace.

"Are you well?" Natan asked, his voice rough.

Aiden saw pity and love in his hazel eyes, and all his defenses slipped. "No!" he admitted on a broken sound.

"You will be," Natan promised gruffly as Aiden wept on his shoulder. "Hold on just a little longer."

He quieted as Natan stroked his hair, then drew a deep breath as the tangles of fear loosened with his tears.

Natan stepped back. "There's a man at our camp I think you should meet. Ethan has—"

Aiden raised a hand to stop him. "You needn't tell me. I sensed him the moment we crossed into the Northern Territory, as I sense Ethan and your own gentle heart, my friend." He stared into the distance as all the souls of the living pressed on him. He wished them joy and shook back his hair, scattering the energy to a safer distance. He searched his pockets for string, found a bit of ribbon Ellis had tucked in his coat on a walk one day, and smiled as he tied the dark strands off his face. He wondered with awe that such a simple act could remind him so forcefully of his precious husband.

"Are you ready?" Natan urged, relentless.

Anger swept him, then was allowed to flow through and dissipate. "Of course, Mage." He rose and bowed to the ground.

Natan swore in dismay. "I didn't mean to—"

"You are in the right, Mage. I feel lost." Aiden looked around with a troubled gaze. "When Ethan and I used our powers together, Ethan was always there to keep me balanced, focused. Without him, I am always unstable, unsure. I don't know my next move."

Natan touched his arm. "I believe that's why Alek is here, my dear boy. Make use of him."

At the mention of his name, Alek gave Natan a strange look. "Do you think we are all fated to a certain path, Mage?"

"No. We can walk away whenever we choose. But we are here, now, and it would be fatal not to use whatever advantage that gives us."

Alek looked from him to Aiden. "I'm not sure what to do," he stammered.

Natan broke into laughter and covered his mouth. "You two remind me of Ellis and Kayle when I ask them to gut the fish!" His eyes danced. "There is nothing *to* do, Alek. When Aiden needs you, he'll reach for you. Simply let him take what energy he requires."

"Mage?" Fear touched Aiden's heart. "What if I hurt him?"

"Do you love him?"

"As a dear friend, and father. But Mage, I killed my father." Aiden hung his head as darkness crept into his thoughts.

He felt Natan's grip on his arm. "No, Aiden. That was Ethan's work.

There was a madness in him that drove him to kill. There is no madness in you or in Alek."

Aiden was in agony. "But can you be sure?"

"I've felt madness," Natan answered quietly. "On the Isle of Wind. In Camron." He touched his tunic where the scar on his chest often ached. "In Mazzo and the Vice-King of Sennia. In my brother Niko." His face whitened with suffering. "It's not in you, my lad." He let out a hard breath. "Will you come with me?"

Aiden and Alek followed him a good tramp south and east until they reached the rocks that hid Natan's camp. The archer, Carrow, nodded as they passed him. There were two figures at the low fire. One was Korin, but it was the other man that claimed Aiden's attention as pity he couldn't control flooded his being.

He knelt by the fragile shell of the man and gently touched his ashen cheek, dry as parchment. Dark eyes opened, too large in that gaunt face, and for an instant, terror glittered in their depths as Derik struggled upright.

"Hush, Derik. Don't be afraid," Aiden murmured through a throat choked with emotion.

Joy suffused the tortured face, and Derik's smile trembled. "You've come to release me?"

"Yes, my friend," Aiden said gently. Derik's spirit broke, and he leaned, sobbing, into the arms Aiden held open. Aiden's tears spilled on the graying head against his breast, and he stroked the hair that only a short time before had been as dark as his own.

"When the time comes, I'll be swift," he promised fiercely. Dangerous anger flamed to life in him for the monster in Siagan, his twin, but he flung it from him in a wave of energy that boomed through the rocks and burst in the fading sky as thunder. Every face looked up in surprise, and many fell on their knees in fear. Aiden sent his thoughts out, searching…

Ethan looked from the flames on the hearth to the dark shadow of a man standing over him, his brother, and blind terror struck him, instantly stilled. Pride sustained him, and his smile was a grim challenge. Aiden bowed stiffly in acceptance…

Derik gave a small yelp of fear but Aiden hushed him, not sure what Derik might have seen of the encounter between him and his brother. He wrapped a blanket around Derik's thin shoulders and placed him carefully into Korin's arms with whispered words of comfort. His fingers eased the lines of strain from around the sunken eyes, and he sent Derik to the joyous dreams that still lived gallantly in his worn heart.

Footsteps approached, and Commander Tyrel and the Regent Syros entered the camp, meeting Aiden's eyes as he glanced up.

"Syros." Aiden smiled. "Your child is beautiful," he added unexpectedly as he rose and they shook hands.

Syros blinked. "He is, isn't he? I was just thinking of him…"

"Is Governor Basal still at Lord Fredrik's?" Alek put in to cover Aiden's sudden confusion.

Pain fleeted across Natan's face, and his hazel eyes darkened. "Shall we sit?" he asked, then spoke softly of the tragedy at the Hall.

Aiden frowned and leaned closer when Natan mentioned Ashel's name. "This Ashel, he's a cousin of Fredrik's?"

"Yes. All the lords of the Hall are related. Does it mean something?" Natan asked, troubled.

"Perhaps. We know there are some races who can control the energies of the earth more subtly than others. Maybe certain families as well. You fear Ashel has become a threat?"

"Robin thought so, and Korin found out the truth of that claim."

Aiden swore under his breath and eyed Korin sitting quietly with Derik. "Korin never should have had dealings with Ashel, nor gone into Siagan to meet with Ethan. The danger was too great, for him and us. He knows much of our plans."

Natan winced at his cold words. "I believed it was the right decision in both instances," he said stiffly. "We can't fight an enemy we know nothing about."

Aiden sighed in dismay. "I have no desire to question your wisdom. Forgive me. Korin seems to have come out of it intact." Aiden lowered his face to the ground in obeisance, and Natan scrambled to his feet.

"Don't do that."

Aiden raised his eyes. "I shall. You are the Mage, and it is incumbent on me to follow."

Natan turned his face away. "I am no longer that man. Have you forgotten? I gave my abilities to Niko." He turned his burning glance to Aiden. "And now they dwell in you."

Aiden smiled gently. "They are in you still, my lord. Have you not felt the stirring in your blood, the tingle of skin, as if every sense has heightened? Are you not aware of the life flowing in every object around you?"

"I don't want it!" Natan cried violently and covered his eyes as if he could stave off the energy Aiden knew pulsed through him with each beat of his heart.

Syros rose and put an arm across Natan's trembling shoulders. "Sit down," he urged.

Aiden moved to touch the single tear on Natan's pale cheek, drawing his gaze. "There are none here who would have chosen this path willingly, dear friend. But don't fear." He leaned close and imprisoned Natan's gaze, his voice fierce when he spoke, "When the end comes, I shan't hesitate."

Syros frowned. "How can you be so assured?"

Aiden clenched his hands until they whitened, and his words spilled out, "I want to go home!" Hot tears stung his eyes, his desolate yearning betrayed in his broken voice, a longing the others shared to the depths of their souls.

Syros cleared his throat. "The Barkuit army is at your disposal," he said and inclined his head. "Willum will back this."

"Barkuit?" Aiden said, voice deceptively quiet, and all eyes swiveled to him. He rose to his feet, and the air crackled around him as his anger roused. "The Barkuit army?" he sneered, haughty and imperious.

Alek jumped up. "Aiden," he said urgently.

Fury blazed through Aiden. "The Barkuits drove us from our home."

"No, my lad," Alek murmured, and the low tones thrummed along Aiden's spine. "This is not that war, and Barkuit is now our ally. It is the man at the lake we must fight. Ethan. Do you not remember?"

Aiden struggled, and Alek placed his hands on his face and leaned his forehead on Aiden's creased brow. "Remember," he commanded.

Aiden flushed with anger. There was a rumble in the earth, and white agony crept over Alek's features. A crimson drop of blood gathered at his nose and slipped across his pale lips to fall on his tunic. Aiden followed the tear of blood with his eyes, and as it spilled on Alek's breast, he pulled away with a broken cry. "No!"

He gazed around in panic, taking in the frightened faces, seeing the blood on his dear cousin's countenance. "I didn't mean…" Giving a moan of despair, he covered his face.

Natan moved to put a hand on his shoulder, but Alek stopped him, his words reaching Aiden from far away. "It's too late, Mage. I saw his mind. The memory of the earth is long, the last seventy years, the years Karthagans have been in Belega, a mere blink of the eye. The past and present are becoming confused in his thoughts. If we're to take Ethan, it must be soon."

"It will be," Natan swore in a tone Aiden had never heard the gentle man use before, cold as steel.

Aiden took a hesitant step away, then stopped. "Alek?"

"Yes?"

"Ethan is dead, isn't he?"

"No, dear friend."

"But I killed him."

"You saved Cecil's life, and probably many others. But Ethan lived."

"Ethan is in my mind, Alek. I shouldn't have confronted him. I made a mistake in my anger. He confuses me."

"Lean on me, Aiden, as the Mage said. Let me help."

"It will be hard," Aiden warned, distressed. "It will hurt."

"I don't care! If it can end this madness, I would give my life." The cousins stared at each other in the wavering light. "I don't want to hurt Cecil anymore," Alek confessed, his voice choked with tears.

Syros eyed the company. "The time has grown perilous," he said grimly. "Carrow, Tyrel, I have no authority over you, but if you will, I'd have you return to the border and watch for any of Ethan's followers that may slip past us. Be vigilant! The enemy will come in many guises."

"As you wish," Carrow bowed.

Commander Tyrel took a moment to grip Syros's hand. "Take care, my friend."

"And you," he said gruffly.

Aiden watched them in silence, confused, and let Alek take his arm and guide him to their own camp. He knew the Mage came with them, but once at the welcomed fire, he sat and studied the flames, holding off the nightmares waiting behind his eyes. In this, he would not allow Ethan to win.

*

KAVI AND KIRSTIN stood at the ship's rail and watched the approaching shore, the glitter in their eyes as bright as the moonlight. Cecil waited near them, and though he dared not show it, an ache crept into his heart. He knew their madness grew with each league closer to Siagan. He could only pray that they reached Kangar before the insanity swept them all. He'd urged Daran to sail again as soon as they left the ship, not even waiting for supplies, and the captain had agreed with an anxious face.

"Come with us, Cecil," he'd implored, frightened for his friend. Cecil wavered. He wanted to go home. He wanted to wake in the morning in Alek's arms, and all the chaos and suffering to come would be as naught. He wasn't given that choice.

He glanced up to find Kavi's speculative eyes on him and shuddered. Kavi knew him. He'd been there when Cecil had been enthralled by Camron, the Red Twins' cousin, all those years ago. That could be a cruel weapon in his hands.

Cecil took a breath, burying the uncertainty in his heart. His first goal was to get Kavi, Kirstin, and himself on shore and see the ship and Kayle safely on their way to Sennia. Time would deal with the rest.

There was silence on deck as they dropped anchor some distance from land, and Kavi and Kirstin climbed into the waiting dory. Cecil shook hands with the men. In the last moment the captain's daughter, Riana, flung herself into his arms.

"Don't go!" she sobbed, heartbroken by his obvious danger.

Kayle gently drew her away, his face working. "Be safe, dear friend," he whispered to Cecil in a voice raw with pain.

Cecil embraced him. "I'll do my best," he promised solemnly.

"Perhaps I should go with you," Kayle began, but Cecil shook his head, knowing how he worried for his people on Sennia.

"No. There is nothing you can do here. I've seen madness like this before and will be prepared. You need to go home. The insanity is spreading, and they will need your help more than we do."

He took up his pack and went to the waiting dory. Kayle helped him in and stared a long moment into his eyes.

"Give Papa my love," Kayle said at last. "And take good care, Cecil."

"Thank you," Cecil said quietly, with little hope for his own safety.

Kayle's eyes narrowed, and he leaned close. "Trust in the Mage. He'll set things right. Stay alive! That is your only priority. All will be well. Just live to see it, my friend."

They embraced again and Cecil kept his gaze on him, gathering his courage as the dory lowered into the sea. Carefully avoiding his companions' eyes, he rowed to the dark shore. He couldn't think of them as his friends. He daren't, for surely they would use that against him as well. Cecil reluctantly recalled his time with Camron and searched his mind desperately for something to hold onto. He'd been so lost with Camron, his mind a gray whirl of chaos and despair. And the phantoms…

He docked with care, wondering at the emptiness of the harbor. After helping the others from the dory, he tied the boat securely and started walking toward the city.

"Cecil."

Kavi's voice was a soft breath in the still air. Cecil kept moving. If he could make it to the end of the dock and slip into a dark side street…

"I will hurt you!" Kirstin called with manic laughter in her voice.

He stopped cold. He'd gambled they'd be preoccupied and ignore him, but as he turned, he saw the wicked blade in Kirstin's hand.

Kavi strode up and struck him hard across the face. "On your knees," he hissed, and tangled his fingers in Cecil's hair as he knelt. Kavi jerked his head back and searched his face.

"I think you need to be punished, dear," Kavi stated, and Cecil braced at the cruel smile marring his features. A gray mist rose in his thoughts and swirled in and out of the corridors of his mind. Time grew strange. He came to himself in a room in Siagan, pressed against the wall by a cruel hand at his throat.

Fingers slipped through his hair. "You didn't tell me he was so pretty."

The raspy voice slithered into Cecil's head, twined down his spine. Camron raised Cecil's chin and touched his face. He whimpered as the fingers stroked his bruised throat. What did the sorcerer want?

He screamed as the fingers seemed to push into his head and crawl over his brain on spider legs until he thought he would go mad. Camron was in his mind! He cried out in terror and wanted to push him away, but he was frozen in place. Camron caressed his tear-streaked face and kissed him on the mouth...

Cecil shivered with cold and reaction. He'd left Camron far in the past, but the memories had been stirred—of terror and confusion and degradation. He blinked gritty eyes. Some time must have passed, with Kavi or Kirstin leading him toward the city. They were at Kangar's gates with soldiers barring the way, torches held high. The Karthagans stood with proud, mocking faces but made no move to challenge the soldiers as of yet.

"What's going on?" Cecil managed to ask, though his throat was so tight he could hardly speak.

"Were your dreams pleasant, pet?" Kavi drawled and caressed his face. Cecil flushed painfully and lowered his gaze to the ground, but his breaths came quickly and he couldn't help but tremble as a raspy, whispery voice swirled in his thoughts and twined around his spine. His nerves grew exquisitely sensitive until even the soft voices around him became a harsh clanging in his mind.

A sudden bark of laughter escaped him, manic in its intensity, and he covered his mouth with a shaky hand. Tears streamed from his blurred eyes. He'd believed for an instant the Karthagans couldn't break him because Camron hadn't. But it was Alek who had saved him from madness that time, and Alek was far away.

He became aware of Kirstin's quiet voice in his ear, cutting through his panic. "These soldiers have kindly given us horses and supplies. We should be on our way."

Kavi halted him as he turned to the waiting animals. "Hold out your hands," he said harshly and bound Cecil's wrists with a strip of leather.

Kirstin giggled as she put a rope over his head. "Come along, pet," she trilled, and Cecil's face burned as she led him past the gates as if he were an animal. He hesitated, wondering how to warn the soldiers not to follow, but on seeing their expressionless faces in the torchlight, he bowed his head and shuffled along at a tug on the rope. He suppressed a shudder as the gates clanged shut behind them and fought the lure of madness in the whispering voices in his mind, knowing they would only grow worse as they neared Siagan.

*

"INTERESTING," CAPTAIN GAEL observed as they approached the city of Siagan on horseback, the walls and buildings shimmering in the moonlight.

Willum gave a short laugh. "Not the word I would have chosen," he said as he surveyed the dark ranks of Karthagan tents stretching out before them. "Terrifying," he insisted and motioned one of his lieutenants over. "Hold the companies here until I return. Under no circumstances are you to engage the Karthagans."

"Very well, sir."

Willum and Gael approached the slumbering camp and dismounted as three figures rose from the nearest fire. He suppressed a shudder as the Red Twin's features became clear in the firelight, and he heard Gael's soft curse. The golden discs of the man's eyes were cold and empty.

Aiden blinked and life returned to his face. "My lord Governor," he said in a quiet voice, and his braid swept the ground in his low bow.

"Lord Aiden," Willum replied and bowed in turn with a nod for Alek and Natan.

A fleeting smile crossed Aiden's face. "I must apologize for entering the Northern Territory without permission. If things had been otherwise… But we are sorely pressed for time."

Willum swallowed his surprise at the courteous tone. He'd looked for hostility.

"Word has reached Barkuit of Siagan's insurrection. We're here to put a stop to it. Will you aid us in that?" Willum asked cautiously.

Aiden looked troubled. "Willum, will you dismiss your people and take council with us? It would be ill-advised for our two armies to join, and yet we must work together."

"As you wish." Willum inclined his head. He drew Gael aside. "Have the companies move a quarter league to the north and set up camp. No fires. I'll be there shortly."

Gael frowned at the dark tents over Willum's shoulder. "Should I not stay with you?"

Willum flashed a grin. "I'll be safe enough, Gael."

"Yes, sir." Gael saluted smartly, and then his brown eyes widened. Willum glanced back at Aiden and caught the strange glimmer in his liquid eyes that must have startled Gael. He knew, suddenly, that the Karthagan walked the edge of a dagger between sanity and the madness engendered by the lake.

"Gael, move the army, now."

"At once, my lord." Gael leaped to his saddle and galloped off. Within a heartbeat, the Barkuits were marching at a brisk pace to the north.

Willum let out a held breath and greeted Aiden's companions, taking a knee to Natan. "Mage. It's good to see you again."

Natan's flush was plain to see in the soft moonlight and Alek chuckled. Willum rose, stifling his sudden irritation. He hadn't expected the Karthagans to follow his orders and stay in their city, though it would have been nice. "My lord Alek." He looked around expectantly. "Is Cecil here?"

Alek's face drained of color and Aiden stepped in. "Come to the fire, Willum. There's much to discuss."

Alek stirred up the coals and added more wood, and the four men sat close to the flames. Aiden made a vague motion with his hand as he settled on the ground, and by the sharp tingle on his skin, Willum knew a barrier had been set between them and the camp.

He laughed shakily, and Natan looked at him. Willum studied his open face. Exhaustion was there, and fear, but under it all was a grief barely contained. He reached an impulsive hand. "Natan, what is it?"

Natan swallowed painfully and glanced away.

"It's Kavi and Kirstin," Aiden supplied, and Alek moved restlessly and fastened his gaze on the fire. Aiden spoke of Kavi and Kirstin's growing instability and their subsequent taking of Cecil.

"I believe they started out with good intentions," he continued. "But the nearer they come to the lake… And yet they're too far away…" He sighed helplessly. "I can't protect them until they draw closer." Willum noted the tremble in his hands as he clenched them together.

"You're not responsible for everyone. No one blames you," Natan told Aiden in firm tones.

"But it's Cecil, the one kind person when everyone else was cruel, who always stood by me. I can't help him." Aiden fisted his hands in anger, and they all jumped at the crack of thunder overhead. Willum's scalp prickled, and he searched the sky for lightning.

"Let it go, Aiden," Alek said gently and placed his hands on the white fists. The golden eyes blazed, but Alek never flinched. Sweat broke on his brow, lines of agony ran his face, but his gaze never wavered. With a sudden sharp cry, Aiden's anger broke, and he stared at Alek, appalled. He turned his head, and a single bitter tear slipped from his tightly closed lids.

Alek drew a deep breath and wiped his face with his sleeve. "Well," he gasped, "That was unpleasant. I guess it could have been worse."

Aiden laughed abruptly. He made to speak when a loud boom from the city sent them surging to their feet. They looked at each other in amazement and concern, and the four of them scrambled up the nearby slope.

Willum threw himself beside Aiden on the cold earth and watched in horror as a man raced from the city gates, a wall of flame chasing behind him. The fire was quickly gone, and they heard wild laughter as the figure halted and whirled to face Ethan silhouetted in the archway.

"Ashel," Natan muttered.

Aiden sucked in a breath. "Natan?" His voice was low and anguished, an urgent plea.

"At once, my lord." Natan sprang to his feet, and he and Aiden sprinted into the night. Willum watched in confusion and turned to Alek. The lord's face was white and set.

"What is it?" Willum asked, desperate for answers.

"They've gone to aide Ethan's Shadow," Alek answered brokenly and explained what Ethan had done to the soldier, Derik. He bowed his head as grief swept his features. Willum didn't understand all of it, but Alek's pain was clear enough, and he knew the tragedy of war had begun. Not knowing what else to do, he stood.

"I'll keep an eye on Ashel," he offered. At Alek's nod, he drew a steadying breath and strode into the darkness, not at all sure what he could do against such power.

Chapter Twenty-Two

KORIN JUMPED AT a loud crash from the city and met Syros's shocked gaze across the fire. Instantly, Derik convulsed in his arms as if waking from terrible dreams. Korin gently drew the trembling man closer. *What was happening?* The sunken eyes fluttered and opened, and wonder crept across Derik's stark face. "You're here."

Derik's voice was a wisp of air on his cheek, and Korin could hardly breathe as pity tightened his throat. Didn't Derik remember where he was? Tears blurred his vision. Derik's feverish eyes seemed to drink him in, and then he blinked and looked uncertain. He pressed his face to Korin's shoulder.

"Don't look at me," he said, anguished, and Korin's heart twisted.

"Derik." He turned the ravaged face to him. "You're beautiful," he murmured and brushed a kiss over the blackened lips. "You always have been."

The whisper of a laugh escaped the tired man.

"Liar." Derik gave the faintest of smiles and closed his eyes, settling more comfortably into Korin's arms as if content to spend his last moments there. Korin slowly rocked him, overcome with grief, and wept as he felt the young life slipping from its useless body.

Running footsteps approached, and he heard a sharp cry of dismay. He knew that voice. "Mage, what…" He couldn't continue. He couldn't breathe and held the shriveled body close to his aching heart, not wanting to let him go. Only a sudden stillness in the air and the firm tread of a man awash in power kept him from the dark pit forming in his mind.

"Derik, I'm here," Aiden said and knelt beside them, folding Derik's tortured hands in his own. Derik's lids fluttered, but he didn't seem to have the strength to open his eyes. But a smile trembled on his cracked lips and peace settled on his face as he sank further into Korin's embrace.

Another boom echoed from Siagan, and Aiden gently pressed his forehead to Derik's. "Are you ready, dear friend?"

"Yes," Derik breathed, and Korin's heart bled a river of pain for him as his emaciated body jolted, Ashel's renewed attack on Ethan smashing into him. But Aiden must have instantly transferred the energy to himself. White agony contorted his face, and he released Derik's hands, sitting back on his heels as Derik collapsed.

"No," Korin murmured, clasping Derik in his arms as Derik's final breath brushed against his wet cheek. He hadn't been able to save him. He'd wanted to save him! Was there nothing he could do right? Not one small thing against the horrific end coming for them all? He wept, holding Derik to him as his mind slipped toward despair.

"Let him go, Korin," a stern voice said—Aiden—and he had no

choice but to let Derik be taken from him. Fingers pressed on his temples.

"Let me in," Aiden crooned, and Korin whimpered as Aiden slipped easily into the passageways of his thoughts. The Red Twin was cruel, calling up each scene spent with Ashel: the dark moments of forced passion, the small tortures on his white skin, subtle manipulations. Also, the horror of the time he spent with Ethan at the lake, the terrible fear and helplessness. He cried out when Aiden took him to his childhood and relived every degradation and black seduction…

Korin was aflame! He burned with humiliation, anguished and tortured with memory. He wept in shame. How dared he offer his heart to anyone? He was degraded and stained, a loathsome man not worthy of the life that pulsed within him.

He felt a searing pain and opened his mouth to scream but gasped instead. It was gone—the oppressive weight of guilt, the shame. He felt renewed. Joy spilled into him, and he opened bewildered eyes.

Aiden was beside him and he smiled. "Your friends accepted you long ago, Korin, as you are. Do you forgive yourself?"

"Yes!" he cried out with a laugh and found it was true. Aiden nodded and lifted his hands, and the black mass he held swirled into the night and dissipated. Tears slipped unheeded from Korin's eyes, and he glanced at Aiden helplessly, not knowing how to thank him. The Red Twin reached over and pressed his hand.

"Live," was all he said, but Korin thrilled at the passion behind the word and nodded. He brushed at his eyes and looked a question.

"Come with me." Aiden rose and led him farther into the tall boulders. On the far side they emerged into a small glen scattered with rock. A shallow grave had been quickly dug, and Derik lay in the rich soil wrapped in Syros's cloak. Korin knelt.

"Thank you," he said earnestly and ran gentle fingers over Derik's ravaged face, remembering a comely young man with pretty eyes who'd trembled as their hands brushed. He placed the first rock beside the still body, then stood on the edge of the glen and stared into the darkness with burning eyes while the others built Derik's cairn.

It was nearing completion when Willum trotted into the glen. He stopped in dismay. "He's killed him, then."

Aiden stared at the grave, deep sorrow in his eyes. "I spared him much of the pain, but it still proved too much for his fragile heart." He swore bitterly. "Ethan was to have used Derik as a barrier against my attack. Instead, Ashel—" Aiden broke off his words, fury turning his eyes molten. He flashed a look at Willum. "Did you catch Ashel?"

"No, sir. He drew quicksand to the banks of the stream, and I couldn't cross." Willum turned suddenly to Korin, who blushed without knowing why, though Willum only asked if he knew where Ashel might hide.

"No, sir," he stammered, distressed. The great lords were watching him, and he felt out of his depth. Only Syros's sympathetic face kept him from running. Natan must have guessed something of his discomfort and suggested they go back to the fire and talk.

Korin said a last goodbye to Derik, placing a hand on his grave while the others trailed after the Mage. Syros stirred up the glowing coals of the fire when they returned to camp and put water on to heat, and they settled wearily around the comforting blaze. Korin roused with effort and turned as Alek came up beside him. Concerned by his tired features, Korin asked, "Are you well?"

Alek smiled faintly and nodded, but Korin could see the strain in his eyes.

Natan spoke into the troubling silence. "Kavi and the Lady Kirstin are in growing peril, as is our beloved Cecil. And they are still out of Aiden's reach. Korin, you seem somehow untouched by the insanity that claims us, though you have been closest to the madness in Ashel and Ethan. It is a blessing. We'll surely need you."

"We?"

"Ashel will need to be dealt with shortly. He must have learned much during the few days he'd hidden in Siagan. We need to know his plans. But before that, Syros and I are going after Cecil. Will you come?"

Korin studied him across the fire and surprised a sadness in his face. "When do we leave?" he asked quickly.

"In a few hours. They're close, but it will take half a day of hard riding to reach them."

"I'll be ready, lord," Korin said. Syros handed him a blanket, and Korin settled on his side close to the fire, his heart aching for Derik, his young life cut short so horribly. His mind drifted toward darkness and sleep, knowing the desperate morning would come soon enough. The others spoke awhile longer, then dispersed to their separate camps.

Silence descended, the air cooling into night. Korin held his breath, and in a moment Syros nestled down behind him, fitting their bodies together. Korin drew a shuddery breath, but Syros hushed him.

"Sleep now," Syros commanded and put an arm around him, tugging him closer. Korin's thoughts raced; then Syros placed a gentle kiss behind his ear, and the terror and grief knotting his chest eased. The warmth of Syros's body seeped into him, and he sighed and fell into welcomed sleep.

*

THE KNIFE IN Kirstin's hand glittered in Cecil's eyes, filling all his sight, and she giggled when he flinched back. Thin ribbons of blood already marked his chest, sliding down his sweat-drenched skin.

"Kirstin, stop playing and cut him down."

The blade flashed in the afternoon sunlight as she severed the rope suspending Cecil's arms to a high branch, and he dropped heavily to his knees. Sensation rushed painfully back to his numb limbs, and he retched, hanging his head until the dizziness passed. Blood trickled down his chest like tears. Cecil absently watched the crimson drops fall on the dirt. They'd been traveling for days, and when they finally stopped with the sun at its zenith, Kavi quickly strung him up. Pain and grief kept him from any rest.

Fingers threaded in Cecil's hair and wrenched his head back. He clenched his teeth at the coldness in Kavi's eyes. "I feel Aiden reaching out to us, Cecil. What does he want?"

Cecil blinked in surprise, and Kavi gave his hair a sharp jerk. Kirstin knelt beside him and slid her fingers over his throat, tightening the noose on his neck. His head swam, and she only let him breathe when Kavi glared, though her nails continued to stroke his skin.

"I can't reach through their barriers. Is Aiden setting a trap?" Kavi caressed Cecil's face, touched his lips. "Call out to Alek, dear. What are their plans?"

Cecil shivered. He would never betray Alek, so Kavi would kill him, and he didn't want to die.

Kavi leaned close. "He doesn't love you, Cecil." His voice slid silkily into Cecil's thoughts. "Why not yield?" His voice dropped low. "You shame him."

Kavi laughed at Cecil's efforts to push him from his mind, painfully aware of Kavi's glee as every indifferent glance, harsh word, and turned shoulder that Alek had given him over the summer played through his thoughts until he fled wounded from Kavi's mocking eyes. He came up hard against a door deep in his mind, sank to the cold floor, and leaned his tired head against the wood.

He slowly became aware of a warmth on his face and body where it touched the door. He pulled himself to his feet and leaned his length against the wood. He smiled. Alek's love lay beyond. Kavi's sharp questions and growing anger warned him not to pursue it, but he felt strengthened and reassured.

A stinging slap roused him from his internal struggle, and he found Kavi's contorted face inches from his own when he opened his eyes.

"Call to Alek," Kavi hissed. Cecil gave him a contemptuous glance. Kavi's face mottled with rage, and he raised trembling hands. "You're blind!" He struck Cecil beside his eyes. Blood roared in his head, and Cecil gasped in terror as the world went black. Panic swept him, and he struggled to gain his feet. Kirstin cut off his air with a cruel twist of the rope.

Kavi's voice came from far away. "Will you call Alek? I'll let you see again if you call him."

Cecil's head pounded, and he thought his chest would surely burst as Kirstin kept a tight hold on the rope choking his breath. His senses were going, and he said a little goodbye to Alek in his heart.

Kavi wasn't merciful. He struck Cecil's face again and again until he roused from his stupor and could focus his thoughts. "Kavi?" His voice sounded small and lost and bewildered to his own ears, and Kavi hesitated.

But then Kavi laughed mockingly before Cecil could hope.

"We have all day, love." Kavi stroked Cecil's aching face, surely bruised. "You'll give Alek up soon enough."

Cecil screamed as Kavi burst violently into his mind, bringing phantoms from Cecil's own memory. A soft lisping voice, Camron's, wound slowly down his spine and into his heart, bringing despair. He hung his tired head until Kirstin tugged at the rope. She pulled until he sat against the tree, and in glee, she ran the rope several times around the trunk, looping the cord around his neck and knotting it. His breathing was a desperate wheeze past the constriction.

Kirstin knelt beside his splayed body and drew the slim knife from her belt, giggling as she caressed the sleek muscles of his chest, marred now by the thin bloody cuts in the white skin. She added another and laughed in delight at the shudder that ran through his body, the groan stifled in his throat.

"Kirstin, leave him be," Kavi growled.

Cecil was drifting slowly into unconsciousness when he heard a stealthy movement behind him and came awake, heart racing.

"Not a sound," a voice warned in his ear, and his chest heaved with his first deep breath as Syros cut the rope at his neck. His heart pounded as Syros deftly cut the rest of his bonds and took a precious moment to trickle water into his parched mouth. Cecil made an effort not to beg for more.

"We must hurry. Natan will distract your captors, but we need to be gone from here."

Cecil shook his head. "I can't go, Syros. I can't see."

"Let me aide you," Syros murmured gruffly. He put a hand under Cecil's arm to help him stand and led him into the underbrush. A cry of rage rent the air suddenly, and Syros abandoned stealth, leaving Natan to deal with the Karthagans. He held tightly to Cecil's hand, and they fled into the trees, Cecil fearing every moment the Karthagans would simply burn the forest around them.

They traveled at a swift pace through the woods, Cecil's heart faltering when a tangle of underbrush hindered them. He stumbled as the ground dipped at his feet. As he scrambled for balance, someone called from the trees ahead of them and they halted.

"Natan's alone. I'm going back. On your life, don't leave him!" Syros cried, and Cecil panicked as Syros left his side. He tensed as an arm slipped around his waist, urging him to his feet.

"Let me help you, my lord."

Cecil's blindness terrified him. "Who is it?"

"It's Korin."

Cecil let out an anxious breath. "I'm sorry. I didn't know your voice."

He was aware of Korin's shock, realizing his blindness, then Korin cleared his throat. "Trust me, Cecil," he said and began to lead him carefully in the opposite direction from the one Syros had taken.

*

A HEAVY SILENCE fell on the forest as Natan faced Kavi and Kirstin's anger across the glen, Syros having gotten Cecil safely out of the way. Quick as thought, he raised his hands. The ground trembled. Wind sprang to life with a roar as energy pulsed in the air and flew toward the two at his bidding.

The grass flattened in its wake. The Karthagans looked startled, Kavi crying out as the pulse struck and passed through them. He blinked, dazed, and fell to his knees. Kirstin looked down at him, then sat beside Kavi, a vacant look on her face as if she couldn't comprehend what had happened.

Natan sprang to them, his energy straining as Kavi pushed back. Coming to a halt, he bent the earth to his will. "Sleep," he demanded. Kavi opened his eyes wide in surprise, then collapsed to the ground in a heap. Natan was vaguely aware of Syros running up to him.

"Cecil?" Natan asked sharply.

"I got him free. He's with Korin."

"We need to go, now, while Kavi's…" Natan's voice broke, and he cleared his throat.

"Of course, Mage," Syros murmured. He watched Natan anxiously, but Natan kept his focus on Kavi.

"Go ahead, Syros. Take Kirstin. I'll look after Kavi," he said and knelt beside his husband, his heart aching. "My love." He touched Kavi's dear face and brushed the dark hair from his eyes. He stood abruptly and sent Kirstin a distraught look; she leaned against Syros as they made their way into the forest. What was he to do with them? He slipped his arms under Kavi's knees and shoulders and lifted him, then followed Syros under the trees.

An involuntary smile touched his face as he came upon Cecil and Korin, Syros assisting Kirstin to a nearby log. He lay Kavi on the grass beside them, pressing a kiss on his forehead as Kavi slept with a look of peace on his face. Cecil sprawled against a stump, looking utterly exhausted, while Korin bound his torn wrists as gently as any healer. Korin's face was intent, copper hair gleaming against Cecil's white skin where it brushed his arms. They had a small fire going with water heating for tea, and Natan sat cross-legged beside it and warmed his hands. "How are you, Cecil?"

Cecil flashed a smile, though he struggled to speak, his voice raspy, "I can see, Mage. Kavi's spell is gone. That's everything, for the moment." He sighed and leaned his head back against the tree. Korin cried out at the angry burn across his throat from Kirstin's tight ropes.

"It doesn't hurt," Cecil softly assured him, but his voice cracked, and he winced, giving lie to his words. Korin made tea with clumsy hands while Natan went over and touched Cecil's face, searching his eyes for signs of fever, or worse. He shuddered as a shadow moved in the gray depths.

"Cecil?"

"Can you make them go away?" Cecil asked brokenly and covered his face with shaking hands.

Natan swore, furious and grieving. "Syros, will you help me?" He moved Cecil's hands from his face, and Cecil leaned back against the tree, trusting as a child.

"Hold him still," Natan instructed and waited until Syros and Korin knelt on either side of Cecil and gently took his arms. They exchanged a worried look, Korin giving Syros a shaky nod. Natan placed his hands on Cecil's temple. The air crackled as energy sprang to life under his fingertips and flowed into Cecil. With grim determination, he hunted down every dark memory and nightmare Kavi had stirred in Cecil's mind.

It took some time, and Cecil was weeping by the time he'd finished. Korin helped him drink a few swallows of tea, and then he slumped to the ground and was instantly asleep.

Korin watched him, his face grave. "What happens now, Mage?"

Natan rubbed his gritty eyes. "We can't stay here long. Kavi sleeps, so it's easier, but we must get him and Kirstin to Aiden before I lose control."

Korin looked at the cousins. "What did you do to them?"

Natan rose to his feet, reluctant to speak of it. "I sent a burst of energy at them that's left them confused, unable to focus their thoughts and use their power. I can keep them thus for a short while, but we need to move. Can you help me with the horses?"

"As you wish." Korin put his cloak over Cecil and rose.

Syros touched Natan's shoulder. "We'll find the beasts, Natan. Rest a moment."

While they gathered the animals, Natan went over to Kirstin where she sat. The expression on her face was vague and dreamy, and she hummed a childish tune under her breath. Natan feared suddenly he'd broken her mind.

"It's time to go, dear," he said kindly.

"Are we going home?"

"Soon, Kirstin. We'll go home soon." He took her hand and helped her into the saddle of the horse Syros brought up. He then picked up the drowsing Cecil, while Korin swung onto the back of a second roan, and handed him up. "If anything should happen, you're to take Cecil far away. Don't look back. Run."

"I don't understand."

"Look at him, Korin."

Cecil lay on Korin's shoulder, pale from loss of blood, eyes bruised, in pain, fragile as he slept.

"What if Kavi or Kirstin held him hostage again, and Alek were to witness—"

"He'd do anything they asked," Korin said on a breath. Syros gave Korin's knee a reassuring squeeze, then mounted the remaining horse.

Natan went over to Kavi, who sat up groggily, and helped him climb in front of Syros. He feared having Kavi in his own arms would be too distracting.

Leaping on the mount holding Kirstin, he led them at a quick trot toward Siagan. He fretted at the pace, longing to race the horses, but with an anxious glance at the others, let the wish go. Kavi already drowsed against Syros, and Cecil had groaned and fallen unconscious at the first jolt of his mount. Kirstin babbled merrily to herself. Natan put a protective arm around her and cast his mind in search of Aiden. He found him immediately.

"How soon?" Aiden asked.

"Morning, at the earliest."

"You need only make it to the plains, Mage. I'll have them then."

Natan felt his reluctance to hold their contact, so he quickly explained Kirstin's condition and Cecil's illness. Aiden assured him he would send for Tessa, next only to her mother in healing. Then with a soft word of affection, Aiden was gone. Natan sighed in frustration, calculating the leagues still to travel before they reached the rocky terrain outside of Siagan.

*

THE AFTERNOON PASSED as they traveled, and a welcomed sleepiness came over Natan, bringing relief to tense muscles and comfort to a sore heart. The very ease with which he slipped into dreams panicked him, and he jerked awake, taking note of his companions. The horses had slowed to a walk, and he discovered Korin blinking sleepily against Cecil, and Syros nodding in his own saddle.

Kavi was alert and laughed in triumph, eyes brilliant and wild as he shoved Syros from their mount. Syros fell hard as Kavi kicked the animal's flanks and disappeared into the trees.

"Go, Korin!" Natan cried, desperate to have them out of Kavi's reach, as he handed Kirstin to the ground and bid her stay with Syros, who'd staggered to a knee. His temper flashed as Korin hesitated. "Flee south, but no farther than the edge of the plains. On your life, Korin, wait for me there."

Cecil stirred and Natan saw his eyes. He rode close and gripped Korin's arm. "Don't let him sleep anymore," he hissed. He cast off all thoughts of them then. Tucking low in the saddle, he gave chase to the Karthagan who was slowly tearing his heart to shreds.

"Find them," Natan whispered to his mount, who laid back his ears and ran. They crashed headlong through the brush, quickly gaining on Kavi, but then the horse reared, neighing in terror as they plunged into quicksand.

"Hush." Natan stroked his neck, quieting his panic. With a flick of his hand, the earth began to firm under them until they could struggle from the muck to dry ground. Dismounting, Natan took a cloth from the saddlebags and methodically wiped the clinging mud from the trembling animal, talking quietly until he calmed. Natan pressed his face to the warm hide, gathering courage.

"I know you're there, Kavi," he said, not raising his eyes. It took all his will not to cry out when he heard a step, and Kavi's fingers slid up his back, touched his neck. Kavi moved Natan's braid aside and pressed a kiss to his nape in a way Kavi knew would send a shiver of pleasure through him. It squeezed his heart in a vise this time, stirring memories he'd do better to suppress. Kavi's mocking laughter hurt.

Natan turned until they stood eye to eye. He touched Kavi's face, and

Kavi impatiently pushed his hand away. "Don't. Your touch was never as clever as I could wish."

Natan watched him, wary. Kavi was very strong. Natan could feel the energy radiating off him. It would take all his concentration…

"I never loved you!"

Natan laughed outright and pressed his body up against Kavi's. "You know that's not true."

"It is," Kavi sneered though he didn't move away from him. Natan's heart pounded. He felt the madness stirring in the air. If he could get Kavi unbalanced, he might have a chance. Though Kavi was a danger to him like this, wild and beautiful, so alluring…

"What of our children? The family we've made together? Kayle and Tillie? Ellis?" Natan brushed his lips against Kavi's cheek.

"They don't mean I love you."

"Maybe not." Natan flung an arm around Kavi suddenly and pulled him tight against his body. "But what of our nights together?" he murmured roughly in Kavi's ear. Kavi gasped, and a deep flush mounted in his cheeks at the memories Natan sent him, their bodies slick, twined, moving as one in growing heat and pleasure.

Kavi's eyes narrowed, and he jerked free, aware of what Natan was doing, but Natan shouted in elation. It was too late. He'd slipped into Kavi's mind along with the images. Kavi turned and fled into the labyrinth of his thoughts, and Natan leisurely followed. Kavi had nowhere to go.

He found him in a secluded room under a blanket. Natan peeked at him and smiled fondly at the mussed hair and flashing eyes.

"I hate you!" Kavi screeched at him.

"Of course you do," Natan answered and kissed him. Kavi stared at him in confusion. Natan tucked the blanket around his shoulders and went out the door, locking it securely behind him.

"Natan?"

He stopped, though his better sense said to keep going, aware of his danger.

"Let me out, sweetheart. I'll behave."

He winced at the tenderness in Kavi's tones.

"Darling?" Kavi's voice was soft just beyond the door. Natan longed to be his darling again, feel his touch, secure in his love. He blinked and returned to himself to find Kavi asleep in his arms. He held him close a moment and kissed him, grief a hard knot in his chest. Then he laid him carefully on the forest floor and went to find the horses.

Natan's hadn't strayed far, coming to him when he whistled, but it was a moment before Kavi's mount trotted up. Looping the reins of the spare roan over the pommel, he lifted Kavi into the saddle and swung up behind him, nudging the animals onto the trail leading back to the others.

He found Syros sitting where he'd fallen from the saddle, patiently handing stones to Kirstin who stacked them into towers, then clapping when they toppled. His face was pinched with worry as Natan approached. "What's happened to her?"

Natan shook his head. "I don't know. I thought she'd come back on her own." He ran a shaky hand through his hair. "Let's get to where Aiden can reach us. I see no hope for us otherwise."

"At once, Mage." Syros rose to his feet and held out a hand to Kirstin. "Time to go."

Kirstin smiled at him, and keeping a few stones in her hands, let him help her into the saddle.

Evening had advanced to twilight before they left the forest and spotted Korin's fire. They soon reached it and dismounted, Natan settling Kavi on the blankets Syros spread by the fire. He searched Kavi's sleepy face and kissed his brow.

Cecil sat with Korin against a boulder near the fire, and he gave Natan a wan smile as he approached them.

Natan knelt. "How are you?" He felt Cecil's flushed face. Korin helped Cecil sit up, murmuring worriedly as he swayed.

"I'm all right," Cecil said, though he panted, and his gray eyes blinked repeatedly. "Korin won't let me sleep."

Korin gaped. "It's the Mage's fault!" he protested with raised hands. Cecil's lips twitched into a small grin.

Natan bit his lip as their eyes turned trustingly to him. He looked at Kirstin where she hugged her knees and sang to herself at the fire, Syros squatting beside her. Kavi still slept. What was he to do? Cecil burned with fever, his body too weak to fight the infection seeping into his blood.

He sent his frantic thoughts out in search of Aiden and was startled to find him in the rose garden in Karthag on a summer's afternoon. Aiden sat on a bench doing nothing in particular, enjoying the sun.

"Hello," he called, and Aiden gave him a warm smile and waved him over but put a finger to his lips for silence.

"Ethan is here," he whispered as Natan sat beside him, and he nodded his head toward a dark mist in the garden. "Talk softly."

"We've entered the plains."

"That's good news." Aiden's smile faded. "What is it, Mage?"

Natan swallowed painfully, and Aiden touched his face and entered his mind a brief moment.

"I'm sorry, Natan. It's been hard on you." Aiden seemed to study a crack in the cobblestones. "I'm not sure I can help Kirstin," he admitted reluctantly. "Perhaps, with time…"

There was an odd note in his voice, and Natan gave him a close look. "Have you slept at all?"

Aiden smiled slightly. "A little, but Ethan is always here, so there's small comfort in it."

Natan rose and drew the Red Twin to his feet. "I'll be with you soon, Aiden, and we'll end this."

"Yes, Natan."

Natan gave him a fierce embrace. "Believe it, Aiden. My patience has almost expired."

Aiden nodded wearily. "Go back, Natan. Clean Cecil's wounds. I'll find a way to elude Ethan and will be there shortly to lend what strength I can."

"Thank you," Natan said fervently and returned his thoughts to the others. Korin was watching him with raised brows, and Natan shrugged. "Will you help me with Cecil?" he asked by way of distraction.

Syros joined them and they soaked the bandages drying on Cecil's chest. Natan winced as they exposed the raw flesh, aflame with infection.

"How can this be?" Syros asked as he helped.

Natan met his puzzled eyes. "Kirstin must have covered her knife in filth, knowing this would happen."

Kirstin joined them at that moment, sitting opposite. "What happened to him?"

Syros hissed angrily, but Natan lifted a hand. "He's been hurt, dear. Will you help us?"

"If I can."

"That's my girl. Hand me another cloth."

They bound Cecil's wounds loosely, the soldier falling asleep before they'd finished.

"We can let him sleep," Natan assured Korin at his frightened expression, then continued, "Aiden will be with us soon. We should all try to get some rest. It's still some way to Siagan."

"If you say so," Korin said dubiously.

They at last slept, Korin on one side of Cecil and Kirstin on the other. Syros gently brushed the hair off Korin's face and received a sleepy smile in return.

At the purposeful snap of a twig behind them, both Natan and Syros rose to their feet as a figure entered the glen. Carrow. Natan's wild heartbeats slowed while Syros sheathed his knife.

"Didn't mean to startle you," the archer said though his lips quirked with a suppressed grin.

"What are you doing here?" Syros asked, taking a step between Carrow and the others sleeping on the ground, a soldier on alert.

Carrow looked between him and Natan and slowly raised his hands, palms up. "Commander Tyrel has me keeping watch once again on Siagan, and I spotted signs of Ashel passing this way."

"Ashel is close?" Syros took him up sharply, his gaze going to Korin, whose breath had caught at the mention of the hated name. Korin leaned up on an elbow, his face pale in the firelight.

Carrow glanced at Korin as well and nodded reluctantly. "Yes."

Syros's gaze swept to Natan, who nodded after a brief stillness, his eyes closed. "He speaks the truth."

Carrow blinked, the only betrayal of his surprise, and he bowed. "Thank you, Mage."

"Syros?" Korin whispered, slight panic in his tone.

Syros flinched though he kept his attention on Carrow, his face growing hard. "Then I will come with you. I would see that monster dead."

Carrow inclined his head. "As you will."

There was silence as Syros fetched his pack. Then he looked at the others, Kirstin and Kavi and Cecil, and dismay crossed his face. "Mage—"

"Go, Syros." Natan gave a short laugh. "Aiden is close. Even I should be able to get us the remaining distance to him."

Syros returned his smile. "Of course, Mage. Forgive me."

He went over and knelt by Korin. Natan turned his head while they held an urgent, whispered conversation. He looked back in time to see Korin grip the front of Syros's cloak and pull him down for a fierce kiss. Then Syros rose and nodded to Carrow, Syros doing nothing to hide his distress, and strode into the forest behind the archer.

Natan's heart ached. The world seemed full of pain. He sighed and gathered several sticks of wood for the dwindling fire. Korin settled back down beside Cecil, his tears glistening as the moon rose over the treetops.

*

NATAN STOOD IN the quiet camp a moment, watching Kavi sleep, then made his way into the moonlit landscape. He found a slide of rocks to screen him and settled in the short grass, resting his chin on his knees. He was anxious for the morning though he feared what he might see in Kavi's eyes. A star burned across the sky, its beauty tearing his fragile heart.

He gasped suddenly and raised his head as a clean breeze swept the darkness from his thoughts. Aiden! He was aware of the Red Twin's light touch across his mind, gone, but leaving hope and renewed strength.

There was a step in the quiet behind him, and his blood surged. He shivered, waiting. Kavi knelt at his back and ran his hands over Natan's tense shoulders, caressing his neck with his strong fingers. He undid Natan's braid and loosened the heavy chestnut strands. His touch sent shivers through Natan. Kavi pulled him back against him, and Natan could hardly breathe from the tightness in his throat.

"Darling," Kavi crooned, tilted Natan's head, and kissed him. Natan caught fire. He had no pride and would have taken Kavi in his arms, but Kavi turned his head.

"I love you," Kavi began hesitantly, and Natan drew away and sat cross-legged facing him.

"I know," he said with effort when Kavi didn't continue.

"Oh, darling, I hurt you. I didn't mean to. I never would have…"

Natan waited while Kavi struggled for words. It was a beautiful night, and he would forgive Kavi anything if only he cared a little.

"I love you, Natan. But there is a darkness in my mind, trapped in that room you locked it behind, clawing at the door. Chaos and hatred and power. It would destroy you in a heartbeat, and anyone else in its way. I don't know how long I can hold it back, even with Aiden's help—"

Kavi sucked in a breath, raising wet eyes to Natan. "You captured my heart with the first glance from your beautiful eyes all those years ago. You're the best man, the most precious— I don't want to hurt—"

His voice broke and Natan pulled him into his arms and kissed him over and over until it became more expedient to simply share their love rather than waste another word on it. Kavi's soft, adoring smile as Natan caressed his skin nudged the last drop of pain and doubt from his heart, and he eased Kavi onto the grass, kissing his face, his neck, thrilling at the taste and heat of his skin. Tears blurred his vision. He'd been afraid he'd never have another moment like this with the man who was his life.

Natan slid a hand under Kavi's tunic and grazed his fingers over lean muscle, thrilling when Kavi gasped into his mouth. Encouraged, he reached lower, loosening Kavi's pants. Kavi's moan encouraged him, and Natan swallowed that as well, losing himself in the tremble and urgency of the strong body under him as he worked his way downward with lips and tongue.

Chapter Twenty-Three

AIDEN YAWNED AND stretched a kink from his back in the cold morning air. The camp was not yet stirring, but he felt restless and ill at ease. He'd hoped Natan would have returned by now. It had been over a day since the fool had gone…

He smothered the thought. He had no right to question the Mage's actions. He smiled a little at Natan's insistence that it wouldn't be him that directed the coming conflict. He was wrong. They were all pawns in a cruel game that only Natan, with his true heart, could bring to an end.

He stretched again and felt the energy that flowed through him without conscious thought, glorious and terrible. Nodding to himself, he walked to the edge of the small rise overlooking the city of Siagan. It was time.

The camp awoke with a thought, and the Karthagans stood in ranks behind him as the sun rose on the far side of Siagan. The sight stirred something inside him. He realized he'd been dulled to emotion for a long time now. Many of the people with him wouldn't survive the day, and he hadn't given it any notice. He looked over the city below and welcomed the numbness as it returned.

Alek shifted restlessly beside him and gave Aiden a cool stare. "Will you sacrifice us all?" he asked bitterly.

Aiden put a hand on his shoulder. "Cecil is alive, my friend. Let's fight today to keep him thus."

He watched in detachment as tears filled his cousin's dark eyes, content with the sharp nod of his head and the squaring of proud shoulders.

The Red Twin took a step toward Siagan, and his people followed.

The sun was a red disc in the sky, and Aiden smiled as the city's gates burst open and Siagan soldiers poured into the clearing. The Karthagans behind him roared, the sunlight flashing like blood on their swords. They leaped forward and the armies collided with a crash of thunder. The sky ripped open, and lightning flashed in the clear dome overhead, bolts striking Karthagan and Siagan soldiers alike.

Aiden passed untouched through the battle and stood at the open gates of the city. Alek stumbled to his side, blood on his face that was not his own. They entered the city, and Ethan walked up to them.

"Will you let them all die?" Aiden asked him in cold tones. *Why can't I feel their loss?*

"Would it matter? What are they anyway?"

Aiden studied his twin, and a frown gathered on his brow. He moved suddenly, intent on striking, but the thing he clasped turned to smoke in his hands. The fumes rose to choke his breath.

"Run, Alek!" he managed, even as he fell hard on his knees. Giving a startled cry, Alek turned and fled. The gates crashed together behind him, and Aiden fell on his face as darkness took him.

*

ALEK SWAYED AS the gates clanged shut and watched in disbelief the horror unfolding before his eyes. The lightning had stopped, leaving untold dead, and an acrid smoke rose from the charred bodies and torn earth. The Siagan soldiers had brought nightmares with them. Their faces were white masks, eyes glittering, full of hate. They filled him with dread. They ripped the earth apart! Tar boiled to the surface engulfing friend and enemy alike. Fire leaped from one soul to another. *Stop!*

A clear note pierced the air as Alek heard the thunder of hooves. Horsemen sprang among them, and the Karthagans were lifted from danger and swept into the rocky terrain, lost from view. Alek raised his face, numb with shock as a rider stopped before him, and he met Willum's flashing eyes. He gripped the governor's outstretched hand and swung up behind him, and they raced across the plains as howls of rage and sharp hailstone chased after.

They were more than a league from the city when Alek roused, mind clearing, and he begged Willum to stop.

"Not yet," Willum said through clenched teeth.

"Please! Aiden's—"

"Not yet!" Willum snapped. Alek fought the rage that burned him, seeking clarity. Willum must know somewhere of relative safety.

Willum pulled rein at a clearing encircled with high rock, a place the soldier in Alek conceded they could fortify. He slid from the horse and stood on trembling legs and had to grab the stirrup to remain upright as terror and grief caught up to him. Little more than half his people gathered there, and of these, many appeared seriously injured by fire, tar, or sword. Just like on the Isle of Wind.

The thought drew him up, calmed him. He knew this war. He'd lived it before. He straightened his spine as Willum dismounted at his side. "We're in your debt," Alek told him.

"Indeed. I lost good men back there." Willum looked over the soldiers with a grim face. "What is your plan, lord?"

Alek gave him a close look, and Willum smiled faintly. "I'm not a Karthagan, nor do I have any powers to speak of. This is your campaign, Alek. I'm sorry."

Alek took a breath. "Very well." He motioned, and a young soldier immediately left the wounded and hurried to him.

"Temm, take ten of our people to keep watch." He gripped the lad's arm. "If you see the Siagan soldiers approach, don't hesitate. Open a pit at their feet, or if they're spread far, use the wind. No fire. They'd only turn that against us."

"At once, my lord." Yet he hesitated, anxious eyes returning to a girl slumped against a boulder.

"I'll see to her, Temm," Alek promised. The lad bowed and hastened away, calling others to his side. Alek knelt by the girl and touched the part of her face not burned and bleeding.

"Kimra," he called softly, and the girl raised eyes dazed with pain. "Sleep, child," he said in a choked whisper. The heavy lids fluttered and closed, and Alek helped her gently to the ground, laying his cloak over her. He spent some time with the injured, both Karthagan and the Barkuit soldiers, and Willum stayed at his elbow assisting where he could.

Alek looked up suddenly from splinting a broken arm. "They're coming. Willum, keep your men here. If the Siagan soldiers should win through, kill the wounded and flee. Try to circle back to camp and wait for the Mage."

"Alek—" Willum shut his teeth at whatever was showing in his face and bowed low. "As you wish."

Alek put a hand on his shoulder. "Trust me, Willum. These soldiers of Ethan's? They've given their lives to him. I saw it in their eyes. They won't stop now until we are dead, or they are. They would gut the wounded to hear them scream… You must survive to warn Natan. This war will be more nightmarish than we imagined."

"I will," Willum swore and gripped his hand. Alek nodded and strode away with the fleeting thought he'd just said his last goodbye to the man.

A wild cry went up from the rocks towering overhead, and the ground lurched violently, throwing him to his knees. He sprang up and raced to the opening through which they'd entered the clearing, calling his people to follow.

He grimaced as they gathered on either side of him. *So few!* And then he didn't think of them further. The ground appeared to have been shoved into a high mound before them, and he scrambled up the tangle of mud and rock and brush. He flung himself on the summit and peered into the deep pit Temm had opened. Good lad! Broken bodies lay in the dark soil, some still, low moans coming from others.

He cried out as the ground crumbled out from under him. *Fool!* He berated himself as he dropped, pale faces across the pit watching in silence. Pain exploded through him as he landed hard at the bottom, the blow driving the air from his lungs. He scrambled on hands and knees to escape the sliding earth, and his leg stuck in a jumble of rock. He yanked it loose, tearing flesh. Surging to his feet, he flung his arms out. The dirt rose in a wave and crashed upon the Siagan soldiers. *Madness!* The earth screamed in Alek's head.

He climbed and backslid and scrambled up the churned embankment and heaved himself over the top. There was the roar and heat of fire below him, and he watched, dazed, his cheek pressed to the rich soil, as flames engulfed the ravine, catching the few of his people who had followed him. There were screams of terror from the trapped and wounded Siagan soldiers as well, quickly stilled.

He rolled to his back and stared at the black smoke dissipating into a clear sky. Footsteps fled into the distance, south. He should follow. The sun warmed the chill from his bones and he allowed the energies of life to flow through him, gathering his strength and courage.

"Alek?"

He blinked into Temm's young eyes, soft chocolate, and longed suddenly for gray eyes that could see through his every pretense…

He rose impatiently to his feet, thrusting off thoughts that could be dangerous with Ethan so near. His people were picking their way across the charred gully, some already on the embankment.

"How many survived, Temm?"

"Almost sixty, my lord, counting the eight wounded."

Alek closed his eyes for all the lost souls. "Leave two with the wounded, and have Governor Willum follow us back to camp, if he will."

"As you say, my lord."

Alek turned his face to Siagan and started back. There was pain with each step, but it hardly registered in his churning thoughts. How could he win Aiden the time he needed? Perhaps if he gave in to the madness dancing on the edges of his perception… He hadn't gone far when swift hooves approached and Willum slid from the saddle to his side. "My lord."

Alek studied the young governor. Lithe and comely, he had his mother's looks, but his father's ruthlessness was in his eyes that morning. All the better. "How is your luck, Willum?"

"Sir?"

Alek flashed him a cunning glance. "I'm attacking Siagan again. Are you willing to aid us?"

"To what purpose? They've beaten you back once."

Alek's smile turned sly. "That is for the Mage to reveal in his own good time. Is this not going how you planned in the garden long ago?"

Willum scowled, and they walked in silence until Willum touched his arm. "Your leg is injured. Please, ride with me."

Alek looked at his leg in surprise. He limped noticeably, and blood soaked the dark leather of his breeches as it seeped from the lacerated calf muscle.

"Thank you." He inclined his head. They took a moment to bind his leg in a cloth from Willum's saddlebag, then mounted, and Willum kept the horse to a fast trot. Willum's soldiers followed, each taking a Karthagan to save them the long march across the plains. Alek kept his face averted as they passed Siagan. Aiden was in there, with Alek helpless to give him aid. He clenched his hands and forced his heart to stone. He had to think clearly.

Relief swept through him at the sight of tents and cooking fires at the old camp, leaving him weak. Perhaps some of his people had fled this way. They rode up to a fire, and he could have wept as the Mage rose to his feet, finally returned.

Willum helped Alek from the saddle, and Natan clasped his arm, noting the tightly bound leg. "Are you badly injured?"

Pain touched Alek's soul. "It's of no consequence." He spoke haltingly of the nightmare battle and Aiden's capture.

Natan listened in horror, then he sighed and wiped a sleeve across his forehead. "I should have been here," he murmured on an exhale. "But Lady Kirstin, who can help with the wounded, is with us." He watched Alek intently. "Cecil is here as well."

"You brought him here?" Joy flamed inside him, and then Alek recalled himself with great effort and turned on his heel without another word. He stormed through the settling camp, fighting the wild beating of his heart. He found Cecil at a fire under tall pine trees on the outskirts of the tents. Korin was feeding sticks into the bright flames. Alek ignored him.

"What are you doing here?" he barked and saw Cecil startle at his harsh tone. Good. The fool… Cecil raised his face and Alek's heart flipped over. His lover seemed tired to death, dull pain in his wide, vulnerable eyes.

"You've endangered us all," Alek stated in defense.

Cecil flinched, then nodded as if accepting the burden and covered his face with trembling hands. Alek fisted his own hands. He turned away and caught Korin's furious gaze as he crouched by Cecil's side and slipped an arm across his shoulders.

All the better. Alek didn't need Cecil—certainly not the distraction, nor the danger of Ethan exploiting his weakness. He crushed down the hurt, but the image of Cecil's fair hair twining with strands of radiant red as Korin bent over him returned often with its cruel barb.

He skirted the tents to the outcrop of rocks overlooking Siagan and waited impatiently for Natan to join him. The Mage would take control now as Willum had planned long ago.

"Did you find—" Natan began.

"We'll not speak of him," he said harshly. "Ethan listens."

Natan looked at him in dismay, and Alek stirred restlessly. "Ethan has found a way into my mind." He lowered his voice to a ragged whisper. "Into all Karthagan minds. But don't worry, Mage. This day, we'll be free—or die."

Natan put a hand on his shoulder, and Alek allowed the comfort of long friendship and shared peril. "I've sent Cecil with Lady Kirstin to see to the wounded where you left them," Natan told him. "From there they'll make their way to Commander Sadie holding the border. With any luck Kirstin's daughter, Tessa, will rendezvous with them and see to any further wounded this day may exact."

Willum and Kavi joined them, the latter clasping Alek's shoulder.

"Well met, Cousin." Alek smiled into Kavi's face. "This will become a terribly familiar day for us. Are you ready?"

"I am." Kavi lifted his hands, and Alek felt the prickling of power in the air.

Natan took Kavi's face in his hands. "You'll use caution, love? Don't lose yourself."

"Of course." Kavi sounded surprised but then looked thoughtful. "I understand. I'll not let it get out of control." He nudged Alek with an elbow and flashed a smile. "Remember how we used to send Kayden's people fleeing?"

Alek gave a wicked chuckle, and they shared a grin that was not lost on their companions. Willum coughed slightly, and Alek sobered. "Are your people ready?"

"Captain Gael is seeing to it," Willum assured him. They fell silent and studied the quiet city they would once again engage in battle. Willum exhaled on a sigh. "Natan, I'm sorry—"

"No," Natan cut him off sharply. "Doubt will weaken us. Your plan is sound, and we move forward from here. No hesitation. Aiden is waiting within the city for us. We end this today."

A thrill shot through Alek at his words. He firmed his lips. They would end it, and he'd take Cecil home and spend his life seeing to his happiness, if it was his good fortune to do so.

*

SYROS PLUNGED ONCE again into the bog and roundly cursed the archer as he shook the dank mud off his boots. Carrow bit his tongue on a laugh. He couldn't help it. The Northerner was so terribly serious. How Korin must torture him whenever they were together.

"Careful on that stone," he said an instant too late. Syros missed his footing and stepped into the muddy, stinking water yet again. Syros's gray eyes glinted dangerously, and Carrow focused on finding a clear trail. As the sun approached midday, they stopped and shared a cup of precious coffee and some grain and fruit from Syros's pack.

"I heard you have a child," Carrow began diffidently, wanting to make peace.

"My little Dani." Syros's smile warmed his somber face. "He was only a few months old when I left. It's strange how such a tiny person captured my heart so thoroughly." He paused, his expression tender. "Are you married?" he asked in a moment, and Carrow winced though he should have expected the question.

"I was, sir, but I buried her long ago." Carrow stood abruptly. "We should go."

He grabbed up his pack, but Syros rose and gripped his shoulder. "Will it help to tell me?"

Carrow scowled. "She died in childbirth." It was unexpected, but the pity and understanding in Syros's eyes didn't hurt, and there was comfort in the hand on his arm.

"Are we all mad?" he asked a little desperately.

"Who can say?" Syros flung his pack over a shoulder. "With the Karthagans stirring up the old powers, how can we tell?"

They kept to a good pace down the sluggish creek, slowing only when they picked up Ashel's winding trail toward Siagan. His tracks were easy for Carrow to read, and they trotted along the sandy path.

They traveled in this manner for many hours, the day stretching out before them in endless leagues without rest or water or thought, until Carrow stumbled and pitched headfirst into the rich moss and needles covering the forest floor. He was utterly spent and fought for each breath with lungs that burned. His throat was raw and he tasted blood in his dry mouth. Wrapping his arms around his heaving sides, he struggled to sit up.

What had happened? He blinked in confusion. When had they entered the forest? It was late afternoon, and he couldn't recall anything beyond the first hour of travel. A sudden cough seared his throat, and he spat blood, then drank from his water skin with trembling hands.

He struggled to his feet and swayed on shaky legs. Where was Syros? He had trouble concentrating, and it took a moment to find his own clear trail on the springy moss. After a few steps, he fell to his knees and hadn't the energy to stand again. Fear drove him, and he crawled desperately back along his path until he was sobbing with anxiety, barely able to drag his worn body another length.

At last, he pulled himself the final steps to Syros's immobile body. Gathering his strength, he rolled Syros onto his side, out of the muddy pool he'd sprawled into. He swore as Syros emptied his stomach and coughed up water from his lungs, though he didn't waken. Carrow gathered nearby tinder and small branches and patiently worked with flint and knife to start a fire. Shivering uncontrollably, he gave an unrestrained cry of relief when a spark finally ignited the kindling.

He babied the tiny flame, fed it larger strips of wood until it crackled and sprang to life. As he warmed numb fingers, a fierce drowsiness came over him, and his heavy lids drooped. He floated, surrounded by warmth, feeling as though he slept a long time.

"Wake up, Carrow."

Parting his lids, he barked out an oath and scrambled to his feet, pulling the bow from his shoulder. He had an arrow notched before doubt assailed him, though he knew to his soul it was Ashel who gazed at him from across the fire. But it was Lyra's dear face he saw, his wife's sweet voice that said his name with the delight and eagerness she'd always shown at his return.

"You've been gone so long, dearest," she murmured as she rose and went to him with outstretched hands. "Have you forgotten us?"

He gave her a puzzled look. Taking the bow from his numb fingers, she then placed his hands on her swollen belly. The child moved, and Carrow gasped his surprise and wonder.

She smiled in deep fondness. "Will you stay with us, Carrow?"

"Forever," he whispered brokenly and bent his head to kiss her.

She turned her face with a sneering laugh. Steel glittered in her hand,

and Carrow twisted aside, Ashel's knife slicing through his forearm rather than plunging into his body. Before he could recover his wits, the dagger's handle struck hard behind his ear, dropping him to a knee. He watched Ashel flee into the trees with blurred vision.

Grief shook him, remembered loss. Forgetting Syros, he threw off his pain and sprang after Ashel, berating himself for a fool. Lyra had gone long ago. Despair opened at his feet, Ashel's doing, and he clung to his sanity while he fought a longing he'd overcome once before, the aching loneliness without her.

He bent all his thought on Ashel thereafter and followed the clear trail with grim determination.

*

CAPTAIN SADIE PACED the camp on the border as evening drew on and frowned, unseeing, at the soil under her feet. News had come of two travelers, Carrow and the regent, Syros, stalking a third across the wildland outside of Siagan. Her scouting party had just brought Syros in, unconscious and burning with fever, though muttering Ashel's name with horror. She'd sent the soldiers along with Commander Jaden—who'd arrived the previous day to help her, much to her relief—back to the area, fearing for Carrow if Ashel found him first. She chewed a nail, an anxious habit. These were troubling times.

At that moment, riders walked their horses into camp, and Sadie let out a relieved breath. "Tessa?" She studied the girl's blue eyes, honest and clear, and smiled in welcome. The madness hadn't reached her, at least not yet.

"Captain Sadie. May we come in? Aiden sent for me, asking for my help with any wounded."

"You are most welcome. Please." Sadie motioned them down. Tessa's companion dismounted, and Sadie held out her hand, her smile broadening. "Devon! What brings you so far from home?"

Devon grinned in return. "Just making sure our girl arrived here safely."

Sadie was dismayed at the signs of illness and fatigue around his kind eyes. "Come to the fire," she invited and linked her arm with his.

Tessa looked at them curiously. "You're close friends?"

"Of course. The council leader has often invited my garrison to his house for the night while we're out on patrol."

"Have to keep an eye on you soldiers, don't I, while you're in Amara? No telling what wickedness—"

"Devon!" Sadie protested, her heart lightening at his teasing. They shared a simple meal, Sadie enjoying the stolen moment of peace.

"How is Governor Robin?" she asked and delighted in the soft blush that crept over Tessa's fair complexion. She and Devon shared a grin while Tessa's color deepened.

"He's well. Worries for our people. It was hard to leave him—"

She broke off at Devon's low chuckle, then raised her chin, showing her Karthagan spirit. "He's anxious to do well by our people, when with all his heart he wishes to be here, doing what he can."

Sadie touched her arm. "Of course. We all love him, and Robin is exactly where he should be in these hard times—home where the people can see him and gain courage and hope."

"Thank you," Tessa murmured, the distress leaving her face.

Noting her weariness, Sadie rose. "Let me show you where you can rest," she offered kindly.

Tessa spent a moment with Syros before going to her tent, though she had to admit his illness was beyond her strength.

"We have to wait for my mother," she said and went on at Sadie's questioning face. "Natan has sent Kirstin and Cecil here to help with the wounded as they come in. They should be here at any moment." She fell silent, her expression bleak.

Sadie controlled a shudder, unused to the Karthagans' ability to communicate in thought, but also knowing the number of wounded would be great. "We'd better prepare tents for the injured," she said practically, and sent a runner for her surgeon. Tyrel's voice suddenly rang out, and she glanced across the clearing as he hailed a group approaching camp. Excusing herself, she hurried over to join them as Kirstin and a Northern soldier climbed from their horses.

"Lady Kirstin." Tyrel bowed. Kirstin dimpled prettily. Tyrel's face changed, becoming serious as he met Cecil's eyes. "My lord, will you come to the fire? There's a hot meal ready."

"Thank you, Commander," Cecil said, clearly uncomfortable with the man's attentiveness to his poor health.

Tyrel motioned to Sadie. "Commander Sadie, I'd like you to meet my good friend, Lord Cecil of Karthag."

Cecil blushed furiously as Sadie sketched a bow. "Please, I'm not a lord," he protested.

She smiled kindly. "No," she conceded, "you're the celebrated Commander of Karthag's trade ships. Did you think we hadn't heard of you in Nagal?"

Cecil was saved from answering by Tessa's approach with Devon.

They exchanged warm greetings, and Tessa took her mother in her arms. "How are you?"

"Tessa?" Kirstin's smile trembled. "I'm lost, dear."

"I know." Tessa wiped her tears with her sleeve. "But it won't be for long. Aiden will come soon. Will you come now and help me with our friend Syros?"

"Of course." Kirstin hesitated as she took her daughter's arm, glancing at Devon, who'd remained in the background.

"We're friends, aren't we?" she asked and held out her hand, a faint anxiety on her face.

He flushed, and Sadie heard his quickly drawn breath. The gentlest of smiles touched his lips. "We certainly are, my lady." He bowed over her hand without touching her. "Go with Tessa now, dear, and perhaps we may speak later."

"I should like that." She smiled, and he dropped his gaze, hiding his expression.

Sadie led the healers to Syros's isolated tent, and the surgeon quickly ushered them in with relief. Syros burned with fever, his skin dry and hot. "Earlier, he thrashed and called for Sharana, begging her to come to him. He's fallen into unconsciousness since," he told them.

"Are you ready, Mother? We must use great care," Tessa warned, fear in her voice.

Kirstin couldn't speak past her tears. She merely held out her hands for Tessa to guide as they searched out Syros's illness. Sadie watched them a moment and then left them to their work.

Chapter Twenty-Four

AIDEN SMILED TO himself in the gathering darkness of late evening. Life's energy was all around him. He tasted it in the air, felt it in the pulse of his blood. Magnificent life! The Mage was a fool if he thought… He pushed the dangerous response down, crushing it to dust. He would not betray Ellis's father.

Picturing his husband brought a smile to his lips. He could think of him now. Aiden was already in Ethan's trap, the danger of it passed. He wondered how Ellis fared, hoped he wasn't afraid.

Aiden wanted to go to him but resisted. When it was all over, he would return home and never leave him again. He reveled in the dream. They'd been together for such a short time when Aiden wanted an eternity. He still hadn't studied all the shades of color in Ellis's eyes or what emotion each one portrayed. But he thought he knew the color of his joy, his deepest pleasure…

Aiden brought himself back to the present with a jolt. Opening his eyes, he could see in the darkness as if it were day. His mere thought could become reality this close to the lake. He laughed and heard the arrogance in his tone. He was chained to the wall of a small room, Kirstin's room, with Ethan at his feet. Laughter rose in his throat. More fool Ethan if he thought to take energy from him!

Ethan raised his head from the floor, and their eyes clashed. Fury mottled Ethan's features, and he leaped to his feet and struck Aiden hard in the face, then tangled his hands in Aiden's long hair.

"You *will* concede to me," Ethan avowed, a glitter in his stare. Unexpectedly, his knee came up into Aiden's abdomen, driving the wind from his lungs. Ethan fluttered his fingers, and the chains fell to nothing, but before Aiden could gain his breath, Ethan shoved and dragged him through the doorway and forced him to his knees at the lake. A heavy blow landed on Aiden's back, knocking him face-first into the icy water.

Ethan straddled him as he floundered, forcing his head under. Aiden tried not to breathe, but the inky blackness of the lake clung to his mind and confused him. He swooned as water entered his lungs.

In time, consciousness returned to him, and he suffered from the cold that became an ache in his bones. The lake lapped quietly at the shore, almost touching him, receding, returning. Power leaped into him, and he sent it back. It wasn't time.

A boot caught him in the ribs and pain exploded through his body. Ethan grasped his hair and forced him up to his knees. Aiden kept his eyes on the sand, fighting an overwhelming desire to retaliate. It would be so easy...

Ethan drove a fist into the side of his head, and Aiden's ears rang. He spat blood, clinging desperately to his shreds of control. His scattered thoughts cried out for the Mage to hurry, or it would be too late. He'd lose control, and death would take them all after that.

He screamed in exquisite torment as Ethan thrust into his mind and tore apart the barriers he'd set in place. But then Aiden let out a satisfied breath as his twin stepped into the labyrinth he'd constructed in his thoughts. It was a game he could play forever, though madness would be the final outcome for them both.

*

KORIN WAITED ON a high rock overlooking Siagan as drums sounded and the gates were flung open. Without a sound, Siagan's troops poured forth, over thrice that of the Karthagan army standing silent before them. He trembled in an agony of helplessness as Kavi and Alek lifted their hands in unison. The sky cracked with thunder, and a tornado leaped from the earth and air and struck the emerging soldiers, swallowing them in screaming masses. The two Karthagan leaders allowed it briefly, and then let it dissipate, their people rushing the remaining Siagan army.

The ground shook and opened in their midst, and steam and ash billowed out to scorch fragile bodies. Lightning gathered, and many threw themselves to the ground as the heavy bolts struck randomly amongst the soldiers of both armies.

Korin couldn't tell which side called forth the fire, but he cried out in horror as it swept the battlefield, watched in mounting fear as the Mage disappeared through the open gates of the city. How could this be happening? It was every nightmare come alive, the screams of terror, the burning bodies.

The ground heaved, and he fell hard on his knees as a rent opened in the earth. A pool of boiling tar lay beneath and swallowed a pocket of soldiers. The acrid smoke reached him, burning his eyes. He retched, then struggled to stand, cursing himself for not leaving with Cecil when he'd had the chance. He was a fool for thinking he could be of any use here.

A horse neighed in fright as a stray bolt of lightning struck near Willum's men waiting behind the Karthagan army. The crash of thunder was instant and deafening. The animals ran blind in terror, some to the open plains, others to their deaths in fire or the pits. Korin cried out in agony, frantic, fearing the remaining horsemen couldn't hold the line.

His heart thundered as Willum stepped his mount a few paces from his men and stood high in the stirrups, virile and handsome in the black and silver uniform of Barkuit. His banner bearer rode close and unfurled the silver crown on its dark field. A roar came from the horsemen, and with a cry, Willum leaped to battle, his soldiers a glittering wave as swords were drawn, firelight flashing on steel.

Korin sank to the stones and covered his eyes at the butchery of war. Anguished screams from the injured and dying and the shrill squeals of terrified and wounded horses rang in his head. The crack of thunder bruised his ears. He prayed it would end, but it went on and on—an eternity.

The silence that followed shattered him.

He raised timid eyes. Swirling smoke spiraled high and dissipated into a star-filled sky. The nightmare before the gates stood revealed, and he swallowed the bile that rose in his throat. Taking a breath, he scrambled from the refuge where Willum had sent him.

"But I want to fight," he'd argued at the time, despite the glint of temper in the governor's eyes.

"You've already done more than your share," Willum had countered, then added, "Besides, you are of no use to the Karthagans and would only hinder any of my men who would take you on their mount. Stay here. We'll have need of you soon enough."

"As if I can be of any use," Korin muttered now and climbed down to the scorched fields to lend what aid he could.

The strange quiet endured, the last of the injured horses mercifully killed. Willum's soldiers stood dazed with shock, blinking eyes unused to such horrific use of nature, as the Karthagans waited by silently. Korin kept his gaze averted from the dead, the unnatural twist of limbs or blistered skin, the blood.

He knelt by the first wounded soldier he came upon, a young Karthagan. Temm, he thought his name was. The man's left side and arm were charred, and he writhed in the dirt in soundless agony. Tears stung Korin's eyes as he knelt beside him. There were many more in like condition, and he didn't know where to start or what to do.

A comforting hand touched his shoulder, and he glanced up to see Alek's tired smile.

"It's good to find you alive, my friend," Alek told him and crouched beside Temm. Sadness touched his face.

"Sleep." He brushed his hand over the young man's eyes, and Temm sighed as the white agony left his face. "We'll wait for the litters to move him to camp. Will you assist me with the others?"

"Anything, my lord," Korin stammered.

Alek looked at him in pity. "Courage, Korin. This won't be easy for any of us."

"Tell me what to do," Korin begged. He spent the remainder of the night at Alek's side, aiding as he could, lending comfort whenever possible. They met Kavi in the midst of the carnage, and the cousins embraced in joy. Korin bowed to him, overcome with relief. They'd lost so many already.

Kavi touched his arm. "Will you help with the litters?"

They hastily removed the wounded from the field, and Alek sent fire among the dead, burning them to bone and ash. While the fire smoldered, Alek stared at Siagan's walls.

"They're alive," Kavi assured him. "There's still hope."

Willum joined them, a scowl marring his face in the predawn light. "A handful of the Siagan beasts have escaped into the plains. We'll leave immediately on their trail."

"The Karthagans can—"

"No, my lord Alek, if you please. There are few of you left, and my horsemen can cover more ground."

He nodded suddenly to Korin, startling him. "Will you ride with us?" He flicked a look at Alek. "I think you would be safer away from here."

Kavi laughed outright, almost frantic. "It's true, my friend. With the Mage so near the lake, anything can happen."

Korin impulsively pulled him into a quick embrace, then did the same to Alek, who sputtered in surprise.

"Take great care," he urged them and hurried after Willum. The call went out, and the Barkuit soldiers took to saddle with a leap and shout, sweeping across the plains after the escaped Siagan soldiers. Korin rode in their midst, fear a hard lump in his chest.

*

AIDEN PULLED HIMSELF up on his elbows, then struggled to his knees, his head pounding. It had taken the remainder of the night to thrust his raving brother from his mind. He wasn't sure what would come next from Ethan. His twin was insane beyond any doubt, his soft gibbering touching on the edge of Aiden's hearing.

He flinched at the eerie cry that started low and rose to a shriek in the cavern, echoing off the walls and arched ceiling, thrumming in the lake until his bones hurt with the pressure. There was a rush of feet, and Ethan's heavy body slammed into him, sending them both sprawling in the sand on the edge of the lake. Water splashed on Aiden's sweating face, and he screamed in pain and shock as Ethan sank his teeth into his neck. He heaved his body upward, and the terrible hold loosened, only to have the sharp teeth bite his neck behind his ear, rooting for a hold.

Ethan's mad grunts resounded in Aiden's head, driving him to a frenzy. Hard fingers clawed at his face, groping for his eyes. Aiden felt his control slipping as the slavering mouth clamped on his neck again.

"Mage!" he screamed, reaching his limit. As if in answer, footsteps pounded down the passageway and into the cavern.

Natan's desperate breathing filled the air. "I'm here, Aiden!"

Aiden fell back on the sand, and let his body go slack. It was done. Power unequalled filled him with joy, intense pain, and the aching beauty of life. Ethan was a mere twig in his hands. He clasped the struggling body to his breast.

"Hush," he murmured and stroked his twin's lank hair absently as Ethan sobbed in his arms. Energy flowed from his brother, and Aiden drank it in until there was nothing left, yet still he took until Ethan's life was a mere flicker in the darkness—then gone.

Aiden pushed the body from him in sudden panic and scrambled to his feet. Glorious, devastating power had filled him for one brief instant, then surged out, taking his own powers, as well, with a blinding quickness.

"Mage?" His voice rang in the silence of the cavern. Natan went to him and met his eyes in fear.

"Ashel?" Natan asked with dread, and Aiden nodded in dawning horror.

*

ASHEL CREPT THROUGH the underbrush, each twig tested to be sure it wouldn't snap under his weight. Carrow had run him to the ground, and he could hear the man's labored breathing from the copse of willows ahead. If he could just…

He eased aside the branches of a sapling and met the archer's eyes in the faint morning light. Both men recoiled, then Carrow pushed into the small clearing, pulling the bow from his shoulder.

Ashel played his cruel trick again. "Carrow?"

His voice trembled with fear, uncertainty, and he watched with satisfaction as the archer's face softened into bemusement.

"Is it you?" Carrow asked in wonder. Ashel gave him a tremulous smile, his illusion perfect, and Carrow went to the image of his wife and pulled her gently into his arms. "Won't you tell me what's wrong, dearest?"

She buried her fair head against his breast, weeping softly. "I've had terrible dreams. I thought you were dead. I thought our child was dead, and I was all alone in the world. My heart was breaking!"

"Hush now, Lyra. I'm here." Carrow held her folded to his heart and ran fingers through her silky curls. "It was only a bad dream."

She didn't answer, and he raised her face, bending his head to tenderly kiss the trembling lips. Her soft laugh turned mocking, and she pushed against him until he let her go. She stepped away and looked at him with contempt. It had been too easy.

"Lyra?" Carrow held out a hand, bewildered.

Ashel gave a sudden start, listening intently. *What is it?* A piercing joy flashed through him, and he raised his arms to the sky. "It's time!"

He flung open the barriers of his mind, emptying himself of all thoughts and emotions, letting his senses free. He became the perfect hollow vessel, to be filled by the link he'd forged with Ethan, the one he'd made when he'd slipped into Ethan's broken mind as Ethan chased him from Siagan with fire. Ethan's life force sprang from its useless body, passed through his brother, and raced to fall into Ashel in torrents. He cried out with the ecstasy of it, unsure if he could hold such power. Then he could. He was a living flame! He laughed aloud and waved his arms. The earth trembled. He could do anything!

The first arrow caught him in the breast, and he glanced at it in surprise, still dazed with rapture and unable to focus his mind. He thought to admonish the archer and glanced at him, and the second arrow struck him between the eyes. It couldn't be! His spirit fled screaming in fury even as his body fell lifeless to the ground.

*

NATAN KNELT AT the lake's edge and trailed his fingers in the water, emptying his mind, thinking only of the icy liquid against his skin. There was an energy deep in its cold heart, the pulse of the earth. His own heart slowed, steadying to the same rhythm.

Settling cross-legged on the sand, he placed his hands flat on the still water, losing all awareness of where he was, no longer conscious of Aiden where he sat close by. Time drifted away, as did thirst and hunger, fear and joy…

He merely existed, letting the energy of life flow into him, out, back in with each breath he took and each ripple on the lake, the soft lap of water on the sand.

A screech shattered the stillness, a far-off discord in the peace of the cavern. He winced as it drew closer, piercing ears grown sensitive. Natan surged to his feet as it burst into the cavern and surrounded him, confusing him with terror and anger and the lure of a wild madness. Caught up in the chaos, he laughed in amazement, and had already taken several steps into the lake before a sharp blow on his cheek roused him.

He stared into urgent eyes, unable to hear the man's words, but Natan knew him, somehow. He focused on the concern and deep fondness in the golden depths, fighting to gather his scattered wits. It was hard, with the shrieking wind raging around the lake, the water itself beginning to match the movement. His spirit wanted to be free, to fly with that wind…

He swirled viciously when Aiden struck him again.

"You must end this, Mage! Can't you see Ashel's trying to draw you into his nightmare so he can take control? End it now!" Aiden's breath caught on a sob. "I want to go home."

Aiden covered his face, and Natan's confused mind fought to understand. He put his hands on the bowed head and felt Aiden shake as he wept without restraint. What was wrong? He didn't want Aiden to be sad. Tilting his head, he listened to the wailing, lonely cry in the cave, a spirit lost. He didn't want there to be sorrow, not on his account. He opened his arms.

"Come to me," he called with love, gentle as a father, adamant as stone. With one final lament from a wounded heart, the energy crackling in the air poured into Natan. He cried out with the wonder and agony of life, which nearly overwhelmed him, but not quite. Drawing a breath that filled his lungs, he smiled and sent his thoughts out into the wide world, meticulously gathering the errant strands of power that belonged to the earth and had been so brutally plundered and corrupted by thoughtless children.

He came upon Kayle in Sennia, standing on a balcony of Sambola's castle looking out at a world in chaos, a terrifying madness in the air taking his people one by one. Kayle fixed his gaze on him, tears streaming from his dark, sorrowful eyes.

"Do it now, Papa, I beg you," he urged, grief and fear trembling in his voice. "So many have already fallen. It's taken Tillie. I don't know her anymore. Please, remove this dreadful power. I support you. I love you."

"Yes," Natan told him. A promise. He returned to himself and waded waist-deep into the icy lake, then hesitated, infinite sadness touching him. He sent his spirit out one last time.

He found Kavi on a group of rocks overlooking Siagan as the sun broke above the horizon. Alek paced, the air around them charged with an energy they dared not use and left them anxious and unable to find peace.

Kavi jolted as Natan appeared. "What is it?" he asked in terror.

Alek drew a quick breath, peace settling on his features. "The power has never truly been ours, Kavi. Let the Mage have it." He opened his hands and willingly released his gifts to Natan's keeping.

Natan held out a tentative hand to his husband, but Kavi drew back, alarmed and unsure. Though Natan had expected resistance, it still wounded him, and he dropped to his knees. Kavi sat beside him and held him close as Natan buried his face in his shoulder.

"Natan? Darling?"

Natan shook his head, strangely helpless, and Kavi ran his fingers through his unruly curls and raised his face.

"Will you hate me?" Natan asked in a whisper, sure Kavi could see straight to his heart, the frailest crystal in Kavi's hands. Kavi bent and placed his lips against Natan's, intensely sweet.

"I'll love you forever."

A thrill raced through Natan as Kavi's energy flowed into him, but he drew back when Kavi would have kissed him again. "Afterward," he pleaded and pressed Kavi's hands. He rose.

"Come to me," he urged his lover, then flung his spirit back to the cavern. Natan took another deep breath as he once again stood in the lake and thrilled at the power swirling within him. A smile of wonder touched his lips.

"I want to go home," he softly repeated Aiden's words, longing for Kavi's arms around him. He drew one more deep breath, then plunged into the icy depths of the lake. The air in his lungs froze, the cold stabbing him with cruel knives. He sank into the darkness of the water, and life's energy flowed out of him, filling the lake, pouring into the heart of the water. The earth drank it in, healing, becoming whole. Then, as if done with him, the lake swept him onto shore, and Natan fell into the black abyss in his mind without a second thought.

*

IT WAS THE knowledge that Kavi waited for him that brought Natan back to consciousness. He forced his eyes open to find Aiden hovering anxiously over him.

"I feared you had left us, Mage," Aiden said gruffly.

Natan tried to raise his head, then dropped back to the sand, weak with exhaustion. With a muttered apology, Aiden picked him up and carried him through the dark tunnels to the cellar and then up through the kitchen to the entrance hall of Siagan's castle. A fire glowed on the large hearth, and Aiden set him on the warmed rug before it, draping him in soft blankets from the couch.

As Aiden built up the fire, Natan struggled out of his sodden clothing, wrapping again in the blankets, feeling frozen, aching with cold. Hot blood stung his face when Aiden knelt at his feet and began to rub life and warmth back into him. It took time and patience, but healthy color slowly returned to his skin, as did life and warmth. He smiled into Aiden's eyes in sudden excitement. "We did it!"

"Yes, we did," Aiden agreed in elation and tucked the blankets tighter around Natan's trembling body. They both jumped when the front door banged open, and Aiden let out a shout as a vibrant form swept past him straight into Natan's reaching arms. They fell in a tangle of blankets, Natan kissing Kavi's cheeks, eyes, anywhere he could reach.

"Kavi," he whispered over and over, tears blurring his vision. He dashed them away impatiently, needing to see his lover. Kavi's own tears wet his beautiful face, and Natan kissed them, then took Kavi's lips again, needing the connection desperately, both of them weeping with the joy of the moment.

He was hardly aware when Aiden retreated to the doorway where Alek waited with a wide grin.

"I take it Natan is well?"

Aiden chuckled. "He will be."

They spoke more, but Kavi's hands slipped under the blankets and Natan didn't hear another word they uttered, losing himself in Kavi's tender ministration and growing ardor.

*

CARROW BRUSHED AT his eyes as he dug a shallow grave with his knife and bare hands. The sun rose while he worked, and his gaze strayed again to the body a few paces away, though he'd promised himself not to look. She still lay there, his precious girl, with his arrows in her tender body. His heart constricted, and he went back to his task, grieving, and didn't know how to bear the pain of it.

He finished and went to her, and just for a moment he sat with her in his arms and pretended she was alive and warm and awaiting his love. He knew. He *knew* it was Ashel he held, but his heart wouldn't let him believe it.

Carrow gently laid her in the ground when horror suddenly crept up his spine. It took all his courage to place his hands on her belly, and he wept anew in desperate relief. At least he'd been spared that nightmare. Ashel had lied about having the child within him.

He hastily covered Lyra with rock and dirt, then grabbed up his bow and plunged into the woods. Day was breaking and he hadn't slept, but stubbornness kept him moving, and it was solely his skill that led him to the border many hours later. He stumbled to a fireside and sank to his knees in exhaustion. Thoughtful gray eyes met his across the flames and narrowed in concern. In a moment, a mug of hot tea was pressed into his hands. Sadie's softly spoken questions finally penetrated the numbness gripping him, and he sobbed out his story, and her honest pity at last let him sleep.

*

TESSA PACED THE camp, unable to settle. The injured had begun to trickle in that morning, larger groups coming soon afterward. She knew so many of them. Hearing her name called, she approached a nearby fire and met Sadie's anxious gaze. Carrow lay beside her, and Tessa crouched, noting his torn and bloodstained clothing. "What has happened?"

"He's killed Ashel," Sadie answered as she wiped the blood from Carrow's drawn face. "Will you fetch the doctor? I don't want to leave him."

"Of course." Tessa rose and hurried through the camp, rousing the surgeon from his cot in the tent with Syros. She lingered a moment after he'd snatched up his pack and gone, putting her hand on Syros's forehead. His fever had broken, and she and her mother had driven the poison from his lungs. He slept naturally, and she felt sure he would recover fully in a few days.

Restless, she returned to the fire she shared with Cecil on the edge of camp and found him still sleeping. It had been a late night for them all. Devon and her mother slumbered close by, and the sight of them in each other's arms warmed her heart. Though Kirstin's memory was slow to return, she had known Devon last night and accepted his kiss.

There were other small victories. The young Karthagan couple, Temm and Kimra, survived. As did Carrow and Cecil, many others. She would cling to the hope this brought.

Tessa added wood to the fire when a rough hand clamped over her mouth.

"Not a sound, sweet one. I need a hostage, but any of you will do."

She shuddered at the hot breath in her ear. The Siagan soldier removed his hand from her mouth to grip her wrist, and her quick glance at his face clashed with eyes black as midnight, that without Ethan's influence, showed the madness taking his mind. She swallowed the cry on her lips. The blade in his hand was less bright than his glittering eyes.

The soldier looked her over, hunger in his gaze. "Yes, you'll do nicely," he murmured and began to pull her toward the trees. She struggled then, throwing all her weight to the ground, trying to break his hold. She screamed as he hauled her against his length.

"None of that, pet," he warned and laughed as he kissed her, cruel and vicious. He raised the knife so that it shone in her eyes, then rested the blade against the soft skin of her cheek.

A shout startled them both and someone caught the Siagan soldier in a clumsy tackle. They went down hard, but the soldier was up with a snarl. Cecil scrambled to his feet, sucking in frantic breaths. Tessa exchanged a frightened glance with him as her attacker gave a manic laugh and tossed the knife from hand to hand.

He made a sudden lunge for Tessa, and Cecil dived for him again, catching at his legs. The soldier twisted in Cecil's grip as they fell, the knife flashing in a wide arc, slashing into Cecil's forearm. They broke apart and gained their feet. Tessa screamed for help as blood oozed through Cecil's fingers clamped to the wound. Footsteps pounded toward them—Tessa didn't look to see who, keeping her gaze on her crazed assailant—then a yell rang above the others. Hoofbeats approached, and a rider swept into view. The Siagan soldier turned on his heel, but Willum caught him in two strides. His sword flashed as he swung without dismounting, and the man fell, his head cloven by the vicious blow.

Willum leaped from his moving mount and sprang to the soldier, turning him with a boot to see his face. He nodded in grim satisfaction, only then looking at Tessa. "Are you well, my lady?" He sketched a bow at her nod and straightened as his company rode up.

"Did you finish him?" Captain Gael asked as he drew to a stop beside them.

"Indeed." Willum seemed to lose his strength and leaned heavily on his bloody sword. "Was he the last?"

"I believe so, if my count is correct." Gael dismounted; his exhaustion evident as he clung to the saddle a moment.

Willum wiped a hand over his face. "We need rest," he murmured. "Let us sleep a few hours before we decide our next move." He sighed in relief as Tyrel, along with Commander Jaden, rushed up to them.

"My lord," Tyrel bowed, with a hasty glance at the dead Siagan soldier. "My tent is yours when you are ready."

"Thank you." Willum looked at the body at his feet. "I'd better—"

"I'll see to him," Jaden promised. He motioned, and several of his men came up to escort the weary Barkuit soldiers to tents hastily prepared for them and to see to the horses, while Commander Tyrel walked with Willum and Gail through the camp, talking urgently.

As they departed, Korin turned his mount toward Tessa and slid from the saddle, flashing her a smile before hurrying to where Cecil knelt in the dirt awkwardly binding his arm with a bit of torn shirt. Korin knocked his fumbling hands away and deftly wrapped the wound. "Alek needs to take better care of you or someone else will," he muttered.

Tessa smiled at Cecil's flushed face and beckoned him and Korin to the fire. "Welcome, Korin. And thank you for aiding me, Cecil."

"At your service," Cecil said warmly. Korin gave them a sleepy smile as he settled by the warm flames, though horror lingered in his eyes. Tessa set about making tea and something hot to eat, perhaps a porridge, wondering how many friends would be reunited that day. How many would have to go on alone.

Epilogue

THE MORNING PASSED slowly into afternoon, and Cecil grew increasingly anxious. With Ethan vanquished, the Karthagans should have left Siagan and come to the border. But there was no sign of them. He found it hard to sit still and lent a hand around camp, folding up a tent, packing a bag. He was on hand to help the surgeon when Syros left his tent for the first time since his illness.

"Thank you, Commander." Syros smiled through his pain as Cecil settled him by the fire where Willum sat sharpening his knives after too brief a rest. Seeing his frustration with his obvious weakness, Cecil took a moment to whisper, "You're alive, sir!"

Syros let out a rueful chuckle. "You're right, Cecil. I shouldn't complain." Willum reached over the fire and shook Syros's hand, then went further and embraced him.

"It's good to have you back," Willum said gruffly, and Syros visibly swallowed a lump of emotion. Sadie and Carrow joined them, bearing dried fruits and cheeses.

"To celebrate," Carrow told them, and Syros inclined his head and looked embarrassed.

Cecil listened to their desultory talk, then rose, wanting to walk as restlessness took hold of him again.

"Stay with us," Korin called from a stump close by where he'd been sitting, blatantly waiting for Syros, his red hair catching the sunlight. "They won't be here for hours yet."

Cecil blushed slightly at their attention but lifted a shoulder. He walked a few paces away, when the unmistakable sound of approaching horses came to them. The camp roused to either welcome or fend off the newcomers, arrows notched and swords drawn as the group rode into camp.

"Goodness." Kavi's smile turned brilliant as he gazed at the tense soldiers. "All this for us?"

Willum's quiet laughter eased the moment, and Kavi slid from the saddle. Merry greetings were exchanged, and at Willum's bidding, the Karthagans were led to food and soft pallets, the wounded to tents made ready for them.

Willum gave a low bow to both Aiden and Alek as they dismounted. At that moment, Commander Jaden trotted over, and a broad, happy grin slipped on his face as he came up to Natan. "We did it!" he murmured fiercely. Natan nodded, and moisture glittered in his eyes. Jaden laughed even as he embraced him. "No tears, Cousin."

Natan shrugged, unembarrassed. "I'm happy," he said simply as he took Kavi's hand.

Cecil watched Alek. His lover's dark eyes were eager, expectant, as they searched over the gathering. They lit on him, and Cecil thrilled at the slow smile that spread across his face. But concern followed as Alek crossed the distance to him and pulled him into the trees. Alek's face was pale, his clothes stained with blood, both his own and other's. His lean body swayed with exhaustion.

"I've come to ask if you can forgive me." Alek looked aside. "I'll go away, if you wish."

His humility hurt. What had become of the proud lord Cecil had given his heart to?

"Well…" Cecil drawled, allowing his voice to trail off as if he had to think it over.

They stared at each other a long moment, and Alek's brows drew down. He raised his chin and Cecil grinned. There was the arrogant man who infuriated and charmed him!

"We'll rest the horses, then start for Karthag in a few hours," Alek told him brusquely, a flash in his eyes. "Is there a quiet place to sleep?"

"Of course. There are tents set aside for you."

Cecil started to turn away, but his heart thumped as Alek took his hands and drew him closer.

"Just a moment, Commander," Alek murmured, heat in his voice, and Cecil exalted as the haughty mouth claimed his own.

*

KORIN WATCHED AS Alek led Cecil into the trees, and his heart pounded. While the others were busy settling the newcomers, Syros and he had been momentarily left alone. It was now or never. Korin slid off the tree stump and crouched across the fire from Syros. Syros looked at him, pain smudging his lovely, piercing gray eyes.

Korin shifted restlessly in the silence between them. Had he been mistaken? Syros had seemed to care…

He gave an abrupt laugh, looking aside. Of course he had cared, an easy fuck on the battlefield. But Syros was a Northern lord while Korin was…nothing. A whore in Fredrik's Hall since he was a child. What would a decent, honorable, wonderful man like Syros need with him?

"It is good to see you healing, lord," he said huskily, wishing with all his might he had continued across the border when the others had stopped. He could have been far into the Southern Territory by morning. Perhaps Nagal could use another soldier.

"Look at me," Syros said, voice laced with underlying pain and weariness, but the command was clear enough. Korin glanced up, trying to keep emotion from his face. But Syros smiled, melting his heart. "You're too far away." Syros patted the ground beside him. "Come here."

"I should go…" Korin tried.

"Now."

Syros hadn't raised his voice, but hot blood flooded Korin's cheeks. Heart thumping, he moved to Syros's side, kneeling in the rough grass. Syros tsked and put an arm around him, pulling Korin onto his lap despite his sputtered protests.

"Better," Syros murmured contentedly. He clasped Korin in his arms, cupped his chin, and kissed him, silencing the protest hovering on his lips. Korin relaxed against him, exactly where he wanted to be.

*

AIDEN STOOD ON the edge of camp as the sun lowered toward the horizon and sighed in the fading light. He'd slept a little, but tiredness still weighted his limbs. And his spirit. They'd won the day but had lost many friends. Not everyone was returning home. He could wish…

Alek stirred beside him and held his gaze, searching. "We did all we could, Aiden."

Aiden looked back steadily, curious as to what he saw. Cecil sent him a kind smile from Alek's side.

"I didn't take very good care of them, my lord," he observed when Alek remained silent.

Natan watched them, his hand clasped in Kavi's. "You did more than anyone else could have, Aiden," he said firmly.

Aiden's glance included them all. "But, like a fool, I walked into Ethan's trap and left our people undefended."

"And you were where you needed to be and brought Natan to the lake where he *had* to be." Alek gripped his arm. "Aiden! You gave up everything for us. You protected our bodies and shielded our minds from Ethan. You saved us! Never think otherwise."

Aiden brushed at the tears he couldn't control. "We left Karthag a hundred strong. Less than half of us remain. I don't believe…"

Alek shook his head. "There's no one I'd rather have at my side. Please come back and help me protect and guide the remaining Karthagan people."

Aiden swallowed, unable to speak. He nodded and blushed a little at Alek's fond expression.

"Let's go home," Natan told them and motioned for the horses to be brought up. Aiden felt a new excitement in the air. They were going home to a world healed of their madness.

Tessa stood at her mother's side with Devon and Commander Jaden as they wished them farewell. Aiden went to her.

"Come to us soon, cousin," Aiden urged, clasping her hands. Alek echoed his words and embraced her, as did the others with smiles and tears.

"Give Robin our love," Natan teased, then turned to Kirstin and embraced her in turn. "Be well, dear."

"I will be. I feel more myself every day." Kirstin smiled, happiness shining in her eyes, and twined her fingers with Devon's, who hovered over her protectively.

"I'll see they get home safely," Jaden promised. "Goodbye, cousin. I'll see you soon," he told Natan, and they hugged in farewell.

Syros shook Willum's hand as Willum made ready to depart for Barkuit with his soldiers while Syros would head to his city of Kangar on the coast. "We'll set runners between Karthag, Barkuit, and Siagan, my lord," Syros informed him.

"And between Nagal and the other cities in the South, if Robin will permit it. We'll keep in touch," Willum added. "There's no reason for us to be divided any longer."

Syros nodded. "Excellent. Better times are coming, my lord."

They embraced and Willum climbed into his saddle. "Goodbye, my friend."

The Barkuit soldiers and Karthagans traveled together for some time, diverging to their separate cities after a brief halt to rest the horses near dawn. Aiden sensed the eagerness and exhilaration of his people as the morning progressed and they drew near to Karthag. The forest he'd played in since childhood seemed unusually beautiful. He couldn't wait to see Ellis, hold him once again.

They rested once more in the late morning, then spent the long day in travel. In time, they reached the city, where a joyous homecoming awaited the weary Karthagans. The gates stood wide, the people cheering as they approached. Aiden's heart came near to bursting when he spotted Ellis in the forefront of the crowd, arms opened to greet him.

Jumping from the saddle, Aiden went straight to him, crushing Ellis in his frantic embrace, until Ellis laughed against his chest and nudged him back, smiling into his face, his amazing eyes bright with tears. "Let me breathe, darling! Welcome home."

Aiden couldn't speak, choked with emotion. He could only pick up Ellis's hands and kiss them over and over while Ellis openly wept with joy.

The animals were taken to the stables, and the company dispersed, the soldiers going to their separate homes, while the cousins gathered in short order in the garden in the soft evening light. Cecil had a meal brought out while Alek built up a fire. He drew Cecil to a bench and sat with his arms loosely around him, smiling in contentment. "It's good to be home."

"It certainly is," Natan agreed and stretched out his legs and wiggled his bare toes. He'd changed into a loose tunic and breeches that unintentionally showed his lithe body. Kavi pulled him into his arms, and Natan rested his head back on his shoulder. There was such peace and happiness in his face it did them good to see him.

Aiden took a breath of exquisite joy. He'd bathed and washed his long hair, and Ellis was helping him untangle the strands with his slender fingers. Aiden leaned against him, stole another sweet kiss, and grew light-headed from his smiles.

"We could just cut it off," he offered at a particularly stubborn knot,

not caring either way. He drew a quick breath and reddened slightly when Ellis tilted Aiden's chin up to meet his gaze.

"Don't you dare." Ellis ran his hands through the dark silken mass, and Aiden couldn't breathe as he watched Ellis's eyes darken with unspoken ardor.

"Can we go home?" he asked gruffly under cover of the conversation around them. Ellis blushed even as he took his hand, and they rose to their feet. With a quiet goodnight to the others, they made their way from the garden, already lost in each other.

*

ALEK WATCHED KAVI a moment as he gazed lovingly into his husband's eyes and placed tender kisses on Natan's upturned face. He exchanged a look with Cecil, who chuckled and slipped with him from the garden, leaving the warm fire to the couple oblivious to everyone but themselves.

They ran like children through the streets to the stables and borrowed two horses. Alek felt young and alive as they raced to the beach, Cecil laughing as he kept pace. They rode in the moonlight as waves crashed on the shore. Alek turned his mount, followed the winding path toward their unfinished house, and thought his heart would burst as Cecil leaned from his saddle to kiss him.

"Welcome home," Cecil murmured against his lips. Cecil lifted the flap of the leather pack he'd snatched up at the stables, giving Alek a glimpse of a brightly colored blanket and a dark wine bottle. He lifted his gaze, pulse racing, and met the fire and promise in Cecil's eyes. Cecil kissed him again, making Alek's happiness complete.

*

SYROS STRODE UP a cobbled street in Siagan in the late afternoon sunshine, taking in the renovations already begun. Willum had moved quickly, the damaged dwellings reroofed, and the brickwork started. Syros had gone home to Kangar for a week to check on his city and see his son, bringing Dani back with him. Commander Davis would return to Siagan next month to resume stewardship of the city, but in the meantime, Syros would take over repairs.

After leaving Dani and his nursemaid in the rooms prepared for them, he made his way through the city to find Willum. A loud boom startled him, and he hastened up the street, only to come to a halt at the castle and stare in amazement. Willum straightened from the huge catapult in the square.

"Our relief is here," Willum called to someone out of sight. He spoke a few words to Captain Gael at his side, then came up to Syros. "Well met."

"Hello," Syros replied with a courteous bow, then turned an interested gaze on the demolished castle. "You're burying the lake," he surmised, and Willum inclined his head in agreement.

"Indeed. We'll turn the space into a garden, perhaps. I'll allow no dwellings to be built here." Willum motioned along the street. "I believe a meal is being prepared for us, if you care to come with me.

"Commander?" Willum called as they passed the war machine, and a lithe figure hidden behind it stepped forward.

"Sir?"

"Send the men to the barracks and join us at the Hall if you will. We'll finish here in the morning."

"At once, my lord. Thank you." The man swept a low bow, and his copper hair gleamed in the sunlight. Syros eyed him in confusion. What was Korin doing in a Barkuit uniform? And had Willum said commander? Syros fumed. The bastard could have met him at the gate…

Korin's beautiful eyes lifted to him, bright with joy, and he forgot his anger. Syros smiled at him but kept his questions for later, conscious of Korin's gaze following him up the street as he hurried after Willum.

They were to eat in the garden. As Syros took a seat beside Commander Gael at the fountain, he noted it was still a pretty spot, though not as well kept as in Davis's time. His heart skipped as voices approached on the pathway, and Korin entered the shaded area along with Dani's nursemaid carrying Syros's young son. Syros rose hastily and took the little boy into his arms.

"Everyone, this is my Dani," he said with pride, and Willum and Gael shook Syros's hand, exclaiming over the boy. Dani's tiny face crumpled, and he made soft little noises of distress at the attention, turning into his father's shoulder. Overwrought, uncomfortable, his cries grew louder until Syros felt utterly helpless.

"Here, give him to Uncle."

Syros's heart jumped on hearing Korin's voice at his elbow, unaware he stood so close, but handed over his precious treasure without hesitation.

"None of that, little man," Korin cautioned as Dani sent up a wail. He sat on the bench Syros had vacated and laughed in the boy's red face, then bent to murmur secrets in his ear. Dani's eyes opened wide, captivated by the vibrant face above him, and he gurgled and smiled as the attractive voice whispered excitements.

"Korin, I'll not have you weaving your little plots with Dani," Syros said lightly though real concern smote him. As if stung, Korin rose and placed the child in Syros's arms, then he took a knee to him.

"I would never harm the boy, Regent. And I pledge now, in front of everyone, that if need be, I would give my life to protect him."

Syros eyed him a moment, then held out his hand, deadly earnest. Korin stood and solemnly gripped his hand in a promise. He was unbearably handsome in the dark Barkuit uniform, making Syros's heart turn over. Korin widened his eyes at his scrutiny and, thoughtfully, took a seat beside him, staring at his boots as the conversation went on around him.

"Will you walk with me?" Syros asked quietly after they'd eaten, and Korin took a quick breath and nodded. They said a polite good evening to the others; then Syros handed Dani to his nurse and led Korin on a winding path to a bench hidden in the roses. He asked Korin to sit, then lost his courage and took a restless turn about the clearing, coming to an abrupt stop before him.

"Syros?" Korin asked, puzzled.

"Why are you here, like this?" Syros waved at the uniform and the Northern city around them, buying some time.

"Willum said he could use me, and I had hoped…" Korin drew a deep breath and plunged ahead. "I had hoped you'd want me to stay." He flinched at Syros's sharp inhalation, and his gaze grew wistful and strained. "I understand. After Ashel…you must despise me." He rose to his feet.

Syros put a hand out to stop him. "I want you, but then you'd be tied. I don't share. Darling, can you bear that? Shouldn't you be free to—"

"Free to what, Syros?" Korin lowered his voice, his face bleak. "Free to go back to empty nights and meaningless affairs that leave me hollow and aching and alone? Syros! I only see you. I want only you if you'll have me."

Syros's blood rushed through his veins. "Yes." He jerked Korin up against him, touching his face in awe. Korin gave a shout, laughing, and his joy swept over Syros as well—more so when Korin pulled him to the soft grass and threw his cloak over them both.

*

CECIL HAD BEEN home a week when the schooner he'd been waiting for slid into Karthag's harbor. He boarded the ship and strode across the deck to grip the captain's hand, a grin spreading on his face. "It's good to see you safe, Daran."

"And you, Commander. I had my doubts."

"So did I," Cecil confessed. He took a breath and stretched his lean body. It was a perfect morning for sailing. The water was calm and there was a faint breeze to send them on their way. He and the captain went forward to check the rigging, and a glad shout went up from the sailors at the sight of their commander. Cecil bowed even as the blood rushed to his face.

His heart skipped on hearing a familiar voice behind him. "Alek?" He hurried to him as he came up. "Is something wrong?"

"No." Alek gave him a tentative smile. "I wanted to say goodbye."

Cecil drew a startled breath. Alek never saw him off like this… He stepped back and bowed deeply. "My lord."

A soft whistle blew, and the sailors stopped their work and gathered on the deck as Natan and Kavi came aboard.

"You don't have to leave so soon, Mage," Cecil chided gently.

Natan smiled. "Yes, we do. I'm anxious to be home and check my nets, and also see how things are progressing in Sennia. With both Niko and the Vice-King gone, many are asking Kayle to accept the kingship. He will need my help, whatever he decides."

"Is there any doubt, Father?" Aiden asked as he and Ellis strolled over. "Kayle is capable of meeting any challenge. He won't let them down."

"He loves his people," Natan agreed.

Ellis's voice quavered when he spoke. "We'll miss you. Come visit us soon." He tearfully kissed Kavi, then turned to Natan and gave him a fierce embrace. Tears filled Natan's bright eyes.

"Thank you, Ellis," he murmured and hugged him tightly. "You can't get rid of me this easily. I promise I'll come back often."

Aiden wrapped an arm around Ellis's shoulders, holding him to his side. He placed a kiss lovingly on Ellis's forehead, then sent a glance to Cecil. "Remember, dear, Cecil travels often to Sennia. There's no reason we can't visit the Mage and Kavi whenever you'd like."

Ellis drew a hard breath and nodded. Natan embraced him once more, then let go with reluctance, and a general leave-taking ensued.

While the others were distracted, Alek took a moment to draw Cecil behind a lifeboat.

"Take care, dear," he stammered and seemed to find words inadequate for all he wanted to say.

"I'll be home soon," Cecil promised with a catch in his throat.

"I'll be watching for you." Alek touched Cecil's fine silken hair, and his ardent glance warmed Cecil's heart long after the ship departed.

*

IT WAS THEIR sixth morning at sea when Natan stood at the prow of the ship and let the ocean spray wash over him. They would be home that day. His eyes were drawn to the tall mast and the small basket on top, and a sudden longing to be up there took hold of him. He missed the power of the earth at his fingertips—no, they were better off without it. Happier. But standing at the top of the world was the next best thing.

Kavi came to his side, and he slipped an arm around him, but his eyes strayed again to the crow's nest.

"Are you going up?" Daran asked, strolling over.

"No!" Kavi answered quickly and shuddered. Natan was unable to hide his disappointment, and Kavi touched his face. "Would you like me to go with you?"

Natan's heart surged. Kavi had been acutely gentle with him on the voyage; Natan shouldn't take advantage. And yet…

"I won't let you fall," he promised, feeling utterly selfish. But to have Kavi in his arms, up there… It would be a memory to overshadow all others.

He kept Kavi in front of him as they climbed the rigging with Daran beside them offering encouragement as needed. In short order, they swung into the basket, and Daran left them with a grin and a warm light in his eyes, clearly pleased for Natan's hard-won happiness.

Natan studied Kavi's strained expression and closed eyes, Kavi gripping the basket so tightly his knuckles whitened. He wrapped his arms around Kavi and pulled him back against his chest, then laughed lightheartedly and pressed his lips to his cheek.

"Relax, sweetheart. You're safe with me." He added solemnly, "I will never hurt you, Kavi. You have my heart and all my love."

"I know that, Natan. And you have mine." Kavi drew in a breath and opened his eyes. The ocean stretched wide and beautiful before them. Natan stroked Kavi's hair and murmured soft words of devotion and eagerness in his ear until Kavi eased back against him with a contented murmur. Delight spread on his beautiful face as he gazed at the sea, and Natan's heart swelled. He raised his eyes to the glorious horizon, shouting his joy as the wind flew them home, the world safe for the moment, and he secure in Kavi's love.

Summary of Characters by Name

AIDEN: Oldest of the Red Twins, leader of the Karthagan people after Alek

ALEK: Commander, Kavi's cousin, and leader of the Karthagan people before Aiden

ASHEL: Fredrik's cousin. Wants the Karthagans' powers

BASAL: Governor of the Southern Territory

CAMRON: The Red Twins' grown cousin

CARROW: Archer stationed at Fredrik's Hall

CECIL: Camron's captive. Later, Alek's lover and Commander of Karthag's trade ships

DANUL: Mazzo's follower and later Vice-King of Sennia

DARAN: Sea captain traveling between Sennia and Belega for trade, friend of Natan

DAVIS: lieutenant in Barkuit army. Works with Syros. Later Commander and council leader of Siagan

DERIK: Soldier stationed in Siagan. Aids Korin. Ethan's 'shadow'

DEVON: Amara Council Leader

ELLIS: Natan's adopted son. Aiden's husband

ETHAN: one of the Red Twins with his brother Aiden

FREDRIK: lord of his Hall. Wants the Karthagans' power

GAEL: Barkuit captain. Works with Willum

GREGOR: Mage of Sennia. Kavi's mentor

JACKSAN: Nagal Commander stationed at Fredrik's Hall

JACOM: Vice-King. Leader of the Sennian people

JADEN: Lieutenant in Nagal army and Natan's cousin. Later made Commander

KAVI: Gregor's apprentice, Natan's husband

KAYDEN: Kirstin's brother and leader of Rodrik's people. Father of the Red Twins

KIRSTIN: daughter of Rodrik, freed from unnatural imprisonment. Healer

KORIN: Nagal soldier stationed at Fredrik's Hall

KAYLE: Gregor's son and Natan's adopted son

MANDEL: Council Leader. Wants the Karthagans' power

NATAN: Sometimes scout for Southern army. Hand-picked by Gregor to be Mage

NIKO: Natan's friend. Aubre's nephew. The Mage after Natan

ROBIN: Basal's son and heir. Later made Governor of the Southern Territory

SYROS: Captain turned Regent of the Northern Territory

TESSA: Kirstin's daughter. Robin's fiancé

TILLIE: Gregor's daughter and Natan's adopted daughter

TYREL: Commander stationed at the border between the North and South

WILLUM: Gargary's son. Present governor of the Northern Territory

Acknowledgements

Thank you once again, NineStar Press, for giving my magical world of Belega a home. And hats off to my wonderful and talented editor, BJ Toth, whose discerning comments and questions helped me add more depth to both this story and its myriad of characters.

About the Author

Dianne is the author of paranormal/suspense, fantasy adventure, m/m romance, the occasional thriller, and anything else that comes to mind. She lives in the beautiful Willamette Valley of Oregon with her incredibly patient husband, who puts up with the endless hours she spends hunched over the keyboard letting her characters play. She says Oregon's raindrops are the perfect setting in which to write. There's something about being cooped up in the house with a fire crackling on the hearth and a cup of hot coffee warming her hands, which kindles her imagination.

Currently, Dianne works as a floral designer in a locally owned gift shop. Which is the perfect job for her. When not writing, she can express herself through the rich colors and textures of flowers and foliage.

Email

diannewrites2@hotmail.com

Facebook

www.facebook.com/diannehartsock

Instagram

www.instagram.com/diannehartsock

Website

www.diannehartsock.wordpress.com

Other NineStar books by this author

The Karthagans Series
Belega

Shelton in Love

Birthday Presents

Luka

Little Match Girl

The Mirror Maze

Callum's Fate

Sweet William

www.ninestarpress.com

www.facebook.com/ninestarpress

www.facebook.com/groups/NineStarNiche

www.twitter.com/ninestarpress

www.instagram.com/ninestarpress

bsky.app/profile/ninestarpress.bsky.social

www.threads.net/@ninestarpress

www.ingramcontent.com/pod-product-compliance
Lightning Source LLC
Chambersburg PA
CBHW060305100726
47907CB00002B/289